HIGHWIRE MOON

Books by Susan Straight

Aquaboogie

I Been in Sorrow's Kitchen and Licked Out All the Pots

Blacker Than a Thousand Midnights

The Gettin Place

Highwire Moon

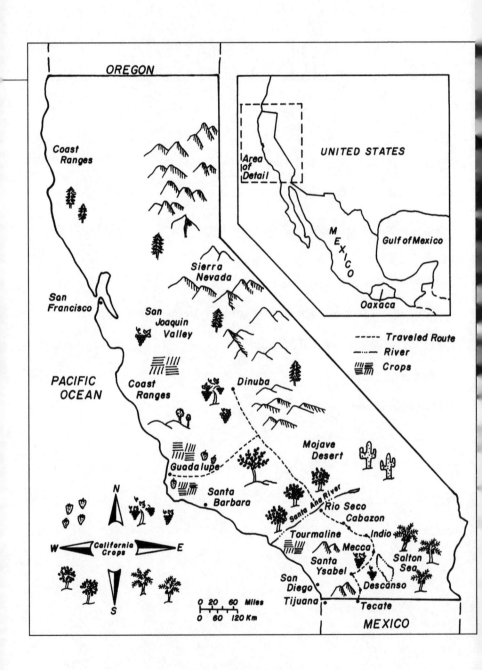

HIGHWIRE MOON

A NOVEL

Susan Straight

HOUGHTON MIFFLIN COMPANY

Boston   New York   2001

For information about permission to reproduce selections from
this book, write to Permissions, Houghton Mifflin Company,
215 Park Avenue South, New York, New York 10003.

Visit our Web site: www.houghtonmifflinbooks.com.

Library of Congress Cataloging-in-Publication Data
Straight, Susan.
    Highwire moon / Susan Straight.
       p. cm.
    ISBN 0-618-05614-9
    1. Migrant agricultural laborers—Fiction.   2. Mothers and daughters—
Fiction.   3. Teenage pregnancy—Fiction.   4. Illegal aliens—Fiction.
5. Birthmothers—Fiction.   6. California—Fiction.   I. Title.
    PS3569.T6795 H54   2001
    813'.54—dc21   00-053878

Book design by Anne Chalmers
Map on frontispiece by Susan Ruman
Typefaces: Electra, Franklin Gothic Condensed

Printed in the United States of America
QUM 10 9 8 7 6 5 4 3 2 1

Fontanel: The soft spot on a newborn's skull.

Just as the child is born with a literal hole in its head, where the bones slowly close underneath the fragile shield of skin, so the child is born with a figurative hole in its heart... What slips in before it anneals shapes the man or woman into which that child will grow.

—Jane Yolen, *Touch Magic*

Acknowledgments

Many thanks and muchas gracias to all those who helped me in Oaxaca and in the United States:

Diana and Renee Carr, Nick Dolphin, Institute Welte, and Dr. Eduardo Cervantes in Oaxaca, and especially Isabel Martinez Maldonado, Gaby, and Angeles in Santa Maria de Atzompa.

Richard Parks, Elaine Pfefferblit, and Pat Mulcahy in New York. In the country of mothers, Holly Robinson, Elizabeth Eastmond, Beverly Johnson, Charlotte Carrington, and Gail Watson. In the wild life, Jeff Watson. In the computer universe, Juli and Jason Gladney. Thanks also to Arabella Meyer, Michael Kearney, and Gordon Johnson.

Grateful acknowledgment goes to the John Simon Guggenheim Foundation and the Lannan Foundation for their generous assistance, which enabled me not only to write, but to spend time with three invaluable sources:

Gaila, Delphine, and Rosette, who got me a life.

A glossary of Mixtec and Spanish words is on page 306.

Prologue

SERAFINA HELD the Virgen de Guadalupe curled in her palm. The blue-robed woman standing on a bed of roses was still warm. Larry had torn the oval picture from the glass candleholder, the veladora Serafina kept burning all day to assure the Virgen's gaze upon her and her daughter.

"This ain't Mexico," he had said, eyes red as pomegranate seeds, and then he roared off in his blue truck.

Without the image, the candle flame shook small and lonely as a glowing grain of rice. Elvia stared at the wick through the bare glass. Serafina watched the tiny fire reflected in her pupils. The little duplex room had filled with the purple light of summer evening.

Serafina smoothed the stained-glass edging around the Virgen. This was not enough. She had tried to make an altar inside the kitchen, but she needed to pray inside a church, with santos looking down upon her, to ask what she should do.

"Náá?" Elvia called to her mother in their Mixtec language. "Nducha yúján nuní yīhi?" She wanted Serafina to make atole, to heat the milk with ground-corn masa and sugar and cinnamon.

Serafina waited, her eyebrows raised. "Please," Elvia said perfectly. She had just turned three. She could say many words. Serafina picked her up and carried her to the kitchen so she could feel the small hands fluttering like moths on her shoulders.

Serafina knew Please. Thank you. Money. Pay. Fuckin cops. Fuckin truck. American. Speak English. Okay. Sorry. She could say "sorry," but she couldn't form her lips properly around any of the other words. She had said "sorry" a few hours ago to Larry, when he had whirled around the house and torn the Virgen from her veladora and shouted, "Ellie's American! My kid's American, okay? Quit this shit!" But her "sorry" didn't sound right. She tried to whisper it now, but her throat wouldn't cooperate. She was crying. She wanted to kneel inside the church at home, to touch San Cristobal, the patron saint of her village, to rub Elvia with flowers and then lay them on the altar as an offering, to pray about what kind of life Elvia would have.

"Náá?" Elvia crooned now. "Cap'n Crunch?"

It was almost gone. It was very expensive. But Serafina poured the yellow pillows of cereal into a plastic bowl. She knew she would have to drive the car. Elvia could carry the cereal. Elvia reached up with a golden square between her fingers, offering it to her mother, and Serafina crushed the sweet powder with her teeth.

Maiz. Nuní. It was corn, she knew. She stirred a swirling brown veil of cinnamon into the atole. The steam rose from the thickened milk and clouded her eyes for a moment, and she saw home. The mist descending from the mountains, softening the harsh light of here. California.

"Náá?" Elvia said from near the TV. "Sesame Street."

Serafina kneeled next to her daughter, blowing on the mug of atole, trying to imagine herself driving past the fence. The television said, "A. Apple. A."

"Apple," Elvia said. "Náá—apple."

Serafina nodded, closing her eyes so the steam couldn't collect there and make tears that would frighten her daughter.

"B. Balloon. B." A boy was carried away by the blue circle.

"C. Cat. C." The yellow cat's whiskers shivered when he grinned.

Outside in the twilight, she held Elvia on her hip and touched the hot door handle of the black car named Nova, almost like a bride. Novia. The car was Larry's bride, with heavy-lidded jeweled eyes. Serafina studied the dusty hood. The car always stayed in the driveway, facing the street to hide the blank square where the license plate should be. When Larry came home, he worked on the insides, tangled like pig intestines.

He had tossed the keys at her and laughed. "Drive back to Mexico," he'd said. "Get a life."

Now Elvia slid onto the front seat, laughing, holding her bowl of cereal. She loved Larry's truck; sometimes he let her turn the steering wheel. Last week, when Serafina began to ease the Nova up and down the dirt driveway, Elvia had explored each dashboard knob. Her short brown legs stuck out stiffly over the edge of the seat.

Serafina placed the mug of hot atole in the black plastic tray on the seat between them. When she turned the key in its silver circle, the car closed a dark hull around Serafina, and suddenly she couldn't breathe. The floor trembled. She closed her eyes, then opened them, afraid. She had come to California in the trunk of a car. The rumbling under her cheek had stayed inside her brain for days. The oily air had stayed inside her throat.

Black gas step. Black stop step. She pushed on them, her own short legs reaching with difficulty. Elvia screamed with delight at the jerking movements of the car down the driveway. The cloud-haired old woman from next door came outside, waving, pointing to something on the ground. Serafina looked away. *I don't have her money,* she thought. *Rent. No rent.*

The car jostled off the curb and into the street. Serafina made herself breathe. A white tower. She thought she had seen a white tower when they had first moved here. She hadn't been past the corner store since. She pushed down on the black gas step and the car moved slowly into the darkness, the engine growling like a large dog in her ears.

At home, the church sat on the highest knoll, where people could see the cross and blue door from miles away. The church was always lit by candles, the door always open, in case someone needed to pray or give an offering.

What did I bring? Serafina stopped the car with a decisive jerk at the corner. *I have nothing to offer.* She saw two cars approaching, and her heart ticked like crickets trapped in a jar. The cars went past, the street was empty, and she turned onto the avenue. Moving the wheel was hard. It was slick and bumpy, not like wood, not rough and cool like stone.

Serafina pushed each step in its turn, and Elvia reached forward to play with the dashboard knobs. The Nova bucked and moved down the street until Serafina saw the white tower and cross, lit bright. She turned the wheel again, and it fought her. The Nova went into the parking lot, where bumps in the asphalt made the car rise up and then fall.

Elvia said suddenly, "*Ñuhun.*"

Fire? Serafina glanced at the dashboard, where Elvia pointed. The knobs and lights and vents were like a strange altar. One knob suddenly pushed itself back out, and Elvia pulled out a fiery-red metal eye. Serafina snatched it quickly, and the car swerved. Darkness rose before them, and Serafina tried to push the stop step, but the car's mouth hit something hard, like a fist against teeth. The windshield was black with leaves, buried in a thick hedge.

Elvia screamed, and at the same moment Serafina felt the burning pang on her arm. She stared at the knob in her hand, but the heat had subsided to an ashen black circle.

The atole had flown from the mug when the car hit the hedge. The thick white splatter on her own arm stung like the bite of a thousand red ants. She saw one large drop on Elvia's wrist, and immediately put her mouth to the burn. The hot sweet milk disappeared under her tongue, and she licked and then blew on Elvia's skin, licking and blowing, cooling and kissing and breathing on the burn, saying she was sorry, she was so sorry she had made Elvia cry.

Elvia had cried only two times in the past year. Once, a boy with hair red as chiles had thrown a rock from the street, hitting her in the back. And once, Larry had driven away in his truck, and Elvia cried because she wanted to drive again.

Serafina whispered to the wound, watching the angry red welt glisten with her own saliva, and then Elvia shuddered one last time and tucked her head into Serafina's chest. Serafina heard scraping, settling in the hedge, and she twisted the dangling keys. The engine-muttering stopped. Elvia pointed to the black knob and said, "*Táā*—Daddy's *ñuhun.*"

Serafina dropped the lighter into her pocket. Then she put her hands together on the black wheel and laid her cheek there until Elvia said, "*Náā?*"

Serafina ran her finger around the mug sides, collecting the now-cooled atole on a finger for Elvia. She whispered to Elvia that atole stayed hot forever, so it was the best drink for cold mornings and nights at home, in Mexico. You could carry a mug of atole to the field and sip it every now and then, and the warmth would seep into your chest.

Bells sounded in the church tower, but Serafina lost count. Elvia yawned and laid her head on Serafina's lap. Serafina felt the hard lighter knob against her thigh. Now it couldn't hurt her daughter. Elvia would sleep, and Serafina would go inside to pray.

"*Cusū,*" she told Elvia, whose eyes were blinking slowly. "*Cusū, sēhe síhí.*" Sleep, my daughter. She waited until each small breath was like a cloud exhaled.

Serafina hid the keys under the seat. She got out of the car. Elvia slept, curled on the black vinyl, her hand cupped like a tiny ladle. The leaves of the hedge were dark and sharp. A light went on in a building nearby; a head was silhouetted behind a curtain. Serafina saw a triangle of glass, a set of fingers when the curtain was pulled back. Then the window went black again.

She tried the small door on the side of the long church, then the double doors in front. Every entrance was locked. No wide blue door slanted open, no welcoming golden candle flames. Serafina glanced back at the car, which was like an animal grazing peacefully in the leaves, and she went around to the other side.

Far across the huge lawn, the woman stood.

White stone. She had no blue veil or golden robe or dark eyes. But her hands were held out in supplication, Serafina saw when she drew close. She was a santo.

The statue's face was paled by passing headlights, and Serafina stood on the base, close to the hard lips, and touched their icy coolness. The eyes were blank circles, but Serafina whispered, "Help me. Tell me what to do, and I will do it."

She lowered her face to the hands, breathing in their chalky scent, laying her cheek against one wrist. "Tell me," she whispered. "Tell me she will have enough to eat if we go back."

She heard a short whirl of sound, and the stone blushed. The white skin was suffused with red light, the lips and cheeks translucent, pulsing. She heard her own language, soft and humming, when she reached to touch the robe now flashing blue, like the Virgen's.

"Home," she heard then. "Go home."

Footsteps landed on the concrete behind her, and a man's voice said, "Hey, time to go home." His flashlight was in her face, the blue lights twirling into the stone eyes. She turned and ran.

The policeman tackled her on the grass and lifted her by the elbow, and she dropped her shoulder and began to run again. Her tongue rose in her throat, and she gasped for air when he caught her again.

Another policeman watched while the first held her skull between his hands and said, "ID? ID? You got ID?"

"Mydotter! Mydotter!" She screamed the words, felt their strange shape pull the cords in her throat. "My! My dotter!"

"Okay, okay, you need a doctor. In Mexico. Get a doctor in Mexico." He held her wrist with one hand and pulled her up slowly. She hit him in the shoulder. She hit him in the face. She had to run back to the car, around the corner, to the dark lot where Elvia waited.

But he pushed her down gently onto the sidewalk until her cheek rubbed the rough cement. "Damn," he said when she twisted against the handcuffs, kicking him as they carried her across the street to the flashing car.

Serafina screamed. She couldn't see the car. They were taking her away. "Elvia! *Náá*, Elvia, mommy, my dotter . . ." The words spilled wrong all across their forearms until one policeman shifted his sleeve over her lips.

"No habla español," he said softly, shaking his head like a father. She understood those words. But she screamed again into the fabric until the harsh red light circled close to her eyes, pumping like blood from a deep cut when they laid her in the dark back seat.

The police car began to move. She screamed into the vinyl as her body floated away from her daughter who was sleeping, her head cushioned by braids. Serafina struggled to raise herself, to see, but she saw only the red light glaring, draining her, flashing in the same rhythm as her heart.

Moths dove in and out of the streetlight beam, banging against the window near her, then veering away in bursts of blurry white.

Branches and leaves covered the windshield, pressed tight like a blanket of black knives. Elvia wasn't to touch knives. Her mother used knives to take the spines off the green cactus pads. They could eat the cactus then. Her father had gotten angry when he saw the cactus today. Once Elvia had gotten spines embedded in her finger, and her mother had pulled out the tiny red needles with her teeth.

Elvia studied the red circle of burn on her wrist. Her mother had kissed the burn. Elvia licked it herself. Her mother would lick and cool it again when she came back.

The crickets resumed their shrill scraping in the black leaves all around the car. Elvia had awakened in the front seat. Her mother was gone. The keys were gone. Her father had thrown the keys, flying with silver wings and landing on her mother's chest.

Ndéchi náá? Where was her mother?

Ndéchi Barbie? Where was her Barbie? That was what the kids next door said to her through the silver fence. Cap'n Crunch Barbie

Dandelion Stupid Beaner Mescan Hey Crickets Shut Up Ice Cream Truck Bye.

Her father had brought her the Barbie. Then he had gone back outside to the blue truck that roared behind a silver nose. She loved to steer the blue truck. She touched the dashboard knobs now. She had been inside this car only a few times. Her mother drove up and down the driveway. Barbie was on the ground, next to the hedge by the old lady with dandelion-puff hair. But Elvia didn't cry. They were only riding up and down the driveway.

Tonight the car had bounced over bumps and made Elvia scream and laugh. It rocked and pitched like a huge, low-slung animal raising its back over the humps and then drawing in all its bones with a jarring tremble when they were over. Like a wild horsie ride her father had let her ride at the store. One time. Today?

Where was her mother?

The silver knob had turned fire-red and her mother had taken it away. *Ñuhun.* Her mother's lips were red as the glowing circle. As though pomegranate juice stained her mouth. *Chīhló*—with sour red jewels inside. And her mother's eyes were covered with blue sky.

The moths bumped harder against the glass, and Elvia peered out the window to see them dancing crazily in the light, dipping in and out of darkness. She saw the parking lot, empty and gray as if she were inside a cloud. *Vico nuhu*, her mother always said, pointing up at the clouds.

Her mother. Elvia was afraid now, and she ducked down into the cave under the dashboard. The well of space was warm, just the right size when she drew her legs to her chest. The floor felt like evening sidewalk against her legs. She twisted her braid into a pillow for her head. She could smell her mother's cinnamon.

Something pale bumped the other window, harder, harder, and she looked up. The sky was light. The moths were gone.

A pair of white hands pressed like a snail's underside against the glass, around a wide face bright as the moon. Elvia screamed and screamed when the man opened the door. She screamed while he pulled her out and carried her away.

Then she was quiet, and she didn't open her mouth for months. "Where is your mother?" the man kept asking. Then a woman asked, "Where is your mother? Your father?" Behind her glasses, the woman's eyes were huge and dark as plums. Her hair was a nest of yellow. She touched Elvia's hair and said, "Pretty braid." Elvia pulled away. She said inside her head, *Lasú*. The woman touched her fingers and said, "Little hands." Elvia put them under her legs. She said inside her head, *Ndaha*. The woman put her in a car.

At the first house, the mother was big. All Elvia could see was the hem of her flowing shift. The rest of her was so wide and full of loose curves that she seemed to take up the whole front room where they stayed, day after day. Elvia watched the edge of material sweep past her on the floor where she sat. It collected carpet strands and lint and crumbs and bits of paper. The dusty, furred hem of the dress looked like the bottom of her mother's broom after she swept the kitchen. Elvia used to sit on the floor then, too, her face close to the sweet-smelling straw as it traveled near her, teasingly close to her bare feet. She would look up at her mother, who pretended she didn't see Elvia's feet, gliding the tickly points of straw just past the soles.

Elvia waited for her mother. She didn't move from the floor. She didn't speak. The woman talked all the time. Another boy came. He had a bruise red as a *chīhló* on his cheek and a thick white sock on his wrist. But it wasn't a sock. When the big woman went to the kitchen, he hit Elvia across the back with the sock, hard like a stone wrapped around his bones. She didn't move. He threw a truck at her. She didn't move. The big woman tried to feed him. He ran from the chair to the television to the couch to Elvia, touching each one with his good hand stiff and flat, running to the next.

She said nothing at the house where the mother had tongue-colored hair, where the many children pinched one another over individual Cheerios and fought about every hot dog.

She never answered at the house where everyone had braids except the father, who had a silver stripe in his black hair. The braids made her cry. The boys and girls had brown skin. The father talked gently to her, repeating, "Habla español," but she couldn't stop crying.

She was silent at the house where the woman washed everyone's hair in the bathtub and Elvia's long black hair swirled around the others' legs like wet roots. She said nothing when the woman cut off her braid the next day. The black braid lay like a glistening snake in the white bottom of the kitchen sink.

She remembered her fingers wrapped around her mother's braid while her mother carried her on her hip. She remembered the smell of cinnamon and corn. She touched her bare neck.

The woman kept staring at Elvia's eyes, frowning at her brown skin, the scissors rasping. Elvia closed her eyes, remembering her father. His eyes were green, like faded palm fronds. Like hers. He used to say, "My kid" to his friends in the yard. Her father had yellow hair like dry grass, tied in a ponytail. Not a braid.

The woman threw Elvia's braid in the trash. Elvia looked at the picture of Jesus on the wall. Her father looked like Jesus, if Jesus wore his hair in a ponytail and cut off the sides of his beard so only a yellow paintbrush hung from his chin, if Jesus took off his shirt and got mad.

Every night, in every house, Elvia waited until the woman or man put on the porch light. The moths gathered around the glass-paneled brass lamps or bare bulbs, and Elvia stayed on the porch as long as she could, watching the blurry white bodies circle and pause and hover. If she sat still enough, they would brush past her cheek or shoulder. She was quiet, listening to the hum and quiver of the moths, waiting for her mother to come back.

Tourmaline

ELVIA PARTED her hair down the center and braided it tightly, to keep it off her neck and to piss off her father and his girlfriend. She would run in the desert, even if she fainted again and woke up with sand-coated cheeks and eyes full of black mist. If she ran long enough, sweat pouring from her skin, August heat coursing through her veins, maybe she could melt away the baby.

If there was a baby. She was dizzy, her head ached, she felt too hot, as if her blood ran faster than she did. But she felt nothing in her belly, and she wouldn't look down. She wouldn't even touch her skin near the navel, because what if there was a baby and it felt her fingertips? Thought she loved it?

But she didn't; there wasn't anything to love. She was dizzy because it was 110 degrees today in Tourmaline and she'd been washing clothes in the bathtub. Her father's girlfriend, Callie, had said, "We can't walk to the laundrymat in this heat, and anyhow we ain't got the money."

She had seen a pregnancy test in the medicine cabinet. Callie must have used the other one. Elvia wasn't going to pee on a stick. There was no baby.

She was tired because yesterday she'd run five miles to the arroyo where Michael Torres used to live in the plywood shelter. She had been looking for him for four months, ever since he'd disappeared in April. She'd heard he and a guy named Hector Perez had been arrested. Grand theft auto. Last week she'd seen smoke rising from the tamarisk-branch roof. But only Hector had come outside, and she didn't know him. She'd been too scared to ask where Michael was now.

This morning was so hot she sat in the cottonwood shade, head aching. Babies made you tired and weak. She wasn't having a baby. She wasn't going to have it and then leave it someday, like her mother had left her, under a dusty windshield with only the sound of moth wings against the glass.

She remembered strange fragments: her mother's candles and bowls, her hands always moving like trapped birds, the crescent grin of white at her brown heels. Useless things. She couldn't even imagine a mother. She wasn't going to be a mother when she couldn't even make one up for herself.

Her father wouldn't tell her anything. "Why talk about somebody when she's gone?"

"You told somebody she was Indian."

"I did?"

"I heard you. Talking in the yard. Explaining to Dually how your kid got your eyes in a brown face. Dually hates Mexicans, remember?"

"Ellie. You're just tanned."

Her father never called her Elvia. Never. "You said she wasn't even regular Mexican. She didn't even speak Spanish. You said she talked some kind of cavewoman words."

Her father had gotten mad then. "And you're not a regular kid. Always askin about things that don't matter. She's a gone Indian, okay? That kind. I'm a right-here dad. Lot of kids don't get that. You're lucky."

She guessed she was lucky, compared to most kids in the desert. Her father always brought food home, he had never hit or even touched her, and he hadn't disappeared.

My mother disappeared. She left me at a church. Like some old Bible story about a baby wrapped in a blanket and stuck in a basket headed down the river. Except I was in a car with no license plates in the parking lot. Too damn embarrassing to explain. I'm not even supposed to know, it's so pathetic.

She knew from overhearing a foster mother talking on the phone, years ago, about the pitiful new kid. "Green eyes, but brown as a berry, and you know she might not even speak no English. I can't tell, cause she won't talk at all."

She listened to everything, and except for the parking lot story she learned nothing else about her mother. She had nothing to say, so she hadn't talked for months. She remembered floors and counters. The broomlike hem swishing over speckled linoleum, the angry orange worms of someone's shag carpet, the fiercely polished wood cool against her legs when she lay in a hallway. Then Sandy Narlette's Formica counter. White with gold freckles. Every day, Sandy Narlette had sat Elvia on the counter and talked to her while she mixed things in a green bowl. But Elvia said nothing. The social worker had taken her away after a year, left her at the skunk man's house. Four years later, she'd brought Elvia back to Sandy Narlette's, and Sandy put Elvia on the counter again. She had said, "Some people think dumb kids don't talk. But I think smart kids don't talk until they have something important to say." She would measure salt like sparkling sand in her palm and motion Elvia to watch it disappear into the flour. Over and over, she let Elvia drizzle honey from a spoon back into the jar, and Elvia stared at the golden thread spool into itself, distinct for a moment, then melting into nothing. *Chīhló,* she would say to herself, looking at the bowl of pomegranates on the counter. *Yoo,* she would whisper, watching the moon rise in the laundry room window. *Nunī,* she finally murmured to Sandy Narlette, pointing to the canned corn.

She had stayed at Sandy Narlette's house for four years. She had moved from so many foster homes that at first she wouldn't let herself like the bedroom of girls, each with her own pillowcase, slippers, toothbrush, placemat, and napkin. Elvia's were blue. She wouldn't let herself like Sandy, her brown ponytail and blue eyes and chapped lips. But Sandy waited, patient and not falsely cheerful, never pinching in places social workers didn't see or portioning out food with vengeance or as a reward or with pity.

Sandy had given her a birthday, since she didn't know hers. Elvia picked August, since nothing was celebrated then, and Sandy said, "Smart move. All the attention for you. Who wants to share with hearts or fireworks or witches?" So now she was fifteen, according to the made-up date she'd gotten used to, along with everything else, before her father found her.

He'd shown up at Sandy Narlette's house three years ago, when she was twelve, a total stranger with dust-covered boots and a dragon tattoo. He said he'd been looking for her for a long time. Elvia turned her back on him, but Sandy Narlette said, "Just give him a chance."

"How did you find me?" she finally asked him on Sandy's porch during a visit.

Her father looked at the foothills and said, "I got un-lost. After you and your mom bailed, I took off. Texas, Wyoming. Drivin trucks, layin pipe. I thought she took you back to Mexico in the Nova. Then last year, some guy saw my car in a police tow lot. I had stickers on the back. Bad to the Bone. Highway to Hell." Her father stroked his yellow goatee. "I thought if the car was in Rio Seco, you might be, too. I went downtown to social services and started asking. It took a long time."

When he finally came to pick her up from Sandy's house to bring her to the desert, she'd stared at herself in the side mirror. He didn't even know her birthday. He said, "I was gone then, too. Colorado. Gas lines." He turned down the radio and said, "When is it?"

She made another one up right then. "Next week. April 20." And he grinned. He bought her a Walkman and some CDs to keep her company while he was at work on the golf courses, hauling pipe.

He wouldn't tell her anything else. And Elvia couldn't remember enough for even a face. Michael had said if she wanted to dream about her mother she had to empty her mind and then drink the special medicine he was going to brew from a plant. "Then you get another level of dreams," he'd said, back in the spring. "What do you remember about her?"

Elvia hadn't wanted to give away the few things she recalled: the moths whirling above her like tiny, furious angels, the glowing circle of dashboard light, her mother's blue eyelids.

What kind of Indian was she, then? When Elvia ran, her long braids pounded against her back like those of a Tarahumara running along the mountain paths in Mexico, near a cave where her mother made tortillas. She'd seen a TV show about Tarahumara Indians when she was eight and living in a foster home. The other kids asked her, "What are you, with them spooky eyes and you're brown?" In the crowded living room, she pointed to the TV and imagined herself in the cave. Clap, clap with her palms. Her mother showed her how to lay the tortillas over the fire.

Now she tied her braids with leather shoelaces, leaning against the cottonwood trunk. It was better outside than in the house. Bracelets of gold light from the leaves fell onto her arms. Her father hated the braids, hated the leather ties. "You're not Mexican," he said, over and over. "You're not Indian. You're American. Wear your hair like everybody else at school."

"Shave it off?" Elvia offered. "All the guys shave theirs. Whatever they are."

Callie, her father's girlfriend, hated the braids, too. "I could curl all that hair for you, make you look gorgeous. But you want to pretend you're a cross between a squaw and a boy."

Elvia shrugged. She liked looking strange, like someone no one would want and no one would want to mess with. In some of the foster homes, the nicer she looked—the more the foster mother brushed Elvia's hair and lotioned her legs and put her in dresses— the more other kids tried to beat her up. When the foster mother had cut off her braid and thrown it in the trash, she'd curled her fingers into a fist, knowing her real mother had had a braid. She remembered riding on a hip, holding on to a long braid.

By the time Elvia was eight, she'd grown her braid back and never let anyone touch her, not her hair or her cheek or her hand.

Until Sandy Narlette's house, where she'd finally let Sandy comb her hair, touch her forehead to feel for fever.

When she cried as her father drove her away, he said, "She was a nice lady, Sandy Narlette, but she wasn't your real mom, like blood family." Like one of those dumb kids in a dumb movie, while she rode in his blue truck away from Rio Seco, she figured he would finally tell her about her real mother, maybe even take her to visit this woman who'd given her black hair and maple skin and Indian running. Maybe they'd fall in love again, like in the movies.

But her father refused to talk about her mother. He didn't talk about much. They'd moved around so much in the past three years that she'd gone to six different schools. Palm Springs, Cabazon, Indio: she didn't look like the rich or poor blond kids or the black kids or the kids who'd just gotten here from Mexico. And everyone asked, "What are you, anyway?"

"I'm late," she'd say, her voice hard and fast like her father's.

Someone would say, "You look Hawaiian." Elvia would shrug. Someone would sneer, "I hate when girls get green contacts that don't even go with their skin."

"Try pullin these out then." Elvia would fold her arms and glare.

Her father's eyes. Her mother's skin. She felt dizzy again. She wondered if she had her mother's heart. A heart that would let her leave a baby.

She wasn't huge. A quiltlike layer of soft fat surrounded her ribs and hips, that was all. She wore baggy jeans and big tee shirts, like always. She and her father had always gone to the army surplus for clothes. Her uniform—thin frame, two braids, and his mouth, when she needed it.

"Hey, Señorita Beañorita," a blond boy said. "You can fuck me for a green card."

"Bend it backwards and fuck yourself in the ass," Elvia said. "Then you don't have to make small talk with a stranger."

She had run to the arroyo again and again. Each time she got close to the plywood shelter, she thought Michael would look out from the car windshield he'd found beside the freeway, where months ago, the moonlight had turned the shattered glass into sparkling silver webs.

"We got walls, Ellie. I work hard to make sure we got walls and AC, and you're always hangin outside like a wino."

Her father's work truck idled on the street. She hadn't seen him cross the yard. When he crouched beside the cot, his knees turned the frayed jeans into circles of white.

"Yeah," she said, her head aching. "You put up with jerk bosses and wetbacks at work so we got food and walls. I know."

"You catch a bad attitude from Callie? It's contagious?" He stood, lifting the grocery bag. "I got one more run today, but I'm droppin off food."

The ground was so hot it shimmered, and she knew no one else was outside in the wavering blank heat. "I know, I'm getting too damn dark out here. Like a Mexican," she said. "How come you never answer my questions?"

He looked surprised. His goatee was blond and stiff on his chin. "She probably went back to Mexico, okay, cause she didn't like it here. Look, I'm not doin this. Why talk about the past when it's over?"

Elvia looked at his boots, covered with ochre dust. The grocery bag sat in his arms, just below the tattooed dragon. "We say that same shit in history class, but nobody listens."

"Watch your mouth, Ellie."

"Why didn't she take me, then?" She nearly shouted it.

He moved his boots in the dirt, and a tongue of smoke licked at the heels. "How the hell do I know? Maybe she wanted you to stay with me."

She stared at him, and he didn't look away. Green eyes, pale as drying foxtails in the fields. Just like hers. *Maybe she hated me every time she saw me*, Elvia thought again.

"Why are you askin about her again? It's been a while," he said softly. "And I said I ain't goin away. I feed you every day."

"We go away all the time," she said. They'd left the house in Palm Springs when he came home with the blue-roped backs of his hands swollen from a fight; they'd lived in the Sands Motel when he had speeding tickets and a bad license plate; they'd left Cabazon when some woman attacked their apartment door for no reason. They'd been here in Tourmaline nearly a year, this desert valley that stretched all the way to Arizona, to Nevada, to Mexico.

Her father shifted the grocery bag. "She left. When I go away, I take you with me." He headed to the house; the truck engine roared and the afternoon was white again with silence.

Why am I trying to dream about her? She stared at the circles of light dropping from the trees. *Because I don't want to be pregnant. And I wonder if she hated me from this minute. I want to ask her. Straight up. If she wished she could have left me before I even showed up.*

A hollow wail sounded across the yard, and Elvia squinted at the small brown stucco house. Maybe Callie's son, Jeff, was crying. But it was the desert wind swirling over the mouth of a beer bottle on the ground. The house had been silent for hours, and Elvia knew Callie was winding down. She hadn't slept for three days, and she'd probably given Jeff a tablespoonful of sweet orange Benadryl to knock him out before she dropped into her own coma.

Did Callie dream after she'd smoked the white pellets turned to embers, after she finally collapsed into unconsciousness? Elvia usually slept against Jeff's damp back, while he thrashed and draped his arm over her face. She wondered if her father dreamed, maybe of her mother's long black hair, so different from Callie's straw-pale strands.

Maybe speed burned up all their dreams. It fried the edges of their brains. All this time she'd lived with her father, he hadn't figured out that she was older. He still thought she was young enough to believe he and Callie sat in the truck at night smoking regular Marlboros.

Elvia saw kids smoking speed in every high school parking lot. She recognized the powdery grains Callie palmed from Dually, who came to the house in his huge black truck, two sets of tires rumbling through the sand. Callie tucked the speed in her pocket, and she sat next to Elvia in the dark, watching Mariah Carey or Fiona Apple on MTV.

"Even though you dress like a boy and try for ugly, Ellie, you're still pretty. You could be a model, or a dancer. Mariah Carey's like a mix of something and something else."

"So you're calling me a mutt?" Elvia rolled her eyes at the swirling, twirling girls on TV.

"Hey, if I had your looks, I know I would. Dance. Sing. Make some money."

"I don't live in New York. I don't dance. I like to use my head. Rocks, okay? Geology."

Callie stared at her. "That's what you're doin out in the desert, huh? Just collectin rocks. Better be sure you don't pick up somethin else. Cause your dad would kill him."

When her father came home from work, he and Callie sat outside in his truck cab, each of their inhaled breaths making the chalky embers in the glass pipe glow red as night-animal eyes.

They stayed awake for days. Her father took the clouds of smoked speed and drove his truck, hauling concrete pipe for new golf courses in Palm Desert, Rancho Mirage, Indian Wells. He came home with overtime money, his fingers coated with cement dust and his lips gray as ash.

Callie took her clouds and whirled around the tiny stucco box. She'd moved in six months ago, and Jeff's hands could reach higher now on the paint and doors, leaving tracks like snails. Callie's hands were red and dry, like tiny beached starfish, scrubbing the stove with a toothbrush and then spilling coffee, brushing off the baby-boy fingers in downward sweeps as if they were ants on her legs. He followed her everywhere, calling, "Maa! Maa!"

Elvia heard him now. She felt sweat trickling down her neck, black spores drifting from her eyes, and she followed the hot chain-link fence toward the house.

"Maa! Kips! Kips! Doggie!" Jeff called. He was in the doorway. She knew he wanted potato chips in a bowl, and he wanted his mother to find his stuffed Dalmatian. Elvia couldn't figure out whether Callie even liked her son. She watched Callie do whatever Jeff yelled that first day, after she'd breathed in sharpened smoke delivered by Dually. Then she twisted and swerved away more each hour, until now she was screaming at him. "One minute, okay? Leave me alone so I can pretend I have a life for one goddamn second? One?"

That's why I'm not going to do this, Elvia thought, watching Jeff's open mouth, his tiny teeth. *Because I like him. I don't want to hate a baby. For making me crazy.*

"I'm right here, Callie," Elvia said, crossing into the shade of the eaves.

"You out in the heat?" Callie paused near the wall, skinnier than a Barbie in her denim shorts and shirt. "Gonna tell me you're lookin for rocks? Don't you think you got enough rocks?"

Elvia looked at Callie's pale skin, shiny as wax with layers of sweat built up over her forehead. Callie's cheeks were scored with purple marks. Speed bumps, everybody called them.

Elvia went inside without answering. The house was a dark furnace, clothes everywhere and the swamp cooler clattering and cups from 7-Eleven like sweating sentries on every table and counter. Callie was always thirsty when she was sketching.

In the bedroom she shared with Jeff, there was only a mattress and a white plastic dresser, so she put her rocks on the high windowsill, out of his reach. Quartzes, pink and white. Red sandstone. Black onyx. Mica-studded granite. Elvia tied her sneakers. Near the foothills, where the cool air settled first when the sun began to fade, rocks glistened in the slanted light, much brighter than when the daytime glare turned the desert into a white blur.

She touched the three jewel-like stones from Sandy Narlette's house, the first she'd ever found. When no social worker came to move her, she'd begun to play in the orange grove, where she found a beautiful blue rock, then a green one, and a brown. Sandy bought her a rock book, and she tried to identify the stones. Lapis. Jade. Amber. But they were broken glass: milk of magnesia, wine, beer. They'd been dulled to stonelike softness by the rush of seasonal rain-water in the arroyo. She kept them to remind herself that everything wasn't what it seemed.

"Ellie!" She heard Callie's shout.

Callie was staring absently at the light wavering along the pale asphalt road. "Shoot, I was in Blythe two years, and I'm still not used to days like today. Gotta be 113."

"Yeah," Elvia said. Jeff butted his head against Callie's thighs, his calls high as a mockingbird's. She knew he was hungry and Callie was coming down hard.

"Ellie? Keep him outside for a minute, sweetie, so I can hear myself think? One minute, so I can call a friend?" She sighed. "I was gonna make biscuits. You love biscuits, right?"

Her voice tumbled like pebbles into a jar. Callie's blond hair was thin on the knobs of her shoulders, and her blue eyes pale as desert-faded denim. Elvia took Jeff's soft elbow and made a detour inside for Honeycomb.

When the cereal was in an old margarine tub, Elvia sat with him in the narrow corridor of shade along the east wall. Even though he was sweating, his head smelled sweet. She had given him a bath yesterday. Jeff trickled dirt through his damp fingers. Elvia leaned against the stucco and felt tiny bumps of fire through her shirt. Could you tell how hot it was by touching a wall, the way Sandy Narlette used to touch her forehead and recite a temperature?

Her head swam with tears again and she said "109" to Jeff's na-ked pink belly. She remembered how to tell if a baby was hot, which she had learned at one of the foster homes. She had taken care of kids she knew would eventually disappear. Just as she had always dis-appeared, been taken to a new place. She touched Jeff's back, cov-ered with heat rash like a mist of spray paint.

She couldn't remember her mother's fingers on her. Just beans in a bowl. She thought she remembered the clicking nestle of beans in a bowl, dropped from her mother's hands. She remembered the blue eyelids in the car. Did that mean her mother's eyes were closed because she was crying? *Had she been crying before she left me? Because she was leaving me?*

Elvia heard the trilling sound Jeff made at the back of his throat, the constant noise that drove Callie crazy. He was almost two. She used to be alone when her father was at work. She'd walked in the desert, watched MTV, gone to school. But now, since Callie and Jeff had filled this house with clothes and crying and whirling noise, Elvia felt lonelier than before, because when she held Jeff or touched his plump foot with toes like pale moth cocoons nestled in a row, she thought, *What did I do? What did I do when I was little like this, to make her leave me?*

Jeff's blue eyes followed Callie like tiny headlights, his cheeks slapped-red from the heat. Elvia thought, *Was I like this? Is that why she left? Because I drove her crazy?*

She'd heard girls talk at school about getting rid of problems. One girl had whispered, "You can't do that. It's alive."

Another girl answered, "No, it's not. It's just cells. A blob."

"It sucks its thumb inside you," the other girl hissed.

Jeff crunched the cereal, humming and trilling. She drank a glass of water, watching Callie's nervous fingers offering Jeff the Dalmatian. "Swear to God," Callie said into the phone.

Elvia began to run at the end of the crumbling asphalt road. Her father's house was the last on Fourth Street before the date groves. The huge date palms were planted in rows, with tunnels of gold between their trunks. Elvia saw the men climbing the trees now that the heat had settled; they covered the golden clusters of dates with paper bags to protect them from the searing sun. She heard them call out to one another in Spanish. Past the groves were the workers' houses, a colony of pale blue shacks in rows, too. Women hovered on almost all the tiny porches, sorting things in bowls, sweeping dust from the warped boards, laughing at someone's words. In one doorway, Elvia saw a cloth-draped, candlelit altar with a plate of food and a huge bouquet of flowers. On the next porch, a mother combed her daughter's hair into a puffed crown.

Elvia pushed herself harder, as if she were training. She'd never joined a track team, because then she'd have to practice and show up for meets. Since Callie had moved in, often Elvia never even made it to school. She had to help Callie with Jeff. And since her father had started smoking with Callie, half the time he forgot to pick her up after school. He didn't want her riding the bus with all the Mexican kids from the date groves. She waited at the parking lot fence where the sketchers smoked. With pencils, they pushed grains of speed deep inside their Philly Blunts. One day Michael had let out his smoke, passed the cigar, and tugged on her braids.

"I could make trenzas better than those," he said, grinning. "So you think you're Indian, huh, with those braids? Your people hunt buffalo, right?"

"What are you talking about?"

"That's what everybody says. When they're wannabes."

"Fuck you."

"Why'd you braid your hair then?"

"Fuck you."

"It's all loose and sloppy now. Here, let me do it. I'm an Indian." He rolled his eyes. She didn't move. He twisted gently, making her a single braid neat as his own. Then he put his palm on the back of her neck, and she couldn't believe he would touch her in front of all those people, with fingers that felt like a mother's.

She started to cry, right there, hiding her eyes from the smokers, and he said, "I was just jokin. For reals. Hey, I'll walk you home. I don't see your dad in his truck."

"My dad?" Elvia spoke into her fingers.

Michael laughed. "He makes sure everybody sees him when he comes."

The previous fall, her father had seen a boy hovering around her in the parking lot. He'd shouted, "Hey, road kill. Touch her and I'll fuckin flatten you."

Michael said, "Your dad ain't been around this week, huh? Come on."

His cheekbones were like turtle shells under the skin, and his forehead was brown as date palm bark. His hair fell the length of his spine. He said, "Trenzas. Braids. You don't speak any Spanish? You're not Mexican?"

"Half," she said.

"Me, too. Half Mexican, half Indian. Half the year here, half in Dos Arroyos. I'm half crazy, and I do a half-ass job at school. And I like to stay half stoned. All the time." He grinned and led her under the freeway bridge into the desert. In the dry arroyo, he showed her the shelter of branches and plywood, the windshield. The late-afternoon sun was hazy as water.

"So you can braid hair," she said. "Big deal. Dutch people wear braids. Blond ones. And Africans wear cornrows. A million braids."

"Your dad's a cowboy, right?" he said. "Blue '62 Ford. Your mom's Indian?" She didn't answer. He lit a cigarette and stared at the smoke. "My mother used to catch moths. Brown ones. She took the dust from their wings and put it on her eyes. Here." He touched her eyelids. "Like sparkly makeup. Cause she lived on the rez. No money. No car. No nothin."

"Did you see her catch them?" Elvia whispered. He drank something from a sports bottle. Everyone at school carried their alcohol that way, frozen each morning, slushy by lunch, potent after classes. When he offered it to her, she made herself swallow it. Hot plastic and sour apples.

"No." He studied the smoke. "My grandpa told me. I have to, like, imagine how she looked."

"Why?" She knew the answer. That was why he'd brought her here.

But he said only, "I brew up this medicine and then I dream about her for days."

"I want to try that," Elvia said quickly. "To dream about her."

"What happened to her?"

Elvia had never said the words out loud to anyone. Foster mothers had the paperwork; they already knew the story. Her father must have explained it to Callie. "She left me in a church parking lot, in a car with no plates, no ID, nothing. She was from Mexico." Then Elvia took the cigarette so she wouldn't have to talk. She didn't like the taste, never had when she'd stolen them from her father's pack, but she liked to hold them, liked to hide her face with the smoke.

She'd stayed in the arroyo with him several times. Once Callie had made scratch biscuits, and Elvia had taken four to Michael. He ate the biscuits and said his mother had been taught to grind acorns on a hollowed-out stone to make bread. "She laughed. She wouldn't do it. Said she'd rather eat dry Jell-O dust than acorns. My grampa said she didn't want to be Cahuilla. She went to Coachella to pick grapes and met this Mexican guy. He moved on to the cotton up north, and she had me. Then she died. Ten minutes later."

He cried, because he missed his mother, and he held Elvia tightly in his arms, smelling of sand and smoke. He took off her shirt and fit his collarbone over hers. He whispered, "I don't want to hurt you." She tasted blood when she bit her own lip. It hurt. No one said it took only a few minutes. That it hurt. That you could barely tell what the hell was going on.

A mother was supposed to tell you. She was supposed to give you something to drink in a teacup with flowers, even if it wasn't coffee like on the commercials, and then she'd tell you about feminine protection and where you put perfume and also, by the way, this is what happens when he takes off your shirt. He doesn't even have to take your pants off all the way.

Not the sex ed classes, where you couldn't act interested or pay attention with everybody else joking and sleeping. You were supposed to have done it already. You were supposed to put on nail polish, real bored, like the other girls who knew everything. Who had mothers.

Real mothers. Sandy Narlette had flowered teacups. She put Ovaltine in them. She sat the girls at the wooden table and told them about deodorant and breasts and monthlies.

You couldn't ask a father, she thought angrily, her feet crunching on the fire road, the sun a red Frisbee hovering over the mountains. *You couldn't ask a father anything.*

She had tried to see something of the movies he had watched late at night with his friend Warren, back when they lived in the Indio apartment. Warren would leave, and her father would fall asleep on the couch. When she crossed the room for a drink of water, the TV showed breasts like basketballs and men holding their penises like red batons. She would stare a moment, until her father's fingers relaxed on his beer bottle and it bumped against his wrist hard enough to make his eyes twitch. Then she'd slide back to her room.

She had seen nothing of Michael's body, only felt his mouth on hers, the sour-apple taste of his tongue after he'd drunk Everclear, and his hands in her hair. She felt wetness and pain and his eyelashes against her cheek.

She ran faster, harder, the white heat scorching her neck, her blood hotter and thinner, shaking loose the pulse in her stomach. *Melt, melt—just disappear*, she prayed, racing past the date palms and accordion music and laughter.

"Don't you love me?" Callie's whisper was flat as a sandal sole. Elvia stopped against the side wall, between stucco and fence. She could hear them in the kitchen. Her father was home. "I'm windin down, and Dually ain't shown up," Callie said, her rubber thongs brushing ceaselessly over the kitchen floor. "Come on, Larry, you're the best at makin em. Fastest."

"Ellie's back there sleepin?"

"Out running again. Says she's lookin for rocks. Larry, I like her and all, but she don't listen to nothin. Too grown."

"She's still a kid." Her father was eating something.

"She's just skinny. She ain't as little as you think."

"She's barely a teenager."

"Hell if she ain't." Callie laughed. "You don't know, huh? You said she was yours." Elvia heard Callie's teeth cracking ice. "Why you got her anyway? For reals?"

"I didn't want her in a foster home." Elvia stared at the dim blue roots inside her wrists. He always said that. "Didn't want fuck-up people messin with my kid."

"That's love, huh?" Callie's voice was so soft Elvia closed her eyes to hear. "When I first met you, and I seen this Indian-lookin kid, I thought no way that's his daughter. I thought you must a took her or bought her."

"Bought her?"

Callie said, "Yeah, except she's brown. Most times people only want . . . babies that look like mine." She was quiet for a minute. Then she said, "But after a while, I knew you weren't lyin. She had to be your kid cause you didn't pay no attention to her. If you'd a stole her or bought her, you'd be watchin like a hawk. Touchin her arm, messin with her hair." Callie laughed low.

"Hey," her father said, the word hard as a shovel. "Like you're a fuckin expert."

"Not me," Callie said. "I'm wound down, and Dually's either busted or packed up. This girl Lee, she's cookin her own out near Sage. Come on." The screen door slammed, and Callie was carrying a bag of something that tinkled like bells. "Lee said if you do those up for her, she'll take care of us."

They were in the yard now. Elvia scraped her back against the stucco, peering from the corner of the house. "Shit, Callie, I worked all day. I'm fuckin tired," her father said.

"Don't you love me?" Elvia heard Callie's whisper again, exactly the same, like a recording.

"Not much of you left. You're gettin so skinny," her father said.

"My tongue's not skinny. I'll do you good later on. Okay?"

"Shit." Her father grabbed his toolbox from the truck and clanked to the back of the yard.

"Maa? Maa! Maa!" Elvia listened to the tiny palms slapping the door inside. Jeff was awake. He couldn't reach the doorknob yet. She slipped back along the fence, in the darkness gathered by spindly mesquite bushes that grew near the wires where traces of water dripped.

Flames sprayed like purple tongues from her father's hand. She edged closer. Car air fresheners—the cardboard labels were strewn on the sand. Pine. Vanilla. Baby powder. Elvia had seen the bag in the kitchen and wondered what it was for.

Her father was intent on the torch. The glass tubes, empty of scent, lay in a pile like clear macaroni. He lifted a tube with delicate fingers, like a woman, dipping it to the flame twice, the glass like a drunk moth. Then he pulled it to his lips and the glass expanded into a golden bubble. He drew it through the cooled night air as though he were directing music.

Elvia stopped in the darkness. The glass bulbs would hold white pebbles of speed. When someone inhaled, the pebbles would glow and melt into the quick vapor and smoke.

The flames licked out under her father's thumb. Michael had built a fire in the arroyo to burn wild tobacco, the branches with yellow tube flowers the same size as these glass pipes. Michael had said, "Everybody needs fire, caveman on down to now. Every wino and bum's gotta have a fire, right? And everybody needs something to make em stoned. Get em through the day."

If she found Michael, how could she bring him here, to explain a baby to her father while he was bent over sparkling bubbles and broken glass? A baby browner than both of them? With thick black hair and eyes like onyx? Her father would probably try to kill Michael.

"Larry!" Callie called from the back door. "You ready?"

He didn't answer, squatting now to check something on the torch.

In the kitchen, Callie stared at her. "Shit, Ellie. Lookin for rocks? Show me what you found today." Callie's eyes were hot as the blue torch flame, her fingers red on Jeff's legs when she changed his diaper. From her pocket, Elvia took out the three glass-stones she'd had since Sandy Narlette's house. Callie glanced at her palm, and Elvia knew she didn't recognize them.

"Them three are enough for tonight," Callie said. "Cause I

don't trust you here by yourself. You and Jeff are comin with us. We're goin to visit a friend."

Elvia rode in the truck bed, watching the few lights of Tourmaline disappear as her father drove up the highway through ash-dark mountains. The road twisted through pines, dropped to another desert valley. Elvia saw only an occasional trailer or house on a ridge.

The truck's dust trailed them like a gold river. She wished she were driving. Her father had been teaching her to drive for years on dirt roads. He said she'd loved cars since she was a baby. She did love the metal cab, like a turtle shell that fit perfectly around her. She liked making her father grin when she stopped smooth, no jerks. "Like there's a low-rider dog on the dash and he didn't even nod," he always said. "Yeah."

Maybe you bought her . . . that was what Callie had said. Like people bought babies, kids, all the time. White kids. Like hers.

She looked at Callie in the front, Jeff's head bobbing on her shoulder while he pounded on the glass. One night, when Callie got drunk on tequila, Elvia had awakened on the couch to find her sitting nearby, touching Elvia's foot. Callie whispered, "My little girl. How'd you get so grown? You been out in the sun? I ain't seen you since they took you away." She pulled the sandal strap up over Elvia's heel. "I'm sorry. Oh, I'm so sorry. I hope they been nice."

Callie must have had a baby girl, long ago, and given her away. Callie fell asleep on the floor, and Elvia cried quietly into the couch, imagining her own mother touching someone else, crying like that. In Mexico. In Rio Seco. Wherever. Telling someone she was sorry.

"I'm sorry," Elvia whispered, but she still couldn't touch her belly. *You punched me. Do you have hands? Do you?*

Tiny rocks pinged under the truck. They stopped on a dirt slope, and when she stood up in the truck bed, dizzy, her father's hand reached for hers, his palm hard as a stone.

"Why'd you stop all the way down here?" Callie peered up the hill. The house was a brown wooden shoebox, with a few matchbox-sized cars parked nearby.

"I ain't takin the truck up that hill," her father said. "This is close enough. I don't know what asshole might be hangin out, might steal the toolbox."

"Always hopin for the best, huh?" Callie said, hoisting Jeff's bottom onto her side. His thin white legs clamped around her like twist ties. "So we gotta hike."

A lone mulberry tree stood like a feather duster in the yard when they made it up the hill. Elvia saw small toys scattered around its roots. A man blocked the doorway, calling, "Who you lookin for?" His voice came hard from inside his beard; his hands were tucked inside a jacket.

Elvia watched Callie smile. "Lee," she said, like a lullaby. "Lee called me up. She said come by and bring her these." The glass clinked inside the bag.

Her father said, "All I'm lookin for is a beer and a quiet place to sit down, okay?"

The man grinned, bone under the reddish hair. "You and me both, man. Them kids in there are drivin me crazy."

"Ellie here's real good with kids," Callie said quickly. "Come on, sweetie."

Her father and the other man walked toward a car, their hands gesturing in a secret code.

The house was hot as sleeping breath, the darkness a yawning mouth. Elvia smelled something sharp: Windex or pee, or coffee burned on the stove. Lee talked into a telephone balanced on her hunched shoulder while she bent over a box on the floor.

"Shit, times are hard," she said into her own shirt. "I'm only takin care a myself and a couple friends." She nodded at Callie. "Dually's been gone a week. You think Dean's gonna do any cookin?" Lee laughed. "Women always gotta cook, no matter what, right?"

She hung up the phone. "Hey, Callie. Help me start on this damn box. The government's keepin all the ephedrine locked up. Some's comin from Mexico, but now I hear the damn Mescans want all the business for theirselves. They're truckin the shit in, but they only sell it to Mescans." Her eyes landed hard and gray on Elvia. "Who the hell's this?"

"Larry's kid." Callie bent to whisper, "She ain't Mescan. Her mom's Indian or somethin." She turned around. "Where's your kids?" Lee bent her head toward a doorway. "Take Jeff on in there, sweetie. Lee's got some chips, don't you?"

From the kitchen doorway, Elvia saw the huge blackened pots on the old stove. Lee handed her a bag of Doritos, then knelt again by the box, pulling out packets of pills. "I got these from some Iranian dude at QuikStop. We got Sudafeds and Efidac."

Callie began pushing the pills from their foil packets, her thumbs curving as if she were snapping green beans on the porch. Elvia guided Jeff's narrow shoulders toward the blue light coming from the bedroom.

A baby slept in the crib against the wall. Elvia bent to see the tiny chest rising and falling fast as she could blink. She smelled vinegar, milk, salt.

"That's my baby," a little girl said.

She was about three, with blond hair curled thin as spiderwebs around her ears. She wore Pull-Ups hanging low. "And that's my brother." She pointed to a two-year-old standing near the bed. His diaper was heavy and long as a white beavertail behind him. *These kids, they'd look better naked*, Elvia thought. *Naked, and their moms could hose them off when they peed or pooped. At least they wouldn't have to carry it around all day.*

"That's mine," the little girl said then, pointing to the chips, and Elvia handed her the open bag. She had silvery tracks on her red-hot cheeks, like traces of fairy dust.

The boy cried, "Chip!" Jeffrey examined the trucks and dolls lying near the TV. The little boy grabbed the bag, and the little girl chased him to the kitchen. Lee said, "Get back in there and share them chips! You know better than comin in here when I'm real busy. Shut your door."

The little girl closed the door. She stared at Elvia, letting the chips fall on the floor, her hands splayed stubborn as a doll's. "How old's your baby him?" The little girl settled next to Elvia, stretching out her short legs.

Elvia was startled. Then she saw Jeffrey concentrating hard on a truck with no wheels. "He's not my baby. But he's a year and a half. Older than your little baby."

"He sleeping. My baby." The girl put her back against the wall like Elvia, legs stiff, thumb in her mouth.

They watched TV kitchens and laughing people. Elvia heard her father outside. *He hates being inside. I hate it, too, but nobody asked me. I get to be the pretend mommy again.*

She could smell chemicals threading through the air now, like incense sharpened with burning metal. The little girl eventually slumped to her side and put her head in Elvia's lap. The boys ate all the chips, picking the smallest triangles like confetti off the floor, and then they lay beside her, too. The baby hadn't stirred, but Elvia could hear his raspy breath. All the breaths rose around her like slow crickets caught in the children's throats.

Pretend you're the mommy. She arranged the sticky-sweet arms and legs around her, pale and sweating, shiny as candy canes with the red stripes sucked off. *I don't want to be the mommy yet,* she thought desperately. She tasted Cool Ranch on her tongue, felt a swaying under her ribs.

She must have fallen asleep for a minute. The acrid air pushing under the door stung her eyes open. Elvia moved the arms and legs as gently as she could, trying to breathe. Lee's baby was awake and snuffling, his round head bobbing against the crib bars. She picked him up. His arms and legs were soft and wet as damp paper when she carried him out of the room.

"Hey," Callie said from the couch. "Come sit down. I see a bottle right here. And I was gonna do your hair, Ellie, cause it looks a mess."

The air was better near the open door, and Elvia gave the baby his bottle. He snorted and snuffled. Callie swayed behind Elvia, her voice faster and happier now. "Don't that feel good?" Callie said, loosening the braids, stroking the brush bristles gently around Elvia's skull. "I always wanted somebody to brush my hair, cause it feels nicer when somebody else does it, huh?"

Elvia stared at boxes of Red Devil lye. Callie's voice tumbled like spilled soda. When she was sketching, she would talk all night, about what she would cook if she had money and how men were different animals. "I mean with different blood, sweetie," she'd say. "Like lizards."

Now she said, "Seventies stuff, you can find bell-bottoms at the thrift store if you look hard enough. Cheap, I mean real cheap." The baby finished his bottle and, instead of being satisfied, started to scream. "Take him to his momma. I'll get a diaper."

Elvia went slowly to the kitchen. Lee hovered over the stove, tiny blue crowns of flame under the pots. The shimmering air enveloped Elvia, prickled her ears and lips hot. She said, "Here."

"Just put him down for a sec, cause I gotta do one more thing," Lee said. "He'll be okay."

"I don't feel good," Elvia whispered, taking off the sodden diaper, and Lee laughed.

"You sure look Mescan to me," she said bitterly. "I wish you were. You could hook me up with somebody in Tiajuana. What I need's over the border. They're hoggin the good stuff."

Elvia turned to leave. Callie came in, Jeff sleeping on her shoulder. Lee's baby was rocking on his hands and knees, his moon-white butt in the air. "Here's the diaper," Callie said. "We're on our way, cause I bet Larry's half dead now. He was half dead when I met him. Tequila, see, that's not the best thing for him, but he likes the taste."

Elvia couldn't breathe. Lee turned from her stirring to take the diaper. The baby's eyes were gleaming circles of wet in the dim light from the burners. Elvia moved outside, to the cool dry night past the front door.

The cars were darkened hulks except for a pinprick of light from the other man's cigarette. He leaned from a window, pointing down the slope, a flat rush of smoke pouring from his beard.

Her father was asleep in the cab. When they saw his head thrown back, his goatee pointing out like stiff fingers, Callie said, "Well, shit, what a lightweight. Always afraid somebody's gonna rip off this old truck he's had since creation, and now he's knocked out . . ."

"I'll drive," Elvia said.

"Just cause your dad's been lettin you fool around on our street don't mean you're good enough to get us down that slope."

But Elvia shoved her father toward the passenger side. She found his keys and threw the beer bottle on the road, hearing the dull pop and trickle. "We gotta get home, and you can't drive at all," she told Callie. "How come you never learned? You like other people takin you places?"

Callie drew her head back. "Well, shit, no, I don't. But nobody ever taught me."

Elvia started the truck, the engine mumbling under her. She could smell Callie beside her, the vapor on her hair and arms.

"Nobody taught me cause we left Arkansas when I was little, ended up in Blythe, okay, pickin crops and our car broke down. Been tryin to get to LA, but this damn number ten freeway takes you through the desert forever. I keep stoppin in places like Tourmaline."

Elvia moved the gearshift, and the truck eased down the dirt slope. Then the house roof leaped toward the sky in a shower of light. The explosion thumped the truck door, reached in to knuckle-burn Elvia's cheek.

Elvia's father knocked his head on the door frame. "Shit," he said. "What the hell?"

"Shit, oh shit, she blew it up," Callie said, holding her neck, wrapping her fingers around it like a collar.

The dark car raced down the knoll and past them, no headlights, a black cockroach skimming the dirt and heading off the mountain. The house was burning like a lone jack-o'-lantern.

"Go!" Elvia's father said, hitting the dash. "Drive home, god-damnit. Go, Ellie!"

"Fuck, the cops gonna smell it when they come," Callie said. "But I seen all the boxes in his car. Lee and them kids wouldn't fit—they weren't in there. Go back up there, Ellie, go on."

Elvia imagined the kids in the bedroom, their pale arms and legs twined around each other as she'd arranged them when she'd stood up. She pushed her foot carefully on the gas and turned the wheel, and the truck rumbled up the slope toward the waves of heat.

"Shit, I forgot about the kids," her father said. "What the hell were you and Lee doin?"

"Cookin," Callie said, eyes red and wide.

Elvia turned the wheels as he had taught her to do to park on a hill. The hot air was a scalding tongue on her arm. She opened the truck door to look for someone, anyone, who'd gotten out. The heat forced her into a crouch, and then the little girl's tiny figure floated like a moth past the tree. Her hands came first—then her arms gray, her hair singed, her cheeks red.

"My mommy told me run. She get my brother and my baby."

But the house was falling in on itself, fierce traces of blue streaking the flames. Elvia saw the girl's eyes shining empty and silver as dimes.

Her father grabbed the girl and pushed Elvia into the truck. He started it, spinning the wheels, as Elvia pulled the girl onto her lap. The hair curled black near her small ear, her thumb was in her mouth, her eyes closed to the embers floating in the sky while the truck roared down the hill.

San Cristobal

EVEN AFTER all these years, the hurt was so fresh Serafina felt a sting like nopales spines along her ribs each time she thought of her daughter. Every day, when she washed the lime water from the corn, the husks rose to the surface like small translucent fingernails. When she whirled the wooden molinillo to beat smooth her uncle's hot chocolate, she smelled Elvia's palm, where she let candy melt before she licked it. And when she washed shirts in the stone basin and saw a wasp float past, its legs dangled loose like Elvia's when she used to sleep carried in Serafina's arms. Then the pain was so strong that she rocked back on her heels. Her daughter's legs dangled, didn't cling tight, because she trusted her mother to fly her safely to bed. *And instead I left her*, cried Serafina.

Back then, she had tried to sit up, to see the Nova, but the police car turned the corner and she banged her head on the door handle. When the pain inside her forehead receded, the men were pulling her from the back seat and walking her slowly toward a building.

"Green card? ID? You got ID?" a green-shirted man said inside, and she swayed.

"Habla, habla," he said impatiently.

"My dotter," she said.

"Her doctor must be down south," the policeman said.

The green-shirted man was la migra, she realized. Immigration.

He led her by the handcuffs into a small room. Tears slid down her throat like hot beads while he rolled her fingers over ink, the way her father and uncle had always signed their names. *But I can make letters*, she thought, confused. Then in a large room filled with men in work-stained clothes, a man spoke to her in rapid Spanish. She shook her head. He said, "Ahh—Mixteco?" He pointed to the green bus outside. "El camion."

Then she saw herself in the bus window and wanted to smash her own face. The bus lurched down the highway. She touched her pocket. She still had the lighter from the Nova and two silver barrettes that had fallen from Elvia's hair earlier. Elvia must have awakened by now—she would touch window glass this dark, whispering for her mother. Serafina rocked forward, hitting her forehead on the metal edge of the bus seat. Elvia would cry. She would scream for her mother. *Náá! Náá!* Who would find her? What if no one found her, and the sun rose, and inside the hot car Elvia's sweat evaporated and her breathing grew dry and short?

Serafina's own breath buckled in her chest. No. No. She kept the screams inside her throat, so no one would hear. As soon as this bus left her over the border, she would come back.

She saw only carpets of flat dark, then scattered lights and outlines of rugged mountains. How could she plot her trail back to Rio Seco? She had come here in a car trunk; she had seen only blackness, smelled only oil, felt each piece of gravel pinging against the metal box.

The Nova had felt like that, when it moved forward, like the dark car trunk, with sickening jerk and groan. How had she thought she could drive? Elvia was curled on the black seat, her small hand flung out as if waiting for a gift. She swallowed another scream and glanced at the men. One knee was spiderwebbed with oil; one neck was burned into red mesh from outside work. Their work boots or tennis shoes were splayed, their grimed hands uncomfortably still, their heads thrown back in uneasy sleep. They would return to their jobs. She would follow them.

When the bus descended from the mountains, she saw the tangle of signs and city lights. The men began to talk: Tijuana, Tijuana. The blinding lights of the border stations loomed like a row of open refrigerators, and then the bus was past them. Serafina felt the pains ricochet between her hips, as if she were having Elvia again. Her fear always gathered there now, lived in those belly muscles. She stood and pushed with the men. *Let me out. I have to go back.*

The stream of men filed past the green shirts and onto the asphalt beyond the chainlink fence, and then they floated away like dandelion spores. Serafina followed two men in blue coveralls and baseball caps who strode with purpose along the fence.

She could barely walk without the warm fingers pinching cloth behind her arm, without the chubby legs holding her waist and the braids touching her shoulders with each step. Elvia's hands at her knees every day, her nose a damp knob when she hid her face at the bend of Serafina's legs. She had never been away from her daughter longer than the hours sleep had separated them with dreams, and even then their hands and hair touched on the sheets.

She stumbled, holding the fence, and someone called, "Borracha," thinking she was drunk. She followed the men toward the levee that separated them from California.

The bank was crowded with people arguing and comparing, women selling tortillas and tequila for courage. Night was the time to cross. She had stood here before, with her brother Rigoberto, when he wanted to cross the wire. Serafina had shaken her head, saying she would stay with their mother in the hills near the dump. But after Rigoberto had gone, Serafina folded herself into a priest's car trunk, her mother looking down with a face pinched and stricken under her black rebozo. Everyone was dead, she said. How could Serafina leave her, too?

She turned slowly now, looking back toward the hills that led to the dump, five miles away. *No,* she told herself. She didn't even know if her mother was still there. And she knew Elvia was in the car, sobbing by now, crying for her to come back.

She heard only rushing blood in her head. The two blue-coveralled men clambered up the metal wall in a surging wave of backs, and then they were gone, dropping off with thuds. A woman was lifted up nearby, her pink blouse like a floating carnation. Serafina clawed herself up the metal wall, fitting her feet and fingers into the grooves, pausing at the top, so dizzy she nearly fell. Would someone shoot her up here? She saw the maze of arroyos and ravines, and dropped onto the dirt of the other side. She followed the dust of rubber soles and ashes, the sounds of running. The trails were lighter than the soot-scarred dirt, the lines stark as if a giant finger had carved them for these feet.

She kept the pink blouse-back in sight, wanting to follow a woman. Branches scratched her arms. They were running down a tunnel of brush into a ravine, where she heard shouts echoing. Bodies came from behind her, knocking her hard into the crumbling dirt wall. Sand filled her mouth and she spat in the rustling. Thumping blades dipped close like giant wasps, and she ducked into a damp hole in the arroyo bank, curling herself there for a long time.

When the helicopter faded to faint whirring, and more voices emerged from their own holes and bushes, she began to run again. She saw only black shapes cartwheeling past her and out of the canyon's mouth, like sheets of burned paper blown by the wind. She ran faster, trying to leave the dank moisture of the arroyo, and in the open space flashlight beams danced like blue needles. The white headlights of the truck that roared across the plain pierced her eyes, her chest, pinning her down like sharpened broom straws.

They sprawled on their bellies, in a pinwheel shape, and Serafina could smell the beer breath of the man next to her. His eyes were slanted fierce and red as chiles. La migra counted them. Then the Bronco jostled back to the same dirt road just inside the fence. Two of the caught men laughed as if it were a game, but the chile-eyed man cursed, spitting on the floorboards. Serafina's teeth were coated with dust. While she lay in the dirt, the Nova's lighter poked her thigh and she thought, *I should just die, die now, and then I would be an angel. I could be in the Nova in a few seconds. Elvia wouldn't be afraid. I would be there with her.*

She stood on the dirt road near the border station, the Bronco rumbling away. She wasn't an angel. She was the worst mother in the world. Her own hands on the steering wheel, her own eyes distracted. Her own fault, all of it. She prayed that Elvia was still sleeping, that she wasn't afraid, that the hedge shaded the car. She struggled off the fence and walked.

"Puta," someone whispered when she passed. "Puta mixteca."

Makeup like a whore. She had forgotten the eyeshadow and lipstick. She had wanted to look like a magazine woman. Her jeans cut into her waist. She clambered up the levee again, where fewer people were shifting at the edge. No tiny warm hands to pat her, shape her, steady her. No narrow chest resting against her collarbone, heart tapping against her own. She wasn't connected to the slope at all, and her body careened down into the foot-pounded darkness again.

She knew it was a different arroyo, but she breathed the same dust, the soot-black earth of campfires and shoes and running. A faint line of light hovered on the horizon, so she knew she was heading east, and a few voices echoed from further up the ravine. Then the hard arm shot out from a crevice and snapped around her neck like a clothesline.

One man knelt on her legs, and the other ripped her blouse open. "Dinero," he said, tearing at her bra, where women kept their money. He slapped at her breasts, and Serafina screamed.

"Nobody cares if a fucking pollo screams. People can hear you but they don't care. You don't need to cross now. You can stay here, where fucking Indians belong. Scream some more."

It wasn't enough that one lay on top of her, grinding her back into the earth. The other one waited at her head until her eyes rolled back and then he struck her skull, sideways, over and over. Other women screamed, whirling seagull cries, and more shoes scraped hurriedly past the crevice. The man she couldn't see hit her again, the bones of his hand like a shovel, and she heard nothing after that.

When she woke, she couldn't see. She felt her blood seeping into the ground. She felt her soul leaving, floating from beneath her breastbone, and then she wasn't tethered to the earth. She was eating the earth. She lay on her face, her teeth grinding the grains of stone left from the thousands of footsteps rushing the other way.

When she tried to shift her legs, she felt the sharp poke of metal. Her jeans were bunched around her knees. She tried to pull them up, but her left arm didn't work at all. The fingers on her right hand were too weak on the stiff cloth, and she felt the air on her thighs. Something sharp at her hip. Her knuckles brushed the barrettes. She slid them up her leg. She couldn't see. It was all she could do to rub the barrettes until the silver warmed her fingerprints under the black of la migra's ink and the drying blood of her own face, fading to nothing.

She had awakened in white sheets, a tiny brown hand on her shoulder, the knuckles brushing her cheek. She was dead, she'd thought joyously, and Elvia was here with her. She reached for the small hand, but the fingers were hard and thin as cinnamon sticks. Not baby-plump. Then her mother's face hovered nearby, creased and brown as a walnut. Her mother's joyous cry rang out, just as Serafina's liquid happiness drained back into her chest.

She couldn't move. Her head was hollow as a dried-out gourd. This was the bed where she'd been born. In Oaxaca. Her mother called, "La Virgen has brought her back! My daughter!"

Serafina moaned then at the cold hands of the statue, suffused with red, at the car hidden in the hedge, a forehead pressed against the window. Her mother bent low and soothed, "Who? Who? There is no Elvia here. Don't worry—no one will hurt you now. You are home."

Adobe walls—home in San Cristobal. Not the plywood of Tijuana. Her mother said, "Cuehē cuū-yō! Dead! Alba's son Gabriel found you like a little animal, your mouth full of dirt. He carried you up to the dump. Your head was covered with blood. Your hair was hard as stone."

Serafina felt plaster around her left arm and splinters of pain in her side. "Your ribs were broken," her mother said, touching the tightly wound strips of cloth. "Your arm was broken, and your ankle. We took you to the clinic in Tijuana, and the doctor said you might never awaken. So I borrowed money from Alba and brought you home."

Her head hurt so much that black filled her eyes, like rising smoke. "Elvia," she tried to say. A nun might have taken Elvia inside the church to wait for her. Elvia could say "Mama." She would tell the kindly old sister, "Mama come back." It might not be too late. But her tongue didn't work; it squirmed heavy in her mouth, like a trapped creature.

"Don't move. Don't talk." Her mother frowned. "*Sēhe síhí.* Daughter. You nearly died. Your *anima* tried to leave. Your soul had already flown. You have been gone from this world nearly a month. It is October now. Only la Virgen's gaze brought you back."

October? Serafina looked down at her arm, trying to remember. She saw the scar, a spatter of silver like shooting stars. Elvia's atole.

"Atole," her mother said, pointing to the altar beside the bed, the row of veladoras trembling, watching, the bouquets and incense perfuming the air. A clay bowl of sweet thick milk steamed nearby. "I made this every morning, to send your favorite smell past your face, to help you become hungry again," her mother whispered, picking up the bowl.

The cinnamon scent floated to her. She couldn't lift the casted arm to touch the scars. Elvia was gone, carried away from the church, waiting, waiting. Giving up. Serafina cried out, not even words, just a spiral of hoarse barking that made her ribs hurt, her breastbone, her marrow.

For days she tried to form words her mother could understand. They swirled in her head—Cap'n Crunch. Apple. Atole. *Sándoo.* Elvia.

Please. Money. Please. Her mouth could not form them. Her vision was full of black-lace veils, as if the man's blows had loosened something in her skull. She kept her head turned away from la Virgen de Guadalupe, hanging over the altar. The tilted face made her cry again until the pain shot through her head like agave thorns. *I was looking for you*, she thought. *I was praying to you, and they took me away. My baby was sleeping in the car. How could you be so cruel? I wanted to come home, but not without her.*

She listened to her mother's grateful prayers to la Virgen: "Thank you for bringing my daughter back to me. Make her stay. There is only evil in the north. Make her stay forever."

Uncle Emiliano studied her briefly before he left for his corn fields. He was over sixty now, her mother whispered. The old women of the pueblo filed in to look at her, to shake their heads at the evil in Tijuana, in the north. Her mother counted the dead: twin babies in the tomato fields of Culiacan, her husband and eldest son in the Tijuana dump. Even their spirits were not here, in the mountains of San Cristobal. No one was left. Everyone was working in America, disappeared like Rigoberto and Serafina, four years ago.

Serafina stared at the whitewashed adobe walls. She chewed tortillas. She felt the cotton *huipil* blouse on her chest. Her jeans were gone. She had nothing now, just like when she'd left. The barrettes?

"*Sēhe síhí*," she finally murmured. "Elvia."

Her mother was incredulous as she spooned broth into Serafina's mouth. "Elvia? A daughter? You were fifteen when you left me in Tijuana. I sent you to your brother. You were promised to marry Rogelio Martinez. He was in the strawberries. Rigoberto was supposed to find him." She leaned close. "You were not married. A daughter?"

It took Serafina a long time to tell her everything. How the car trunk felt, how she couldn't breathe, how the sickening thuds and jerks made her dizzy. Then she was standing on a sidewalk, nearly fainting, and her brother, Rigoberto, took her inside a garage where ten men lived. He said Rogelio Martinez had left months ago for the vineyards past San Francisco. Rigoberto said nothing was the same here in California, nothing was like San Cristobal; he gave her store-bought tortillas and cheese and a blanket for his mattress. He said she had to put away her skirt and wear jeans. He would find a job for her. He said, in a bitter voice, that jobs were better for women.

The next morning, the woman in the front house took Serafina to the Angeles Linen plant, where she folded towels and sheets, her heart beating wildly in fear until the fourth day, when she was comforted by imagining that the steam swirling around her was the mist of San Cristobal. That night, Rigoberto told her he was leaving for the grapes in the desert, in Indio, that he would be back in three months, that she should be careful. She looked at him uncomprehendingly; he was her only brother still alive, and he was supposed to take care of her. But Rigoberto said there was no work in Rio Seco for him, and he needed to make money to send to their mother.

"He left?" her mother said, disbelieving.

"He said he needed to make money. He said grapes were quick. Thirty-five dollars a day. He said Uncle Emiliano needed a new roof." She stared up at the corrugated tin Rigoberto's money had bought. She whispered to her mother, "He left in a truck with the other men. I was afraid in the garage, but I went to my work with the woman. I didn't know the street. I only knew the hands on the wall."

Angeles Linen was a pale blue building with hands folded—as if in prayer—painted on the side. Serafina stood with the other women pulling sheets and towels and uniforms scalding hot from the huge dryers, folding and stacking. All around Spanish words flew too fast. Her hair was tucked into a blue mushroom cap.

A young man waited outside for his truck to be filled with clean laundry. He smiled at her a few times, his eyes green as faded leaves, his mustache yellow and thick. She lowered her eyes, a trickle of fear falling with the sweat down her back. That afternoon, the day Rigoberto left, she folded in the hot fog, and through the wreaths of steam, green-shirted men poured through the narrow doors like wasps bursting from a crack. From her corner, Serafina saw them float against blue chests and brown elbows, she heard screams rise, and she was swept by other women outside. Then she saw the box. Blue backs scaled fences, and she bent herself into the square darkness of the box before the migra men came into the parking lot. She shut the flaps against the light and prayed to la Virgen.

"I asked her to save me from la migra," she whispered to her mother. "And someone picked up the box and put it in a truck."

Larry knew she was inside. He said two words she didn't understand into the cardboard flaps. She remembered the smell of her tears and sweat, drying to silvery webs on the hot, thick paper beneath her face. She felt faint, like in the car trunk. She didn't want to go back to Mexico. She didn't even know her address yet. She had no idea where the truck was headed.

"You went with him?" her mother said, her cheeks etched with disbelief.

In his apartment, Larry had dabbed stinging orange medicine on her knees, pointing to his own scars and scabs. She was paralyzed with fear. She was fifteen. She had never touched a man, hardly brushed her father's or brothers' hands when she gave them food. In San Cristobal, no one held hands or kissed until they were to be married. Larry's ponytail draped like a corn tassel over her wrist as he painted her knees.

She remembered the green couch. "I didn't know where to go. Rigoberto was gone. I didn't know where Indio was. Only strange men were left at the garage. The woman in the front house was caught by la migra. I saw her on the floor." She remembered staring at Larry's TV, which glowed like a square veladora.

Larry brought food from Taco Bell. The cracking-hard tortillas pricked Serafina's gums. She sat awake on the green couch all night, after Larry fell asleep in the chair across the room. Sirens blared down the street, red lassos of light reached through the curtains to circle the walls, and the sound sent pain and fear to collect like a nest of bloody threads in her head. The tomatoes she had picked in Culiacan, the seedy red acid on her hands, the blood-smeared bundles of her dead baby sisters, the exploding rockets soldiers had fired in Oaxaca to make her uncle and the other old men leave, the torn hole like a dark rosebud in one old man's temple. The webbing of red at the corners of Larry's eyes when he applied the Mercurochrome. She was afraid to move, afraid to look at his long, pale feet sprawled near his boots.

In the morning, she kept her eyes closed. When his delivery truck pulled away, she looked down at the avenue with cars rushing past. If she left this room now, where would she go? How could she find the garage? What if a neighbor saw her and called la migra? What if someone saw her even now, in the window? She huddled on the green couch, staring at the television.

When Larry returned that night, bearing another bag from Taco Bell, he tried to speak a few words in Spanish. "La migra," he said, then swept his arm across the table. "No trabajo." She understood nothing else he'd said but that: No job. No place to go. She put her head down on the table, smelling the unfamiliar beans of the paper-wrapped burritos. Larry pulled his chair close to her, patted her hair awkwardly, and said, "Okay, okay." She understood that. Then he pulled her toward him and kissed her, hands on her back. All she could think of was the way La Virgen's hands felt against her lips, the plaster fingers glowing with the oil of everyone's entreaties, maybe her own mother's lips on her forehead and cheeks. She had no idea how to pull away, how to kiss back, and so she imagined herself a statue when he pulled at her shirt. But his hands were hot and callused.

"You let him touch you? An American?" Her mother clenched her fists. "They have disease! They hate Mixtecos!" She leaned forward and whispered, "You made the gods angry."

Her mother's braid was still black at the end, but the stripe of silver hair at her part was now wide as a panel of lace. When they'd moved to the migrant camp in Culiacan, Serafina had seen prostitutes gather in the fields on payday nights, lying down with men under the trucks. "We don't do that, like animals," her mother said. "You are promised to Rogelio Martinez. When you are married, and you lie down together, his white blood will mix with your red blood. Ten times, and then you will have enough to make a baby."

She understood nothing Larry said, nothing he did. She knew it then, in the dark kitchen. There was no San Cristobal now—her father, who would kill a cow and marry her to Rogelio, was dead. Rogelio was somewhere in the grapes. The things she knew—washing clothes in the river, boiling corn over a fire—were gone. Here was a stove with frighteningly beautiful blue fire, a street with sirens and white strangers, a man smiling, touching the buttons on her blouse. His teeth clicked against hers, his watch ticked against her fingernails, and Serafina understood that these were her only coins: her teeth, her nails, the bones of her spine rubbing the arm of the green couch.

How could she tell her mother about the way the shouts of la migra circled in her brain even now, how hundreds of people watched her from car windows and houses, inspecting her braid and cheeks?

These peeling walls hid her at this moment. Larry fell asleep in a few minutes after he finished lying on her. He was kind for a week, then drunk for two nights, and then he didn't come back at all.

For days, she walked around the two rooms, touching the stove, the TV. She couldn't imagine how to get back to the garage where Rigoberto had taken her, which was filled with strange men from Michoacan. The plywood room near the dump in Tijuana, black flies and white seagulls whirling around her head, a trash barrel flame for cooking ash-specked tortillas, her father and brother buried, her mother sitting stunned on a concrete block. Rigoberto in Indio. Men grabbing her breasts in the dump, saying they would break into the shack to feel virgin blood.

Her head ached in the welter of scars like pink yarn stitched on her temple. "I had a baby," was all she could whisper to her mother, whose face crumpled with pain and disgust before she looked away, staring at the flickering candles on the altar.

"I missed you," Serafina whispered. "That morning, I missed you."

She remembered how Elvia's breath had smelled when they woke up that day, soft and milky through the baby teeth, and how Serafina had touched one sharp pebble of backbone. A small stone, shifting underwater at the river's edge when she knelt there to rinse the clothes, her mother humming. She had suddenly missed her mother's smoke-scented neck, her braid thin as an eyelash at the end when it brushed Serafina's arm near the cooking fire. Serafina had slid one finger into Elvia's loosely curled palm, thinking, *I want to go home,* but instead of gripping reflexively, like a baby, Elvia opened up her hand like a flower and pulled it away.

Her mother's hands were on Serafina every day. She spread pastes of turpentine and cloves on her ribs and ankles and wrist, for warmth to heal her bones. But inside Serafina's belly, the pain was sharp— she wasn't touching her own daughter, braiding her hair and washing between her toes. "*Sándoo,*" Elvia used to whisper at her feet. Serafina couldn't even see her own useless feet—her aching brain wouldn't work. It took months before she could walk properly, bend her wrist, look at the sky without seeing black sand. When she finally hobbled up the dirt path, holding her mother's arm, she said, "I have to go back and find her."

Her mother shook her head. "She is gone. They have found another place for her. She is an American now. She has a better life. You cannot leave again."

"I have to go back—" Serafina would begin, each day while she grew stronger, and her mother's voice would rise into a scream, her lips fierce and drawn back like a cat's.

"If you go back, you will die! All my children die! You are the last one." The desperation in her mother's voice edged over to hysteria, and she would scream, "You left me! In Tijuana! All of you. I was there alone with robbers, with floods, but you never came back!"

One of the old women would rush up the path and try to calm her. Doña Crescencia or Doña Elpidia would say, "You must stay, or you will kill her. Your mother has taken care of you. You must take care of her. Why do you want to return to California?"

Her mother's eyes would widen, and Serafina knew she had to be silent.

Her uncle spent days in his fields. There was no word or money from Rigoberto for months, and they ate tortillas with cheese or beans or salt. Her mother cried and said Rigoberto must be dead, too, her last son buried in California. Then he wired a hundred dollars from Fresno, but when she wrote back to him there was no answer.

For nearly a year, Serafina refused to look at la Virgen's face. *How could she make me choose—my mother or my daughter? How could she be so cruel, to expect me to live with a cleaving of my breastbone?* But one night, when her mother lay sleeping beside her, Serafina studied the soft blue robe, the hands clasped in prayer. She tried to imagine Elvia's face, grown thinner or chubbier, fed or not, smiling or sobbing. The tiny teeth. Please. Please. Apple.

She had been found. She couldn't be dead. *I would feel that. Who is feeding her? Another woman is brushing her hair, braiding it. A nun? Do nuns take care of children, in the north?*

What if Larry had come back, and someone had told him about the car? What if Elvia lived with Larry now, waiting for her mother to return? What would Larry have told her? What would he feed her? The nopales paddle had flown into the yard like a green moon of anger.

Larry had a beer glass. *Colorado* was etched into the side. Serafina knew this word, from the market in Nochixtlan, the vats of prepared mole sauces—negro, verde, colorado. Black, green, red. A red place? A red beer?

But the glass was wrapped in paper she had never seen—clear plastic bubbles trapped together. She remembered touching the circles of air, rigid buttons of protection.

Now she prayed, for the first time. But in the fire-glow, she thought that even her prayers were too Mexican to reach California, to touch her American daughter. So she prayed that la Virgen would wrap an invisible blanket of bubbles around Elvia, each dimple of air full of exhaled love.

Today her mother wore a white *huipil*, a dress her mother's mother had woven. Her mother's mother had spun the cotton, threaded it onto the loom, and embroidered the birds and animals with silk. This huipil had been saved for years, to be worn only in death.

Twelve years, Serafina thought, smoothing the fine cloth. *I never left you*. Her mother used to whisper, "I never left you, when I brought you back so sick, in case your *anima* flew."

Her mother had lost her mind a long time before. When Serafina cried about Elvia, or when anyone who visited San Cristobal talked about America, her mother would shout about the devils and the spirits of the north, where even the air was full of evil magic. Then, five years earlier, her mother's left breast had dripped fluid, as if she needed to nurse a baby. Serafina wanted to take her to the doctor in Nochixtlan, but her mother shook her head, a strange blue light around her black irises. "The milk—it has come back," she said.

The breast pained her, but she smiled and said it was a hurt like a baby's lips. Then the pain traveled to her back and her hip, and, finally, when her body began to waste away and her breath smelled like metal, Serafina told her uncle they needed money for the doctor.

She wrote to Rigoberto in the cotton, in the lettuce, in the oranges—all the places from where he'd last wired money. "Please come home. She is very sick. She will leave us soon." Every month she walked the seven miles to the next village, Santa Maria Tiltepec, where she took the bus to Nochixtlan and the wire office that held money for the few people left in San Cristobal. All the men who were working in California and Arizona and Washington put their money on counters there, where dollars disappeared and turned into pesos in Nochixtlan. After almost a year, Rigoberto sent three hundred dollars and wrote back:

> Take her to the doctor in Oaxaca City. I cannot come home. Crossing is too hard. Do you want my face or my money?

"Cancer," the doctor said, after they'd taken the long bus ride to the city. Nothing helped, not teas or horchatas or medicinal rubs, not the prayers and offerings.

Her mother lay in the wooden casket Uncle Emiliano had just made. A small crucifix rested on her breastbone, her fingers wrapped around a tall white candle. Her *anima* had chosen last night to fly, lifting from the open doorway and blending into the mist of the mountains around San Cristobal Yucucui.

Her mother still couldn't be alone. When the sun rose, and Doña Crescencia came to sit, Serafina would make tortillas and take them to her uncle in the field, as always. Serafina knelt on the palm mat near the coffin. She heard Doña Crescencia's thin voice rising from the path. Serafina touched the melting wax so it wouldn't drip on her mother's fingers. Doña Crescencia was wrapped tightly in her rebozo, her brown face small and round like sweet bread.

Doña Crescencia sat down on the palm mat and said, "Five years of suffering. She chose last night to leave because your brother didn't come for fiesta. Eladio Reyes and his brothers came from Santa Monica. They took the bus. Amado Torres brought his sons from San Bernardino. He has a truck. And the Sanchez brothers spent all their money from Santa Barbara on the flowers and candles. They will carry San Cristobal this year."

The fiesta for the town's patron saint was the only time people came back, during the third week of August, when they ate the special moles that sent sweet and spicy steam through every window, when the church was full of flowers that added their scents to the air, when the men carried the statue of San Cristobal on a platform through the streets.

"I asked them all," Doña Crescencia said sternly. "They heard

Rigoberto went to the coast, to the artichokes and strawberries. But no one knows. And he isn't here."

Serafina nodded. "He sends money."

"Money doesn't erase his tequio," the old woman said. Tequio—each person in the pueblo had a responsibility, for the water or the roads or the church, for the fiesta, for the old people. Money would pay someone else to do the work, but it wouldn't dissolve the insult of absence.

"Money isn't life," Doña Crescencia said, moving a pearl of wax from her friend's knuckle.

Serafina glanced at her, remembering the tiny apartments, the feeling of desperation when Larry didn't bring home money, when the only place for food was the corner store. "When you are up there, it is. Up there, it feels like the whole life."

She went into the cane-walled cooking shelter outside, starting the fire under the clay comal, mixing the masa she had ground. The firelight was the only glow yet in the dark. Serafina didn't need to see. She had done this since she was small; she had thought she would teach Elvia.

Her throat hot, as if an ember were lodged there, she kneaded the masa, waiting for the tears. For the first few years, she had wanted to die. Every morning, in the blackness before dawn, she had shaped tortillas, making sure the small maize-yellow suns appeared in her hands before light filtered through the cane-stalk walls, before any words or pictures drifted through her head. Sesame Street. Cap'n Crunch. Náá. Crickets running along the baseboards in Rio Seco. The old woman next door, her bony, pale hands reaching for the jars of pomegranate jelly.

Serafina nudged the suns, laid them gently on the comal. Her mother had stripped dry corn with her in the storeroom, saying, "A San Cristobal man will come back, and you will marry. You will have children here."

Every year, families came from America for the fiesta, but not Rigoberto, not Rogelio Martinez nor his brothers. Every year, the pueblo was empty again except for the old, a few children, and a crazy-eyed girl whose mother ran the soft-drink concession.

Serafina would imagine Elvia's small, dimpled fingers on the glass of the Nova. The fingers growing longer, thinner. Holding someone else's hand. The nun. A policeman. A stranger. Growing in Elvia's blood would be hate. *She will hate me when I go back to find her.*

She washed her face with water from the barrel. Pulling the silver barrettes from her apron pocket, she rubbed them over her lips. She felt the weight of the Nova's lighter in her palm. All she had. What did Elvia have, by now? Had she taken anything from the car? Serafina looked at the adobe walls she had touched almost all her life. Had Elvia had a home? The only address Serafina could remember was Yukon Street. She couldn't be there now. What if she wasn't even in Rio Seco? She could be anywhere in California. Anywhere in America.

When I see her, I will tell her: "Don't hate me. Your backbone lay along my breastbone every night, that close, while we slept. My arm was over your belly, to protect you. To keep you."

She brought a cup of coffee for Doña Crescencia. "All those cities in California named for santos, full of people who never go to church," the old woman said, sewing beside the coffin.

Serafina nodded, carrying the dishtowel-wrapped tortillas and dented thermos into the road. Doña Crescencia's singing followed her on the path to the fields, her words like gauzy trails from a spider. Serafina breathed heavily, but she couldn't see her own air in the cold because the dawn's fog, the sierra's own exhalation, shimmered like thousands of pearly beads.

She paused to look back at her uncle's house, the tin roof disappearing in the fog, and suddenly she felt invisible, too, not watched by the saints of earth and sky, whom she might have ignored for too long. She squatted in the path, nearly panting with fear, holding the tortilla bundle like it was a baby. Her mother was gone. This was how she'd felt in the linen plant that first day, invisible in the steam, sure no one was watching over her.

She pressed the tortillas to her chest for warmth and walked again, up the steep path to the milpas, the corn fields of her uncle. His patch of green was high above, where the valley was very narrow and the flanks of the sierra nearly met. "Rigoberto and the others are collecting someone else's dirt under their fingernails," he always said. "In their mouths."

But Rigoberto had always been angry at the soil while he pulled the plow himself on the steep slope where oxen couldn't maneuver. After the rain stayed away for years, and then a flood washed the soil down around the scattered houses close to the river, he said to his uncle, "Your earth is almost gone." Serafina looked at the palm-frond shelter where her uncle sat sharpening his knife, near the shrine honoring the season's only cornstalk with three ears.

Back when she was eleven, carrying lunches in a basket on her back, her father had promised her to Rogelio Martinez, who was fourteen, and accepted the promise of Rogelio's sister for his oldest son, Luis. During their three years of school, they all played together, until the boys began to accompany their fathers to the milpas and the girls began to grind corn in the yard and wash clothes at the river. She remembered seeing Rogelio and his father plowing or resting under their own shelter, opposite theirs. She glanced at her uncle now, his thin puckered mouth chewing, his eyes far away on the hills. "Ñū'ún saví," he used to say to Rigoberto when they argued. "We are people of the rain clouds."

"Ñū'ún tu cuiti," Rigoberto used to mutter, so only Serafina would hear. He didn't want to be disrespectful. "People of nothing."

When Rogelio and his father left with a truckload of men, her father reaffirmed their promise. "Three years, four," the men said. "When we get the money to come back and build a house."

But a year later, after another dry season with no rain and ears of corn the size of thumbs, Serafina's father took them north to Culiacan, in Sinaloa state, to harvest tomatoes. They slept in a box of tin, in a row of twenty, where the sun was molten all day and the brown water came from one pipe. Her mother's belly was big again. One day in the field they tied tomato plants to metal stakes, their hands stinging-slick with green paste, and a plane flew low overhead. A burning mist dropped onto their hair, flew past their lips, and seeped into their chests.

A week later, Serafina's mother moaned in the tin corner, two other women blocking her from Serafina. In the night, men gathered down the line of doorways, kicking a soccer ball, but her father and brothers sat frozen on a truck bed. In the morning, two cloth-wrapped bundles lay tiny as loaves, faceless, covered blind.

"*Sēhe síhí*," her mother cried, and Serafina ran to her call. Daughter. But her mother saw nothing, murmuring, "*Sēhe síhí, sēhe síhí*," and Serafina understood then. Two girls. Daughters.

They were buried in a row of graves near the edge of a tomato field, under a series of long stones chipped by a man from Puebla. A long row of gray doorways to the sky.

Rigoberto turned his book to the graves and trudged toward the field, where a crew boss screamed. "He doesn't care," Rigoberto said. "More from Oaxaca come every week. More ants. Ants carry so much. They're so strong. And then you step on them."

Their father only stared at him. Their mother didn't eat, didn't speak. Her black hair grew silver at the part between her braids, a stripe of emptiness, of hunger. The tomatoes were hot in Serafina's fingers, stacked in the crates. When the field was trampled and bare, her father took them north again, to Tijuana. Her mother rode silent in the bus, eyes blank until they reached a plywood shack painted yellow near the dump, where her mother's comadre Alba, long gone from San Cristobal, stared into her face. Alba's lips nearly touched her friend's, and then her mother's eyes shifted, glistened, and she began to sob into Alba's aproned chest.

Serafina knew then that only a woman who'd lost a child could receive those tears. She was not old enough yet to cry like that. Now, folding the dishcloth, she knew she was.

Her uncle finally said, *"Nicuvui nuhundeyteta."*

The deceased become the earth. Serafina whispered, *"Ñú ūu cuhu,"* to herself. My two sisters. Her uncle had never seen them, had never left this plot of his earth.

"When are you leaving?" he said.

She looked at the green fields, bending with beaded mist. Her uncle had his corn and the liquor he distilled from the sugar cane he grew in the far corner. *Ndixi* kept him warm all winter, dissolved more and more of his words every year until now he spoke only of ritual. "Soil is the flesh," he used to tell her and her brothers. "Rocks are the bones, rivers are the veins, and water is the blood. If the santos are not satisfied, we will starve."

"You're worried about who will feed you," Serafina said finally, and he glared at her, hearing the bitterness in her voice. She had never spoken to him with heat and disrespect.

"Is that what you think?"

"Someone else will do that. Doña Crescencia will make your tortillas and wash your clothes."

He frowned. "What is it that you miss so much? The money?"

Serafina looked at the sun turning the mist gold. "Tonight we bury her, and I will cook for the raising of the cross in nine days. Then I will leave, whether Rigoberto comes back or not."

"Because you're young, you think you know everything."

"I'm old. I'm thirty-one."

"When people leave, they only go somewhere else and die. Your brother sends money but he doesn't come home. Mixtecos must die on their own land, or their souls wander forever." She turned for the path. "Don't forget the santos, even if you can't see them where you are going."

She bent over the metate in the yard, grinding five huge leaves of yerba santa into a bright green paste. Then she laid cilantro leaves under her stone mano, moving back and forth. To send her mother on her journey to the other world, she would make her favorite.

The green mole sauce with pork. In the stone molcajete where her mother had guided her fingers so long ago, she ground cumin and green tomatillos, garlic, and several jalapeños, mixing in the yerba santa.

A new straw hat, like the ones men bought for the fiesta, floated up the path. She recognized the slumped shoulders and stubbled jaw. "Florencio," she said.

The lines around his mouth were deeper than when she had seen him last, three years ago at the fiesta, when he told her he worked with Rigoberto. He was her brother's closest friend. He turned to look at the cooking pot, and in the firelight she saw only the sides of his neck and his hard cheekbones. He looked so hungry.

"I'm sorry about your mother," he said. "I heard now, walking through town. We have only one letter from you. We've been moving from place to place for months. A bad, rainy season."

Serafina let out her breath. "So Rigoberto isn't coming."

Florencio shook his head. The marks around his mouth were curved, as though someone had cut him with a machete, and three grooves reached from each corner of his eyes. "There were floods all spring in Pajaro and Salinas. The lettuce and the strawberries. No work for weeks; no place to sleep but a barn. No money. Now the oranges are ready." Florencio paused. "I told Rigoberto I was coming back to see my cousin."

Serafina nodded. Florencio's young cousin had lived in Tijuana for a few years, but she had come home alone to have a baby. She stayed in a room at the small store, taking care of the empty soda bottles.

"She is the only family left," he said. Serafina knew his parents had died in a car accident years ago, with Gabriel, Alba's son. The one who had found her in the arroyo. Bandits had chased Gabriel's truck in Sinaloa, causing a crash, then robbed the bodies.

"Rigoberto stayed in the oranges because he borrowed money from the boss. For you." Florencio took out a roll of dollars wrapped tight as a cigarette. "Now he can't leave."

Serafina couldn't breathe. "He knew?"

Florencio shrugged. "He said your letter sounded like you would come soon. It's much harder to cross now, and coyotes charge more."

Serafina shivered, hearing a string of firecrackers from town. Her hands shook when she ladled a dish of mole verde and put it near him. He dipped the tortillas and ate slowly. His face was grave now. "He said you want to go back there. To where you were."

"Rio Seco," Serafina whispered. "I do."

"What happened to you?" he whispered, looking down at the ground.

She went to the adobe storeroom to hide her face. Stripping dried corn kernels into a bowl, she saw herself small, heard her mother telling her not to waste any part, not the husk or even a few kernels, or the ñū'ún would look from the sky, see them lying on the ground, and assume her family had too much corn and didn't need such a large harvest next season.

She tried to remember what she'd been teaching Elvia. A. Apple. B. Balloon. C. Cat. She had chanted the letters to herself for years. But someone would have taught Elvia everything else. Another woman had taught her to tie her shoes, to button shirts, to comb her own hair.

Or Larry had combed her hair. He hated braids. Maybe he cut them off. "She ain't Mexican," he used to say. "Ellie ain't Mexican." He would have told Elvia a thousand times that her mother was someone to forget.

She was fifteen last week. Ocho Agosto. She will never recognize me. Serafina bit her lips until they stung. Then she slid sticks across the hearthstones to feed the cooking fire, careful to brush off splinters and dirt from the blackened rocks that held up the iron ring.

The ñū'ún yuu nu'un —the santo of the hearthstone—was the fiercest of them all. Rocks are bones, her mother said, and the rocks burned daily in the hearth suffer the most pain. They are truly dead. Never step over them or place things on them, or you will become very ill. Serafina crossed herself, missing her mother's whisper across the steam.

She bent near her mother's small, dark face on the pale pillow. She had carefully braided the long gray hair, the woven tail wispy as a moth's antenna. She could see the small indentation left by her thumb, at the corner of the mouth, where she had held her mother's dry lips closed as gently as she could, until the body's stiffness settled in to keep them together.

Her mother carried with her the things she needed for her journey to the other world. A soft white cotton bag that Serafina had filled with chocolate and sugar and a tiny wooden molinillo to beat the foam. Two tortillas. Five pesos. A small bar of soap, a small bottle of water.

Her mother's papery, corn-husk voice would be gone when they closed the box. Her soft brown neck, where Serafina had cried so many times, her mother's collarbone wet when she finally let go. Doña Crescencia said, "You will keep your mother's rosary? It is yours now."

The rosary twined in her fingers. "No," Serafina said. "It was her mother's. It is still hers."

Last week, when her mother was fading, Serafina had thought she would call out the names of her husband and sons. Claudio. Luis. Rigoberto. But her mother spoke to her own mother. "*Náā*," she said. When her mother called out the word again and again, "*Náā, náā*," Serafina lay on the dirt floor near the cookstove and screamed into her rebozo so no one would hear. Her daughter would have called for her over and over, screamed at the car window.

When the husk slipped easily from a rubbed kernel, Serafina washed the corn until the thin skins rose into tiny drifting pockets on the water's surface. *Nuñi saha.* She remembered the Cap'n Crunch, the sweet corn dust on Elvia's fingers.

Nine days later, Serafina made mole coloradito, the red sauce, for the raising of the cross. While people sprinkled holy water on the flower-laden cross at the family altar, Doña Crescencia begged Serafina not to leave. "They hate Mixtecos there—remember the Cortez brothers?"

The four Cortez brothers had left for the border last year. The coyote who drove them in a crowded pickup through back roads didn't stop for la migra's sirens and crashed the truck in a ravine. The bodies were sent back to San Cristobal naked, bruised, and bloody, in cardboard boxes. When the lids were removed, the entire pueblo screamed at the disrespect for the dead.

Serafina shook her head. "Everyone else is already gone." August was harvest time, and Serafina imagined the people at the border like swarms of birds, all trying to get through a hole in the straw roof at once, circling and circling while some slipped inside at each pass.

Her uncle lay in his bed; days after he had carried the coffin, his back still ached. Serafina mixed cloves and turpentine in the molcajete, smeared the paste on a cloth, and lay it on his lower back. Before her uncle could speak, she hurried outside.

The church smelled as it always did, of roses and wax and sweet smoke. She would never be home again, in this familiar light, with the tilted faces of santos she had known all her life. "You are everywhere," she whispered to la Virgen de Guadalupe. Serafina kissed the metal lighter from the Nova, the shiny black knob, the circle that had glowed red. She placed it near the candles and flowers and photos. "If you let me get to Tijuana, I will give something else for the rest of the journey. When I lost my daughter, I was only looking for you."

The white-petaled flowers on the cross were wilted by all the touching. Serafina wondered if her mother's bag of possessions had comforted her. In her own cloth bag, she had Rigoberto's money. A few clothes. Her rosary. And at the last minute she had washed the gray stone molcajete, the round bowl with tiny legs her mother had used every day until she gave it to Serafina. She had put the smooth pestle inside and wrapped the bundle with a shirt.

Outside, she touched the stone sink, still wet from her washing dishes, and the comal, still warm from her cooking. Where she was going, nothing was permanent, carved of stone.

She walked down to the main road to Manuel Jimenez's truck. He drove people from Oaxaca to Tijuana now. The men waited, their cigarettes glowing inside the windshield and floating in the truck bed. When her shoulder was pressed to the window and the truck was moving, she kept her eyes closed, not wanting to see what was sliding past the glass, away from her. She could feel Florencio's elbow. She held the barrettes, not needing to see the rubbed shine, the silver bars she had mouthed and touched until they were fragile stripes of light in her palm.

The Sands

"STOP CRYIN, or they'll think somethin's wrong and they won't take her," Callie said angrily when Elvia's tears fell onto the little girl's arm.

Her father and Callie argued in jagged whispers while Jeffrey screamed from the floorboards, angry that another little body had taken his place on Elvia's lap. Elvia stared at the half-sleeping face, touched the leathery red cheek. "The hospital's in Desert Hot Springs," Callie said.

When the truck pulled up at the circle drive, Callie said, "I'm carryin Jeffrey, and nobody's gonna think nothin bad cause I'm a mother. I'll just say we found her wanderin." Her voice was still gravel-edged and fast. "Pick her up."

Elvia carried her, one arm around the ribs, one under the tiny bottom, and she felt the hands on her back. The little girl was limp, but she held Elvia's shoulder blades like they were handles. Then the door slid open and the emergency room nurse was staring at them.

Callie said, "We were drivin back from my mother's house and we seen a fire. Found her in the street, we don't know who she is or nothin."

The nurse said, "I'll be right back with some papers for you." Her shoes squeaked.

Callie took Elvia's elbow with a grip hard as pliers'. "Put her down." Elvia couldn't. The little girl's fingers dug into her bones, holding tight. "Put her down and move, Ellie. Now." Callie pried the fingers from Elvia's shirt with one hand, and Elvia felt the little girl sliding down her side. She bent and put her on the chair. "Don't you cry, goddamnit," Callie whispered, pushing her toward the door. "Don't."

Elvia looked back at the little girl staring at her until the door slid shut and she saw only their own figures moving away from the reflection.

"Don't get out yet," her father said to her when Callie and Jeff went into the house. "Ellie. We're bookin up. Okay? Now go grab what you need. Just one bag of stuff."

In the bedroom, Jeffrey watching, Elvia dropped stones and clothes into a grocery sack. Pain like lightning pulsed through her head. If she'd stayed in the kitchen to put the baby's diaper on, just a few more minutes, she'd be dead, too. She and her own maybe baby.

Jeff poked her legs. "Ellie," he said.

Her father shouted outside. "Ellie!"

"*Okay!*" she yelled back, going outside, dropping her paper bag at her feet. "*What?* What the *fuck* does everybody want?" Callie stopped pacing near the truck bed where Larry was throwing duffle bags. "Oh, I can't cuss, but I can take care of Jeff all *fuckin* day and miss class? I can almost get killed cause you guys handle your speed worse than faders at school?"

"You better watch your mouth, cause you aren't grown," her father said, and she glared at him. *Yeah, I am,* she thought. *You just don't know.*

But Callie was staring at Elvia's grocery bag. "You're takin your little squaw-girl likes to play Indian?" she yelled. "You goin with him, Ellie? This fuckin idiot?"

Elvia's father's smile was square and long, like a zipper under his mustache. "I'm only an idiot cause I'm outta here," he said. "I was a fuckin genius when I was layin pipe all day and you were at the casino, right? You hung out with the Indians runnin video poker. And I was okay drivin you to Sage tonight and you could a got Ellie killed."

"I took care of her better than her real mama," Callie shouted. She turned to Elvia. "Your real mama ain't Indian, she's just a Mes-can. And if she was a good Mescan, she wouldn't a dumped you. Cause usually they don't."

"How do you know?" Elvia said. Her eyes burned, staring at her father.

"Her name's Serafina Mendez. Look." Callie grabbed a toolbox and pried the lid open. She dumped out wrenches and a hammer. "I seen it. Look." She held up a plastic card.

"What the hell are you . . ." Elvia's father began, but Callie held the card out to Elvia.

No picture of her mother. Only words under the dull, scratched laminate.

Clinico Medico de Tijuana
Serafina Estrella Mendez
Miscelanea Yoli
Colonia Pedregal   Tijuana   Mexico

"See," Callie hissed. "And he's got one with a picture."

"No, I don't," he said, his face twisted in anger. "We're outta here. Come on, Ellie."

"I seen her picture once," Callie insisted. "That's her name. For reals. She lives right over the border. Two-hour drive. It ain't Mars. If she wanted you, she could a came to get you."

"Why didn't you tell me?" Elvia said to her father, the card thin as a leaf in her fingers.

"Tell you what?" he shouted back. "That when your mom bailed, she left that and some clothes and some burned-up candles? Big deal. She forgot to pack you, too." He closed up the toolbox, threw the last bags into the truck, then nodded toward the open pas-senger door. Elvia slid the card between her fingers. Her mother—in Tijuana?

"She was an asshole just like you!" Callie said, starting to cry. "Runnin away! I can't believe you're takin Ellie." Her skin was dented in dark-green places at the jaw, her gums were scored with purple marks when she opened her mouth, and Elvia realized Callie hadn't eaten in days. "I don't believe this shit. I've been tryin to take care of your kid . . ."

"I got a job in Nevada, okay?"

". . . and you take off."

"The rent's paid till the 30th."

"You and her," Callie cried. "Choice, like you always say. Real choice shit." Elvia got in the truck. She saw Jeff's fingers appear on the door frame. She waited for the rest of his arm, for his face. He poked his bird-feather hair around. Callie said, "You're pickin her over me."

Elvia's father stopped moving, smiled again. "Wouldn't you pick him over me?" he asked, nodding at Jeff, who stared into the truck wheels.

Callie didn't glance down. Elvia saw her rake her thin hair into a ponytail and tie it into a knot. "Well, shit," she said. "Well, shit. You're pickin for me."

He slammed the door, and when they reached the end of the driveway the sand flew from under the tires and stung Elvia's arm hanging out the window.

When they'd parked in the slot for number 11 at the Sands Motel, Elvia said, "I can't believe we're back here again."

Her father's voice was softer than usual. "We're just here till I figure somethin out."

"You know what I can't figure out?" Elvia couldn't look at him. She felt the ID card against her thigh. "Why we never stay anywhere."

Her father still held the wheel, his knuckles big as dirt clods. "Callie owes this guy money."

"Dually. He fronted her some speed. Like I don't know. Hell, Jeff probably knows."

"You don't know," her father said, rubbing his forehead. "It's not funny. When he doesn't get his cash, he takes people instead. People like you."

Elvia shivered, looking at the row of red doors, bulbs lit near each one like small, angry suns. "This is where we came the first time," she said. "When you got me from Sandy Narlette's. And we still don't have shit."

He leaned his head back, his goatee pointing at the windshield. "I can't believe you drove down the hill. You were drivin when you were little. All you wanted to do was sit in that Nova."

He always remembers me as a little kid, she thought. *Not who I am.* "If I hadn't taken us down the hill, we'd all be dead. Those kids . . ."

"That's their mom's fault, okay?" But his voice shook a little. "Hey," he said, pretending to turn the wheel now. "You used to sit like this forever, drivin wherever little kids drive. Pullin out all the dash knobs. You always wanted me to put you in the car. Your mom couldn't drive."

"Then how the hell did she leave?"

Her father stared at her. "She figured it out somehow. She acted like she didn't know anything, but she figured out what she wanted. Callie's right. If she wanted you, she'd a came by now." He opened the truck door. "Let's go. I gotta be at the quarry before the sun comes up."

He didn't turn on the light, only put his things down on one bed. She sat on the bed closest to the air conditioner. "You're going back to work at the quarry? With Warren?"

"For a month or so. I need some cash."

"I want to go to Tijuana. Look for her." He threw his head back and she knew she had about thirty seconds before he shut down. "I hate talkin about this shit."

"I know," Elvia said, quietly. "But I have to find out." She watched him light a cigarette and lean against the door. He wasn't with Warren or Callie or Dually. Nobody was laughing or arguing; the TV was silent.

She wondered how speed felt in your brain. Like Windex, working on each cell, shining them up, but then so strong it started eating them, too? She remembered the smell from Lee's stove.

He looked at the ID card in her hand. "Why do you want to find her so bad? When somebody doesn't want to be where you are, even if you chase em and catch em, so what? If Callie found me right now, I'd just book up again."

The card was smudged and dirty. She saw a black fingerprint. Big. His.

"You kept looking at this," she said. "Did you try to go there?"

He nodded, smoke drifting from his goatee. "Couple weeks later. I was in jail when she left. Bar fight. Then when I went down to TJ, it was a nightmare, Ellie. All these beggars and kids and drunks. Like a shitty MTV video. I wandered around for two days, couldn't even find the Yoli place. Got my radio and tools rippped off. Came home and figured, why would she go back to that? Take you back to that? I figured she went the opposite way—LA, Frisco. Wherever . . ."

Then he pointed the cigarette at her. "And when I found out you were in foster, then I figured, hell, she didn't go back to Mexico. She decided to start over. She dumped you cause you were a burden, Ellie. Probably ended up someplace a lot better than here."

He opened the door to go, and she said, "Maybe she found another guy cause you were too hard to live with. Maybe she has ten kids now. How old was she? When she had me?"

He was pissed now. "I don't know. Old enough."

"You had a kid with her and you didn't even know anything about her? Way great courtship. Rattlesnakes take a week, you know, cruising around before they do it. How'd you meet her?"

"It doesn't matter." He was facing the parking lot.

"Romantic."

"I was tryin to help her out."

Elvia laughed. "Same thing you said about Callie. Help women out and then dump them."

"Oh, but you're fuckin up there," he said, turning. "Other way around, remember?"

"No shit. She dumped us both."

"Ellie." He threw the cigarette butt into the parking lot and pointed to the card. "Don't set yourself up. Don't expect anything. Ever."

"You already taught me that," she snapped. "Look at where I am." Elvia stopped, stricken by the floating feel under her ribs. In this tiny motel room, he'd eventually notice her soft, expanding belly. And he would be past ballistic. When she lay on the bumpy spread, she heard him lock the door.

The air conditioner hummed in the window. She saw the gray dust thick on the metal slats, like the ash from the fire, and when new headlights shone round and white on the window shade, they were as empty as the little girl's glittering eyes.

Elvia buried her face in her jacket and sobbed until her face was bathed in stinging salt. The little girl had sucked her thumb, her eyes closed, her arms already callused by the fire's heat. She would have marks forever, to remind her of the night her mother and brothers swirled into dark sky, glowing. She would float around in shelter homes, in strange kitchens, just like Elvia had, with no mother to catch her.

She rested her face on the wet jean jacket, breathing through her damp hair. Who would ever hold the little girl's burned-scarlet face again? *We told the nurse we found her. Someone found me, in the church parking lot. Was my mom taking me inside, to leave me on one of those benches? Sandy Narlette said some moms are better able to take care of kids than others, just like cats and dogs. Animals. She said don't get mad.*

She got up now, her empty head ringing, and turned on the TV so the screen could flash videos, but she left the sound down to a whisper, like someone was in a kitchen, at a table nearby. She didn't want to smell the strangeness of the bedspread, so she piled her own clothes around her. She could smell herself. She was scared. She wanted to hear the truck come back.

.   .   .

Her father's boots crunched the sand outside like broken glass. She heard him talking to Warren, who'd lived at the Sands forever. She moved the window shade aside. The motel's horseshoe shape was filled now with cars and trucks. All the shades were drawn, like hers, shielding dim, jumpy light from TVs. The windows flickered amber around the asphalt like burned-low campfires, and the mesquite tree was smoky gray in the center.

Their voices were fast and raspy as the cicadas in the trees. They carried McDonald's bags and six-packs. In the harsh light of the naked bulb outside their room, Warren's brown hair faded flat away from his broad forehead, and he was even skinnier than he was the last time. He had white lines like spiderwebs near his eyes and on his neck. "Man, it's been a while. Hell, look at the fuckin red doors. Indians own the place now, man, live in number one."

"Indians?" her father said.

"Fuckin Indian Indians, bud, with the funny clothes. Ragheads."

Her father opened the door and peered into the darkness. He turned on the small light, and Elvia imagined watching the light from their window fill up the horseshoe so that the campfire circle was unbroken.

He put one bag and a cup on the little table. "Your favorite."

Elvia took the vanilla milkshake and sucked hard on the straw. The grains hit the roof of her mouth like grit turning to snow. Her father had taken her to the snow once, to the top of Mt. San Jacinto. Michael said he'd climbed Mt. San Jacinto with an uncle on the Soboba reservation. He never stayed anywhere for long. She thought of his fingers on her face, his whispering: "You definitely got good blood. Look at you."

She shivered when her father turned up the clattering air conditioner. "I'm gonna drink another beer with Warren," her father said. "I'll be back."

Milk pooled sweet at the back of her throat. She had tasted Callie's beer once, washing bitter gold down her throat, leaving nothing behind. She tried to imagine the vanilla shake raining down on a baby, a thumbnail-sized baby inside her, but she couldn't picture anything even close.

The cicadas had stopped their humming when she turned off the air conditioner and opened the door. She looked at the mountains above, but she had no idea where the moon would rise here.

Every month, the full moon rose in Sandy Narlette's laundry room window. When Elvia had arrived there the second time, when she wouldn't talk, Sandy would sit her on the dryer; while she loaded clothes, Sandy would say, "Elvia, tell me when that fat, bright moon sits on the telephone wire outside. Tell me. I love those few minutes when it's balancing. When it's a highwire moon."

Elvia remembered exactly how it looked—like it could stop going on the same path it took every month, like it could roll sideways instead, suddenly deciding to visit a whole new place, riding the silvery wire, raising starry sparks.

Her father's truck was parked at number 14, Warren's door. *More beer*, she thought, feeling the cooled concrete under her bare feet. He always said, "Never walk around barefoot, like a vagrant. Never sleep outside, like a wino. Never talk to strangers, like an idiot."

But she loved walking in the dark, breathing in the air the desert plants released when they opened up to drink the dew, seeing the gray-gold flash of a coyote. Day was night. Her father had told her that, because he'd been in the desert a long time.

She followed the sound of his laughter now, passing three dark windows to sit against the wheel of his truck. A slice of light from the open slot of their door fell onto the dirt past her feet, but for a few minutes she heard only the loud click of the channel changer. Then Warren said, "Whoa, honey, that's the one for me. True redhead."

Elvia saw a fingernail crescent moon over the mountain now. She didn't want to imagine what the redhead was doing. More than what she'd done with Michael, and nobody in those movies ever got pregnant, she bet. She heard furious clicking, the remote working hard. Warren said, "Turn it back to the redhead, Larry. Come on, gimme the thing."

"Fuckin TV's so beat up you can't see shit anyway," her father said.

"Last time I seen you and that chick Callie, she said you were buyin a big-screen," Warren said. "Now you're broke. What the hell happened?"

"Callie was sketchin, man, she'd smoke anything. Sudafed, Efidac. Her teeth were fallin out—she was bones. Remember Dually, with the Ford?"

"He still movin the stuff out there?"

Elvia remembered Dually's face, in the doorway, on the couch. His beard a black scarf over his neck, his blue eyes threaded with blood. "Dually came around last week, said Callie owed him big time. No more fronts. Cash or crash. I ain't gettin killed for her."

"She's got a kid and all," Warren said, and Elvia heard the remote crash against the wall.

"Not my kid," he said. "My kid's in our room watchin MTV. I didn't hear you feelin sorry for Callie a minute ago when I gave you some of what her friend cooked up. She's hella sorry she let me have it. Callie'd crack your head open to get that outta your brain."

Warren's feet scraped, and Elvia hoped he was only picking up the remote. She heard him sit back down in the creaking chair. The cicadas clung frozen to the stucco. The TV gulped and clicked again, and Warren said, "Yeah, man, the redhead. Go, baby." Her father must have grabbed the remote, because Warren said, "Shit, Larry."

"I'll watch it, but I don't want the damn sound on. They're already screwin, so what the hell's she screamin you ain't heard before?" Elvia heard the rasp of her father's match, the popping of his lips when he drew in the first breath. Blue hairs of smoke reached out the door.

Screwing. That's what she and Michael had done. Not love.

Crying over their mothers. Then screwing. What would he say if she found him in the arroyo now? How would she get that far, walking? Her father and Warren might sketch for days on Callie's speed, work long hours at the quarry. She'd be stuck in the room, where she couldn't hide her belly forever.

"Man, look at that ass. And the tits," Warren said.

"All fake. They probably make ass implants, too."

"Check out the Oriental chick," Warren said. Her face? In the few glimpses she had gotten, Elvia had seen flailing arms and legs, once a screaming mouth stretched thin as a rubber band, but never a face. Her neck was suddenly hot when she thought of how she had opened her eyes and seen Michael's eyes closed, his face empty like he was far away even though he lay on top of her.

"Oriental chick is short. Just like Ellie's mom," Warren said. "I remember her. Real little, black hair down to her butt."

Elvia held her breath. Her father was silent. She tried to imagine a face. A whole face.

"Man, I seen this show about women from the Philippines, bitches like slaves, cook and clean and roll over." Warren coughed. "I don't know how you screwed up with Ellie's mom. Shit, you saved her ass from Mexico. You hid her from immigration, right? Weren't you both workin in Rio Seco, in that linen plant out there on Bellgrave Road?"

Her father was quiet again. Another glowing cigarette butt landed near the first. *He would never tell me this. Because he doesn't want me to find her. Bellgrave Road.*

"I wanted to help Sara out, you know, help her get a life. Be American. She never even left the house, she was always so scared," her father finally said. "But then we show up, after that Wyoming job, remember? And she's got all that goddamn cactus on the table. Why the hell's she feedin the kid cactus?"

"Cause she liked it."

Elvia tried to see herself eating cactus with her mother. *Tell him. Tell me.*

"Cause I didn't give her enough money."

Warren laughed. "We used to party. She was a Mexican. All you had to do was fuck her and give her some dinero now and then. Better than she'd a got in TJ. She should a been happy."

Her father muttered, "That's the thing. She was all sad. Never looked happy. After all that time, she was scared of me. Like everybody else. And I didn't get it."

"She didn't get it. I remember you makin her say her address and she couldn't even do that." Warren made his voice high and slow. "Twanny-fi ten Joo-cow." He laughed. "Wasn't that it?"

"Yukon. We lived on Yukon."

Elvia made herself breathe. Twenty-five ten? Yukon. Maybe her mother had gone back there, left a note. Maybe she was living there again, waiting for Elvia to find her. Why wouldn't he ever tell her the address? Or the one in Tijuana? Now she had three places to look.

"I wasn't doin right back then. But I didn't expect her to bail. Ditch her own kid."

Elvia rubbed her cheek against the tire, feeling grit score her skin. Why would her mother be on Yukon Avenue now, when she didn't want to be there before? *When she'd gotten tired of me, too.* She saw Jeff's chest smeared with chocolate, his gums shiny-red when he cried and cried.

"Why'd you go lookin for Ellie anyway? A girl and all."

"Hey, my dad left my mom when I was a week old. What did I fuck up so bad the asshole had to bail? What did I do?" Her father's words flew hard against the screen. "I never seen him. My mom said he had green eyes. She had blue eyes. That could be a lie. How the hell would I know?" Elvia heard another hissing match. "I didn't want anybody messin with my kid."

He'd said that to Callie, too. Warren said, "Half the time looks like she can't stand you."

Her father laughed. "She's a kid. She ain't supposed to like me. I take care of her, I feed her, but I don't gotta like her all the time, either." He pushed out more smoke. "Maybe Florida's the story, man, start all over. I heard they're lookin for guys to lay gas line in a swamp. Remember we did that in Texas, that one time? Be good to get Ellie outta all this."

Elvia touched the sand on her jaw. She wasn't going to Florida. She was going to find Michael. Tell him about the baby. Then they were going to Tijuana.

Her father was nearly whispering now, and she crouched forward on her knees. "You see all that makeup on the redhead? The last time I saw Sara, she had all this blue shit on her eyes. Looked like she was blind."

She stood up, knowing that she really had seen her mother at the steering wheel, turning with shiny-wet cheeks, closing her eyes like two pools of water under the dark brows. She remembered this. Not a dream. Her mother's mouth painted red. The keys flying. The lighter.

"Change the fuckin channel, man, I'm tired of thinkin about women."

An air conditioner shivered next door. Warren said, "Always a woman fucks you up, Larry."

Elvia padded quickly down the concrete, passing through harsh circles of bulb light. She wouldn't cry. She lay on the sheets that smelled like strangers, burying herself in her loose hair. Soon her father would come inside to check her breathing, to lean near her and whisper, "Ellie? Everything cool?"

"Ellie?" She heard him, like always, before he left her breakfast. "It's on the table."

She twisted from the sheet. He sat in the chair, lacing his work boots in the dim light. "Just be cool till we get situated again, okay? I'm goin to the quarry with Warren. In a couple weeks we'll figure out school. But for now, check out the TV and keep the door locked."

She didn't answer. He said, "Stop worryin about Callie and that girl. That's the past. Soon as somethin's over, it's the past. I learned that real quick in life, and you have to learn it, too."

She heard the truck start up. The breakfast burritos looked like sleeping babies in their thin wrappers. She drank the carton of milk, ate one burrito, and slid the other in the jacket she tied around her waist. He'd left ten dollars. She wrapped her rocks in a tee shirt: the black onyx she'd found near the highway, the red sandstone, the smooth, pearly stone Michael had said looked like her own personal moon. When someone knocked, she froze. Maybe it was Dually. He wanted money, or her father. But a woman's voice said, "Hello?"

Elvia opened the door. The woman's face was dark as her own, her braid so long it twitched over her hip. Between her brows was a red circle.

"You are sleeping here?" the woman asked. Her voice was light as water drops from a fountain. "I thought there was only a man. Would you like me to take your towels?"

Elvia shook her head, and the woman said, "Are you all right, my dear?"

"Yeah," Elvia said. She stared at the paint, like a tiny lipstick kiss on the woman's forehead. Had her mother left a red kiss on her face? Had someone washed it off, when they found her?

The woman's long skirt shifted like sheer curtains at her feet as she turned to glide down the cement walkway. Indians, Warren had said.

"Hector said there's Indians everywhere in Mexico," Michael had told her, the last time she saw him. "Maya, Yaqui, Zapotec. About a hundred kinds. You got no idea what she is?"

Her mother, Callie, her father—they all left people, over and over. Elvia had left the little girl behind the blind hospital doors. She didn't even know her name. Jeffrey—would Callie leave him one day, if Dually or someone else promised her what she wanted? What if Dually found her here? *If he keeps messing up, I'm gonna get killed,* she told herself. *But he never left me. I can't go to Florida, stay in another motel room, get bigger and bigger. I have to figure out what to do. I have to tell Michael.*

The Indian woman sang softly outside. Elvia touched her belly and then drew her hand away. Nothing. She felt nothing.

Michael hadn't left her. He'd been arrested. Elvia shivered, touching the air conditioner slats that shuddered like the truck radiator, as if someone were driving into the room.

She walked in the shade under the eaves until the last room, number 20, and then on the frontage road to the quarry in the hills. She remembered the asphalt, pale as water, the edges crumbled into sand. Brittlebush shook in the wind, and broken glass sparkled so hard it hurt her eyes.

Her father always said no one would come looking for him in this hellhole during August. She stood in the feathery shade near the only tamarisk tree by the quarry fence. The mountains were like heaps of charcoal ash behind the quarry, except where a wide vein of green ran down the valley. Elvia knew from listening to her father and Warren that flash floods laid down enough stones and gravel to sell to contractors who built fake streams through golf courses and retaining walls to keep coyotes and scumbags out.

Standing right here, three years ago, she'd watched her father for hours, sure he would never come back to the motel for her. She'd sorted piles of stones. In Sandy's rock book, she'd found weathered granite, sandstone, quartz. Igneous, metamorphic. She'd decided to be a geologist, like the men she watched who came to the construction sites and tested the soil underneath.

Trucks came and went now; exhaust mixed with dust. Her father and Warren got out of a truck bed and began loading chalky stones heavy enough to make the wheels bounce. Landscaper's favorite: creamy weathered granite, rounded by the river.

Her father saw her when he was finished and stopped to light a cigarette. "Ellie. You're gonna get heatstroke. Go back and watch some TV."

His face was dark in the shade of his hand, like a visor at his brow. Elvia said, "I've got a headache. I left my Advil in the truck. Can I have the keys?"

He came toward the fence. "You okay? Did you eat?"

She wanted to cry again. I feed my kid every day. I take care of her. I don't have to like her. "Yeah, I'm okay," she said, and he handed her the keys.

"Get out of the sun before you fry your brain. Just cause you're tanned dark, you think you can stand the desert during the day. You can't. Bring those back."

She clutched the keys. His voice was still as fast as it had been the night before. His arms and cheeks were dark red, dry as brick dust. She turned when he did, and walked back down the quarry road.

In the sandy parking lot, the sun was like a hot wire on the part in her hair. In the truck, staring at the side mirror, she saw his eyes, her mother's lips. She tried to imagine her father's face if she handed him a baby browner than herself, with Michael Torres's cheekbones like tiny shields.

A finger tapped her on the arm, the nail edged in black. Two Mexican men grinned at her, saying something in Spanish. She said, "Fuck you. Get the hell away from me." The same thing she said when boys spoke Spanish to her at school and grabbed her arm, when white boys said, "Hey, beañorita."

Everybody knows Fuck You. Universal language, Michael's friend Hector had joked.

She turned the wheel so sharply a gold scarf of dust rose behind her. She'd only take the truck for a few days, until she found Michael, until she went to Tijuana. She knew the dust would blend in with the quarry's haze, and her father wouldn't even know she was gone until it was too late to stop her.

Lasso

MENTAL FLOSS. That's what Callie would say.

If you floss with barbed wire. Her friend's home-cooked shit felt like that right now, roaming through his brain, sawing back and forth, catching thoughts on the metal spurs.

Each boulder was thirty, forty pounds. Over and over. Bend and swing it up into the landscaper's truck bed. Weathered granite for some rich asshole in Palm Springs. Then Ellie asked him for the keys, and he stared at her braids. Her face through the chainlink fence.

Braids. He used to swing her around, her braids flying, in the yard on Yukon.

Sara used to wear one braid down her back. Like a thick rope backbone.

He'd come back from a long haul to Wyoming one week, and Sara was on the couch with Ellie, braiding her hair. They didn't see him at the door. "Lasso," Sara was saying, and Ellie reached up her hand and touched the braid. "*Lasú.*"

He asked a Mescan guy at work. "Trenzas," Carlos said, shrugging.

"Lasso?" Larry said. "What about that?"

"That? Indian talk."

Now Ellie walked toward the parking lot, and then her back was lost in dust. Larry finished the weathered granite, his head ripping with the movement and heat, a glinting deep inside his brain. The roof had lifted off the fuckin house. Fire burned blue and purple like he'd never seen. All for this barbed-wire home-cooked shit. All gone now. Each pipe somebody smoked, all the dollars they had to give up, and then they had to load rock and load concrete and load pipe and drive, drive, drive all the way to wherever, so some guy could hand them more dollars so they could buy burritos and Bud and more smoke, so they could load more rock.

All day. Every day. Dollars and Bud and smoke. Move it. Let's go. Come on.

"Come on, Larry," Callie always said. "Come on, babe. Let's go. Let's do it."

Jimmy put him on the bulldozer, sent him up the quarry road to pull a load of river rock. Larry drank some water, thinking he'd wait for Elvia to come back with the keys. But Jimmy said, "Come on. Let's get to gettin."

Larry drove the dozer in the fierce swirls of dust and wind and white heat. Ripping back and forth in his brain. Like last night.

When he'd left Warren's room the night before, the half-moon was already out, hanging like acrylic fake rock in the sky. The kind builders loved for edging out a fountain or flower bed. *Fuck. Back here at the quarry. At the Sands. Fuckin August. Square zero again. Start all over.*

Callie's home-brewed shit left a taste like mossy metal on his teeth, in his throat. Callie was probably coming down about now. She was probably cussing him ten ways, hauling Jeff on her hip like he was a big rock, pacing the living room.

She'll find somebody else. Just like she found me. Leave the kid with somebody for a night, comb her hair, tie up her shirt, go to a bar, and tell him all about it. Like she told me—her car broke down in Blythe, and she was just tryin to get on her feet. Rest for a couple weeks, then go to LA.

I listened to that shit. But the next fucker might not. So she can tell him what she likes to do. Get him in the car. That'll work. For a while.

Long as he don't make a baby. I ain't makin no more. Sure as hell, only one I ever made is in there sleepin. Got her MTV and boots and burgers. Nobody can say I don't take care of mine. He swallowed again. Mossy green metal. Like a horse trough. He hadn't seen a horse trough since Colorado. He'd drunk water from one once, when he was about fifteen and desperate. Where had he run from? A foster home. Six or seven boys, all beating the shit out of one another while the mother watched TV in the basement. Ward of the state.

Ellie was never gonna be a ward of the state. She was somebody's daughter. Forever.

His teeth hurt. How did smoke hold the taste of metal? Long fuckin day, longer night. Drove corrugated to the site, smelled that truck exhaust. Made those damn pipes in the yard, smelled that glass melting under the acetylene torch. That air freshener evaporating. Drove all the way to Sage, smelled that shit coming from Lee's house. Her old man talked a lot of shit. Lee's husband was in Tehachapi for two years. Intent to distribute. And this dude sat there smokin those More cigarettes, smelled like burning dirt. Then he took off when the house blew.

Those kids weren't his. What the hell did he care?

Shit. Ellie was in there. She almost got it. All Callie cared about was her supply. Ellie isn't her kid. And she doesn't give a shit about Jeff. Swear one time in a bar, somebody told me she tried to sell him once. White baby with blue eyes—four hundred bucks.

He opened the door and sat on his bed. The dusty, high bathroom window lit up like a dirty headlight each time a car passed on the freeway. *I can't believe we're back here again. Where we were when I first got her from the foster lady. Sandy Narlette.*

He remembered how Elvia had looked the last time he'd swung her in the yard, back on Yukon. A place she'd never see, because he didn't want her to know. Her braids. Why did the braids piss him off back then? They didn't look American. Too long, too tight. Something like Mexican.

He'd thought Sara wanted to be an American. Hell, she crossed over, right? She was working, right?

All those times I fucked up, she didn't leave. Where would she go? I always came back. I always brought dinero. It was so fuckin hard to get that dinero, every week. Layin gas line in Wyoming, fightin snakes in Texas when we put in water pipe.

I wasn't even around when she had Ellie. Where was I? Shit. Warren and I bought something from this dude in Hillgrove. Thought it was speed, but it was PCP or some shit. Took us out of our damn minds for five days. Woke up in San Diego. Couldn't even talk for a week. Not even to the cops. Must a hit one cop.

But when we were settled in that duplex, Sara had nothing but regular American women around. All I saw on the street. Why didn't she hang out, like women did, stand on porches and trade recipes or nail polish or something? I bought those magazines. Even if she couldn't read the English, couldn't she pick out some kind a barrettes, point to the hamburger at the store?

Hell, no. She wanted to eat cactus.

My mom used to tell me about Colorado, when her mom was a kid. The Dust Bowl. They didn't have food for the cows, so they burned the needles off the cactus and fed em that. Cactus paddles. Hell if I wanted to eat that shit.

I left a grand when I finished the Texas job. Was it that much? When did Warren mess with that dude in the bar, and we ended up doin a month? In Denver.

The air conditioner shuddered like a radiator near Ellie. She slept with her back to him.

I used to twirl her around. Every time. I gave her that Barbie. Long hair like hers. She held that Barbie like a regular kid. With a regular mom. Regular dad.

The narrow channel between the beds was black. He felt like his feet were in a ditch. Bare feet. He always felt better with his boots on.

When he was a kid, his cheap sneakers had holes like worms had eaten the rubber soles. He always wore steel-toes now. Every day.

Steel-toes let you kick ass. When you had to. Around Warren, you had to all the time. Warren was always touching people—
women in bars, ones that didn't belong to him. Guys that beat him at
pool. Warren didn't know shit, cause he'd been in group homes all
his life. Ward of the state. All he knew was fightin. And the only sex
he ever got cost money.

But Warren was around in Denver. When Larry's mother left
the bar with some rancher and ended up getting dropped off on
the highway outside town. When she wouldn't do something, or
couldn't do something, or shouldn't have drunk any more tequila.
When she froze in a ditch.

Her bangs must have been icicles. Women had bangs. His
mother's bangs were blond. What the fuck kind of word was that--
bangs? Hair hanging over your forehead. You had to imagine that
shit, what it looked like, if you were only fourteen. Icicle eyelashes.
Black as oil inside. From the makeup.

Sara had had blue eye makeup on that last night. Like a clown.
Ellie had never worn makeup in her life. She was still a kid.

*But she can't sleep in the same room with me for much longer.
She can't be fuckin fifteen. Already. I can't believe we're back here at
square zero again. Shit.*

Air conditioner's so loud I can't even hear her breathe.

He ran the dozer up and down the quarry road. The dust coated his
arms like brown nylons.

His mother always wore nylons when she went out to a bar. The
Time Out. The Drop Inn. She brought back money.

He dropped another load of river rock at the quarry pile. More
landscaper trucks. He headed back up the quarry road. *Ten-hour day,
seven bucks an hour. Shit. Not like running concrete pipe in for the
golf courses. All that money gone. Callie smoked it up, spent it at the
casino. Dropped it in them slots. Indian slots.*

*Then she gets mad at Ellie for running around in the desert, jog-
ging and collecting rocks. Calling her a squaw and shit. Cause she's*

*tanned and wearin them braids. Hell, Ellie's smart. That's all. She
ain't like Callie, droppin out of school. Ellie likes school. And she ain't
messing around with boys. Callie's full of shit. Ellie's still a kid.*

I buy her root beer and burritos and milkshakes. I buy her boots.
Not steel-toes. But if she wants steel-toes, I'll buy em. She ain't a boy.
But she's my kid.

*Callie wanted all the money. Now she'll have to get her own.
That's all they ever want, when you meet them in a bar or at a gas station or wherever. They look at you and see paycheck. Fuck him and get
his paycheck.*

*Drive and drive and get the check and then it's gone by Monday
and you drive again.*

*You have to sit still to hang around with kids. I couldn't do that
part. Ellie'd be on the couch and my eyes fuckin wouldn't stay still.
They were used to driving. Have to watch the traffic, the assholes in little cars, the motorcycles, the cops. The guy behind me lookin to hijack
pipe. Your eyes move around like BBs in a jar. Then you get home and
you have to look at a kid while she talks to you. About school and her
friend Jamie and math and today I saw a hawk and look at these rocks
they're like meta-somethin.*

Kids can tell when you can't do it.

*She didn't bring back the keys? She must a gave em to Jimmy, in
the office.*

*Two years here and shithead Warren's still gotta ask me Can I get
a ride back? Every paycheck goes for beer and hookers. But he's always
around. I told Callie that once. She was on my case about lendin Warren a hundred bucks and I said, "He was around long before you were
and he'll be here when you're gone."*

"Larry, dude, the truck's fuckin gone. Callie must a bought
more shit from Dually."

*Cash or crash. No more fronts. She remembered when I lent War-
ren the money. She told Dually I might be up here at the Sands.
Dually came and took the fuckin truck. And Ellie in it.*

Collateral. Anything's collateral.

*Not my kid. That's not money. That's my kid. Fuckin goddamn
Dually.*

Jimmy's truck peeled out big-time. *Yeah, you don't want to be around.
Dually's house is out in North Palm Springs. Walkin all this way in
the fuckin wind. Barbed wire everywhere. All along the road. Inside my
fuckin head. Never been here before, drove by once. You don't come to
Dually, he comes to you. Fuck him. Pit bulls or a piece? What's he
got? I don't remember.*

His house is all shut up from the heat. No truck. *He fuckin sold
my truck or he hid it. Where's Ellie? Fuck knockin. That's what steel-
toes are for.*

Colonia Pedregal

ON THE STAIRWAY of tires, Serafina stepped into each black circle, dust puffing around her ankles as if the earth were coughing. She looked back at the blue-painted shack perched on the ravine's edge to see if Florencio was following her. She didn't want to talk to anyone yet. Plucking a handful of stones from the crumbling mud bank, she hurried down the streambed toward the dump.

This morning, the sky was already hot, pale as paper at the roof edges, the way Tijuana had looked when she lived here before. But this was a different ravine, because most of the old colonia had washed away in the winter floods last year, Florencio had said. Some of the colonias scattered in the ravines and hillsides around Tijuana were bigger now than the pueblos the first settlers had left. The scrapwood and tin houses clung to the hill like cliff-swallow nests on church walls.

Pedregal. The colonia was named for the rocks, so easily gouged from the earth by fingers or rain, made into walls and boundaries. Mounded onto graves.

She shivered. Fences of box springs glittered with faint dew near her shoulders as she walked. The banks of tires fortifying the slumping dirt thrust out like the toes of giant boots. On a clothesline, tiny socks fluttered in the slight breeze. Someone else had been up before her, washed all those baby clothes and hung them out just now, because no one left anything outside at night. It would be stolen, sold, taken because it was untended.

Even the flies were still asleep. The men in Doña Alba's had all been still as dead bodies after seven days of driving and walking from Oaxaca. Florencio's shoulder had been touching hers when she awakened, and she'd pulled away, confused by the heat of someone else's skin.

Elvia's arm, so long ago—had the tiny elbow rested against her ribs? Could she allow herself to remember it, now that she was leaving tonight to find her? Tonight. She didn't want to stay another day here, where so many people got lost.

The dompe was silent. No trucks circling the steep dirt road, no seagulls screeching overhead, no dogs looking for food, no people picking through piles of trash for bottles, wire, cardboard, for clothes and canned food. But figures began appearing over the crest of the trash hills. Early risers came to claim their spots, where the first bags would be flung and the best items snatched. She saw a man at the far edge, wearing a dirty white shirt like her father had. He was bending and straightening, searching through the pile at his feet. He would turn and see her, she thought, panic rising in her throat. Her father's spirit: waiting for her to come back and pay her respects.

The rubble was still smoldering from yesterday, when the dompe workers would have lit fires to stop the people from walking there. The smoke wreathed the man's shoulders. Serafina squinted, and the thin smoke cleared. Not a man—a white piece of paper, held to the ground by a stick, bending back and forth in the breeze off the sea.

She crossed herself, crouching by the plywood day shelter near the entrance. Years ago, when they'd first arrived in Tijuana and her mother had collapsed into Alba's arms, they'd spent their days here. On the journey from Culiacan, her mother hadn't eaten, hadn't spoken since she'd cried out for her buried baby girls. She sat hunched, hidden in her rebozo, and Alba kept them from starving. Serafina sat near the iron comal, making tortillas for the dompe workers; she patted the dough, while flecks of ash and dirt cooked like pepper into the tortillas.

The pink sweater—she remembered. People had run toward the truck even as it still moved, anxious for the new load of tattered plastic bags to fall. Serafina saw a flash of pink, a knit arm, near the top, and she kept her eyes fixed on it when the trash began to slide. She pulled at the cans and rags and bones, feeling her fingers slide into the soft body of a dog. She winced and moved to the right, and the sweater fell as elbows began to push at her back.

In the shelter, she hid the sweater under a piece of cardboard, planning to wash out the rancid liquids that soaked the sleeves. She heard her father and Fidel, Alba's husband, shouting at the same time. Fidel held up a bottle, flat and curved. He drank, handed it to her father, and then her father gave it to Luis. The bottle glinted, tilting up toward the sun in Luis's hand.

Serafina had been dragging cardboard to cover the sweater when her mother screamed. Her father and Luis and Fidel were shaking, rolling on the ground like dogs with ticks, their backs arching hard against the earth. Serafina ran to her father; Rigoberto tried to hold him down but he jerked away, sprays of thin, dark foam coming from his nose and mouth. Luis's arms were scratched bloody by the broken glass where he rolled, and black drowned his teeth.

Now, Serafina walked close to the spot, but she knew she stood in a different place, the ground much higher with layers of garbage and bones and blood. At a streambed, a cow's carcass lay stripped by dogs, ribs in a curving row where hair clung in patches to the backbone. Close to here, their souls had flown. She dropped the stones, then took from her pocket the pieces of dried tortilla wrapped in cloth. Nuní from San Cristobal, broken into stiff triangles.

Tucking her uncle's corn between the stones, she whispered, "I'm sorry I left you. You never wanted any of us to leave Mexico. But everyone here disappears."

Glimpsing the silvery ocean, she made herself whirl and face the border. The other glitter: the wire fences that snaked across the bare earth near the Tijuana River, a black stripe down the center of the concrete channel and the high sloped levees where already hundreds of people were gathered, waiting. She hardened her spine and made herself look at the hills beyond the border. *I won't remember that part—not right now. My soul didn't leave then. It came back. The other part of it is still waiting for me, on the other side. She is still looking for me, too.*

She bent to push one piece of tortilla back into the stones and then passed the trudging army of people approaching now with their plastic bags and searching eyes.

The men were all awake now, smoking in the truck, in the yard, ash turning bright when they inhaled hungrily. Serafina paused at the box-spring fence, chilled by the bright winks of ember.

That day, Larry and Warren had smoked red embers from a pipe in the truck cab. Elvia pulled her to the duplex window, saying, "*Táá*-Daddy has *ñuhun* in his mouth."

Larry came inside, eyes scarlet, staring at her hands on the nopales cactus. His friend Warren said many things to make him laugh, pointing to Serafina and the cactus. Then Elvia dropped her own nopalito, tears streaming. "*Náá? Vihnchá ndaha!*"

Serafina looked for the bristle of spines, taking Elvia's finger into her mouth and sucking hard, scraping needles off with her teeth. She remembered. Larry shouted, "Ouchie. You got an ouchie." He turned to Serafina. "Sara. Ellie ain't in Mexico. You ain't in Mexico." Then he lifted Elvia to his chest, where she plucked out the keys from his pocket.

"Drive!" Elvia said, and Larry grinned and took her outside. They drove away in his truck, Serafina running to the sidewalk, Elvia's hands turning the steering wheel.

"Don't freak," Warren said, his mouth close to her face. Then he deliberately reached into her blouse, his eyes on her face the whole time, and pulled out the roll of money Larry had given her earlier that day. Warren's fingers brushed her breasts hard, and she twisted away in the settling dust. What if he didn't bring Elvia back? What if the truck hit a tree and Elvia flew out like a doll? Serafina

felt her skin bubbling and rising, floating away from her without
Elvia's tugging, patting fingers on her thighs, shoulder, braid. Then
she knew: *If he brings her back, I will take her home to San Cristobal.
I will ask a santo first.*

Now Serafina approached the men in Alba's yard. "Tonight. I
don't want to wait. I want to leave tonight." She didn't know how else
to begin. The polite words of home had flown from the truck window on the highway. The way she'd begun to speak to her uncle was
the same hard, empty voice she heard addressing Florencio, without
any respectful small talk.

Florencio sat on a wooden chair with a cup of coffee. Serafina
lowered herself onto a slab of concrete. "Did I cause you to feel uncomfortable?" he asked, in the formal tones of San Cristobal, but
with a faint clicking behind his tongue. *He has been in California a
long time*, Serafina thought. *Like Rigoberto. He is my brother's friend.
I have to be patient.*

"No," she said. "I went to pay my respects. Because I am leaving
tonight."

Florencio nodded, his black hair damp in shiny quills over his
ears. "I remember Rigoberto telling me how they died. I remember
him crying. He cried for his mother, he said."

Serafina looked at people stirring in other doorways, in bare
plots surrounded by wooden pallets and box springs and geraniums
in coffee cans. A small boy ran naked, his stomach covered with a
huge burn and purple medicinal wash.

Alba had rebuilt her house after last year's flood washed everything down the ravine. She had left San Cristobal twenty years ago,
one of the first people to claim land here, where she built shacks for
people coming from Oaxaca to Tijuana. She made a living, with her
son Manuel driving people north. The new shacks were plywood
and cardboard and tin, their walls held together by nails driven
through bottle caps.

Manuel crowded Florencio from the chair now. "Move, fingers," Manuel joked.

Florencio had only three fingers on his left hand. The skin at the outer edge of his palm was twisted pale and rosy. Serafina looked at his eyes instead, black as hearthstones, a flourish of etched lines above his cheekbones. He was two years older than she, thirty-three, like Rigoberto.

"The lettuce," he said, eyes steady on hers. "In Salinas. Rigoberto carried me to the clinic. The field was muddy. My machete . . ."

He sat on an overturned bucket near her. "You crossed with the Italian padre the first time."

Serafina nodded. The priest had come every week, with blond American teenagers in two vans filled with sacks of beans, potatoes, oranges, and Bibles. And if someone in the colonia begged hard enough, the priest carried a woman over the border in the trunk of his Volvo. Only a daughter or wife searching for a loved one on the other side.

"This time will be much harder," Florencio said.

Alba came from her house, her arms raised high, the loose fat trembling like flan. "Serafina?" she cried. "You're here? That means she's gone now." Her dress smelled of butane and coffee. "I miss her every day. She was ready? Her *anima* was prepared for the journey?"

Serafina was quiet. She finally said, "She wanted to be with her own mother."

Mattresses filled the front room, and a young woman emerged from behind the blanket covering the doorway to the other room. Four small girls, their hair tangled as birds' nests and their eyes almond-slanted like Manuel's, flew to the young woman, touching her somewhere, leg or knuckle or wrist, and then they were gone. Outside, their screams and laughter grew faint.

Alba said, "Chilaquiles. Help me carry it outside." She put her plump arm along Serafina's shoulders after they put the heavy pot on the outdoor grill. The men gathered in the yard, drawn by the spicy steam of red sauce, Oaxacan cheese, and torn tortillas.

Alba gave Serafina a bowl. "Your eyes are like charcoal. You cried for her."

Serafina nodded, but she knew the dark wells were from her fear. Manuel had driven on back roads to avoid the police in Puebla and Mexico state. Thousands of pesos to let them through, if they saw the truck. And the bandits, the soldiers—all looking for Mixtecos to rob, Manuel said. He had taken them to rest in caves where no one would see them, or he'd paid a farmer for a night in his corn field.

Florencio had whispered to her in the milpas, in the caves, "Why are you going back now?" Her face tingled, in the dark; he was from her pueblo, and he believed in the old ways. She couldn't tell him about the box, about Larry and her foolishness, about her daughter.

She handed Florencio another tortilla now and said to Alba, "I'm leaving tonight."

Alba bent close to Serafina's arm, stirring the chilaquiles, shaking her circlet of gray braids. "It's too hard to cross now," she said. "Half the men used to leave every morning for San Diego. For the gardens. Now there is the wall and more migra."

"Now the Guatemaltecos work the yards," Manuel said. "They work for free, practically, and sleep under the freeway." He ladled more sauce for himself. "And now is Operation Gatekeeper! All day on the radio Americans say, 'Do not attempt to cross the border! Los Estados Unidos will prosecute los illegales!'" He laughed. "And then you hear the music—Los Tigres del Norte, Los Illegales del Sacramento, Los Illegales del Rio Seco! The bandas sing when he's finished his speech!"

Everyone grinned. Serafina remembered the men at fiesta singing about oranges and avocados and lemons.

"Los Illegales del California!" Manuel shouted. "Pick the damn strawberries! That's all I hear now. More strawberries they planted this year, so they need more pickers."

"You lived in San Bernardino once, right?" Florencio said to him. "You never go back?"

"I hate the food up there, I hate the way they drive. I can't go anywhere now. Look at all these goats, with their sharp little hooves."

The small girls were crowding around the table, and Alba handed out pan dulce. "I wasn't smart like you, Florencio. I got married."

"I'm not so smart . . ." Florencio began, and then he bent his head to his bowl. Serafina felt the brush of hair at her own arm, and the smallest girl went under the table after a dropped cup.

"It's even more dangerous than before," Alba said again, pulling Serafina over to her chair under the tree. She whispered, "Your hair was tangled in the black rubber so I could hardly see you. Your mouth was full of dirt. You had been eating the earth. Your mother carried you like a baby. Now she's gone. Stay here and make tortillas again. You're like my own daughter."

Serafina wouldn't let herself cry, but her mouth trembled, and she whispered to Alba, "If you truly feel that way, then you'll know why I have to go. I have a daughter. A baby. I lost her that night. La migra caught me, and she was left behind. I have to go back and find her."

Alba sucked in her breath, hand to her mouth, and said, "No! You told your mother?"

Serafina shook her head. "Not for a long time. Then I couldn't leave her." She stared at the girls running through the yard, braids swinging. On the hilltop, dust clouds rose from the dump. "Her head was sick, she never got better. Like the cradle where the babies grow, inside the body, sent poison up to her skull. She was crazy." She stirred the tortillas floating in the red sauce. "She said we were cursed to lose our daughters. And she would stop the curse with me."

"But your daughter would be—"

"Fifteen," Serafina said softly. *Two arroyos over, where the old colonia was,* she thought, *that's where I was fifteen and I lay down in the car trunk. When the priest closed it, I tried to think I was a baby inside a mother. I curled up. The motor was the mother's heart. I breathed saltwater from my eyes.*

Alba whispered, "She has had another mother."

"She is half American." Serafina put her hand up to silence Alba.

"No. No one knows. But I am still her mother." Getting up to fill her bowl again, she said, "Tonight." She was still hungry, and she wanted to have strength to walk in the dark.

Manuel and Florencio and the others were drawing pictures in the dirt. Serafina listened. They would have to pay a coyote. They had already paid Manuel, though he didn't charge them much since they were from home. The men from Santiago Tiltepec, he charged more. But the coyote wouldn't care where they were from. He would want all their money.

Impatience and her fatigue from sleepless nights made her hands and knees tremble. She couldn't be polite. "Manuel," she said, "if it's so much harder to cross, how much will it cost?"

The men stared at her, surprised by the rudeness of her abrupt interruption. "It used to be two, three hundred dollars," Manuel said. "But now it's eight or nine hundred. La migra is stronger, smarter."

One of the men from Santiago Tiltepec said, "Last time, there were two migras on horseback, and they roped me like a calf. Kicked me, took my shirt and shoes, tied me up and left me while they went for the others. Coyotes could have eaten me from the belly out."

Alba joined them. "You should wait until la migra concentrates somewhere else, in a few months. You should stay here until you have enough money."

Serafina had nine hundred dollars, the tight roll of money between her breasts. Florencio glanced around, and Serafina knew he didn't trust the men from Tiltepec. You didn't trust anyone in Tijuana because there were no rules. And in California, you didn't trust anyone until you were with your own people, in whatever camp they had settled. Your new pueblo.

Manuel handed his plate to his mother. "La migra has more trucks. And los panderillos—the gangs are worse than dogs, tearing people up. You have to go to Tecate, through the mountains and the desert. That's the only way to get through, unless you want to try seven times here and get killed. Fucking August. San Cristobal is unlucky—people have to go back home for the santo's fiesta. But it's the time for grapes, tomatoes, oranges. Everybody's crossing now."

Serafina went inside. She looked at the clothing hung on wires strung from the tin ceiling, at the mattresses, at the dresser crowded with shampoo, lotion, dolls. She tried to pray near la Virgen de Guadalupe on the wall, but she had nothing more to say. She couldn't leave the offering she had planned: the barrettes. She couldn't let them go. Instead, she bent to touch the small socks scattered like crushed flower petals on the dirt floor, and she went back outside.

"I can take you to Tecate tonight," Manuel was saying to Florencio. "But you need a pollero to take you through those mountains, unless you've been that way. That's what I heard. I don't know anybody in Tecate. But coyotes are everywhere. Just like the animals, they find you."

"You were like a little animal," Alba whispered again, crying, thrusting a bag into Serafina's lap where she sat in the truck. "Your mother . . . Please, please, be careful." Alba glared at Florencio. "You—you are responsible for her."

"That's where everybody else is trying tonight, mano," Manuel said, nodding at the levees and fences along the highway. Serafina looked at the Soccer Field, the no man's land of blackened earth where she had pulled herself along the ravine by her elbows.

"Tecate," Florencio said softly, looking straight ahead, not at the crowds of people lining the levee and fences. A wall of backs. "Tecate."

Serafina willed herself away, imagining the feel of Elvia's hand tugging her braid.

After an hour, Manuel said, "Tecate—look at all these trucks. Everybody's trying here, too."

Jaime, from Santiago Tiltepec, said, "A man from home told me of somebody. Ramon. He always wears a black cap of the Raiders."

Florencio looked uncomfortable. He said, "I would rather go ourselves, but I only know Tijuana. I don't know the mountains."

"You're on your own. I have to drive back to Oaxaca. Fucking August," Manuel finally said.

The backs were lined along this fence, too, like drying clothes on a line that stretched forever. The sun was nearly gone, the mountains across the border a jagged black horizon edged with crimson. Florencio glanced at the plastic bag in Serafina's hand. "What did she give you?"

"Clothes," Serafina said, her heart racing. Could she trust Florencio? She barely remembered him. "Spoons. Bolillos and pan dulce for the morning."

A man shouted, "Agua. I have agua in botelos. It's a hundred degrees in el desierto. Agua." Serafina trembled, her fingers on the wire, the mountains melting into darkness.

"Serafina," Florencio said, his voice soft. "I hope you didn't pack anything you can't lose."

She touched the cloth bag slung across her breasts, with her few clothes and things from home. Her own money was tucked into her bra. Florencio said, "The coyote will take your things and throw them away." He moved nearer, blocking her with his body from the pressing elbows. "He'll take them because he can. Because he'll say your money isn't enough."

Serafina reached into the jeans pocket to feel the barrettes. Then she thought about her rosary, her abuela's stone molcajete and mano, the last things from Yucucui. From the two rooms she had known all her life—the fingers on the beads, on the smoothed pestle. She opened her blouse in the shelter of Florencio's arms spread on the chainlink fence, hoping he was safety, and she tucked the rosary under one breast, pushed the mano in the deep valley between, and redid her buttons.

"He must be from Sinaloa," Florencio whispered when the Tiltepec men approached with the coyote in his black cap. *From the north, with his paper-colored face and sharp nose,* Serafina thought.

People from the north don't believe anything we do, think Mixtecos are stupid burros.

"I am Ramon," the man said. "Can you walk thirty miles? I have a truck waiting past the checkpoints. Eight hundred. Each." He stood completely still in the chaos of bodies.

Florencio nodded. "When we get away from here, in the mountains," Ramon said, "you can pay me. Buy some water now. We have to keep moving."

Outside Tecate, the fence gave way to nothingness, to blank sand and dark shapes hurtling past. Ramon stood still again for a long time, more like a rabbit than a coyote. His black jeans and jacket made him nearly invisible except for the white letters on his cap, when he turned to whisper, "Now! Follow me! Now."

She ran behind Florencio. In the distance, the headlights of trucks were like blue machetes swinging through the brush.

Mecca

"I'M ON THE highway to hell," Elvia sang along with the radio. "My way to hell—no stop signs." Then she slammed her hands into the steering wheel.

That was her father's favorite song. She concentrated on the shimmering road, the curves through the valley. *He'll tell Warren, "She's just like her mother—took my ride and left my ass behind." He'll be madder about the truck—he's had it longer than he's lived with any human. But hey—now he doesn't have to feed me all the time. Worry about me. Tell me what to do.*

After ten miles, she looked across the desert floor at Michael's shelter in the arroyo, under the salt cedar trees like gray feathers. *What if he's still not there? I have ten dollars—enough for gas and a couple of tacos. How can I get to Tijuana? By myself?*

She headed down the fire road, skirting the foothills, until she saw a turnout protected by two huge boulders. *Granite, studded with mica flecks, split by water hundreds of years ago,* she thought. *Drops of water, just a trickle.*

She brushed dust off the huge dashboard, like a rock shelf she'd crouched under when she was small, keys dangling like silver birds at the edge. Did she remember this? Or was she imagining it? Hadn't she sneaked out one night to push herself under the dash, to see how it felt?

She turned Metallica up loud, thundering in the cab. Her father used to sing along. Then he'd turn to her, point to the grocery bag on the seat between them, or to her own hands on the wheel while he let her practice driving on the dirt roads outside Palm Springs and Tourmaline.

"Nobody ever did this for me," he'd say.

"What?" she'd say, even though she knew what. She knew he wanted to answer.

"Taught me to drive. Let me pick root beer at the store. Kept an eye on me."

That was the dumbest part of right now—she missed being at the store with him, cruising the aisles making fun of eggplant and Fab and Tidy-Bowl. Picking out Cap'n Crunch and ribs and whatever she wanted.

She sat in the truck bed. *Like he always said, "Why think about somebody when they're gone?" Because I want to remember her, too.* From her backpack, she pulled out a candle and her stones. You could make an altar anywhere. She lit the candle and arranged the stones around the base. She laid out a white tee shirt and the rough, red sandstone she'd found in the riverbed. Scraping with her thumbnail, she made a small pile of coarse red dust on the tee shirt. The color of dried blood. She trickled it out in a thin line on the white cloth, like the Indian man she'd seen on TV drawing pictures in the sand. Navajo. Pushing errant grains into place with her finger, she spelled her name.

When the Navajo man on TV had finished, he said he'd made a design that would heal someone in his tribe. Her father had laughed. "Yeah, hell, he can sell that for big bucks to some tourist and heal his own ass with a bottle of wine."

Her name was dim between her feet. The ID card was stiff in her pocket. She tried to stay awake. She held the small knife Callie had given her, clutched close to her leg. Callie had said, "If a man bothers you, don't show him the knife. Tell him you'll cut off his nuts. Then when his hands go down there, stick him in the chest. I know I'm not your mama, but I'm trying to help you out cause your mama sure ain't." *Every mother said some version of that,* Elvia thought. She was so tired now. She wound her braid in a circle to cushion her skull against the truck bed. She picked up the moon-white stone to rub against her cheek, the same smoothness as her thumbnail across her lip, the way other people did when they prayed.

Elvia heard stones—thumps when they landed in the truck bed, and then a rock fell onto her shinbone. Someone yelled, "You okay? Wake up so I see you're not dead!"

She squinted at a brown face, a black ponytail. Michael's friend Hector, the one he'd been busted with, came closer, pointed to the sand. "What's that?" Elvia smeared her leg across her name. "You're Michael's jaina," he said. "I seen you that one time."

"No, I'm not a fuckin hyena." Elvia casually displayed the knife, holding it loose.

"Jaina. Ruca. His girl." Hector glanced at the knife.

"I'm not his . . ." Her head still wasn't working. What the hell was she, anyway? Girlfriend? No. The mother of . . . Damn. "Where is he?"

"Torsida." Hector was messing with her, using words she didn't know. His eyes lit up like agates. "No habla nothing? Torsida. Prison. St. Jude's Training School. We got four months."

"So why are you out?"

Hector shrugged, his face serious now. "Cause it was my time to go. But mano messed up again on purpose. He wanted to stay another month."

"Michael wanted to stay?" She couldn't believe it.

Hector squatted and put the bag down. "Three hots and a cot, sabes?"

Three meals and a bed. Then Michael really didn't have anywhere to go.

Hector studied her. "He told me you wanted to find your mother. He said you were sad."

"I'm not sad." Elvia glared at him. "I'm fuckin tired, okay? Why'd you guys steal a car?"

"We got tired of walking one day. We saw a Trans Am. We wanted to go to the mountains. Michael knew a secret place from his primo. His cousin. The snow stayed white there forever."

"Did you go?" Elvia looked down at the salt cedar trees turning pale gray in the changing light. The sand was white now, and the truck was in the sun.

"We got busted." Hector stared at her.

"Don't even fuckin think about this truck, cause . . ." Elvia began.

Hector said, "I don't want the truck." His voice was quiet. "You can quit talking like your dad, huh? I heard him in the parking lot before. If you're crazy like him, you and Michael are cool for each other. Drive me out to St. Jude's, and he'll bail from there."

"You ride in the back." She slid the knife into her pocket and held the keys.

"Just like a farmer, eh?" His voice was hard. "Orale, I'm used to hueras acting like big shit."

Hueras—white girls. She knew that from graffiti at school. "I'm not a huera!" she shouted.

Hector shrugged. "You don't speak Spanish. Your dad's a cowboy. I guess you don't know what you are." He climbed into the truck bed and pointed to the freeway.

She drove, furious. *Callie's calling me Indian squaw-girl and this guy's calling me huera. Fuck them. Michael knows who I am. Indian and Mexican. I don't have a mother. I'm like him.*

St. Jude's was ten miles past Tourmaline, five miles from the freeway, in a box canyon. The stucco building was surrounded by a chainlink fence topped with barbed wire, glinting like dew. From where they parked, Elvia could see swarms of boys wearing white tee shirts and navy pants.

Hector squatted under a cottonwood tree. "I'll give him a message, and he'll bail tonight. Most of the guys are from LA. That's why they're way out here. Nobody can find them, and if they jump the fence, they get lost or burned up in the desert. So they don't."

Elvia glanced at his clean hair, his wary look. He said, "Meet us at that green place," pointing to a cleft in the foothills across the freeway.

"Don't get lost," she said, nervous now.

He grinned. "I'm a geographer. I never get lost. And Michael knows the desert."

She drove back down the dirt road. A geographer? Was he making fun of her geology? Maybe Michael had joked about her—or forgotten her.

In a McDonald's, she watched the afternoon light turn the mountains bruise-blue. That first day, Michael had grinned at her, teeth perfect except for one missing molar that left a gap dark as licorice. "My people been in the desert since dinosaur times. Where you from?"

"I've been here three years," she said. "I'm from a lot of places."

The only place she'd ever stayed long enough to know where the moon would always rise was Sandy Narlette's. The laundry room window—the full moon like Sandy's scented soap, above the white dryer cave, and Elvia used to sit on the linoleum and marvel at the gleaming.

It had taken Sandy six months to convince her that the blue things were hers, with her name embroidered on the edge. She'd loved her sisters as much as she could, when they sat around the kitchen table painting fingernails, when Rosalie, Sandy's real daughter, painted stones in sparkly pastels and gave them funny names to go along with the broken-glass gems she held now.

She couldn't believe Sandy Narlette let her go, let this guy show up after four years and said, "He's your father, your biological father, and he wants you." All that time, Elvia had gotten used to the idea that Sandy's house was permanent, the sisters and the slippers and the mother. She was so angry that she had left everything behind except her rock book and these three glass-stones. Sapphire blue, jade green, and cinnamon brown, what she imagined was the color of her real mother's skin.

What if she never saw her father again? What if Michael never came? What if she never found her mother? She stared at the pay phone. She still knew Sandy's number by heart.

She told the operator her name. "Elvia. *Elvia.*"

Sandy said, "Is that you?"

Elvia felt a rush of tears that made her feel like a little kid, and she didn't like it. "The real me. The biological Elvia. I just took off from my biological dad."

Sandy was quiet. Elvia gripped the receiver. She could hear dishes clinking in Sandy's sink, a radio on the counter. "You got a cordless phone?" she asked.

Sandy said, "Okay. We'll just start right up, like I do with my friends when we talk every day. We'll pretend we're friends and I'm not your former foster mother who's been worried for three years about what happened to you, why you never called, whether your dad treated you right." Forks. Elvia heard silverware tinkling in the white enamel sink where she'd washed dishes so many times. Sandy sighed. "Yes. I got a cordless phone."

"My dad treated me fine," Elvia said slowly. "But his girlfriend was getting us in trouble. So we left, and . . . I got tired of moving." She pictured Sandy's face, her blue eyes and narrow brown eyebrows, no makeup, chapstick on her soft lips, her brown hair in a ponytail.

"So where are you planning to settle, if you're tired of moving?" Sandy's voice was light. "Your birthday's next week, right? You're not even fifteen yet. So you're walking?"

Elvia thought, *That's not even my real birthday. Only one person knows when I was really born.* "I'm going to look for my mother," she said. "I have a couple addresses."

Sandy said, "Oh, I hope you find her. I told you—I think she loved you. Maybe you'll find out what happened." Then her voice went soft, and Elvia heard a little kid's question. "Yes, you can have fruit snacks," Sandy said, her words turned away.

Elvia said, "You still have foster kids? Mess-ups like me?" She didn't want to miss it—the kitchen, the linoleum, Sandy's fingers. Only kids missed that.

Sandy laughed. "Kids are never mess-ups. Their parents are." She put her mouth close to the receiver. "Elvia. If you find her, and it doesn't work out, come here, okay? You remember where? Be careful. If you need me, call me again. Please."

She drove into the night, not crying. When she opened the glove compartment looking for tissue, a purple scrunchie fell into her hand. It had fallen from the little girl's hair when she lay on their laps. Callie had shoved it into the glovebox. Elvia put the velvet to her face. The glittery sparkles scratched. The little girl would never see her mother again. Only foster moms. *I hope she got a good one.*

She was at the tangle of pepper trees in the foothills now. Nervous at the silence, she turned on the radio. A Mexican station— swinging trumpets, cheerful accordions, guitars. At one foster home, she'd had her own radio, small and white as a tissue box. She'd listened to Mexican music, trying to teach herself Spanish. "Es mi tienda favorita—Sears." My favorite store. But then her foster mother, a thin woman with glasses like sideways blue teardrops, had said, "You're driving everyone crazy. And Spanish is bad for your schooling."

A man sang, "Por tu maldito amor." For your bad love. *What will I say if we find my mother in Tijuana? What if she's got a nice house, says, "So whatcha been up to all these years?"*

I can tell her about Broom Woman's house dress. TV Woman giving out dinners in trays. Hitting Woman smacking everybody on the butt if they didn't move fast enough, slapping our hands if we reached for food too quick.

I can tell her that Sandy Narlette put me up on the counter with gold flecks and talked to me while she stirred in her green bowl. And that I listened.

Then my dad came to get me. Okay? You didn't.

She remembered the burritos in their wrappers that morning. So long ago. The vanilla shake.

And now I left the only person who ever asked for me, came to get me. I'm waiting right now for somebody who disappeared, too. Like a ghost. To tell him I have a ghost baby inside. To ask him to help look for a ghost woman. Blue-closed eyes and red lips that kissed me good-bye. Forever. If she sees me now, it won't be forever, and she'll probably be pissed.

Gone Woman. Brown feet. Green cactus like hand-sized moons. A sting of spines. Red pomegranates like planets on a tree. White moon when we sat on the porch. She called it *yoo*. Braids in my hair. *Lasú*. Wash up. *Sándoo*. Sleep. *Cusū*.

I heard her say that to me in the car. Then she went away.

You. You went away.

When the night was black and the air was finally moving cool through the windows, she heard heavy shoes crunching on the sand. Her heart stuttered. "Michael?"

He put his arms around her, and she felt the smoothness of his neck like polished stone against her forehead. Then he released her quickly. She thought, *He feels my stomach is bigger. My chest swelling up. I don't want to tell him right now. First thing.* But he patted the truck and said, "You ripped off your cowboy pops? Shit."

"I got tired of walking," she said lightly, and Hector rolled his eyes.

"Last bed check was three o'clock. Mr. Jesse sees I'm gone in an hour," Michael said. But he leaned against the truck and kissed her, put his fingers along her cheek, and whispered, "What I was thinkin, after I first got busted, was you look like you got sand in your eyes. Like when pieces of wine bottle go rollin down a creek, and they get softer? Not so glittery? Like that green."

Elvia whispered back, "When things at my house got bad, I remembered your stories. About the desert, the plants, your mom." The ID card was warm from her body when she handed it to him. "I found an address for my mother in Tijuana. You like being on the road, right?"

"Not in your dad's truck," he said. "I just did five months for that car, remember?"

"I'll drive," she said.

"You got any money?" She shook her head. "We need to make some dinero real quick."

Hector said, "Mecca. We can make some money picking grapes, and St. Jude's won't look for you down south. They'll think you went to Rio Seco or LA."

Elvia started the truck, and Michael said, "Your dad takes good care of the engine. He'd kill me if he saw me ridin up here, huh?"

"Yeah," Elvia said, but she thought, *If my dad knew about the baby, he'd really kill you.* She turned the wheel hard, making a doughnut in the dust and heading for the freeway, the guys slumped low like little kids. The sun edged over the mountains, flat and silver as a pie tin.

The freeway was littered with tire pieces like crow wings. Michael lifted his head to read a few billboards. "Indian Ridge—a Jack Nicklaus golf course. Indian Lakes—an active adult community. They look real Cahuilla." She laughed at the silver-haired people drinking iced tea, riding in golf carts. "So if you're not active, you're dead?" Michael said. "A dead Indian?"

"You're dead, in a bed, or playing golf," she answered, just like her father had said. He used to make fun of the street names—Gene Autry Trail, Bob Hope Drive. Would he really take off for Florida, a new life? Or was he looking for her right now, maybe in Dually's truck? Dually, Warren, and her father—they'd beat Michael and Hector close to death.

Twenty dollars of love. Elvia shivered. Whenever someone owed her father or Warren money and couldn't pay, her father would say, "You can give me the money or I can get fifty dollars' worth of love outta your face. Make me feel better, since I'm broke."

How much love would take care of a stolen truck, a runaway daughter, and a baby?

Michael said, "You're on empty. This old truck'll burn petrol big time down to Mexico."

Elvia pulled off in Indio to spend her last five dollars on gas. Hector said, "We can make forty bucks a day in the grapes, if you guys work hard."

Michael said, "Hey, remember that long-hair dude, Caveman, from St. Jude's? He got out last month. Told me to meet him in Rio Seco if I want a hundred bucks. He wants to try the dreaming medicine, just like you. But he has to pay." He passed his hand over Elvia's braid and said, "Everybody's gotta pay. Except you."

She shivered again, even in the dawn's heat, even though the narrow highway already shimmered, like discarded cassette tape stretched out for miles through the sand.

"You're not in America now," Hector said. "You're in Califas, the brown state." He and Michael sat up straight now. "Nobody's gonna notice us here. No white faces except farmers."

Trucks passed hauling hay, vegetables, and boxes of grapes. Elvia peered at the next tiny town.

"Coachella." Hector pointed at grapefruit packing houses, auto repair shops, Mexican cafés.

"Arabia," he said, when the highway plowed through sand again, surrounded by date groves, the dangling amber bunches covered with paper bags.

Suddenly she saw the grapes, wall after wall of green vines that stretched for acres. Cars were parked along the highway shoulder, plumes of dust rose from trucks driving between fields, and people walked every row. Their faces were covered with bandannas, their heads with baseball caps, and their hands moved quickly as sparrows among the leaves.

"Mecca," Michael said.

"You been here before, too?" Elvia asked Michael.

"Yeah," he said. "Just one time. Doin what you're doin. Trying to figure out how I got here. How my moms met my dad here. How drunk he must a been."

He looked away, and Elvia saw his ponytail like a gleaming black rope in the hot sun coming through the windshield. When would she be alone with him, talk to him about why she really wanted to find her mother? He said, "True hell, mano. You got it marked on your map?"

Hector nodded, tapped on the black leather folder covering his knees.

"So you have maps of everywhere?" Elvia asked, scared now of the whole day, the whole trip stretching before her. "This is the fucking *Wizard of Oz?* What are you looking for, Michael?"

He stared at the fields, not at her. "For some money." Then he grinned. "And a good time. Nothin else."

Mecca was a few stores, a few streets lined with trailers and small houses, and the grapes all around. The smell of burning sugary fruit, fermenting in the sun, nearly made Elvia sick when they got out of the truck at a row of trailers—faded pink, turquoise, and—the one where Hector knocked—pale green as a watermelon rind. But when a man came out onto the single metal step, his huge belly straining against his white undershirt so the material was nearly purple, he frowned at Hector. "Where the hell you been?" he said. "Your jefita gave up on you. In May."

Hector bit his lips. Elvia thought he looked like he would cry. Jefe. Boss. His little boss?

"Where'd they go?"

"She took two or three hermanos up to Watsonville for strawberries. Your pops said, 'Fuck fresas' and went to Washington. Apples, I guess."

His mother, Elvia thought. *She gave up on him.*

Hector said, "Tío, I need some work."

His uncle looked at the clipboard in his huge hands. "Show up when you feel like it? Damn, Hector. Everybody started at five. It's seven now. And it's Thursday. You crazy?" He glanced at Elvia and Michael. "It's 112 today. They picked before?"

"Yeah," Hector lied. "Orale, Tío, I need some money. Please."

"Go see Manuel at Block twelve, off Sixty-sixth," the uncle said. "Tell him I sent you, and don't fuck up. People here are feedin kids. Not just playin around." He handed Hector a bag and slammed the trailer door.

I'm feeding a kid, Elvia thought. She ate the spicy tamale Hector gave her, drank the manzana soda. Apple.

But Michael said, "Mano, if we're gonna sweat our asses off, I need somethin to keep me goin. You know."

Hector said, "My uncle's cousin. Guapo. He does the fields." He looked at Elvia. "My moms doesn't do speed. But her and my pops—they drink a lot, smoke mota. This is where she's from. No nothing. That's why I left last year."

Cars lined Sixty-sixth, and the grapes stretched across the hot earth, all the way to the ash-colored mountains. Hector counted off the blocks, and when she parked he said, "Put a long-sleeve shirt over that. Put on some pants. Or you'll get sunburned and cut at the same time."

He and Michael stood by the truck doors while she struggled out of shorts and into her jeans. Her skin was grimy with two days of sweat and dirt. She couldn't button her jeans at all. She left them undone and let the baggy tee shirt fall over her belly. Then she kicked up white dust on the roadside to keep up with Hector, who was waving at a man under a bright beach umbrella at the end of a row.

It *was* hell. Elvia held the clippers Hector gave her and snipped each stem. Crouching alongside the wall of grapevines, breathing the dust that rose from everyone's steps, from the wheelbarrow's progress, from the trucks that rumbled down the dirt road with boxes, she thought, *Shit, I can do this. I run in the desert all the time.*

But Hector yelled at her after the first box she filled. "Like frosty green marbles, big ones. Not babies. Not yellow. We get our asses kicked if we mess up the box." She worked slowly, dropping the heavy dangles of fruit into the box at her feet. After an hour, she looked up to see the people around her, their faces obscured by bandannas, their heads covered with baseball caps, their hands reaching through the leaves like blackened mitts. She felt dizzy, her back aching already as if her father's acetylene torch prodded the muscles above her hipbones. She could barely breathe, the heat like a thousand fire ants on her scalp. Salt trickled into her eyes, and when she wiped it with her hands, dirt and blood stung even worse.

Hector came by with a water bottle. He poured water into her eyes, into her mouth. Then he and Michael cut and dropped bunches like machines, filling three boxes to her one. Michael carried the full boxes to the end of the long row, where the scale man waited under the umbrella.

Through the stems and leaves, she could hear people talking in Spanish. She tried to look at the women's faces—what if her mother was here, right now, picking grapes? Each pair of eyes squinted, dismissing her, searching for the grapes.

As she touched each woody stem, each bunch of frosty green marbles, she smelled the fermenting juices and breathed the dust. Each breath was sharpened, hot, as if the dust particles carried thorns, and her lungs burned. When she'd filled another box, she bent over, ready to faint, and someone laughed on the vine wall. *Melting—you wanted to melt away the baby. Fine. You'll die, too.* She was on her knees when Hector came again, pouring more water onto her head and face, whispering, "You okay?"

"I can't breathe," she gasped.

Hector said, "There's pesticides on the grapes. You can't gulp with your mouth. Breathe through your nose. Don't give up yet. Come on. At least fake it."

A hand thrust through the vines, giving her a bandanna. Elvia tried to see the face, but she heard only laughter. She tied the cotton square around her nose and mouth, thinking it would suffocate her, but she smelled menthol in the cloth. She panted for a few minutes, then began to pick again.

Lunch was more tamales from a truck, and water. Elvia poured it onto her chest, her neck. She lay in the sandy alley between rows, her head in Michael's lap, her eyes closed. Melting—was the baby hot inside her, glowing like a tiny doll? No—it didn't have hands yet. No feet. It was just cells. Cells that might be disappearing into her aching, pulsing muscles and skin.

She could barely lift herself off the sand when the work began again. The sky and sand and leaves were all white, blinding her as she reached for the grapes, rubbery hot. She panted inside the bandanna. Her mother could be picking beside her. Her mother could be washing these grapes and popping them into her other children's mouths. Elvia steadied herself against a pole until she could see again. Then she turned and followed Hector back down the row, where the late-season vines were sending tendrils across the sand to trip unwary feet.

The green hallways emptied out before dusk, and Elvia was still struggling with her last box.

"So who's your ruca, Hector?" someone said behind her.

"I'm nobody's ruca," Elvia answered, spinning around.

The girl laughed. "You look like nobody. Never seen nobody pick so damn slow."

Elvia thought, *It's not my fault, okay? I'm pregnant.* But the teenage girl came around the wall of vines, in stretch pants and old sneakers, her belly huge, as if she'd have the baby any day.

Elvia was so startled she dropped her clippers, and the girl laughed again. "Clumsy, too," she said. "I was gonna tell Marisela you married Hector so she'd kick your ass."

"Shut up, Tiny," Hector said, grinning. "I'm not here. You're not talkin to me. I'm not really here. I'm headin back to Rio Seco. City college this year."

"Orale, schoolboy, Sally's still in love with you, too," Tiny said. Elvia stared at the women coming down the row, waving at Hector. She couldn't believe he was a big deal here, with his neat ponytail and wide smile, his notebook of maps. He took her box down to the scale man, who was waiting impatiently, and then another girl came up behind Elvia.

"So that's your vato buying crystal?" she hissed. "Spending your money you ain't made yet."

Elvia saw Michael now, leaning into the window of a turquoise Mustang that had been cruising the avenue. Hector said, "Guapo. Michael was looking for him. And he's always looking for somebody like Michael."

Just like Dually, Elvia thought, tired, her feet swollen into her shoes. Suddenly she knew—*Michael's gonna sketch all day and night, like Callie and my dad. He hates the world slow and ordinary, one place you know. Like I wish it was.*

"Everybody looks like fuckin ghosts fadin away," Michael said beside her. The trampled sand, the bare vines limp and bedraggled, the piles of trash and pallets and boxes at the end of the rows—she stared at the retreating backs, and they did look haunted, covered with fine, pale dust and bent by the day. People walked toward town or loaded into trucks and cars.

"Come on," Hector said. "We won't have a place to sleep if we don't book up."

Every parking lot and sandy area was taken up with cars and trucks. People were stretched out on hoods and in truck beds, sleeping or talking, propped against tires, playing cards and starting small barbecues. Elvia jerked the truck into a small island of sand in the sea of cars and trucks and folding chairs in a vacant lot. Hector said, "We gotta wait for Rosario."

Elvia laid her head on the door frame, so tired she could hardly move. A carload of men next to them was listening to the radio. "Por que l'amor de mi alma, solito Mexico . . ." The song spilled from the open windows. "Viva Zacatecas!" someone in the back sang along.

"Sinaloa, Michoacan, Zacatecas," Hector said. "Where'd you say your moms was from?"

Elvia shrugged. "Mexico."

"Thirty-one states, so you better get a clue." Hector pointed. "There's Rosario. The tamale lady. From Cabazon Reservation. See the red truck? Every night she comes. Beef tamales like you never had. And apple empanadas. Like pies but better."

"From the rez, huh? She's Cahuilla," Michael said, peering at the old woman.

Hector shrugged. "She's a cook. She's been coming here since I was a kid. Summer for the grapes. Winter for the dates. Sometimes we lived in a station wagon."

"Well, I ain't sleepin with all these people," Michael said, scowling, three lines etched between his brows. "Cause I don't want to be around when they start fuckin and fightin." His eyes were shiny as night glass. "My moms met my pops here. Probably fucked me into the world in a fuckin parking lot. I ain't in the mood to think about whether my pops is sittin in that old-ass Dodge Dart right there."

"Life's a bitch," Hector said, his voice hard for the first time. "And then you die. But if you got a better place . . . We gotta be back in the field at five, or Manuel ain't paying us, sabes?" He stalked over to the red truck and brought back a bag that smelled of chile and cinnamon.

Elvia felt the sweat and dust drying on her arms and face now that a breeze moved through the valley. "I need a shower, big time."

"Most people take a bath in the canal right there." Hector pointed to the drainage ditch under the bridge.

She shook her head. "Then let's go somewhere else."

Michael pointed her south on the highway, the sun red in the dust hanging over the fields. After a few miles, Elvia saw a glimpse of blue, a huge mirage of a lake. Then she smelled briny ocean. "Where are we?" she asked, at the expanse of water glittering against the sand.

"Salton Sea," Michael said. "Everybody used to fish here, but now the lake's all fucked up. Full of poison and salt from the fields. See the mountains?" He pointed to the purple riven range rising across the water. "Where those stripes are, that's where the real lake was. When my grandpa's grandpa lived here."

Elvia could see the marks, an ancient shoreline. "So this lake isn't real?"

Michael said, "He told me Lake Cahuilla was a hundred years

ago, big water from Indio to Mexico. And people fished. Then this
long drought came and there was just a puddle. The people went
further in the desert or up to the mountains. My grandpa's people
went to Desert Springs. Then in, like, nineteen hundred something,
farmers came and pulled the irrigation water from the Colorado
River. It flooded a few times and the whole river poured in here, till
the railroad people dumped all this junk to dam it up. Now it's the
Salton Sea. A fake lake." His voice was still sketch-fast, Elvia thought.

Hector said, "My grandpa used to come here all the time. He
was from Veracruz. Lived on fish—tilapia and corvina, in salsa colorado. But now all the fish are dying off. Pull in there."

Elvia parked at the concrete shell of a two-story motel, with the
front wall gone and a honeycomb of bare rooms—no windows, no
carpet, no furniture, like square caves staring at the glowing water.

"Desert people took it all for their trailers," Hector said when
they climbed into a room on the second floor, the cement floor and
walls still warm. He opened the tamales.

Michael was restless, sweeping trash from the floor with a palm
frond. "What would your pops do if he saw his truck right now?"

"He'd probably try to kick your ass. Both of you."

"What if we kicked his ass?" Michael said softly.

"What?"

"You ran, right?" Michael shrugged. "Like you never want to
see him again. Was he treatin you bad? Messin with you? Is he your
real dad?"

She remembered what Sandy's daughter, Rosalie, had called
him, that day he came to get her. "Yeah—my bio dad. He never
messed with me. He messed with everybody else."

Once, at the Tourmaline Market, a man had leaned into the
truck window while she waited for her father. He asked what time it
was, how hot it usually got. Her father came outside and punched
the man in the face, then rubbed his skull in the hot sand. He said,
"Get in your fuckin Honda and drive. If you can't drive cause your
face hurts, I'll drive you someplace. My choice."

She couldn't say to Michael, *I left him because I was gonna get bigger and bigger from a baby with your eyes. Your skin. And I was scared of everything.*

"You seem like him sometimes."

"Maybe. Sometimes. When I'm driving."

Michael didn't smile. He took out a cigarette. "And who knows what you got from your moms, right? See, Hector can't figure out what he got from his parents. He's like alien boy."

"Look," Hector said, turning to Elvia. "There's twelve of us. A dozen eggs, okay? I'm number ten. My parents, they work hard wherever. Like today. You do that every day, and then you gotta have some beer. They get drunk, they fight, they have another baby, they move on. But you know what? My mom—she works all day in the field, and then she's gotta cook somethin for everybody, gotta wash out the clothes and hang em up. I don't blame her for gettin high. She's like, so tired, I don't know what she was when she was herself."

"So now they're gone?" Elvia said.

Hector nodded. "I miss my mom. But last year, I worked the grapes. And then they were going up north to Parlier and Dinuba for the rest of the grapes. I turned seventeen. I figured it's like my last chance to finish school. So I stayed in the arroyo with Michael and went to Tourmaline High. Now I want to go to college. Geography." He looked embarrassed, holding out his hands for the cornhusk tamale wrappers. The apple empanadas were doughy, spicy with cinnamon. When Hector went out with the trash, Elvia lay on her side. Every muscle ached, in her thighs and along her back and even her wrists. Inside her lungs, she felt a washing sting like Listerine. Poison. Dust. Heat. She couldn't do this every day, for the rest of her life.

Michael squatted beside her, his hands dangling from his knees. Elvia studied his face in the glow. He broke open a cigarette, sprinkling the tobacco on her hand. "You need this for your prayers." Then he lit another cigarette and sucked hard, passing it to her. She shook her head. "Just hold it," he said, pulling her hand and putting the cigarette in her fingers. "You feel the warm?"

She nodded. The ember and the smoke. "I didn't know it was like a tiny heater. I always hated them cause my dad smoked so much." She lifted the cigarette to her lips and took a puff, feeling the burn in her throat, and then pushed the smoke back out.

"Just say no, right?" Michael laughed. "You know what? When I'm sittin outside, specially in the winter, and I'm feelin strange like I miss somebody, I always light up. The smoke looks like people sometimes. Check it out."

The swirling figures hovered near her, outlined in blue. *Maybe that's why my dad always had a cigarette,* she thought. *He was lonely, even when he was with Callie or Warren. Or me.* She remembered her father's blue smoke reaching from the motel room, and she wondered whether, now that she was gone, he was lonely or relieved or so high he couldn't think.

"And you got something in your hand. I mean, like you're holdin something," Michael said, staring at the cigarette.

"Like a finger," she whispered. "Like babies hold somebody's finger."

"Yeah." Michael sucked on his own smoke. "And the finger gets shorter, and the ash keeps your hand warm." He lay beside her and buried his face in her neck; then he kissed her, and she tasted her own sweat and the dirt from the fields. She thought her belly would move, would protest, but when he ran his hand down her back, tracing her spine, she felt nothing below her ribs. Only his mouth again, warm and smoky.

She pulled off her jeans, scared. *If we do it now, then in a couple weeks I can tell him I'm pregnant. He can get used to the idea.*

He rolled on top of her, and she fit her arms around his neck. Their cheekbones slid together. That was what she liked, the first time he lay on top of her, the slants of bone beside each other, the smooth skin. Until his heart beat loud, and his chest seemed to open and bloom against hers.

But now she couldn't breathe at all. Something was sliding back over her lungs, her heart, and she pushed at him for a second. He said, "What? You scared? Didn't we like, do the wild thing before? I always pulled out, right? I was so fuckin drunk I can't remember."

Elvia tried to breathe again. Did the baby have lungs? Did sex feel like this before? This didn't hurt. It felt hot, but separate from her, like she was watching someone else in the ceiling shadows. It wasn't like the arroyo, when she'd tasted his neck and thought of their braids tangled together on the sand. This time, it was like being in a movie she couldn't see. Then he pushed himself away from her, and she felt warmth seeping onto her thighs, like blood.

She kept her face close to Michael's ribs. He'd say she couldn't be pregnant, he'd pulled out. What if that wasn't him, on her thighs? What if it *was* blood? From the baby's—cushion? Didn't babies grow in blood, at first?

She waited until he fell asleep, then pulled her jeans up over the moisture. She had to pee. From the edge of the room, she saw Hector sleeping in the truck bed.

Her bare feet were swollen and burning on the cooled sand. She hurried toward the derelict swimming pool and crouched beside an old water pump in a shed. She saw no blood on her thighs. She ached between her legs now, too.

Flickering lighters floated inside the dry pool, and two girls rose up the steps like zombies.

"Where you from?" the thinner girl shouted angrily, standing in front, folding her arms.

"Nowhere," Elvia said, recognizing this gang question from school.

"You one of the Mexicans?"

Elvia didn't know what to answer. She didn't know what she was in their eyes. "No."

"You sure?"

"My mom's Mexican," Elvia said, trying to keep her voice strong.

"Shit. I'm talkin about them," the girl said, pointing at the graffiti all over the pool sides, the shack, and the nearby cement wall. THA MEXAKINZ. A line was drawn through MECCA.

"She talks like a gabacha," the larger girl said.

"Where you from for reals? Lift up your shirt," the thin one said. She raised her shirt with one finger, and Elvia saw MECCA tattooed in dark blue letters on her flat stomach.

"Nothing on my stomach. I'm pregnant," Elvia blurted out, afraid.

"So?" The biggest girl lifted her shirt and said, "I'm on my second and I work faster than you." The letters of MECCA were faded and stretched into pale blue wavers. Elvia recognized her voice. Tiny. She had been across the vines. "She's the one with Hector, Lena."

Lena studied Elvia. "You stayin in Mecca?"

"No." Elvia thought, *I never had anyplace, or anyone, I cared about enough to want it in my skin. I'm out here floating around.* "Does it hurt? The tattoo?" She thought of her father's dragon, how she'd touched it when she was small.

"I can put your vato's name on your arm. If you don't got a barrio," Lena said.

"You want his name on you? Just remember, when he turns asshole, it's hard to burn that shit off." Tiny laughed, then showed Elvia her forearm, where she had an angry raised scar like a fat worm.

Elvia thought, *A tattoo would remind me of someone. A place.* "Nobody's name. Could you do a picture?" She glanced at the dark caverns of the motel.

"You sleepin there? Damn. I'll do you a small one for free," Lena said.

When they got to the tiny wood-frame house lit by candles, an old woman squinted at the door. "Tranquilina?" she called.

Lena made Elvia sit in a chair. Herbs hanging from strings were everywhere. Elvia took her shirt off, touching her left shoulder blade. She said slowly, "*Luna* is moon, right? And a kind of moth?"

Lena said, "Abuela's from Guadalajara. She says *palomas de la luz.* Doves of the light."

The windshield, the white moths dipping over her; Michael's

story about the sparkling dust on their wings, then on his mother's eyelids. "Three of them," she whispered. "Three moths."

The alcohol on her shoulder blade was stinging cold. *The only clean skin on my whole body,* she thought, sitting hunched over in the chair. *Shoulder blades are like handles. I must have held her bones, when she carried me around. When I was a baby.*

When the needle pierced her skin, she felt an answering tingle inside her, a cricket scuttling over her hipbones, even scarier than the burning on her shoulder. "Calmate," Lena hissed.

The cricket feet answered the pain, step for step, until Elvia was numb with fear, until she was prodded from her haze by Patsy saying, "She got a firme design. I never seen it before."

"Firme?" Elvia whispered.

"Cool," Lena said, rolling her eyes. "Here. It won't look real good for a couple weeks."

She handed her a mirror, but all Elvia could see was red skin coated with Vaseline. She couldn't see the moths yet, their colors. What was on her skin now, what was inside her skin? Had she painted a memory of leaving into the baby even before it was born, the ink going into her blood and straight to the tiny feet climbing the ladder of her ribs?

It seemed she had just fallen asleep when he woke her. The sky and water were lavender, heavy with heat. Her shoulder was crusted and throbbing, and, when she was alone, she rubbed the grandmother's salve on the tattoo. She waited, still, for the cricket feet again, but she felt nothing. Maybe she'd imagined them, to take her mind off the pain.

The sun turned the fields and sand brilliant white, and the workers staggered down the hallways, dropping boxes, adjusting bandannas. She recognized Tiny and Lena now and said "Hey" through the leaves. Hector and Michael stopped cutting to look at her, and the girls laughed.

"He doesn't know," Elvia whispered into the tendrils. "The moths were for me. Thanks."

"Damn, you're crazy," Tiny said, working her way to a different row. "No wonder you hang with crazy vatos." Everyone clipped furiously, moving much faster than they had the day before. "Friday," Hector said, racing away, too. Elvia worked alongside Michael, breathing the winy dust. The hours passed in a blaze of heat, salt in her eyes, dust drying her nose, and her feet and hands feeling swollen as cactus pads. *If I find her, will I have to do this forever, just to stay with her?* She clipped the grapes, remembering her father pointing to the date palms and saying, "You want to work like that? See why I make sure you stay in school? I want you to have a good job someday. Not like a Mexican." Then one day he added, "Not like me. Workin in the sand with pipes ain't any better. I'm just as dark as them. Right?"

She reached for the grapes again and again, the fruit itself hot and swollen as her fingers, her eyes. The bandanna smelled like her own chile breath. The sun, the dusty leaves, the pale green fruit— everything blurred as if she were moving underwater, just trying to stay alive.

The sun was still high when the block of vines was finished. The man at the scale spoke to Manuel, who gave Hector and her cash for their boxes and Michael's. Hector went to find Michael, who was with Guapo.

She was holding seventy dollars. *I can buy what I want at the store anyway. I don't need my dad or Michael or anyone else right now.* Tiny and Lena folded their paychecks, slid them into pockets. Tiny said, "Be careful. Watchate, huh? For you and . . ." gesturing to Elvia's belly.

Then they got into an old station wagon with several other women. *I never had girlfriends, but I had sisters at Sandy's. We painted fingernails all the time.* Lena and Tiny would be laughing, putting makeup on, combing each other's hair for Friday night. Like a family.

Michael was sketching again, leaping into the truck and announcing, "TJ tomorrow. Camp in the desert tonight, away from here."

In the open desert south of the Salton Sea, she left Highway 86 and headed slowly down a faintly marked road. Hector said, "There's a checkpoint for illegals on the highway. What if la migra got your mom? Way back then? What if she had to go back home?"

Elvia looked at the smoke trees and creosote bushes; just this, all the way to the border. "Maybe they caught her, but why didn't they catch me?" she said. "Why wasn't I with her?"

Under a salt cedar, they ate the tamales and empanadas again, and Elvia laid her head in Michael's lap, staring at the stars. The cicadas were furious now, making the night hum as if a giant generator were parked somewhere in the sand. "My dad said Tijuana's crazy. What if we don't find her? Then we come back?"

"Back where?" Michael said. "I'm goin to Rio Seco, so I can brew the medicine you want to try. And I'll make that hundred bucks from Caveman. All I got left is forty."

"Cause you gave half yours to Guapo," Hector said, and Michael only grinned.

Hector lay down in the truck bed, his map folder under his head. Michael bent his head to Elvia. "You see the baby smoke trees, down that arroyo?"

Elvia nodded at the small puffs of silvery gray. Michael said, "The smoke tree drops the seeds, but they have to get beat up by rushing water, like knocked into rocks and all, before they can take root. So the babies are always like way downstream from the mom."

She thought about his mother's moths, about the coyote dropping palm tree seeds in the desert; this was why she'd loved him, back in Tourmaline. "So you're saying forget Tijuana?"

He shrugged. "I'm just sayin sometimes that's how it's gotta be."

This is a good time to tell him, she thought. *About the baby*. But he said, "You hear something?" He stood up. She thought she heard faint barking, hoarse, maybe a dog. "Get up in the truck," he whispered, and when she lay down, opposite Hector, he said, "Shhh." He paced around the clearing. She heard only the millions of cicadas.

Elvia awoke with a start when Michael said "Hey" and poked at her shoulder blade.

She screamed at the pain, felt a scurry of cricket feet in her belly, and sat up. Dawn made the salt cedar into a fountain of light. Michael said, "How'd you get hurt?"

She held her breath. The feet stopped. *Do you try to run away when something hurts me?* she thought. *Do you run like a hamster around and around my belly? A damn exercise wheel?*

"Elvia?" Michael said. "Somebody beat you up in Mecca?"

She lifted her tee shirt, and he said, "Damn."

"Moths," she said. "Are they like the ones your mother caught? For the dust on their wings?"

He took in a sharp breath. "They're cool. I don't know if they're like something real or not."

In the truck's side mirror, they were small, puffy. One was yellow, one green, one blue. She let her shirt fall. She liked imagining them, hovering above the windshield, a glimmering blur. Michael said, "I heard shooting last night."

Hector nodded. "We're way out here in the Chocolate Mountains. Navy gun range."

Michael looked east toward the sunrise and said, "Something weird out there, too. Not coyotes. Like a bird, screamin all raspy. I never heard anything like it. Stopped a while ago."

He started the truck and drove down the faint dirt road until they saw a dark heap in the sand, like a pile of clothes. Hector said, "Shit. La migra didn't get him. The desert did."

Michael said, "Look under the cedar tree. That's who was callin."

Four people lay under the branches. Elvia followed Hector and Michael to the unmoving shapes, and she saw that one of the bodies was a woman, curled on her side, her brown face pulled tight and shiny and hard as a doll's, her eyes just as unblinking.

God of the Hearth

"BAJANSE," the coyote hissed, and they all crouched down, motionless under the thick stand of brush that still held the day's heat and smelled of tar and sage. Serafina breathed light and fast as a baby. She heard rustling jackets and breaking branches as another group trudged up the path to the top of the hill. Then she heard the whine of the helicopter like a wasp.

The beams circled like lightning, making her dizzy, but the coyote said, "Don't move." She wanted to run, before the icy light touched her head. The running feet and whipping blades pushed dust into her nose, her mouth. *You are in California. You are breathing it again. Eating this dirt, Uncle would say. Don't move. Don't move.* The helicopter hovered at the top of the hill, and they heard someone else yell, "Bajanse!" An American. Then more Americans shouted, and Serafina shrank down into the bark of the large bush.

But the shouts faded, truck doors slammed, and after a time, the coyote said, "Andale. Move now." Her legs buckled from fear and the blood stung when it moved again inside her skin.

When they reached the top of the hill, they saw the trucks receding down the dirt road. "Sensors," the coyote said. "Migra plants them in the dirt, and somebody stupid trips them. Then they wait at the arroyo. I always wait until they're finished. Go."

Florencio whispered to her in Mixtec what was said in Spanish. She could understand the coyote some of the time. She walked behind Florencio, the darkness like the inside of a shuttered room. They moved along dirt roads, through ravines that left Serafina breathless with fear. The steep crumbling banks, the branches catching on her shirt—she remembered everything now from the last time, even while she walked. A hole torn in Florencio's jacket let a patch of white tee shirt show through—a ragged floating star. She tried to follow it.

They hiked for hours and hours without stopping, upward through forests. She smelled pine resin under their feet. The dirt road was littered with branches and stones. "Where are we?" Florencio asked once, ahead of her, and she heard the coyote laugh.

"Where I take you, indio," he said. Then, after a time, he said, "Los Pinos."

Even in the blackness, she was afraid of the eyes. Like before, in California. She was afraid every moment she moved. She wanted a room again, a room she could never leave. If she found Elvia, and found a place, she might never go outside the door.

Except for corn, she thought, trying to comfort herself. She was so hungry her stomach felt as small as the mano between her breasts. *I would grow corn in the back yard, behind a fence, where no one could see me watering the plants. I wouldn't need anything else. Tortillas and masa and atole. I would have a chicken for eggs.*

She stumbled on a root in the path. Her head hurt, a stabbing pain. She was afraid of the eyes of la migra, of eyes that might be hiding in the gullies or caves. She was afraid of the coyote, Ramon, when he stopped and stared at them all, then listened in the darkness. Once more they heard people running, after they'd crossed a highway like a river of black asphalt. They ducked down in the brush near the road, smelling urine and trash and stagnant water, and they heard a radio. Static, harsh, and spitting. When it was quiet again, Serafina looked at Florencio near her, his eyes like wet black stones, his mouth open. The coyote seemed to know where he was going. "Walk," he said to them again. "I never get caught. They look for you indios all the way to Temecula, and I never get caught. Go."

On the highway above them, a lit sign read SANTA YSABEL 29. She could read santos' names.

They didn't talk all night, only grunted when they tripped on stones or passed under thorny manzanita on a thin trail. They headed into brush so dry and heavy that she smelled the fragrant oils on her sleeves after she pushed through the branches. The night grew cool, paler, and she could see Florencio's back more clearly than the star patch.

"*Tiñū'ú xíní*," she whispered to him once, and he looked up. *The stars here are the same as they are at home*, she thought. *But not as bright, as if the air is different.*

The coyote's thin, papery face floated beside her suddenly, and he gestured for Florencio to pass, then the Tiltepec men. Jose and Jesus and Guillermo. Their eyes were on the trail. The coyote said, "Speak Spanish, india. You better not complain."

She was silent. He said, "The one with three fingers isn't your husband. And the others aren't your brothers. Verdad?"

Serafina kept walking, hearing him just behind her. "You aren't married. Answer me."

She took a breath, trying to remember the right Spanish pronunciation. "Where are we?"

"We are still in Los Pinos. We will sit down for a minute and eat. Then walk again. Wherever I tell you to walk."

His voice was soft behind her. She smelled ashes now, old smoke hanging in the air. She saw a small clearing ahead, a flat place inside the trees. He knew where they were going. He said, "Sit down and give everyone some food. Ten miles to Descanso."

They sat on stones blurry in the slight haze of dawn. Serafina passed around the bolillos and pan dulce. The coyote sat apart and shook his head when she offered him food. "I don't need to eat," he said. She watched the men leave one by one to pee. She chewed her dry roll, drank the water Florencio offered. The coyote took something from a small bag, and then he bent over a match flame.

She saw the small glass pipe. Like the one Larry and Warren

had passed between them, she thought suddenly, the same tiny red ember that glowed strong with sucked-in breath. She remembered how Larry's eyes had been clear and kind, his mouth twisted in a smile, his frame stretched over the couch while she cleaned sometimes. But when he smoked outside with Warren, his body and eyes and mouth and anger moved constantly, like restless dry wind.

She had imagined Larry returning to the duplex. Was he relieved that they were gone? Had he grinned and gone back to the red place, Colorado? Or had he found Elvia in the parking lot or a hospital, fed her hamburgers, told her Serafina was a bad mother?

Serafina let the crumbs fall from her fingers. The coyote stared at her. He ate smoke.

When Florencio came back, the coyote grinned at Jesus. "Where are you going?"

"To piss," Jesus said, hesitantly. The coyote laughed.

"Where are you going here in el norte? To work, chingaso," he said.

The men were quiet. The coyote said, "Algodon? Fresas? Naranjas? Uvas?" He pointed a different way for each, a cigarette now held in his fingers. Cotton. Strawberries. Oranges. Grapes. Serafina watched Florencio.

"Do you even know?" The coyote's voice was fast now, harsh. "Or you're just going to wander around? Hope you find work? Shit. Everyone from Oaxaca is here. From Zacatecas and Nayarit and Michoacan. You better know where you're going if you want money. You, payaso?" He pointed the cigarette at Florencio.

"Naranjas," Florencio said finally, glancing at Serafina. She knew he didn't like to talk. He said you couldn't trust anyone once you were here.

"You say you been here before," the coyote said. "Where did you work?"

Florencio rested his hands on his knees, like he was displaying his nubbled skin on purpose. "San Diego. Santa Barbara. Santa Maria. Guadalupe."

"En Mexico?" Guillermo said. Serafina knew he hadn't been here before.

"No. In California," Florencio said.

"Guadalupe?" Guillermo whispered. "A city here?"

"Yes. Fresas." Florencio looked at the coyote.

"Fucking fresas," the coyote said. "I'm so tired of playing cat and mouse with la migra. Every day. If los gabachos don't want you Oaxaquenos to pick the fresas, why did they plant so many this year? Fucking stupid to run around like this. Hiding. They want you to work your pinche indio asses off anyway. They must eat fresas every fucking day."

It was quiet for a time, the men only chewing and smoking. Serafina felt their eyes on her when she handed them the last sweet bread. She didn't sit down again. In the yellow light dropping from the trees, she saw now the burned grass and earth beneath their feet. A fire had swept through this place. The soil was charred black, the tree trunks webbed charcoal.

Serafina stood up then, and walked carefully the other way, far from the men's voices. She paused to hear if anyone said her name. No one did. When she reached out to steady herself against a blackened tree, the puzzle-bark smelled acrid, and she thought suddenly of the gods her mother and uncle had always prayed to outside—clouds and sun and wind. All the santos' names had just rolled off Florencio's tongue. San Diego. Santa Barbara. She remembered now. California was full of saints, all dead, the green freeway signs like their tombstones.

Dizzy, she made her way to a charred pine tree near a steep cliff. She didn't want to pull down her jeans anywhere near the men. Serafina felt the barrettes sharp against her leg. She touched the blackened bark, bent down, and relieved herself. Then she zipped the jeans with clumsy fingers, turned and saw the two faces, mouths stretched open, gaping, empty eye sockets staring like little black caves.

She screamed, over and over, and Florencio came running. The burned men lay tangled in the pocket of earth between the tree and the cliff. Their skin stretched tight and black over their bones, shiny and hard as the tree bark. Their faces were silver in the morning light, like metal masks.

The coyote said behind her, "Campfire got out of control last month. The whole mountain burned. They got caught sleeping. Or they were just stupid. Stupid indios."

Florencio took her wrist and helped her over the stones. He stayed close behind her when they began walking. "Don't worry," he whispered. "We are closer now. We are almost there."

She didn't answer. Her feet throbbed inside her shoes, and with each step, pain knuckled up her back. Descanso, he had said. Someone had given these places Spanish names so long ago. Everywhere. *Descanso* meant rest. Soon they would rest.

"Answer me," he said, behind her again. Florencio was just ahead, ducking through the brush. The coyote's hand twitched the end of her braid.

"I am going to my brother," she said. "Florencio is his compadre."

"You're going if I take you to the truck." His voice was pleasant and soft, like a priest's murmur near the altar. "You're going to fuck me a hundred times first, if I want you to. If I fucked you and then cut your throat, no one would know. No one would even find you for a year. Like those two back there. And when they found you, they wouldn't give a shit."

Serafina didn't let herself stumble. She watched each foot, then glanced up at the men ahead. Florencio had stopped now, had turned his face toward them. She could see the slash of his teeth through his breathing-hard mouth.

"When we get to Descanso, we have to stop. For the heat. And wait for the truck. You can sleep. And dream about what I'm going to do to you later. Because there's nowhere for you to run. If you leave the trail, you're going to die. I want you to dream about that."

She walked. All this time, she had dreamed about Elvia. Milk and cloth and the sweetness of the skin on her neck. The sweat stung her eyes. She couldn't think of Elvia because it made her soft and weak. A little animal. She had to think only about the trail, about the man behind her. How would she live if he hit her in the head again? What if he hit her in the same spot? Her temple would collapse like a sugar candy skull. When the coyote threw her onto the ground, what could she do so he wouldn't hit her?

He was probably right. She was alone. These men wouldn't help her. None of them was her husband, or brother. She didn't look at Florencio's back. She didn't look at his hat. She stared at the trail five feet in front of her. The coyote passed her easily, not touching her braid, and began to whistle.

The truck was not here, in Descanso. They were in a clearing at the summit. The mountain air was so thin Serafina felt dizzy.

The coyote, so angry now that his neck was suffused with red, stalked around the packed dirt where Serafina could see that people had camped many times before. A trash heap was piled in the trees, and the remains of several fires were scattered in the sandy field. His friend was supposed to meet them here with ten more pollos and the truck, he muttered. They must be in Santa Ysabel. Twenty more miles. Fuck walking. They would wait here, through the night.

"Make something to eat," he yelled at Serafina, pointing to the battered nopales near a boulder. He tossed a knife onto the dirt. Serafina cut the green cactus, scraping off the spines, trying to calm herself.

Elvia had gotten tiny thorns in her finger, that last day. When Larry and his friend Warren had come home, Serafina was cleaning nopales, moving the knife blade over the tiny red spines, shirring off the needles to leave the pads green and smooth, dappled with blind white dots. She loved few things more than this motion, this skin like a baby's, this comforting heap of food that grew anywhere, even here.

Larry's eyes were paler green than shorn nopales. He'd been so angry that day, when Serafina was cooking the cactus, when Elvia said in Mixtec that the thorns hurt her. Larry threw the keys, like a metallic dragonfly. "Get a life. Speak English. Drive to Taco Bell."

Warren had laughed, after his thick red fingers reached inside her blouse, brushing her breasts and pulling out her money. Larry spun a cactus pad out the duplex door like a green plate.

Serafina glanced up at the coyote, who was impatiently watching her finish the nopales. He picked up the knife and snapped it shut. Florencio built a fire to roast the cactus on sticks. Serafina sat near the flames, watching the sun drop into the far bushes.

The coyote was thirsty. He drank much of the water. Then he said, "I need the money now. Before the truck comes. Because then we have to leave in a hurry. Give me the fucking money now. Let's go."

"Five hun—" Jesus began.

But the coyote said, "Give me what you have. All your fucking money."

The men gave him folded bills. He walked over to Serafina and said, "Come here."

"She—" Florencio stood up, and the coyote pulled a black gun from his waistband.

"Come here," he said again.

When she was in front of him, he grabbed her by the braid and said, "This is how you move los indios. By la reata." She didn't know the word, but he used her hair as a leash, pulling her head so sharply she felt her cheeks shiver like gelatin. He pushed her into the brush.

They came out in another ravine, steep walls of sand and a large cave where rushing water had scoured out a shelter. Blackened stones set in broken circles meant people had camped here, too. The sun had faded to gray shadow. The coyote's mustache was thick and black as burned rope. He jerked her around by her braid. She pulled out her roll of dollars and gave it to him.

"Kiss the money," he said, grinning. "That's all that matters here."

He shoved the dollars toward her mouth, pushed the paper between her teeth, rubbed her tongue. *I have been here before*, she thought. *I know about the money. This money.*

"And this," he said. "This is the only other thing that matters."

He pushed the gun at her mouth. "Put your tongue inside it, fucking india. Kiss the fucking gun. No. Put your tongue inside now."

He pushed hard, and her tongue bled. He scraped the metal circle on her lips, and she closed her eyes. In church she kissed her thumb when she made the sign of the cross. This metal was only a thumbnail against her lips. He hit her in the jaw with the gun. She fell. *Descanso,* she thought. *Rest. I will rest. If I knew Elvia was dead, I would cut my own wrists and let the blood flow out of me until I was so light, I would rise up to meet her. And my mother. So light.*

She heard him urinating on the fire circle. Then he nudged her with his boot. "Get up."

She stood up, her jaw loose and hot, and her hand went automatically to her pocket.

"What do you have? Silver. I saw you take something from your pocket." He shoved her fingers down and made her pull out the barrettes. "Shit. Nothing. You have nothing."

He slapped them from her fingers with the gun, and they fell in the sand. Pulling her braid so tightly her eyes blurred, he pushed the barrel of the gun to her forehead, twisting and rubbing again. Leaving a mark, she knew, from a tiny sharp edge that scored her skin.

His other hand clutched her blouse front, just as Warren's had, and anger blurred her eyes. The barrettes were lost now. He bent to unzip his pants again, and Serafina touched her forehead. She saw smudges of black on her fingers. The god of the hearthstones. She pulled the mano from between her breasts and hit him in the temple with the heavy stone, which rested perfectly in her hand, as always.

He dropped the gun, and she swung again and again. When he was on the ground, his eyes blank, she pounded at his head until the mano was covered with blood.

She dropped the stone pestle and her whole body trembled. The ravine was silent. She couldn't hear anyone. The men were afraid of the gun.

But Florencio stumbled through the brush tunnel. "I thought

he would shoot you, if I came," he said. His eyes widened, and he reached toward the cut on her mouth, but she pushed his hand away. Something was wrong with the way her jaw hung. She knew she couldn't talk.

He flinched at the blood on the coyote's teeth, the pants gapped open, the stone mano lying nearby. But he listened, bent to touch the man's neck.

"Alive," he whispered. He reached for the money on the ground, the bills folded soft and thick as a doll's pillow. Serafina remembered the barrettes.

She scrabbled for them in the sand and put them in her pocket. Her fingers were crusted with dried blood. Florencio said, "Go back." He didn't look at her, but at the ground near her feet.

She moved quickly to the black gun that had left the dent of a circle she could feel on her forehead. She threw it down the ravine into a tangle of brush. *No. No gun.* She tried to say the words, but only a deep, muffled bleat came from her mouth, and she shook her head in frustration and pain.

"Serafina," Florencio said. He let his fingers sway toward the boots. "He will come after us, if he lives. Find us. We have to get to Yuu Sechi."

Rio Seco. The mano was in her hand. Sticky with drying blood. "If he comes after us, he'll kill us," Florencio said. Serafina dug a hole in the sand and covered the mano. Then she ran back to the fire, where the others were waiting, staring, until she hid her head in folded arms.

When Florencio emerged into the clearing, his face was gaunt, his hands black, and she knew he'd lifted soot-covered rocks over his head. A killing pile. He stared at her, and said, "Now we have to walk the rest of the way."

The Tiltepec men grew angry on the second day of walking to Santa Ysabel. "No truck now, no way to get to Los Angeles. We had a ride to Fresno. We can't walk all the way to Fresno."

"Shut up," Florencio said finally. "He could have just as well shot us as given us a ride. I gave you back all your money. So shut up and walk."

She couldn't answer for herself. She couldn't talk. Her jaw was swollen big as a fist. She could barely walk, her ankle sore and misshapen as dough. They couldn't hike along the highway shoulder, because Florencio said people in the mountains hated Mexicanos so much that they ran them over, shot at them from cars. So they fought through the brush and creekbeds in the day, rested when the heat became overpowering, and then tried to hug the highway at night.

The sun beat down until she could smell the oil burning on the asphalt underfoot and in the greasy bushes by the road. Skeletons of small animals were dry and flat. The faint, stinging circle on her forehead reminded her of how close she'd come to dying.

Death seemed to hover over all the California mountains as she stumbled, Florencio holding her arm. When she felt she would faint from the heat, Florencio said, "Water. Look." He led them to a nearly dry stream, and the men drank from the brackish puddles. She couldn't bend over. With his hands, he funneled water into her mouth, and she tasted moss and earth and oil.

"Down there," he said, pointing south, "in the desert, people die all the time because they have no water. The coyote drops them off and says someone in a truck will come. Just like this one didn't come. The people wait forever, and the sun kills them."

Guillermo said, "We're not in the desert now. If we had the gun, at least we could shoot a rabbit for food." He studied Florencio suspiciously. "You have it. You want to sell it."

"No," Florencio said impatiently. Tiltepec people didn't always like San Cristobal. Serafina didn't look at their eyes on her. No one trusted anyone here, in California.

They saw the cabinlike store in the evening. Santa Ysabel was tiny. There was no truck in sight. Florencio bought water and crackers and a few cans of soup, and they left hurriedly. In another dark clearing, they rested. Eventually, the Tiltepec men slept in a row, their beer cans like candles at their heads.

Serafina's jaw felt hotter, as if a bright marigold of pain were fastened to her bone. "You still can't talk?" Florencio whispered. She shook her head. "Did he hit you with the gun?" She nodded, pointed to the place on her jaw.

Florencio said, "You have to open your mouth enough for water." But just separating her lips made tears stream from her eyes. She took the bottle and dribbled water past her teeth.

He knelt and put his fingers on either side of her face. "When I was in the hospital for my fingers, everyone got hurt in the fields that month. I saw a nurse put one man's jaw back. Someone hit him with a shovel. She said if she didn't put it back, it would always hang wrong."

He lifted her jaw like a shelf, and pain tore through her skull, flared as though the marigold were on fire. Then he tore a tee shirt into strips and wrapped them around her jaw and mouth. "It will keep you warm." He made a pallet of their clothes and said, "Put the good side of your face here. I will stay awake. I am used to not sleeping. When we pick the naranjas, we pick all night. The boss parks the trucks so the headlights shine on the field. I don't need to sleep."

His voice faded, and she slept.

When she knelt at the stream, the blackened blood came off her hands revived and red again from the water. She washed the barrettes, dried them, smelled the metal. She had always cried for a blanket of Elvia's, a shirt, anything that would smell of her skin and breath. But a blanket would have been shreds by now. The barrettes glowed in her palm until she put them away.

They walked parallel to the highway, in the blistering heat of lower land. Serafina saw trucks pass by with people brown as she, and a crumbling adobe house with brown children in the dirt yard. "Indios. Californios," Florencio whispered. "Mixtecos can survive, too. We can make it."

Her tongue, swollen in her mouth, throbbed with thirst. She was glad she couldn't speak. Maybe she would never have to talk again. She drank a few sips of water when they stopped, and the pain of moving her lips washed her forehead clean of thought.

In the clearings, she saw how many had come before them by the piles of plastic water jugs and trash and ashes. Serafina knelt near the fire circles in each place and prayed, *"Ñū'ún yuu nu'un.* Thank you. I will not burn your stones." She laid two wildflowers at the edge of the blackened rocks.

If they didn't get to Rio Seco soon, she would have to wash clothes in a stream. Find wild plants or something to cook. They would live more primitively than in Oaxaca. She thought she was delirious. Her head swam with heat. Maybe she should go home. But she couldn't get home. Never again. She would never see San Cristobal again.

They descended from the forest into brush and chaparral again, stopping beside a river. SAN LUIS REY, the highway sign read. The land was flatter, golden and parched in places.

"We are near the highway to Rio Seco now," Florencio said. Serafina saw more adobe houses, more wooden shacks, Mexican people living near an avocado grove.

Florencio went to a cardboard shack near the trees and paid a woman for some tortillas and water and beer. In the dark, Serafina took off her jeans. She washed her legs and arms in the swirling puddles of river. Now she was home. *I am delirious,* she thought. All the santos were here, and the stones at the river's edge, and she was nearly naked, hungry, praying.

Rest

GOLD TEETH. They had gold teeth. The Mexicans brought him here. From the date grove. *He dumped me out there in the trees.*

All he saw was Dually's knuckles and a baseball bat. Dually said, "I'm not gonna waste bullets on your fuckin loser ass."

The Mexicans put two teeth in my pocket. I guess I spit em out. On the sand.

The nurse kept saying, "You awake now? Hmmm? That's very good, that you wake up. You been sleeping so long. Let's check your pulse, okay?"

She looked Indian, like the woman at the hotel. She said, "Tajinder. That's my name. You call for me, okay? Push the button if you need something."

His jaw was fuckin wired shut.

How long? Where's Ellie now, if Dually was hidin her? He said, "I don't know what the fuck you want, asshole." *He said it in my ear, when I was down. He said, "Your bitch is gone."*

I must a said, "Ellie?"

He hit me in the mouth again. Swear to God, he put a fuckin paper bag over my head. From the grove. The ones the Mexicans put on the dates.

"I ain't sellin your bitch nothin, cause her ass is gone. Bustin down my door lookin for money. You got the wrong strategy, asshole."

He must a hit me in the head. I can't move. My arms are strapped down. Fuckin tied up like a dog. How can I figure out where Ellie is if I can't move?

*Dinner in a hose. In my arm. Shit. How long? Did he have Ellie
or not? He was talkin about Callie. Your bitch is gone.*

Ellie's not—she's my kid. He knew that.

Tajinder has a long braid. Warren called em ragheads. Indian.
Ellie's mom was Indian. Tajinder's short like her. But her face is
rounder. "Mauritian," she said. "I am from an island. Here it is too
hot for me. I need some rain. But the wind blows only sand here.
There. Now your IV is hooked up again."

*Guess since I ain't talkin, she'll just jabber away. Like any
woman. Except Sara. She could go hours and not say shit. Only to
Ellie, when they were alone. She taught Ellie those cavewoman words.
Like for moon. Yoo-hoo. I remember that.*

*Ellie could go for hours, too. Just like me. Didn't have to say shit.
Didn't have to jabber. Callie jabbered all fuckin night. Every woman I
been with talked all the time. Except Sara. Ellie was always askin
about her lately. Why? Where the hell did she go?*

"Hey. Jinder. Yeah. How long I been here?"

She frowns. He couldn't believe his fuckin tonsils were talking.
"How long I been here?"

"Ten days. You woke up for a few minutes before, but you were
unconscious most of the time. You need to rest. You look like—like
you had a hard time. You need to rest now."

Fuck.

Ellie booked. She took the truck and fuckin bailed.

*When I first got her, she used to stare out the window at the moon
and look all sad. I couldn't figure it out. Then one time, I asked her,
and she said the full moon always came up in this one window at the
foster lady's house. I said it's better to have variety in your life, to wonder where it would come up this time.*

"You need to rest for a long time. Mr. Larry Foley. You have a
broken nose, broken jaw, stitches in your head."

*I can't drive fifty-five. I can't drive at all. I better find her fast. Be-
fore she gets in trouble. Tied up like a dog, fuckin truck is gone, and I
can't move.*

Tijuana

THE WOMAN'S FACE was dry and taut, ageless, brown as a palm-bark mask. Elvia threw up near the truck tires. *What if that's her? What if she crosses every year from Tijuana to work grapes, and now she's just bones?* She leaned against the bumper, and Michael wiped her forehead with his tee shirt. "Come on," he said softly. "They're already dead, okay? I'll call 911 when we see a phone. We can't hang around in a stolen truck."

When she turned the truck around, she caught a glimpse of a blue tennis shoe. "Maybe they were from Tijuana," Elvia said.

"I saw a wallet in the sand," Hector said. "Pay stubs for last February from Sun-Picked Farms. Jose-Luis Ortiz was heading for the grapes, wherever his home was. For reals."

Miles down the highway, at the gas station in Ocotillo Wells, Michael went to the pay phone. Elvia began to fill the tank, still seeing the woman's bronzed cheeks. The nozzle was old, and she could smell the fumes, taste them collecting in her throat. Then suddenly she thought, *The baby! Doesn't it breathe my air? I can't remember. What did Sandy say?*

She saw them all sitting at the table one night, playing cards. Sandy had gotten a new foster baby, and she said softly, "You're all different. You were different when you were babies. And mothers never know how each kid is breathing in dust, air, information, how their blood and cells circulate those things around. Where they stay

137

in each kid. Some people get sick, some don't. Some are good at math, some aren't. But you have to pay attention to figure it out. In each kid."

I have to be careful because it's breathing in everything, she thought. *Oh, my God. I'm the mother. Right now.* When Michael touched her arm, she jumped.

"You look like you saw a ghost," he said, laughing, and then his whole face changed. His cheekbones lifted and he handed her the rest of his money. "You keep this. I'm a ghost, half the time. Half, remember? Feel like I'm half dead already."

Elvia felt his fingers tracing her eyebrows. "You look live to me. You just need some sleep," she said.

He leaned against the truck. "That's what I mean. I can't sleep at night. Every time I fall asleep, I think I'm gonna die. So I like to stay awake long as I can. Or sleep just a little while. In a safe place. See this?" He lifted the hair over his ear, and she saw a pink scar like a piece of yarn. "I was walkin on the rez, when I was little, and a bullet went around my head."

"Somebody was shooting you? How old were you?" Elvia touched the skin.

Michael's eyes were fierce on her. "I was ten. They probably weren't aimin for me. Just shootin. Not even on purpose, and I almost died." He glanced around. "Like my mom misses me. I swear. Like she wants me with her. In the other world." He bent close to her neck. "Don't tell Hector or anybody I said that. Never."

She loved the way his face changed when he told her secrets; everyone else looked the same all the time, bored or high or angry, but Michael's eyes would open wide over his cheekbones and he'd look closely into her face like she was the only one who listened to those stories. "We're like, floating out here. I like floating," he said. "Wait till you drink the kikisulem. Remember, I told you about it way back when?"

"The dreaming medicine," she said, trying to imagine the next level.

"When I drink it, I see how my mom looks, and I know she can't wait to see me. Some guys drink it so they can gamble better, or just to trip. But I drink it so I can be in the other world."

If my mother's not dead, how will I see her? Elvia thought, trying not to remember the face in the desert. *Will her spirit just want to talk to me? Alive? In Mexico, or Rio Seco, or wherever?*

Then Michael pulled gently at her shirt, looking at the tattoo. He said, "I can't believe you remembered the moths." The metal ridge of the truck bed dug into her side, and she thought, *Now—I'll tell him about the baby now. If it's a girl, he can rub moth dust on her eyes someday.*

But Hector whistled, and Michael jumped into the truck bed. "What if your dad called the cops on us?"

Elvia shook her head. "He'd never call the cops. For anything." Elvia hesitated, looking at the drops of sweat on Michael's collarbone. "He's been in too much trouble. And we were running in the truck last week. From . . ." She sighed, thinking of the little girl's hair under her fingers, the glow in the sky ". . . from a speed lab."

Michael grinned. "For reals? Your dad was tweakin? You get some?"

Elvia said, "I don't sketch. Never."

"Too bad," he said. "Cause I'm fallin out." He stretched in the truck bed, using her backpack as a pillow. "My favorite mattress. A movin truck."

Elvia nodded. Her father loved to sleep in the truck bed, too. When she started it up, Hector slid onto the bench seat. "Your dad taught you to drive, right? So he knows you took his troca."

She pulled quickly back onto the road, guilt sharp as fingernails denting skin. "No," she said. "He doesn't think I'd do that to him. He always says he expects a knife from strangers—not from friends." She drove toward Mexico, thinking, *When I first lived with him, he always forgot I was in the truck, when he'd tell Warren or whoever, "Gas, grass, or ass—nobody rides for free." Then he'd remember. He'd look at me and say, "Except my kid."*

She held the wheel tightly while the big truck nosed through the curves. She saw the dead woman's face. Her hair had been loose, wavering on the sand.

"She's probably dead," she whispered to Hector. "That's why she never came to find me."

Hector rubbed his face and said, "A lot of people die in summer, down in the desert. They die in the winter, up here. My uncle got killed about twenty miles from here, in Julian. Some skinheads saw him walking and beat him up real bad. They left him in the snow."

"Snow?" Elvia looked at the dusty pine trees. "People come this way, too?"

Hector said, "They come all the time, all year. And they can't cross at Tijuana anymore, cause of Operation Gatekeeper. The government put more border patrol in San Diego and San Ysidro. Now everybody comes this way or through the desert. It's a lot harder." He polished his folder cover. "My uncle in Tijuana, he wanted to visit my mom in Mecca."

Gatekeeper. It sounded like some evil video game to Elvia. She thought of all the bones and spirits that could be scattered around them.

Hector said, "Pull in there. Viejas Road." He laughed. "Old women road. What a name. We're by Descanso. Take a break. I can show you how close we are."

She and Hector got out. Michael was close to the wheel well; he didn't wake up. "Mano stays awake for days, sleeps for days." Hector shook his head.

"Yeah, I know the drill," Elvia said, looking at Michael's open mouth. He and her dad were alike. Constant motion or dead trance. Jumpy and restless or still as a coma. Only really happy when they were driving, driving, moving along.

Hector sat at a scarred, half-burned picnic table. He opened the black folder and laid out hand-drawn maps, talking carefully, as if he was nervous to show her. "Last summer, I went to this special program for migrant kids at Rio Seco City College. This one teacher, Mr. Trevino, he liked my maps. He said I should go to college."

Elvia peered at all the lines drawn in colored pencil. Hector said, "This one's all the cities with Spanish names, and I put the English words next to them cause it's funny. The San and Santas are easy. Then you got Borrego. 'Sheep.' Escondido, over the mountains there. Means 'hidden.' And Encino means 'oak trees.' Up north, see Los Baños? 'The toilets.'"

He showed her another map. "Crops," she said, tracing the tiny, precise pictures he'd drawn on California. Almonds and peaches and walnuts in the middle. Strawberries and lettuce and broccoli near the coast. Grapes and raisins where his mother was.

"I saw an atlas when I was little," he said. "The states all had pictures like the Statue of Liberty on New York, cowboy boots on Texas. California had trolley cars by San Francisco, Hollywood by LA, and sailboats by San Diego. I wanted to put the real stuff I knew for California."

She saw strawberries everywhere in the south, grapes and oranges and lemons in the desert. She touched Mecca. A small red heart there, too.

"Your girlfriend, Marisela?" she said, pointing to the heart.

"I'm not making any feria. She needs money, so she found somebody else."

"You'll make money someday. With maps. I'm gonna make money with geology. Check construction sites, have my own truck." Elvia blushed. She hadn't even told Michael her plan. The ID card was warm in her hand. "Miscelanea Yoli," she said. "That's the city?"

Hector sighed. "That's just a store. Colonia Pedregal means, like, neighborhood of stones. People don't have addresses or mailboxes. So what if you find her, and she doesn't want you?"

"I thought about that." Elvia bit her lip. "She probably won't even recognize my face. But I can say I saw her, one last time. Then I can try not to be like her."

Hector's eyes glinted. "You mean so you won't—"

"What?" Elvia stood up. What did he know? "So then we'll come back . . ."

"You keep wanting to say 'home,'" Hector said, raising his brows. "But you don't."

"I don't know what home is yet," she said. She didn't want to talk anymore.

Down the narrow path, she looked for a place to pee. The ravine was strewn with trash and blackened fire pits, and something smelled horrible. Nervously, she went behind a boulder. Then she saw a strange pyramid of stones.

Hector called, "Where are you?"

"Come down here, just for a second," she called back.

They stood looking at the pile of rocks. The earth had been dug up around the rocks, and coyote or dog paw prints were tracked in the sand. "Some kind of Indian good luck memorial?" Elvia said, but Hector shook his head.

"Some kind of burial," he said, and she turned away, shuddering, nearly stumbling on a gray-black stone the size of a hand, covered with dark-crusted sand.

Hector was nervous. "You two got ID? For when we come back across?"

Michael rubbed his eyes. "Driver's license." He was grumpy. "Hey, we could head down to Chihuahua. All my grandpa told me was my moms was sixteen and she met some dude named Jesus from the dog place. Jesus went up to the cotton, and she went to heaven." He threw out his arms. "He might a felt bad if he knew I was around, but Jesus was off the hook." He looked at Elvia then. "Just like your moms. Free and clear. You sure you want to do this?"

Elvia said angrily, "You can catch a bus right now, if it's too much trouble, okay, Michael? You'll be free and clear. Off the hook." She stopped, realizing he might figure out what she meant. "I have a library card, from when I lived with my foster mom," she said.

Michael had the license, so he drove. Men in sunglasses motioned them forward. Hector shifted nervously in the middle, and Elvia felt the breeze on her wet face. She'd washed up in a Del Taco bathroom. So her mother wouldn't think she was dirty, homeless, lost.

Even though I am, she thought, glimpsing at herself in the side mirror. She looked past herself to barren lots, shabby buildings, and then a bridge. Her father had said he had come here after he found the clinic card. His tools had been stolen.

Hector motioned Michael to turn down a broad avenue. "Up there is the tourist stuff," Hector said, pointing to shops lining the streets, where people carried bags and wore huge sombreros. Small, dark women, heads covered with black shawls, hovered at corners with hands held out for money, their kids with tiny hands outstretched, too.

"Mixtec Indians from way south," Hector said. Elvia stared at a woman against a wall, blouse open, a baby at her breast, her eyes on the car, her fingers lifting a white cup to rattle it at them.

She felt a pain shoot through her own breasts. *That could be my mother. Is that why she didn't want me to come? Back to nowhere?* She slammed herself back against the seat.

The tourist area was gone, the highway crowded by stucco houses and wrought-iron fences and run-down buildings just like parts of Rio Seco or Los Angeles. Hector said, "Look on the other side." Cement banks led up to huge fences, and people wearing dark clothes, their faces gaunt and watchful, sat along the metal panels. "They're waiting for night to jump the fence. But Operation Gatekeeper catches everybody. So people try the desert and the mountains now."

Elvia leaned out the window, thinking, *She stood here, I know it. She crossed here, with all these other people. What's on the other side of the fence? Where do they go?* She saw mostly men, squatting, leaning, like they'd been waiting for weeks, years. A few women pushed carts or walked with boxes slung around their necks, selling things, while a few others waited with men, their shoulders hunched, their hair hiding their eyes.

Suddenly they'd left the crowded houses and repair shops and clinics and were entering a steep-walled canyon. Hector said, "Turn here."

Elvia was shocked by the bareness of the earth. No trees, no bushes, no wild sunflowers or foxtails like the roadsides at home. The powdery dust and rocks looked like they'd been sifted and dropped back down by giant hands. People slid down paths and walked along the roadside.

Then she saw the first crosses. At a junction of paths near the roadside, five iron crosses, with plastic flowers attached, stood forlorn, the wind from passing vehicles whipping the petals.

Elvia said, "They look so sad."

Michael said harshly, "Hell, no, it reminds you people were right there, cruisin or laughin, and then they died. On that spot. It's like, their place. You could go visit the cemetery, but that's just dirt they bought. Their soul left right there, by the cross. You can't forget."

"Yeah, look," Hector said. At the end of a ravine, two more crosses, white wood, with notes and flowers attached, leaned in the wind.

Elvia understood then. "Like the people in the desert, somebody's taking their bodies away. And nobody will ever know how long they walked, where they came from, when they gave up."

Hector nodded. "If you hung around the fields, you'd see crosses all over California." He pointed again, and Michael turned in to an immense valley where shacks and fences clung to ravines and hilltops. Laundry waved like flags everywhere.

People were everywhere, walking in the dry riverbed below, descending the ravines on tire stairways. Elvia said to Hector, "Pedregal is on one of your maps?"

He shook his head. "Nope. You can't make a map of this place. Everything's hidden up in the hills, or it washes down the arroyos when it rains. Sometimes bulldozers come through and erase whole neighborhoods. And then the people just settle someplace else, call it Colonia something-else." He looked at her with solemn eyes. "I'm trying to find Colonia Aguilar, where my dad's aunt lives. I haven't been here for a long time. The barrios look bigger, like more people keep coming. New places all over the hills." He glanced across the valley.

Women were everywhere, carrying babies in shawls, carrying plastic bags and baskets. Their feet raised dust on the paths, the cars pulled the dust into veils, and the whole valley seemed hazy. "Fuck it," she cried, putting her hands over her eyes. "We'll never find anybody here."

Michael put his hand on her shoulder, saying, "We came this far. Maybe your mom and my dad are gettin happy right now, drinkin Tecate beers, and we'll see them at the liquor store." He reached a finger to her jaw, tracing a line.

Hector said, "Watch the road, mano. Turn down here, I think. See that big water tank?"

They crossed the dry riverbed on a dirt track, and the truck bounced hard in the deep ruts, then labored up the steep road. Elvia saw houses covered with painted tomatoes; the walls were metal sheets, the roofs corrugated tin with rocks and tires thrown on top.

"This is Colonia Aguilar. Eagle's Nest. Tía Dolores has been here for twenty years." Hector looked around. "But I haven't been here since I was about six. Too hard to cross now."

"For you?" Elvia asked, puzzled, but then the truck skidded to the left, and Michael said, "You hear that? Tire's gone. Shredded."

Hector said, "Don't mess up the rim. We can walk."

Michael got out, crouching near the left front tire. "I ain't leavin the truck to get ripped off," he said to Hector, who nodded.

Slowly, she followed Hector up the dusty hill. Women hung laundry, watered cactus plants in coffee cans, stared at her. She stared back. *I don't even know what the hell she looks like.*

Two men working on a car engine glanced up at them, frowning, and three little girls came up to a fence made of rope-tied sticks. Elvia saw their smudged cheeks and dusty braids. *That's me*, she thought, looking at the smallest one. *Me.* "Hi," she said, and the girls laughed and ran away.

Breathing hard, she read the sign in the next doorway. MISCELANEA ROSITA.

A plywood counter stretched along the windowsill, with sodas, candy, and tiny bottles of shampoo and lotion and perfume. A woman watched them impassively from her doorway. Behind her were shelves with cans and bags. A store. Miscelanea Yoli was where her mother maybe got her mail. *Probably a hundred of them around here. We'll never find her*, Elvia despaired, panting, dizzy.

"There—my aunt's place," Hector said, pointing to the house next door, green like pistachio ice cream, behind a fence of strange curly wire that looked like lace panels. Elvia leaned against one of the wooden poles. Suddenly she didn't think she could go any farther. Her skin was coated with layers of sweat and dirt and grape, her hair was matted and filthy, and her breastbone felt hollow as a straw.

She hadn't felt the cricket feet tapping her bones since Lena put the needle into her shoulder. She'd thought fear and pain made the baby kick, but she'd been scared many times since and she'd felt nothing. She must have hurt the baby, breathing in speed vapors and gas fumes and poisoned grape dust, letting tattoo ink flow into her skin. Into her blood.

It's a baby now. Not just cells. It won't melt or disappear. That's so fucking stupid. How could I think that? It's like igneous rock—pressure just changes it. It's got feet. Or hands. Something that thumps. I probably pressured it into something bad. Deformed. It can't even thump. I really fucked up. Like my dad said, fuck-up's in my blood.

She held on to the fence wires. Tires held up the walls of the ravine, stacked like big black pennies against the crumbling mountainside, and all around this yard tires were painted yellow and planted with red geraniums. *I give up*, she thought, sitting down in the dirt, the curly wires poking her back. *My mother's a ghost, just like Michael's mother. My dad's probably in the wind, off the hook, just like Michael's dad. And Michael acts like he wants to be a ghost, too. So this baby didn't have a chance.* She had a sudden vision of a tiny skeleton, curled inside her. She started to sob, throwing her head back to the sky. She thought she saw shimmering white angels, stiff and swaying, hanging from the trees above to mock her.

Ticuāá–Butterfly

SERAFINA saw the creamy-white butterflies rise from the cauliflower field, like the little spirits of children. She lay in the bed of eucalyptus leaves in a farmer's windbreak, delirious with fever and pain. The smell of the fragrant bark and silver-knife leaves made her remember.

Yukon Avenue. The dead end of the street, where these ghostly trees shivered in the wind, where Elvia loved to peel the bark and then touch the tree-skin underneath. The smell in her fingers those nights, when Serafina washed her in the tub. Her backbone showing through her skin like a rosary.

She fumbled for the rosary under her breast. She touched the beads. Each bone, a prayer under her own now-swollen fingers, under the soapy water she remembered, under her tears.

Please. Take care of her. Keep her safe. Let me see her again.

The men slept. Florencio's rattling breath was nearby. Only her eyes moved. The hot wind scoured the field and the butterflies were disturbed, moving jagged in the currents of air, trying to settle.

She had dreamed when she slept of the tiny white dress. Back in San Cristobal, a girl named Guadalupe had buried her baby girl in a shimmering white dress. She had had a fever. She was only three. Like Elvia, the last time Serafina saw her.

The sharpest pain, sharper than the pain in her jaw or her feet or her stomach, ricocheted between her hipbones, the way it did each time she saw the small back in the tub, the almond-colored cheeks and eyes, the smile when she lifted her face. The hands at her knees, on her back. The terrible untethering from the ground of Serafina's whole body without those fingers in hers, on her, holding her.

She opened her eyes. A few of the butterflies rested on the eucalyptus trunk nearest her. She saw that some of them were yellow, a pale buttery color she didn't remember from her time here before.

Two more nights, maybe, if she could walk again. That was what she thought Florencio had said, though her jaw sent ringing into her ears and the constant walking jarred her hearing even more. They were closer. Rio Seco.

She made herself think of that night, the feel of her body floating away from the car in the parking lot, so that she would get up when this darkness fell, tonight, so that she would make herself walk again. She had to feel those fingers, even if she just touched Elvia's hand, even if the hand was larger than her own. She had to see her daughter's eyes. Some woman had to have taken care of her, all these years. Someone had to have taken her place.

It hurt to think that, but it hurt more to imagine that the soul had flown into a small, winged spirit trying forever to find a foothold.

Baby Teeth Like Little Opals

SMALL WHITE DRESSES, shrouded in plastic, hung from the ceiling. Through the doorway, Elvia could see the larger dresses swaying in the trees, like ghosts rocking babies.

At least she fed me—I was born, Elvia thought wearily. *Wherever she was when she was pregnant, here in TJ eating tortillas or in Rio Seco eating cactus or whatever—she didn't fuck me up with drugs or starve me.*

So last week I would a been happy. I thought the baby was tiny and it would melt. But it must be like a geode now—a hollow sparkly place inside a bigger rock. Like a secret. Blood drying into crystals. No. What a fuck-up way to think. What do they do, if they die? They don't get smaller and smaller till they fade away. They just stay the same, floating there?

Hector's aunt stood near her now, asking her something in Spanish. Elvia didn't understand. The aunt's hair was short and curled into black waves, stiff and sprayed, and in her housedress and glasses, with her wobbly arms, she looked like any American grandma.

Elvia heard her talk to Hector in faster Spanish, then a long trickle of laughter. *What the hell am I doing in Mexico?* she thought. *What will I do if I find her? I don't even know her.* She rubbed the moths on her shoulder, made them burn.

Suddenly she wondered what her father would think of the tattoo. *Probably get mad, even though that's the first thing I remembered about him, back at Sandy's house.* She watched the plastic-shrouded dresses sway. *This is it. If I don't find her here, there's just the two places in Rio Seco, and then what?*

Hector said, "Me and Michael are tryin to find the right tire." He put a bowl of beans on the tiny folding table near her. "Tía Dolores says, 'Are you okay?'" he said, squatting close by, peering into her face.

She didn't want to look weak. "So I eat beans, act like I'm Mexican, and then Jesus will let me find my mother?" Elvia lifted her chin toward the religious portrait on the wall.

His aunt sat in the other corner, picking up her sewing. She murmured a long sentence in Spanish, ending with something Elvia understood. "Pobrecita."

"I'm not a fuckin poor anything," Elvia hissed at Hector. "I heard girls at school teasing each other like that. And even if I find my mom, I'm not turning into a beañorita."

Hector yelled, "No, you're just gonna be a—a witch."

"You mean a bitch!" she yelled back.

"I don't use that word. A bitch is a female dog. You're not acting like a dog."

Hector's aunt stood up, the satin slithering from her lap. "Shut up. Two of you. Nobody talk that in my house. Respect. Hector, aquí es el dinero para llantas."

She handed him money, and Hector went outside without looking back. His aunt turned to Elvia. "Your body es tired but your mouth okay." She picked up her sewing. "So don't eat beans. Who cares? I make frijoles todos las dias." She hesitated. "Every day, all gone."

Elvia felt stupid and scared. She hadn't known the aunt spoke English. And now Hector was mad. She went to the doorway, peering through the dresses. Hector walked down the street toward the truck. Michael was a faint figure down the hill.

She realized suddenly that Michael was more worried about

the truck than about her. He had fallen in love with the damn truck. She was just another friend. Fool around. Get high. Kick it. But the truck—he was guarding that like treasure.

She studied the dresses hanging outside in the tree—large or small, each dress was made with white satin and lacy ruffles, pearls and sequins. Even the babies would look like angel brides.

"The dresses in los arboles, that for your quinceanera," Tía Dolores said. "You had one?"

"Quinceanera?"

"For when you turn fifteen," she said, frowning.

"I'm fifteen ," Elvia said, staring at the red-brown beans. *I guess I am*, she thought. *Who knows? Who cares?* She remembered seeing a girl her age in a white dress, in the date worker houses. People were clapping and taking her picture.

"Beañorita," the woman said suddenly, like she had read Elvia's mind. "Who is that?"

Elvia was embarrassed. "Girls who just came from Mexico. To California. Where I lived."

Tía Dolores frowned. "Funny joke. You don't think I speak English? But I work en San Diego. Ten years. I watch three kids, clean the house, cook everything. I take two buses from here, then walk. Back then, the border was nothing. How you say—a pain. Now is Operación Gatekeeper. People go around to the desert and back to San Diego to work. Estupido."

"People from Colonia Pedregal?" Elvia asked. "My mom lived there."

"I don't know Pedregal. Maybe in the new colonias by the dompe."

Elvia paced in the doorway, thinking of the dead woman in the desert, the eerie smells of the mountain ravine. She looked down the street. The truck's cab was a pale blue skull facing up the hill, all alone.

Colonia Aguilar—Eagle's Nest, Hector had said. Dust devils began to dance in the road, and from this hill she saw the wind pick up trash and tongues of dirt in each ravine and colonia.

In the west, the sun hung like an old coin in a pall of rising smoke. Hundreds of seagulls wheeled like white crosses in the air, and something floated high above like white jellyfish. Hector's aunt stood beside her now. "The wind come from the sea. Over there. By the dompe."

"The dump?" Elvia stared at the floating jellyfish, lazy and then vicious with the wind. Plastic bags. That's what they were.

"People live en el dompe. They live everywhere. Maybe you don't find her. So many colonias, so many people." Elvia smelled strong perfume, felt fingers patting the moths on her shoulders. "Sit. For the llanteria take a long time. Sit. I work, and I cook. Not beans."

Elvia felt bad for a minute. "I'm sorry I said that. People called me beañorita before." She sat down and ate a spoonful of the beans, the flecks of red chile stinging her lips and mouth like pinpricks. "These are good." Hector's aunt smiled then.

A taxi labored up the road, bringing a brown cloud to the doorway. "Dolores?" someone called. Two women and a girl of about fourteen came bustling inside. *They want a dress for that birthday,* Elvia thought. But they put a bridal veil on the girl's head, laughing and nodding.

The girl glanced over. "Novia?" someone said. Hector's aunt shook her head, starting a long speech—Elvia heard "Pedregal" and "madre." She hated the sudden pity in their eyes.

She went outside. The taxi had turned around in the dirt lane. *What if the guys come back after dark, with no tire? I don't want to hang around for days—I want to find her now. Or not.* She stepped out to the street, trying to remember what Hector had repeated. "I want to go—me voy al Colonia Pedregal."

The driver, a pale man with a faint mustache like iron filings clinging to his lip, shrugged. "No se Pedregal."

Elvia took out ten dollars and said, "Me voy al—todos—las colonias. Please."

He nodded and she got in. She could do this herself. Now or never.

·   ·   ·

The taxi driver picked up people everywhere, standing by the dirt roads criss-crossing the main ravine. Everyone spoke in rapid Spanish. Two men were crammed into the front seat with the driver, and packed against Elvia in the back were four women, one holding a boy on her lap. Only the boy stared openly at Elvia. His eyes were slanted and dark as shards of slate. His mother wore a loose dress and a long, messy braid, and her plump body sat on stubby legs. *Indians?* Elvia thought, watching the boy.

The car headed back toward the main part of Tijuana. The taxi driver called out, "Clinica," where the boy and two women got out. Then the cab picked up a whole group of people and headed back into the valley. Elvia said loudly, "Colonia Pedregal?" to the driver, who answered back impatiently. They wound through neighborhood after neighborhood, a hundred dirt roads lined with a thousand plywood and tin shacks, and Elvia looked for stones. She saw box spring fences everywhere, their wires turning to pink coils in the sun, and wooden pallets made into houses and corrals for goats. Tires were piled like stacks of Oreos; Michael and Hector had probably found one for the truck by now.

The driver said to departing passengers a sentence containing the word *Pedregal*. People shook their heads, until one man shrugged and let loose a torrent of words ending with "dompe."

The cab was finally empty. Seagulls and plastic bags whirled in the near distance, and she smelled smoke. She was afraid now. They were heading farther away from Tijuana, even from Hector's aunt. He had to know she was American, even though her grimy jeans and big tee shirt made her fit in here. He glanced in the rear-view mirror as the cab bumped up another hill, another washboard path.

She stared at a group of white crosses with fresh flowers in a deep ravine along the road, and he said, "Agua," pointing to the hills. "Muerto."

Water, she thought. *Death. Floods.*

"Mucho?" he said. "Much cross." He pointed to shacks, to the sky. "Fuera. Y frio." He pretended to shiver. Fire. And cold. People had burned in tiny houses. And frozen to death. "Niños," he said finally. He put his hand out, low.

Children.

Now she hugged herself. Was he giving her a clue? Was he taking her someplace to dump her? For ten dollars? How much was that here, where she didn't even know what a peso looked like?

They shuddered slowly up the hill, the driver shaking his head ominously, and she realized they were in a pall of thick, dark smoke. One or two shacks, low to the ground like tunnels covered with wooden pallets and cardboard, hugged the ravine not far from the crosses. At the top of the hill, he stopped the car, and she looked out onto the dump.

Dompe. Mountains of trash lay like distant whales breathing smoke from invisible blowholes, and then she saw people walking on the mounds, poking with long sticks, dragging sacks. At the edge of the dump were cardboard shelters and houses, people peering out at the taxi. Children with faces black-smudged as if they'd slept in embers, women with sandaled feet, also black. Three men came up to the taxi, and the driver spoke for a time.

Elvia sat up, heart rising painfully, sweat trickling down her back. She saw a few stones, piled in a wall, littering the ravine. One man peered inside at her and said something that made the men laugh roughly.

The driver had never moved from his seat. Now he leaned forward and pointed to the crosses in the ravine. "Pedregal. L'año pasado." He spoke slowly, staring at her.

Elvia clutched the seat. Año was "year," she thought. Pasado? He gestured behind him. Passed? He said, "Mucha lluvia," sprinkling rain with his fingers. Then he wiped away all the houses with the back of his hand.

Elvia was stunned. Gone? The whole neighborhood? Was her mother a cross in the ravine? The men said something else, and the driver nodded, holding up one finger in a gesture of waiting for Elvia. He maneuvered the cab around the shacks and along a canyon encircling the dump. The seagulls cried like screaming women. Elvia laid her head back against the seat.

"Pedregal," he said. Banks of tires flanked another arroyo, and a nest of houses perched along the ridge. Cardboard shacks, a few cement-block houses with protruding iron bars like antennae, and across the arroyo, a blue-painted tin house with blurry red geraniums in coffee cans.

No Miscelanea Yoli. No store or dress shop or anything except houses and people trudging down the arroyo, coming from the dump with bulging sacks and smoke-etched faces.

The driver called to a woman who'd come out of her shack holding a baby, suspicion tight at her mouth. Elvia leaned out her window, stuttering, "My madre. Serafina Mendez."

The woman frowned at Elvia. Her baby was wrapped completely in a black shawl, like a dark cocoon set against her shoulder. The woman shook her head.

"No. Serafina? No."

The other shacks were dark. When the taxi turned around, Elvia looked at the woman hovering in her yard, watching. Someone's mother.

The sun sank into the dump, the far-away smoke settling now, turning it into a small, unimportant apricot. She could see it from Aguilar, when the taxi dropped her off.

She was done. She couldn't imagine looking elsewhere in Tijuana, among the hundreds of arroyos and pedestrians and miscelaneas. Hesitating in the yard, she thought, *Maybe she had to come back, and she didn't want me to grow up like this. Did she want me to be American?*

Tía Dolores gave her a murderous look when she stepped inside the house. It looked like a jade palace compared to the dump and Colonia Pedregal.

"Wash your clothes. If you sleep here." She still sewed, brown fingers like plump Tootsie Rolls against the white satin. Elvia saw that her hands were swollen. "The boys get a llanta and I tell them you go. They go look for you. I don't know where. Now wash. Everybody wash at my house. No dirt." She sucked at her teeth. "Maybe your novio don't come back."

Elvia folded her arms. "Novio? My boyfriend? He wouldn't leave."

She humphed. "Novios go away all the time. Especially in Tijuana."

Elvia laughed bitterly. The woman thought that would scare her? "Happens all the time in California, too. Big deal. I'm a fuckin expert in 'go away.'"

Tía Dolores said, "No dirt. No dirt words." Then she said gently, "Hector tell me she go away. Because she was American then. Not Mexican. Mexican mama, she don't leave a baby. Your mama es in California. An American now. You find her easier on the moon. Use a—"

"A telescope," Elvia said, sighing.

"Sí. She es alone up there, stick out like a pin." She held up a pincushion crowded with silver heads. "But here a million are come and go. So many lost. My nieto—Hector father, I find him. His mother is kill. A car. I find him on the street when he is four, five. He live with me all that time, then he go across to California. To work. He get married to a crazy woman. Hector mama. And they have so many children. I never have any. Only him." She pointed to Elvia's clothes, to the backpacks and bags piled by the door. "Limpia."

"Limpia?"

"Wash."

Sándoo, Elvia thought. She said, "My mother was Indian. Indio. She said sándoo for wash. Yoo for moon."

"You hear her say these?"

"I guess. My foster mother told me I said all these different words."

"Foster?"

"Like, my mom for a while. Five years."

"Why you didn't stay with that mother?"

"My dad came to get me." Elvia added quickly, "She wasn't my real mom."

"Real." Tía Dolores put down her sewing. "I am not the real woman for Hector's father. But the one feed you, take you to la clinica for sick, wash the clothes, who is the mother. The one hold you for—suenos malos."

"Bad dreams?"

"Sí. Who worry about the teeth. That's the mother." Tía Dolores paused. "If she is Tarahumara or Mixtec or Maya, you think what life she have. Before. Sur." She pointed toward the south. "Look the indias here—" She held out her hand, as if begging. "Los niños tambien. If you find her in the street, so—" Now she lifted a cup, as if seeking money. "What you do? Go? You are happy then? Maybe she know you, and you—" Tía Dolores hesitated and thought a long time. "You leave her. Like she leave you. Sí? You break the heart. El corazón."

Elvia had no answer. She tried to picture her mother on a street corner, tried to decide how she would know this woman. Hector's aunt was right.

Tía Dolores said, "I leave a dress for you. Outside. Go wash."

In the dirt yard, Elvia found a stone sink under a loquat tree. An old-lady print dress hung from the tree. The concrete-block shed had a toilet and shower head. With the rough soap, she rinsed off the tears and dirt and grime of Ventana, of Mecca and the desert, of today's colonias. She hadn't taken a shower since the Sands Motel.

He was the real father, she thought. *He fed me and took me to the doctor. He's worried about me. I've been gone for five days. I better call him.* Naked and dripping, she rubbed the towel on her shoulders and winced. She found a mirror on a plastic shelf. The tattooed moths were smaller than her father's dragon. She remembered touching his dragon's scales.

She tried to touch her moths' wings. Under the scabbing, she thought she could see colors. She tilted the mirror. It looked like the moths had antennae, not wiry like butterflies' but feathery blue. Lena was a real artist.

Maybe she had put a little magic in the moths. Maybe Elvia shouldn't give up. Not yet.

She put on the flowered dress and felt very cool, as if a cloud was skimming her skin. She hadn't worn a dress since she was about six. She didn't look in the mirror again. She heard Michael say, "You look like a Mexican woman now. An old lady . . ." She turned to face him.

"A wet and tired old lady." But his grin faded quickly. He was staring at her belly, pressed against the damp dress.

"Damn. You're pregnant? Oh, shit. Shit. Why didn't you tell me?"

She led him to the truck, and he sat next to her silently. Elvia looked at the windshield where a rock had made a lopsided star. *Does Michael want to be the real father?* she thought, breathing out hard. She said, "You didn't look like you were ready to hear about a baby."

"How many months?" he said, shaking his head.

She added the week since they left. "About five. Since we . . ."

"In Tourmaline?" *He sounds so surprised,* Elvia thought, pushing in the dashboard lighter, pulling it out to see the pulsing red circle. "You could still get it—fixed, right?" he said.

Those girls in the school bathroom talked about getting blobs fixed, she thought. *This isn't a blob. I felt feet. Even though I don't feel them now.* "I don't know," she said. "Maybe it's too far. So you're scared?"

"Shit, yeah, I'm scared." He flicked the dangling keys. "Your cowboy dad—that's who you been calling on the pay phone? He knows?"

Elvia shook her head. "No. That's why I left. He'd—he'd probably try to kill you. At least hurt you big time. I don't know what he'd say to me." She sighed. "I called my foster mom."

"From way back?"

"Yeah."

"She still remembers you?" Michael looked out the window. Hector was outside now.

"She remembers everybody," Elvia said.

"What about your real mom? You wanted to find her and give her the baby?"

"Give the baby to somebody who left me in a car?" She was angry now. "You don't get it. Your mom died. She didn't get tired of you. I just wanted to know. And I got tired of waiting for you guys today, so I went to the dump where my mom used to live. Not now, she doesn't." Elvia stared at Michael now, at his fingers drumming the dashboard, his eyes far away. "I'm going to Rio Seco to look there. Then we can decide what to do."

"You were always runnin in the desert. Miles and miles. You didn't even act like a—"

"Like a stupid bitch who gets pregnant? It's not anything special. Just a place to put your thing, right?" *Callie knew*, she thought, closing her eyes. "You were drunk anyway."

"Elvia," he said, putting his hand on her arm. "Hey. I'm just sayin I don't know if I can . . ."

"Teach a baby Cahuilla songs and stories," she snapped. "All that stuff you said about being Indian. This baby's part Mexican, part American, two parts Indian. Gone, gone, gone, and gone."

He frowned. "Not songs. Hell, I don't know if we can even feed a baby. Buy all those Pampers. Guys at St. Jude's say Pampers will clean you out." Then he closed his eyes. "We don't even got a place to stay. Maybe it'd be better to not let it have a shitty life, you know . . ."

She stared at his obsidian eyes. *A shitty life? He wants me to get rid of it. Now. He doesn't even know what geodes are, the sparkly hollow stillness inside.*

In Tía Dolores's kitchen, Elvia saw a stone bowl and pestle, covered with dusty spices.

Hector whispered, "You told him? I can see it in his face."

"Wait—how did you know?"

"I been seeing pregnant girls all my life. Plus Tiny told me. She said she didn't think he'd make a good father."

"A father is whoever puts the sperm there," Elvia said. "That's all." She touched the red powder left in the squat stone bowl. "What's this?" She held up the stone that fit into her palm.

"The molcajete? The mano?" Tía Dolores asked.

Like *hermano*? No. Elvia thought of granite boulders she'd seen in the desert, where Indians had left depressions where they had ground acorns.

"Hand," Hector said. "A stone that fits in your hand. My jefita has one. Somewhere."

Tía Dolores cut into a whole fish covered with red sauce, saying, "Your mano take a long time to fit right. Smooth." She touched the stone pestle. "I have that one long time. Years."

Elvia tasted the spicy fish and rice. *Does my mother still have a mano? What if she's so close she can smell this sauce?*

Michael came inside, his hair wet, his face damp and blank. "We gotta get on the road," he said. "I got a job to do. Make some money." He glanced at Elvia.

Money to get ready for the baby? she thought. *Or money to get rid of it?*

Tía Dolores gave Elvia more rice and said, "You stop looking for her? You go home?"

"Home?" Elvia said the word without thinking. She stared at the mano.

Tía Dolores raised one eyebrow, a penciled comma. "You don't go home? To the no-real mama?"

The no-real mama, Sandy Narlette, had said her baby teeth looked like opals; she kept them in a keepsake box. Elvia touched her belly. Did this baby have teeth yet? Nubs of opal teeth in a skull? Maybe Sandy would know what to do.

Elvia went out to the yard and watched Tía Dolores take the

glowing dresses down from the trees. Then, folded into Tía Dolores's dressfront, she felt herself—bigger chest, block of belly—imprinted by the hug.

"I will pray for you," Tía Dolores said. "And I will pray Hector can go al otro lado. He has no papers. He born in the house. Near where you sleep. The only one born in Mexico." She frowned. "He take a big chance for you. To come here." Then she thrust a package into Elvia's hands. "For your baby," she whispered. "How lucky. You are very lucky."

Elvia didn't feel lucky. She felt scared when she slid into the truck and saw Hector clutching his library card. When they passed the shadow people waiting by the border fence, she said to Hector, "Your aunt told me about—no papers. I would have been lost without you. Even in Tourmaline. In Mecca." Hector shrugged, but she said, "For reals." Then Michael edged the truck into the line waiting to cross back into California, and she saw the Indian women.

They stood between the cars, on the raised white dots of the center divider, their faces gaunt. Their babies were slung in black shawls across their fronts, and now and then a small mouth would let go and a black nipple would swing free. The mother's face above it would become defiant, her eyes meeting the drivers', her outstretched hand coming close to the window, her voice an imploring stream of words Elvia didn't understand.

The older children darted between cars, holding trays of Chiclets and candy, yelling, "Mister! Mister! A dollar!" Other kids sang in voices big as car horns.

A woman came close, murmuring, thrusting her baby at the window, and Elvia turned away. She couldn't look at the face, couldn't look at the mouth.

Michael pulled ahead, and the uniformed men peered into windows, asked questions, waved some vehicles through and pointed at others to be searched. Elvia felt Hector stiffening, his shoulder tense against hers. The brown-faced man whose tag read QUESADA, v. said, "You guys just on a visit?"

"Yeah," Michael said.

"Bringing anything back?"

Elvia spoke up quickly, unwrapping a corner of her package. "We came to get a christening dress. For my baby—sister."

The man took the package, nodded at the white satin. "Got ID?" he said, bending to look at their faces. They handed him cards. Driver's license. School ID. Library card.

"Tourmaline, huh? And you go to Tourmaline High?"

They nodded.

"What's your school mascot?" he asked.

"Bulldogs," Hector said quickly. "We suck big-time."

The man laughed and waved them through.

Elvia twisted around in the seat to see the backs of the Indian women, floating black-shrouded in the center divider, hands slanting out limp and curled, a bundle pushed forward, a baby swimming in the sea of exhaust.

Then she felt it. A tracing line on the inside of her belly, not a kick, but something writing a code on the membranes inside her. A secret code, one she didn't know.

Corn Milk

SERAFINA lay in a cave. Florencio crouched over her. She was cold now. The fever was gone. Her jaw was hard as stone, as though scars were turning to veins of silver inside a rock.

She couldn't walk. She was too weak. "One more night," Florencio said.

The Tiltepec men were gone. They had left for Fresno on their own. Florencio and Serafina were alone, in the cave of boulders at the edge of low hills. They had walked through wheat, then up this slope. She heard cows. She smelled manure piled in the grass. She smelled urine in the cave. She curled into herself, thinking that if she stayed here, all anyone would find was a skeleton. And the silver barrettes. They would not melt away with her flesh. They would fall gently through the circle of her bare hipbones and lie beside her.

"Here," Florencio said. "If you eat, you can walk again. We haven't eaten for too long. I found this in the field. Sit up. One more night. Serafina. We are nearly there."

He was sideways in her eyes. He sat on a stone in the cave, scraping corn kernels from a thin cob with his knife. He talked, a low stream, the whole time, as if he was afraid she would slip away in silence. "The Tiltepec men kept asking what happened. Exactly. To you. To him. I wouldn't tell them, and they said Yucucui people ask for trouble. They said we should stay in the mountains."

164

Serafina listened to his soft voice, to the knife striking the stone accidentally. "Rigoberto said he never wanted to see San Cristobal again. But when I told him I was coming for fiesta, to see my cousin, he borrowed the money for you. I was worried someone would rob me, while I was walking. I thought I would just give you and your mother the money."

Serafina wondered if her mother's pain, inside her breasts and bones, had felt like this rigid cording of hurt in her jaw. A corn kernel splattered onto her leg. She felt the drop of milk.

"I watched you when you were a girl. You were promised to Rogelio Martinez. My mother and I lived far past the river, and I only went to school sometimes." He glanced out over the fields. "To say that here, in California, it is almost funny. To say that you were better off than we were. But we came to the store only a few times a year. I saw you. Your braids were long and tied with ribbon. You watched everything. You were so small."

Carefully, she moved her teeth. A horse with a bit. La reata— the coyote had held her braid like a leash. Jerking her head. She whispered, practicing. "Not small now."

He collected the mashed corn and yellowish milk in a cut-down water bottle and held it to her lips.

When the yellow milk leaked from her breasts into Elvia's glistening, angry mouth, Serafina had been afraid something was wrong with her. Milk should be white, or tinged with blue.

Elvia was born in a bathtub. Serafina had been in the tiny bottom-floor apartment for three weeks, and Larry was gone again. She had never left the front door. She didn't know how to get to the hospital. She wasn't even sure how many months she had been pregnant. When the pains came, a loomstrap around her back but inside her skin, she walked around the living room for hours. They went, they came back, they went. Then water poured from her, and she lay in the tub; it was like a white-stone cave all around her.

She must have moaned, even screamed, because a woman

came from upstairs. She shoved the flimsy door in with her shoulder. Serafina had never seen anyone from outside. The woman was hugely fat, so large her skin fell down in folds from her chin and from her stomach, lapping over the tub. Her mouth was tiny in the pillows of her cheeks. "Okay, okay," she whispered to Serafina. "Okay, now." But then Elvia's head came out, and Serafina screamed. The woman reached down and pulled out the rest of Elvia's body, purple as cabbage and black hair plastered like wet fur all along her shoulders.

The woman put Elvia on Serafina's chest and came back with a knife. She labored to kneel again on the floor, breathing hard in her shivery bulk, and cut the pulsing cord.

Elvia screamed then, screamed and yelled until the woman gestured at Serafina's chest. She put Elvia to the nipple, and all that came out was a yellow, thin milk, but her baby was quiet then.

"You cried in your sleep," Florencio said, lying beside her. "You cried over and over. When will you tell me?"

She saw the bottle beside her, the corn milk dried to a hard film. When her mother had explained the Mixtec way, the man's white blood and the woman's red, the baby, her mother paused and pointed to her breasts. The red blood leaves the mother when the baby is born, and the milk comes. The woman's white blood. When the baby drinks that, they are bound together forever. Their bodies are the same. But if the mother has no milk, or she will not feed the baby, another woman can give the baby white blood, and she can then call herself the mother, too.

She imagined the clean corn smell of atole, Elvia's brows collecting the steam, her lips damp with masa-thickened milk the day she was left in the car.

"She is still mine. My blood was everywhere in hers," she said to the grimy water bottle.

She looked at Florencio and said, "*Sēhe síhí.*"

"What?"

"I have a daughter."

She told Florencio everything. About Rigoberto leaving, about the box, about Larry. She had slept with Larry only three times, and she was pregnant. That was how much white blood had collected to make Elvia.

Now he could look at her with disgust. He could forget the past, watching her in San Cristobal. She had not lived the Mixtec way. *But neither has he,* she thought, watching his hard-lined face, his bloom-ended fingers. He had killed someone for her. He had put food into her lips, something no one but her mother had ever done.

She chanted the names to him: *Socorro Street, where she was born. Yukon Avenue, where I lost her. Iglesia de Santa Catarina. I will see that parking lot again. And I will find her.*

Florencio was silent for a long time. Then he said only, "We have to walk again, then." He sounded distant, disappointed.

She nodded. He would take her to Rigoberto. Her brother would be responsible for her then. Not Florencio. He went down to the field to crouch at the edge, like Uncle Emiliano watching his own earth.

When she could finally get up, after midnight, her feet were so swollen she had to carry her shoes in a plastic bag. Her fingers hung uselessly by her sides, also swollen, even though she'd done no work. They were full of blood from dangling while she walked. One more night to Rio Seco, Florencio said over and over. She tasted the remnants of the corn milk on her lips.

Smoke People

IVY-VINE CURTAINS hung from the overpass to shield them, and swallows' nests decorated the cement wall with honeycombs of mud. The sun was rising behind them, turning the narrow stream of water into a shining snail trail through the brush. Rio Seco. Last night, they'd parked the truck on a street near here and walked. From this cave under the freeway, they'd watched campfires like orange blooms in the black stretch of trees, seen shadow people walking on the paths, carrying water jugs and bundles, pushing shopping carts.

Elvia's body ached, her hip crushed into the leaves and sand and concrete under the freeway roar. *I'm here, somewhere near Yukon Avenue and the linen plant on Bellgrave Street. If my mother's here, she doesn't even know I'm coming, so she can't run. My dad said, "If somebody found me, and I didn't want to be with them, I'd just book up again." But I'm the one that booked. I left him. Maybe I should have told him about the baby, taken my chances.*

Michael jerked awake and rubbed his palms over his temples, smoothing the hair that had escaped his braid. "Caveman's stayin down there. He'll pay me a hundred bucks for the medicine." He pointed to the riverbed. The September heat was burning wild oats and foxtails brown. "See the green?" Michael said, moving his finger. "Only thing still living by fall."

Dark vines looked like floating islands in the dry flats, some with yellow balls scattered among the leaves, some with white flowers. *Fall*, she thought. *I've been gone for ten days*. Michael said, "The yellow balls are bitter gourd, for washing your hair. The white flowers wash your brain."

"Why does this guy want it?"

Michael raised his brows. "He loves Indian shit. Says he's part Cherokee. Like everybody says. But he's always got speed. He wants to mix it with dreaming medicine, make something new he can sell for big dinero." He slid down the embankment to the path.

Elvia heard coughing from the cane, and saw a thin plume of smoke. "I'm starving."

"Eating for . . ." Michael frowned, cigarette smoke curling from his mouth. The baby was already trouble to him. He didn't care about food—he wanted speed. He didn't want to be only half high. She looked up at the freeway sign. Razor wire was curled around it like a slinky, and plastic bags clung to the barbs in tattered shreds, like ancient Christmas tinsel.

She slid down just as a bearded man burst from the cane and walked the other way. Elvia's heart thudded with fear, and she felt the circle of a nub-foot again, faster, insistent.

The mist clung to the bamboo like a thousand tiny breaths. Michael nodded at the black water sliding past in the cement channel. "My grandpa and his cousins dug all the canal ditches back in 1910 or something. This canal waters all the groves from Dos Arroyos to Agua Dulce."

Two brown men wearing baseball caps, carrying plastic water jugs, passed them on the trail. Hector said something to them, receiving a blank look. "Guatemalans," he said. "No español."

Elvia thought, *Everyone's here—Guatemalans and Mexicans and us*. Dogs barked at an opening in the brush. Michael said, "They only attack if you head down to their people."

"Lotta people down here, carnal," Hector said. "You sure you know where we're goin?"

Michael nodded. "More camps than I ever seen. But I remember the place."

A shopping cart nosed out from another tunnel, and Elvia stared at a woman who looked like Callie. The woman glared back and called, "The fuck you want, wetback?"

Hector laughed at Elvia, then shrugged. "Just like Mecca."

Michael bent to study a large white stone near another narrow path. "Let's go," he said, and they plunged into the cane. The smell of wet sand underfoot, and pee somewhere, stung her eyes. Michael peered at another white stone. Elvia saw tiny letters marked like graffiti.

"Cool. He's still here," Michael said. "By the big tree." He whistled, and then pushed through the dangling branches of a huge eucalyptus.

Elvia bent to look at the painted letters. H. 8. And a red heart.

Caveman sat in a bamboo chair that hung from a tree branch. Elvia thought he looked nineteen or twenty. He had light brown hair, sideburns, a curly beard like Velcro, and pale blue eyes, like plastic turquoise. He said, "Hey! My man Torres. You're out already? You make the magic potion yet?"

"Man, I just got out. You got the magic powder?"

Caveman frowned at Elvia and Hector, and Michael said, "They're cool." Caveman went inside a plywood shack and came out holding a Christmas cookie tin, his hands white and soft as biscuits from a can. Callie always said you could tell a person from their hands, but all Elvia could tell was that he ruled this place, with his painted sign on every tree. H-8-Red. Hatred.

"So she's cool," Caveman said. "Whoever she is."

"Elvia," Michael said.

Caveman grinned. "You named after Elvis?" he asked her.

She looked straight at him. He sure as hell wasn't Dually. "My dad's not an Elvis type."

"Her dad's pretty scary," Michael said casually.

"So where is he?"

"In Florida," she said coolly. "Where's yours?"

"At home, I guess." A girl came from his shack, her broad forehead pink, her lips closed in a little smile. "Tina Marie must be headed to the facilities," he said.

"Check it out, cause you can't go alone," Michael told Elvia. "Coyotes and wild pigs that weigh like three hundred pounds and have tusks." Elvia looked at Tina Marie's face, placid as a plastic baby doll's, her eyes wide open. "The guys from the other camps—that's what's most dangerous, okay? I can always hear you, wherever you are."

In the bamboo-sheltered place near the small stream, Elvia steadied herself against the tree. She waited a long time for Tina Marie, who stayed behind another tree. When Tina Marie came out, she threw back her head and stared at the sun, as if she wanted to be blind. "Hey," Elvia said. "Don't do that. You'll mess up your eyes."

Tina lowered her face, and her pupils were black pinpricks. Now Elvia could see that her forehead shimmered with small dents, like beaten metal, and the back of her neck was shiny with stripes of scarred skin. Elvia couldn't imagine what had caused them. But Tina Marie reminded her of kids at the foster homes who weren't really in the room—their selves were gone, with only their bodies left behind.

Walking back, Elvia saw a slash of blood on Tina Marie's bare leg. She said, "Here," handing her a tissue-thin cottonwood leaf, and Tina Marie wiped her leg, still silent.

Elvia sat next to Michael under a eucalyptus tree, tucking her stiff, sore legs under her. "Let me do it, man," Michael told Caveman. "I gotta have tobacco in mine. I don't like the pipe, man, it goes straight to my forehead and not like, all around my skull. It's different for Indians."

"What's the Indian word for speed?" Caveman asked.

Michael crushed the white clots and sprinkled them into cigarette paper. Then he added tobacco from a pouch. "My people didn't smoke speed way back then," he said.

"They smoked plants like the one you're gonna get for us?" Caveman persisted.

"Yeah. Sometimes they smoked that one." Michael glanced at Elvia; he wanted her to notice. Indian stuff. That's what Caveman wanted to hear. Chanting and painting faces and mystical dreaming secrets. She hadn't been much different herself when she first met him. Would he tell Caveman the same stories he'd told her?

They drew the smoke deep into their lungs. Their faces were blank and alien while they held their breath, eyes unfocused, like her father, like Callie and Dually. Elvia passed the cigarette without smoking, holding it away from herself. Caveman got his voice back first.

"What's wrong with you?" he said. "That's the quicker picker-upper. I got it from the best."

"I don't smoke." She gave Michael a hard look. She didn't want him telling these people anything about the baby.

"Why?" Caveman's voice was like a fist. "Your scary dad's a cop?"

Elvia said, "That's pretty funny."

Michael took another draw, the ember going purple, but Hector passed, too. "I remember you from St. Jude's," Caveman said to Hector. "You better not be a fuckin narc."

Michael said harshly, "He's my brother." Then he began to cut down tall, straight sticks of arrowweed with Elvia's knife, weaving the wood together with grapevine. When he was finished, she lay on the sand in the gold-striped light coming through the branches. The pepper tree's fragrant berries made her think of meat, but tweakers didn't eat for hours. From the doorway, she saw Tina Marie's face glimmering with sweat. *Like she has a fever,* Elvia thought, wishing she could touch the girl's forehead and know what was wrong. Like Sandy could.

Hector pulled Elvia up and said, "Let's go to 7-Eleven and get you some food. And Camels for mano." Elvia was dizzy, but she checked her pocket for a quarter.

Sandy said, "Hello?"

The blood rushed to her ears. "It's me."

"Where are you? I was so worried."

"Everything's cool," Elvia said quickly. Through the receiver she heard clinking dishes. "What did you do all day?" Her voice came out wrong.

"What do you mean?" Sandy said slowly.

Elvia closed her eyes, seeing the sink, the moon in the window. "I just wanted to know."

Sandy must have heard it. What she wanted to see. "I vacuumed. I washed colored clothes and sheets and towels and hung them outside. It always cheers me up to see them hanging there like clowns jumping around in the wind."

"How come you have so much laundry?" Elvia held the receiver hard.

Sandy paused. "I had a kid who wet the bed a few days."

Elvia felt the hot rush of something in her chest. Jealousy? How could she be jealous of another foster kid? A little one? She remembered the social worker taking her from house to house. She brushed the velvet scrunchie she wore on her wrist, wondering if the little girl was being driven from front door to front door right now. "You don't want a fuck-up teenager. You like them little." She was sobbing like the night she left Sandy's, riding with the window open, rushing through the desert valley, seeing her own green eyes in the side mirror. "Then they go away. And you never have to see them when they're big fuck-ups." She gulped for air. "What church is it? The one where she left me."

"Elvia—"

"You have it in my papers somewhere." Elvia kept her voice hard.

"Saint Catherine's. On Palm Avenue." Sandy sounded like she might cry, too. "Tell me where you are. I'll come get you. Right now."

"Everything's fine here." Elvia swallowed hard. Sandy cried over everyone. Everyone. She'll be fine, as soon as she gets another kid. One that'll be happy to sit in her lap and listen to stories. A little kid. Not a big one, getting bigger, messing up every day.

"I have to go," she said, and hung up as Hector handed her a small red box.

"Raisins?" she said, wiping her eyes. "You trying to remind me of Mecca?"

"You're supposed to eat iron when you're pregnant. I looked at the vitamins in there, but, man—they're five dollars a bottle. Raisins have iron. You call your dad?"

"My foster mom." She twisted the raisins in her teeth. "Where are we?"

"Over there's Agua Dulce." He pointed to pastel houses on a hillside. "This is no man's land. Lemon and orange groves all along the canal. That's why we used to come here." He touched the raisin box—Sun-Maid, with a beautiful olive-skinned woman and a basket of green grapes. "Those grapes are up in Dinuba. Where my moms went. Hey, I'll draw you a rock map. Where'd you get that blue one?"

She reached into her pocket, where she thought she'd put the glass gems, but she had only the brown and green ones left. "Damn," she said. "I lost the blue one." She felt her eyes fill up again. "I got it when I was a kid. Here in Rio Seco."

"Hey. Michael's gonna keep sketching higher and higher. You need to watchate." Hector smoothed his hair off his forehead, looking tired. He said, "I did speed a few times to stay awake for work. I smoked mota in summer sometimes. But I can feel it on my brain. Like fog on a window. I never do anything during school." He nodded at her belly. "And you can't either."

Elvia said, "I know." Michael was good at dreams. But Hector was good at the rest of life.

"I'm just saying, if you find your mom or not, I'll kick it with you like a friend. Mi palabra."

"What's that?"

"My promise. If you learn some Spanish." He grinned.

She almost asked him to come with her—maybe he could talk to her mother, if she didn't speak English. But no—Hector wouldn't know *cusū*. And if her mother was awful, she didn't want anyone else to see.

"I'll meet you back there," she said.

The truck's blunt-nosed grill was cool under her fingers. Dust and wet made rivulets down the windshield when she started the engine. She drove through Agua Dulce, where roosters stalked the yards of pink and yellow houses. Mercado Aparecida—where women carried out plastic bags of groceries and sleeping babies. Carniceria Reyes—where women studied slabs of beef in the windows. She stared at the animated faces of some gathered near jewelry glittering in the window of Joyeria Alvarez.

Serafina Estrella Mendez. What did she look like? Everyone had braids, black eyes, and brown faces. Everyone was a mother. She turned a corner so fast she felt a sudden, squirming shove, like a dolphin was caught behind her navel. Not a kick, but a roll. *Leave me alone! I don't want to think about you right now. Go to sleep.* She heard the ragged sound of her own thoughts, desperate and impatient as Callie and Lee, as the foster mothers' words raining down on the restless limbs of all the kids where she'd shared beds and couches and carpet.

Bellgrave Avenue was a wide street lined with warehouses and blank-faced buildings. Linwood Transmissions. Beacon Electronics. Women gathered in parking lots, black hair in buns and hair nets. Then Elvia saw the sign: two hands cradling a stack of cloth. Angeles Linen.

The low, blue building had windows completely blind with steam. If her mother was illegal, how could Elvia go inside and ask? As if someone would say, "Oh, yeah, she's right there."

She drove to the back. This is where he had found her. She hovered in the open back door, smelling the steam, a wet smoke of bleach and cloth, clouds of white rolling out into the sun.

Pushing herself into the vapor, she studied the brown faces under round caps like blue clouds themselves, rising from the women's heads. Their hands flew across shirts and sheets and towels, turning smoothing patting curling and then sliding under stacks of linen to disappear when they lifted the pile. Twenty, thirty faces, all those hands, the rumbling of huge dryers and women reaching into the gaping mouths, pulling out mounds of cloth that hid their faces.

In Mecca, bandannas hid their faces. Elvia had become Mexican within minutes, Hector joked. Invisible and sweating and moving her hands.

I'll never find her.

Under the thunder of dryers, they were talking. She tried to see past the wreaths of steam. Someone slapped down a load of sheets, and someone else pointed at her. Sharp-boned faces closed like night flowers. She looked for a face like her own, and an older woman with gray wires of hair escaping her cap called to her in Spanish.

"Serafina Mendez?" Elvia called, as loud as she could. "Mi madre? Serafina Mendez?"

"No," said the older woman. She added something in rapid Spanish, and the other women began shaking their heads, their hands resting for a moment like sparrows on the white sheets.

A big delivery truck pulled in, and someone said, "What the hell are you doing back here? Move it." An older man with blue eyes and a Santa Claus beard waved her away.

She kept her mind empty while she drove toward the western foothills. Yukon Street—a little dead-end road. *Don't expect anything. Just see the place.* She passed Vancouver, then Calgary. Men were gathered on one corner, intently watching passing cars. When they saw the old truck slow down at the corner, they jostled around her door. "Trabajo? Trabajo? Five dollars, okay?" Elvia shook her head and they fell away, turning to the next vehicle. She peered at the signs. A woman with long braids tied together at her waist sold boiled corn from a cart on a corner.

The next street was Yukon. Something Elvia had done, that night, on this sad-looking little street, had made her mother lose it. Everything in her body thumped and pulsed now—her chest, her head, her belly, even her fingertips on the wheel. At the curb marked

2510, she stared at two tiny brown cottages, the dusty hedge along the chainlink fence, the green paddles of cactus, the corn and peppers growing on one side, and irises and roses on the other.

But she remembered nothing except the sound of beans clicking in a bowl, the smells of corn and lime and cinnamon, the pale grins of her mother's heels when she left a room and Elvia sat on the floor waiting for her to come right back.

When she knocked at the corn house, a child inside called, "Mami, mami!" A woman with a braid peered from the screen without opening it. "Sí?" she said.

Elvia swallowed, trying to recall her school Spanish. "Hola. Yo, yo soy Elvia. Serafina Mendez, es aqui? Is Sara here? I am her daughter." She tried not to choke on tears.

The woman shook her head and spoke rapidly in Spanish. She saw that Elvia understood nothing, and she added, "No here. Nobody." The little boy beside her touched the screen.

Of course nobody's here. Without thinking, she knocked at the other door. 2512. Fingers curled at the curtain edges, she thought, and she heard faint singing inside, like a radio. She smelled something nutty. Like oatmeal. But no matter how many times she knocked, no one came to that door.

She parked the truck in the street and walked numbly toward the river. She couldn't stand to try Saint Catherine's yet. What for? It was Tuesday. Who would be there? Who would remember anything about a Nova twelve years ago?

This was the only place to go home to, for now. Walking down the tunnel worn by people pushing through the arundo cane, she heard something crashing to the ground, loud as gunshots. Caveman and Tina Marie, with three other boys and a new girl, were looking toward the sky.

Michael was at the top of a palm tree, dancing around the trunk. He slammed a machete blade above him, and three fronds fell, rocking down through the air, landing on the dirt with the rest, scattered like golden lion tails.

Elvia squinted up at him, and Michael laughed, sliding down
the trunk, leaping the last six feet to collapse beside her. "Caveman's
friend had a chete. Been workin palm trees since I was ten. We'd go
down to the flats and trim a whole street. Make some dinero."

Elvia heard the speed in his voice, saw the red mesh inside
the corners of his eyes. The trees he hadn't touched were still shifting and rustling. Michael said quietly, so no one else could hear,
"Hundreds of palms on the rez. The old people said spirits lived up
there. So they could watch us. Down on the flats, people said it was
rats."

"What do you believe?" Elvia said, brushing the slivers of bark
from his wrist.

"Both," he said. "Come on. I saw Caveman's money roll. Time
to be an Indian."

They walked through the brush along the riverbank to a large
field. "You didn't find her, huh?" She shook her head. "You need
some help, to see her. In the other world." He knelt near a sprawling
vine, a kind she had seen in vacant lots near Sandy's house and in
Tourmaline.

"Jimsonweed?" she said, disappointed. "That's the dreaming
plant?"

"If you know what you're doing," Michael said, digging around
the roots in the sandy river soil. "If you don't, it's the killing plant.
Mess up your brain forever." He handed her two huge trumpet
flowers, big as her wrist, faint purple at the throat but white glowing
brighter than the moon. The blooms wilted in her palm, closing
even while she breathed their strange scent.

"Don't put them near your mouth," Michael said. "They're
strong." He cut two roots deep in the soil, pulled khaki-green leaves
from the stems, and wrapped the roots in newspaper. "Don't tell nobody where we got this. They have to pay me. And if they try to make
it, they'll do it wrong."

"Who taught you?" In Elvia's hand, the milky blossoms were
limp as tissue now.

"My grandpa," Michael said. She looked at the roots dangling from the newspaper bundle, felt the scrunchie on her wrist, and thought about the dime-eyed girl. What had the speed vapors done to her own baby, that night? This was only a plant. An herb.

"I better not drink it," she said.

"What?" Michael whirled around. "All this time, you said you wanted to do this. Pray about her, dream where you should look."

Elvia shouted, "I said that a long time ago. Now I'm talking about the baby."

He glanced down at the big tee shirt still hiding her belly. He didn't remember most of the time. She couldn't do like women in commercials, hold his hand to her belly and say, "Feel him kicking, honey?" so he would smile and run out for watermelon ice cream.

"It's not drugs," he said then. "It's medicine. Sometimes they gave it to women when they were having the baby. To help them. To-night I'll take you to Dos Arroyos and you can see."

"I don't need help yet," she said. "I'm not having it yet."

Caveman and the others were drinking beer. "Jared, Ricky, Shawna," he said, pointing to the boys and a girl with a yellow bruise on her forearm and a purple crest of hair. He called, "What'd you bring back?"

"Buried treasure," Michael said, ducking into the shelter.

She sat on the sand after he left again, trying to picture her own insides. Her abdomen. What exactly was that? She tried to remember science class. She'd paid much more attention to igneous and metamorphic rocks than to the body. There were tubes, an egg, and it grew inside a sack. So her stomach was right next to the sack? How did the food and drink get to the baby? Did everything drift into the sack somehow?

Michael came back inside with several large, flat stones. He laid them in a circle, stacked wood, and lit a fire. "Takes a while to dry," he said, arranging the roots and flowers and leaves on the stones. "Then a while to brew. They're all impatient. They want to erase their brains."

Elvia saw the leaves already curling near the flames. "Erase? Nothing left?"

"You won't get erased. I'm not gonna let you mess up. You'll dream to the next level."

She shook her head. "I can't." She wouldn't let herself cry. She was scared. "I breathed vapors in that speed lab. And who knows what else I did."

Michael was silent, poking the fire. Finally he murmured, "I probably fucked up, too. When we did it, I was sketchin big time. And I drank all that Everclear."

Elvia tried to picture the biology book again. "Drugs aren't in sperm."

"Yeah, they are. Your whole life's in there." He poked a shriveling leaf. "Maybe the kid's all fucked up. Like me."

"We're not fucked up," she said. But they were. What did she have now? Not even root beer and Cap'n Crunch, not her father's smell beside her in the truck. Suddenly she wanted to be at Sandy Narlette's. She wanted the laundry room, where the full moon always came up in the window, the gleaming washer turning pale blue as the Mason jars on the shelf. Pillowcases in the dryer, with thread-stitched names that she could read with her fingers in the dark.

She felt nothing under her ribs, and she saw her own face, inside a cage of glittering string. Sandy had said something about a foster kid's ribs. A Christmas ornament. On Sandy's tree. Something she'd made in the third grade?

Michael lit a cigarette. Then he kissed her. "Tina Marie had a baby," he said softly. "That's why she's all messed up. Shawna said she heard Tina Marie had a baby three weeks ago."

Elvia remembered the blood on Tina Marie's leg. From a baby? "Where is it?"

Michael shrugged. "Who knows?"

She wouldn't let herself see it—a baby in the trash. Wrapped in a bag. She tasted the smoke on her tongue, the bitter ashes on her teeth.

Outside, Hector had started a fire, too. He took tortillas, a block of cheese, and salsa from a paper bag that said MERCADO APARE-CIDA. He blistered the tortillas over the fire, and when Elvia ate one she tasted corn and smoke and warmth inside the slightly charred holes. Tina Marie ate a quesadilla dripping with soft white cheese and salsa. Caveman said, "Why didn't you just get three tacos for thirty-nine cents? It's Taco Tuesday."

Hector handed two quesadillas to Elvia. He said, "You're Mexican, you like tacos? That's like saying, you're American, you only eat hamburgers. But I picked tomatoes in Florida, and we ate grits and chicken-fried everything."

"You were in Florida?" Tina Marie said dreamily.

Hector nodded, tucking his black hair behind his ears. "Mexico's a big fuckin country. My mom is from Veracruz people. She eats fish. My dad's from Tijuana. He'll eat anything."

Tina Marie ate two more quesadillas. Elvia hadn't seen her eat at all before. Caveman drank another beer, then said, "Only faggots get off on cooking."

Hector spat into the fire. Elvia could tell Caveman wanted to rule everything, even the food. Michael came out of the shelter and asked, "What smells so good?"

Caveman got out the cookie tin. Tina Marie put her head in Caveman's lap and fell asleep. Caveman said, "This one wants Indian brew right now. Wants out of her head. Thinks she's fat." Caveman touched Tina Marie's matted hair. "But she just had a baby."

Elvia stared at Tina's pale, plump arm thrown over his leg. "Where is it?" she whispered.

"We sold it."

"Sold it?" Michael said. "To who?"

"Everybody wants a white baby," Caveman said. "This one had blue eyes. Bald as a bowling ball. A lady I know gave us three grand for it. She gets like ten grand when she does her deal."

Elvia couldn't stop staring at Tina, her lips pursed against his thigh. "Was it your baby?"

"Hell, no," he said. "She was knocked up when she got here. You couldn't tell, cause her clothes were cool. Baggy, you know."

Like mine, Elvia thought.

"Who was the father?" Hector said.

Caveman shrugged. "Whoever paid for it. That's the father now."

Michael said, "How you know they'll take good care of it? A baby—that's already a person, like with feelings and all, but you don't know what the feelings are. They can't tell you." Elvia felt him going rigid next to her, and she silently pleaded, *Don't tell him. Don't say it.*

She was angry. It was his baby, too. But he didn't want it. Every time he opened his mouth, he sounded afraid. He wasn't afraid in the desert, in Tijuana, even dangling from palm trees. He was only scared of what he couldn't even see.

"They scream and cry," Caveman said. "This one. All of them."

Michael's forehead creased in lines like fingernail scratches. "No, man, I mean you gotta know what to do, figure out what their feelings are, so you don't fuck them up."

"Hey," Caveman said. "If you paid ten thousand bucks for something, wouldn't you take care of it? A car, a motorcycle, a kid. Whoever bought the baby has to be better than Tina. Or some fuckin foster home, some witch mom."

"You ever been in a foster home?" Elvia asked angrily, seeing Sandy's hands on the gold-flecked Formica counter, her nicked fingers, her thumb for a handle to help you jump down.

"Me? Nope. I don't need a rent-a-witch, cause my real mom's the worst one." He looked at the dark trees. "This one was a mom for a minute." He nudged Tina Marie. "Not anymore."

Tina Marie woke up, her eyes clouded like dirty marbles. Caveman put his arm around her.

Elvia heard a rippling call from a tree. "Barn owl," she said, almost to herself.

"How do you know?" Caveman said, grinning at her.

"My sister," she said, without thinking. "She knows the name of every bird, lizard, and bug in Rio Seco."

Michael pulled back to look at her. "Your sister? She's got a place? A house?"

"My foster sister," Elvia said.

"Foster." Jared shook his head. "If I counted that, I'd have a hundred brothers. Shit."

Everyone laughed. Caveman said, "You're Indian? What tribe has green eyes?"

"Crazy-ass tribe. Like my dad," Elvia said. She heard the barn owl call again, remembered the white-faced owls swooping into the field, Rosalie pressing her face to the screen to see.

"If your fosters are so fuckin great, how come you're down here with us?" Jared said.

"Because she's looking for her real mom," Michael said, and their eyes shifted.

Tina Marie's eyes were like blue-burned holes in her face. Like the hottest embers. "Why?" she asked. "No such thing as a real mom. Only fake ones."

"Hell, no," Elvia said, standing up. "Some people are better than blood." She went inside the shelter and opened her backpack. The folded, faded print dress from Tía Dolores. Elvia touched the too-soft material. Tía Dolores had said that whoever feeds you, takes you for shots, combs your hair—that's the real mother.

Michael came inside to move the jimsonweed leaves and roots. "Tina Marie's like a zombie." He looked up, eyes glittering black as rainy streets. "Talk about sellin it—" He turned away. "It's *there* now. Nothing we do is gonna be right. Nothing. We gotta go to Dos Arroyos."

At the crest of the foothills, Elvia saw the brown veil of smog turning violet in the sunset, and the lemon groves in blurred patches below. Sandy's house was in the lemon groves—Elvia had seen these mountains from the yard, brown hills topped with white boulders. "The Sugar Springs Mountains," Sandy said. "Like toast with cinnamon sugar."

Pepper trees loomed ahead while Michael drove faster and

faster to one of the green valleys where she'd always thought there must be water. Two bullet-pocked metal signs stood at a junction — COUNTY WASTE FACILITY and DOS ARROYOS INDIAN RESERVATION.

Michael said, "Right here is where I first saw Hector. He was riding this old bike, and these three skinhead dudes were racing a pickup, chasing him with a baseball bat out the window, yelling about killing wetbacks. I was hunting rabbits for my grandpa, so I shot out their tire. Told them Mexicans were part Indian so fuck off. Told em they were illegals on rez land."

"They didn't fight?" Elvia looked at the broken glass along the road.

"Hell, no. They screeched outta here. And Hector yelled, 'Punkass rednecks!' Shit, I thought he only spoke Spanish. He told me about his college class and showed me his maps. We been hanging out ever since."

A guard shack squatted at the dump entrance, a lit window with a face peering out. "On the other side of the mountain, they grow avocados. The Mexicans living in the grove come over and go through the dump. They recycle for free, but the county gets pissed."

"Like Tijuana," Elvia said, thinking of people sifting through the smoking mounds.

"But way better trash," Michael said grimly, pulling onto the reservation road. "My grandpa works the shack, day shift. Seems like Indians get casinos or dumps. My grandpa picked a dump, forty years ago."

The steep cliffs along the road were covered with brittlebush hanging like small, silvery clouds. After a few miles, the valley widened, and Elvia saw four house trailers perched beside a dry creek bed. Silver shutters blinded their windows, and their walls were rusty and pockmarked. "My uncles are all gone," Michael said. "I haven't seen them in like, five years. They went to LA or San Francisco. Nothing here."

On the other side, an adobe house was nearly invisible on the canyon wall. Michael parked below it, where a small tent trailer sat under a cottonwood tree. Inside, the linoleum floor was clean, the bed was made with an old wool blanket, and a skim of dust covered the little table. "I live here in summer," he said. "It's cool, like being half inside, half outside."

Elvia sat gingerly on the bed, touching the screen windows. "Half is your favorite way."

"When it gets cold, I go see my cousins in Tourmaline. Stay there and go to school. Sometimes. When it warms up, I come back here and work trees."

Elvia heard someone shout outside. "Hey, now! I thought maybe you were asshole teenagers I didn't know. But it's an asshole teenager I do."

The old man's face was brown and wide-jawed, square as a giant walnut. "You steal this truck, Michael? Or she did?"

"It's hers," Michael said. "Not stolen, Pops." He walked around behind the cottonwoods.

His grandfather humphed, looked at Elvia. "Nice braids, Pocahontas. I hope you're not lost up here, looking for Grandmother Willow. We only got palm trees. A few oak."

Elvia felt her braids loosened from the long day, felt her chest tingle with anger. How the hell did she look? Hands scarred by grapes like a Mexican woman. Eyes pale green like an American. And inside? Distant memories of Indian words from a place she'd never seen.

"I can't be lost if Michael brought me up here." She glared at him.

The grandfather's face was so wide on his thin, slump-shouldered body that he didn't look like Michael at all. He shrugged and grinned. "Sorry. But kids come up here, think they're gonna see buffalo and Indians. We don't eat buffalo. Acorns. Chia seeds. You ever see a Chia Pet? Little smaller than a buffalo."

Michael came back to the trailer and said, "I need my equipment, Pops. Me and Hector are gonna work trees." He fixed his eyes on Elvia, and she knew he wasn't going to tell his grandfather about the baby.

A palm-roofed ramada surrounded the adobe house. Blue and green bottles lined the windowsill, glowing from the kerosene lantern inside the single room. "You're half what?" the grandfather said, serious now.

"Mexican Indian," Elvia said. "From what I know."

"Huh. His mother was pretty," the grandfather said. "She liked Mexican guys with low-rider cars." Michael's cheeks were hollowed and dark as he listened near her. Elvia touched his blank forehead. Where was his soft spot, the bones that closed after his mother was already gone?

The grandfather pointed to clay shards, arrowheads, bowls, and baskets on wooden shelves around the adobe walls. "I know Mexican women make a basket like that pale one. Pine needle. Their people are cut off from California by a line. But they talk the same."

Michael said, "When the dozer guys find something old in the dirt, they bring it to him."

"All this junk is mine," the grandfather said. "From my dirt."

Michael moved impatiently. "I just need the chainsaw and the gaffs and my rope." He watched intently as his grandfather went outside. Then he quickly took a red clay bowl from the shelf near him, slipping it into his jacket. When his grandfather came back with a coil of yellow rope, Michael said "Cool" and went down to the truck.

Elvia hovered near the table, where a bowl of hot cereal steamed. "It's not Cream of Wheat," the grandfather said, grinning again. "Michael hates it. Nobody like you likes weewish."

"Like me?" Elvia said angrily. "Not Indian?"

But he said, "Young like you. Young people like Wonder Bread. They like to eat air." He held out a spoon in challenge.

The nutty bitter grain made her throat rise, but she swallowed and her stomach was quiet. "Acorn porridge," he said. "Look, you're not old enough for that truck. Somebody took it. Michael doesn't need more trouble."

She ate another spoonful. "I'm not trouble," she said.

He surveyed the shelves, touching the empty space where the red clay bowl had been. "Don't let him lose the bowl. If he sells it or uses it wrong, somebody up there will punish him. Not me." He stared down at the truck, then said, "He doesn't have a mother. I tried my best."

Elvia was startled, remembering her father say the same thing to Warren one night. "I been trying so damn hard, and I don't know what the fuck is the right thing," he'd said.

Michael honked the horn. She got into the truck, rubbing her eyes. "The bowl is for the medicine?" she asked, and he nodded, but instead of heading down the valley, he drove another two miles or so until the road was only a dirt track among the boulders. They came to a small white-plaster church and baby-tooth stones under the pepper trees.

"This is where I drink the kikisulem," he said, leading her under the feathery branches. He showed her with his eyes. Past a few wooden crosses with no names, she saw the white rock, not a headstone but a long, narrow boulder with a chipped depression and a wooden plaque that read VICTORIA TORRES in burned letters. "I made it in wood shop in junior high. I have to shellac it every year. For the rain."

Elvia sat next to him on the pepper leaves. "When somebody dies, Cahuilla used to burn the whole house. Now they just burn all their stuff. Clothes, everything. So all I ever had was this rock. You're supposed to use your memory for people, but she died like the minute I came out, so what the hell was I gonna remember?"

Elvia felt his heart pounding way too fast against her spine when he folded his arms around her. "But she didn't leave you on purpose." Near the trunk of the pepper tree was a pallet of leaves, a thick cushion long enough for a body, and she knew he slept here sometimes.

He handed her the bowl—the dusty red clay with blurred black designs. It fit between her palms. She touched the narrow rim and wondered how many mouths had drunk there. "When I drink it," he said, "I hear her voice. So will you. You'll see her—your mom. We'll do it tonight. After we see Ruby. You said your whole body is sore, right? She can help you."

From the truck window Elvia heard dull chopping. A huge agave cactus toppled over near the dirt track.

"Aunt Ruby?" Michael called. A small, dark-faced woman, with graying braids so long the ends were tucked into the neckline of her blouse, was holding an ax.

"Michael? Come help me get this one out." Ruby didn't sound at all surprised to see him.

Michael took the ax and cut around the base of the cactus, and when they'd hauled the chunk of agave heart toward her palm-roofed ramada, he put it in the embers of a low fire.

"Easier to work at night, when it's cool," Ruby said. Her thin braids swung like silver reins from her purple blouse. "What do you want?"

"My—Elvia's all sore from working grapes in Mecca," Michael said. "I was thinking tea."

"Ahtukul?" Ruby said, studying Elvia. She touched Elvia's arm. "Creosote. Good for your blood, for women."

"And the bed," he added, glancing at Elvia. "Warm for her muscles."

Bed? Michael led her to a sandy spot near the creek bed and said, "Lie down." Ruby drew an outline around her with a long stick, the sand near her ears making a shimmery sound when the wood parted it.

Ruby sat her on a wooden stool under the ramada, while Michael dug inside her shape. "Is he still drinking the kikisulem?" Ruby asked, leaning close, sunbursts of wrinkles near her eyes.

"The jimsonweed?" Elvia saw Ruby nod. "He's making some now in the river bottom."

"He shouldn't drink it so often," Ruby said. "I knew how to use it. My father taught me. Once, when I was young, I dreamed to the thirteenth level. You have to go to sleep, in your dream, and dream again. My uncle had to come find me, carry me home. It took two days for me to come back. In my mind."

Elvia looked down at the sand near her feet. *If I drink it, and I do it right, I can dream my way back to that night, and I'll know if she told me something about where she was going. What she wanted.*

Michael carried wood into the sandpit and lit a fire, and Ruby said, "Your body hurts, eh? You're not used to hard work?"

"Not like that," Elvia said. "And . . ." She watched Michael poking a stick into the hot glow coming from the hole. Was she supposed to tell Ruby about the baby? Was the tea to make the baby strong? Woman stuff?

Ruby shredded dried leaves into a boiling pot. Elvia could smell the oil. She stared at the fire in her shape, a grave of red that turned to blue, billowing like water for a moment. "We do this for the first blood, and for mothers," Ruby said, and Elvia turned in surprise. "When I was young, we lived in Desert Springs. We had hot springs. Then they made us walk here, a long time ago. His grandfather Antonio, me, the rest of us. They said someone bought the land. But we knew how to use hot sand, too."

Michael raked the coals out of the pit and said, "Come on." His face was still and remote. Elvia stepped down into the darkness, the sand pulsing with heat, and laid her head on the shelf he'd made. Ruby pushed in the edges of the sand bed, and warmth rushed into Elvia's skin, her muscles and bones.

She closed her eyes. The aches melted. Melting. When Ruby patted the sand down hard over her, sealing her inside, Elvia's breasts tingled and hurt as though matches were set to her nipples. Her backbone bucked and heaved, and she felt a fist rising up against her ribs.

"Here," Ruby said, holding a tin cup of tea, but Elvia was thrashing herself out of the sand blanket, her mouth and nose filled with grains of quartz and mica. She nearly screamed, drowning in the sand, a wetness inside her head black and moist as mud.

"You didn't tell me," Ruby scolded later, leaning over her in the ramada where she lay on a blanket. Elvia rubbed the sand from her lips. Michael had walked up the creek bed, disappeared. "We give the mother hot sand after the baby—she nurses while she rests, and the blood comes out better. Don't you read magazines? Pregnant women aren't even supposed to be in a spa. Hot is hot. Bad for the baby. And when you come roaring up out of there, you had your hand right where that line probably is."

"Line?" Ruby lifted her shirt, cooling her belly, and Elvia peered down to see a thin brown stripe like faded Magic Marker below her navel.

"I always think it's like magic," Ruby said. "Your navel, where your mother fed you, and the mark where your baby is right now. But it's not magic to you two, eh?" She shook her head at Michael, coming back down the creek bed, his arms raised and folded on his head like he expected stars to fall and injure him.

In the truck, she shouted, "You tried to get rid of it! You knew!"

"I don't know what the fuck to do!" he shouted back, racing down the mountain. "We can't take care of it right."

"Right? What the hell is right?" She stopped. "I went running every day in Tourmaline, looking for you and hoping maybe it would disappear." She felt nothing now—no cricket feet or tiny heart that echoed her own, in fear or quiet. "But babies don't disappear," she said, almost to herself, brushing more sand from her clothes. "Only parents do."

Michael said nothing, driving fast toward the river. At the 7-Eleven, Caveman and Tina Marie waved, and he pulled the truck into the parking lot. "What do you want?" Michael said dully, and Elvia shook her head.

He went inside with Tina Marie, and Caveman leaned into the window. His pupils were the size of pepper grains, and Elvia knew he was still faded. "You head off to look for your mom?" he asked. When she was silent, he said, "Michael said she's like, Inca or something. How are you gonna talk to her?"

She glared at him, and his face changed somehow, drooped

and made him look years older. His cheeks melted into the beard when he didn't smile. He said, "Sorry, I didn't mean to fuck with your plans. Hell, me and my mom didn't speak the same language. Cause every time she looked at me, she was so disgusted she couldn't say shit. She spoke that bang-things-around language. I'm in the room, she bangs down her cup, bangs dishes, drops my shoes next to me."

Elvia put her head back on the seat, her skin feeling rough and peeled over the still-sore muscles. "Why?"

"Cause I didn't want to be like Mike. I didn't want to be like Bob, either. My dad. Asshole and lawyer. He wanted my socks to match." Caveman rubbed his beard. "Hey, if your mom was illegal and she wanted to disappear, she's an expert. You won't find her. My mom used to send me to Agua Dulce to pick up day-labor guys for the yard. When cops cruised by—vamos. And we had a maid who stole some jewelry once. I looked all over for her. Invisible."

"Touching story," Elvia said, barely able to speak.

Caveman shrugged. "All I'm saying is, you're American, right? Get high. Be happy. If she left, she didn't want you. My mom was sure as hell tired of me. Some moms aren't cut out for the job."

"You talked Tina Marie into selling her baby," Elvia whispered. "You said she'd be a bad mom."

Caveman pulled out a roll of dollars, thick as green pipe. "Hey, all I did was say I'd manage her money. She can't even take care of that."

She looked away from him, at the telephone pole plastered with concert announcements. Los Tigres del Norte. Los Illegales del Rio Seco. Caveman laughed. "You gonna put up missing mother posters? Question everybody? Shit, take Michael's dreaming medicine and just imagine your mom. That's probably better than living with her." He went inside the 7-Eleven.

Elvia looked at the mustachioed faces on the posters. Rosalie had adopted a stray dog once, fed and brushed it. One day, it disappeared. Rosalie had cried for weeks. She was eleven. She put up lost-dog posters on telephone poles all over Rio Seco. Elvia used to watch dogs running loose and think that what made Rosalie cry hardest was knowing how big the world was, finally, seeing how small she and Elvia and the others really were.

Elvia had tried to explain this to Sandy one night, when Rosalie had sobbed herself to sleep, and Sandy had taken Elvia's face into her hands and said, "The world is huge. And even though you girls call Rosalie the brain, some things you're smarter about than she is."

The others piled into the truck, and Michael drove up Palm Avenue without looking at her, though he was pressed tightly against her. Tina Marie was lively now, saying, "I used to fall asleep in cars. My mom said it was because she drove to LA every day when I was a baby. She was a model. On TV. Before me. Then I fucked up her body." She pointed to distant pinpricks on the foothills. "That's where she lives. If she's still there."

Caveman's voice was gentle as Sandy's. "If she's still there, she's still a bitch. She fucked up your body, too. High heels to the forehead. Curling iron to the neck."

Elvia winced. Those scars. But Tina's voice was oddly calm. "She wanted me to be pretty, too. But I was so fat."

Michael turned into the neighborhood of narrow streets and wooden houses, and he parked the truck. Toys and bikes were heaped on porches, pots of ivy hung from hooks, and empty plastic swimming pools leaned against fences. Caveman said, "Fucking losers. A hundred little jails. A hundred assholes stuck in there watching TV and hating life."

Elvia saw laundry hung over a chainlink fence. "Doesn't look bad to me," she said.

Caveman's laugh was a hiss. "So if you got cable, and you got milk, you got a life?"

Elvia was tired of his sketching voice. "Not your life, right? You got a big house. A maid."

"No, my fucking parents do," he said. "I only had money when I was a good little monkey. And I wasn't. Who the fuck are you to decide what's a life?"

"No one gets to decide," she said, and Michael put his arm around her, keeping it there until they reached the river.

Hector was sitting by the fire. He grinned and handed her peeled sections of orange. "Like Tropicana," he said softly, so only she could hear. "Good for the baby's bones."

"Where'd you get oranges?" She put her head in her hands, feeling sand in her hair, under her shirt, in the webs between her fingers.

"La pisca de naranjas," he said. "Picked them. Like somebody's gotta do before you buy em in the store, huera." He winked. "I went down the canal to a grove and this fat dude on a quad chased me out. Seen a guy pop up out the damn ground. He was livin in a cave."

Michael pulled her up by the hand and led her into the branch shelter, where the fire was only a red eye and the leaves and stems were shriveled gray. They sat near the embers, and Michael stared at her. "Look," he finally said. "If somebody paid ten grand for a kid, they'd like, send it to college. Live in a big house, buy bikes and jackets. The kid could be—"

"Our kid. It would still be our kid." She shivered, looking at the coals.

Caveman burst into the shelter, saying, "Jared and Shawna brought some other people, man. They don't want to wait. They want the good stuff, the Indian shit."

Michael sighed. "Extra fifty bucks if we use the ceremony bowl." Caveman handed him five tens. Then Michael said, "I have to mix it by myself."

Caveman stopped grinning. "What if you're just fuckin with me? Putting in dirt and grass instead of the real deal? They want colors and visions like LSD."

Michael said, "I'll be drinking it, too! Close the fuckin door."

Caveman pointed at Elvia. "She gets to watch?"

"She's my people now." Michael smiled faintly, a new-moon crescent.

He ground the dried root with a small stone and strained it into the red clay bowl, his fingers as careful and precise as Sandy's mea-

suring ginger or cinnamon. Then he dripped water from a sports bottle, stirred the paste with a stem, and added more water until the liquid looked dark and muddy as root beer.

Her father used to say, "Which one's your favorite—Barq's or
A&W? I can't tell the difference. Cause I smoke too much. Drink too
much. My tongue's older than your rocks." He'd grin. "So drink root
beer. Not my beer. Got it?"

Callie'd say, "Never seen a man love a kid like this. Got enough
root beer to fill a tub, and he comes home every day askin, 'How's
Ellie?' Like ain't nobody else livin here."

Elvia closed her eyes and began to cry, and Michael said,
"Look, I want to ask her—my mom."

She sobbed, "You have to make up your own mind."

He stirred gently. "Okay. This is for us. Not Caveman. For you."
Elvia stared at the red bowl. "You waited all this time to check it out."

Then she felt the baby trace a small, blurry design on her hipbone. Caveman and the others pushed the blanket door open and
came in. "Time's up, man. Come on."

Elvia didn't see Hector. She said to Michael, "I can't."

Caveman said, "You're punking?"

Elvia shouted, "Me? I been with people cooking antifreeze and
Sudafed. You don't know shit about real life."

Michael picked up the bowl. "Just a sip," he said, as if she
hadn't spoken. "Not like beer. Like Everclear." He took a swallow
and put the bowl into her hands, his eyes like pools of rainwater at
night.

Elvia smelled the swaying liquid, like earth and cave and
smoke. She imagined the vapors settling a veil over the baby, like at
Lee's house; she imagined patterns and visions in the baby's own
eyes—maybe beautiful, maybe scary. *And the baby can't get out of
me—out of* my *skin.*

She put the bowl on the ground and grabbed her backpack. In
the trees that stank of all of them, she vomited. Then she turned and
saw the field of dry grass, covered with circles of spiderwebs. Tunnel

spiders—like in the field across from Sandy's house. The dew collected on the webs to make jeweled nets, circles of stars scattered across the earth. She ran to the tunnel of arundo cane swaying like green bones in the wind.

The truck's dash was cold as stone. "Nobody did this for me," her father always said. "Taught me to drive. Fed me right. Made sure I came home."

Home. Okay. I better go home.

She drove toward the foothills, the green cleft of trees she remembered above Sandy Narlette's house. She wanted to feel Sandy's fingers on her forehead. "You're fine," she wanted to hear. "Damp and cool as a dog's nose. And that's good."

Lemon groves were scattered here, a few houses, and wild oats gone blond in the fall heat. *We made trails through the weeds, all of us,* she thought. *Rosalie first. Then me. She found lizard skins. I found rocks. The rest of them complained about stickers in their socks.*

She turned onto Marquise Lane and saw the arroyo, a wide gash in the fields. The last time she'd been here was when her father drove her away.

Rosalie had asked about the tattooed dragon, after Elvia's father came for his third visit. So she could get to know him. Elvia wouldn't answer, reaching for the plates, staring at the oilcloth sunflowers, at the spoons she touched every day, at the faces gathered like darting birds, waiting to hear about him. Her father. She touched her blue place mat.

Some time during that night, she lay awake, worrying. The floor creaked. She saw Sandy bending near Jade's pink pillow, sliding her hand underneath. Sandy straightened, glancing at Elvia. "You know who I am tonight," she had whispered near Elvia's ear. "The you-know-what fairy. She's the new girl. Can you let her be surprised?" She nodded, and Sandy traced Elvia's hairline with her finger. "Do you remember? When I surprised you?"

Elvia had found quarters, somehow sparkling with glitter, under her pillow.

Now she stared at the small yellow house, the mulberry tree, and then she turned across the street to the pepper tree near the arroyo's edge. Taking out her knife, she dug between two roots, where a hollow had been covered with dirt. It didn't look like kids had been here fooling around in a long time. The tea tin was rusted and black. Inside, her quarters were dirty, but she saw a glimmer of pearlescent pink when she rubbed one with spit. She had buried them so long ago.

Close to the cement porch, she saw how much the house had faded. The dandelion yellow was pale now, the stucco peeling near the foundation where Sandy always watered her plants. She knocked before she could get too scared. When Sandy answered, her face was exactly the same, her brown hair in a ponytail and only shiny Chapstick on her lips. Elvia held out the quarters as if they were payment and said, "You remember?"

"Oh, my God, Elvia," Sandy said, hugging her hard, the familiar smell of baby lotion rising from her shoulders. "I never forget. Never. Oh, I can't believe you came to see me."

Sandy washed the quarters in the old white enamel sink and laid the money on the wooden table. "I used to sit up and wait, sometimes real late because you girls were talking and wouldn't go to sleep, and I painted them with nail polish. Passionate Pink Frost, for sparkle like fairy dust. And you guys believed it, or some of you did."

Elvia stared at the quarters, at the single place mat near Sandy. Yellow. No embroidered name. The house was silent. Before she could ask why, Sandy said, "Look at this."

In the big front bedroom where they'd all slept, there was one bed and a crib. Sandy opened the top dresser drawer. Elvia saw baby clothes and small shirts, and, underneath them, little white envelopes with names. Rosalie. Gabrielle. Bridget. Christine. Elvia. Jade. Lorraine.

The teeth were so tiny in Sandy's palm. She moved them gently with her finger, then lifted her hand to Elvia. "See? They're just bones."

Elvia touched the dull, dry chips, porous and cracked. Sandy said, "They don't look like this when they fall out. I used to hold them at night, after I took them from under your pillows. I never saw anything so pretty. White as could be, like glowing inside. So polished and shiny."

"You always sat on the tub while we brushed our teeth. Every night."

"My teeth were full of cavities. I wanted yours to be beautiful. At least, while I had you." Elvia held a tooth with traces of black at the root, like dried mud. What used to be blood.

"I can't tell you how they looked," Sandy said. Her face lit up again. "Like opals."

"You told me. Opals."

She touched Elvia's hair. "You'll have to find out yourself, when you hold one of your own babies' teeth. But that'll be a long time. You're—you're fifteen now, right? August 20th?"

Elvia felt the sob rise up from the hollow inside her collarbone. Where Michael had put his lips, hot as a piece of coal. Where sand still clung to her skin. The cry flew from her before she could clamp her fingers over it, and then she saw Sandy's arms, the soft folds inside the elbows Elvia used to touch when they shone with sweat. Sandy pulled her close, saying, "Oh, Elvia. Oh, honey, you'll be okay. Come here."

Naranjas

SERAFINA SMELLED smoke rising from campfires in the river bottom, mixing with the fog that rose from earth near the water. It wasn't like the shimmering vapor that descended from the mountains, like home, but a veil that clung to the cane and bamboo stalks around them to keep her from seeing the people who laughed and argued, threw bottles and frightened her.

Florencio motioned for her to be quiet. She knew if these people heard them talk, saw their Indian faces, they might rob them, and when they saw pockets filled with nothing, maybe beat them for sport. Cut them on the face, like she'd heard some norteños did to Mixtecos. This river, where their feet sounded loud on the shredded eucalyptus bark, was no different from the arroyos and ravines she had already survived.

Up an embankment, inside a freeway cave, she smelled not Mexicans, but teenagers. Florencio moved the beer cans and fast-food wrappers and carried up an armload of eucalyptus leaves, motioning her to sit down.

"*Yuu Sechi,*" he said, his voice careful.

She was here, in the menthol scent of Rio Seco. She began to cry, wrenching silent sobs that shook her so hard her spine felt swollen inside the filthy clothes. She was here. Breathing the same air, perhaps, as her daughter. *Still here to be found,* she prayed, pulling herself up to kneel in the loose leaves, looking down the cement bank for flowers. Flowers to make an offering. Near the trail, she saw nodding yellow blooms she didn't recognize. Flowers of California. She stood up, but Florencio leaned over and pulled her down.

He put his arms around her back like a serape, and her heart leapt in fear at his roughness. But he said, "Don't move. Los malditos."

Several shadowy figures passed on the trail, loud voices laughing and talking. Fires flickered in the darkness below them.

"Malditos," Florencio said. "Teenagers. And some men I heard talking. They saw us here. I will stay awake all night, to make sure they don't come." His forearms were hard as cords.

She was so thirsty. "Is there water?"

Florencio said, "Not for drinking. We can't go near the river, or los malditos might see you. Lie down. We cannot go to the oranges until morning. I have to make sure la migra hasn't been to the camp. Rigoberto or Jesus always stands watch. Someone will wait for my signal." He was silent for a time, and then he said, "Serafina, you waited all this time to come back?"

Serafina lay on the bed of eucalyptus leaves and felt the sharp twinge, the rippling ache that somehow still scraped hard as a fingernail inside. Her womb. She had spent all those years sitting with her mother, grinding yerba santa leaves while her mother patted tortillas, washing her mother's hair, her neck, the fold inside her arms— she had never asked if her mother felt that twinge between her hipbones whenever she saw their faces—Luis's or the two baby girls', or Serafina's own face, when the priest closed the trunk door over her.

She would never tell anyone about the border, the ravine. "I tried to get back. A year had passed. Then my mother lost her mind. I couldn't leave her."

He frowned. "But now, where will you look? You cannot go to the government to get her back. You have no papers." He moved closer, whispering near her hair. "Serafina, we killed a man. Someone might have seen us with the coyote. Then without him. Maybe someone in the hills saw everything."

"Maybe only dead men saw it." She remembered the burned

figures, and she thought of how many people had died just to get to this place. She said, "I know where I will look."

She stared at Florencio's black eyes, the black hollows in his face. "Once we get to the camp, I won't travel again until the harvest is finished. I can't take the chance."

Serafina looked away, at the wall of bamboo disappearing in the fog. "Thank you," she said formally. "I will try to repay you. For everything."

"When we get there, to a fire and a pot, you can make me salsa verde again," Florencio said. "You can make me tortillas. Like home."

All night, she dozed intermittently, staring at the lights of the city muted like thousands of lit candles through a veil. She heard laughter and screaming in the river bottom. When the mountains to the east turned silver, she touched Florencio's arm where he had slumped against her back. "I want to go now," she whispered, just as she had in Tijuana. "I don't want to wait."

When she shook the dirt from her clothes and rubbed her hair back from her forehead, Serafina saw the ghostly light come through the ivy vines, filling the impression she'd left on the leaves at her feet. All these days and nights, she had left traces of her skin, her sweat, her warmth, on cornstalks and pine needles and sand and now here, on the sharp-scented leaves fallen from the trees. Near the back wall of the overpass, underneath layers of graffiti, she saw a blue stone.

A smooth piece of glass, almost like candy in her fingers. Bright as lapis from Oaxaca. She slid it into her pocket.

Florencio led her across a wide road, and they were soon walking along the banks of a canal. Serafina was mesmerized by the water gliding green and silent, so when she saw the tiny figure staring solemnly from behind a metal fence, surrounded by small silver leaves, she stumbled with fright. Her mother, a spirit whose black eyes burned, whose fingers held tight to the wire.

Serafina's hands were full of dirt as she knelt on the ground. Her mother couldn't be here to tell her the search was useless. Had she seen something, on her journey to the other world? Had her mother seen Elvia . . . Serafina felt sound streaming from her dry throat and burning jaw.

"No, no," Florencio said, lifting her by the elbow. "Don't scream or someone will hear."

The woman's voice was small as a bird's through the fence. "No, no, mija," she called. Daughter? Serafina made herself look. The woman said, "Yo soy Paz. Paz. Here. For your journey. Buena suerte." Through an opening in the wire, she held two jars of dark olives.

The woman melted into the olive trees that shimmered like clouds. Buena suerte. Good luck.

The canal made a sharp turn into a tunnel of darkness. "Naranjas," Florencio said. "Limóns y pomelos." The trees were nearly black, row after row, and water trickled from squat cement towers. She slid down the canal bank to one of the arcs falling onto the furrows. Cupping her hands, she drank the water tasting of moss. "We are here," she said.

"No," Florencio said. "But nearly."

They walked for several miles through the trees, the silence immense as Oaxaca, only the drip of water and cries of crows and their feet on the dirt path as if they were walking back from the market at Nochixtlan. She looked down the dizzying length of the rows, endless dark hallways.

At the end of one grove, Florencio held out his arms for her to stay. Near a huge ravine, another grove stretched up a hill, with wooden crates stacked along the arroyo. Florencio squatted near the large irrigation tank and whistled, three times, like a mockingbird.

A piece of earth covered with branches shuddered, and a man peered from beneath a piece of plywood, blinking at the morning light. Florencio whistled again, and the dirt rose higher, revealing a hole. "Jesus," Florencio called softly. "It's Florencio."

Jesus scrambled from the hole, lifting the plywood high enough that Serafina could see a pile of blankets. "Florencio!" he said, coming forward. "Welcome back to las naranjas."

"Rigoberto is still here?" Florencio asked, pushing past the brush over Jesus's hiding place.

"Where else, since he borrowed all that money?" Jesus said. "He can barely eat, jefe works him so hard. He thought you weren't coming back to pay off your debt."

Past huge cottonwood trees, they entered the damp ravine. *Another arroyo,* she thought, her heart beating faster. But then she smelled coffee and smoke and saw the first plywood shacks. They were crowded together against the banks, dotting the steep hillside leading up to the next grove. Serafina saw faces peering from plastic-sheeted doorways, and she said, "Rigoberto?"

"Up there," Florencio said, and she saw several men bathing in the canal, their movements and curved backs like home. When her brother raised himself from the water and saw her, his brown chest gleaming wet, she could have sworn he was grinning from the river's edge like he had when they were children.

But he never smiled. He hugged her, stiff and formal, noticing her swollen jaw but keeping his mouth closed tight, and led her into his shack. Then he brought her chicken broth, salty water with slivers of onion and three yellow coins of floating fat.

She drank a few sips. Then she told him about their mother, the last years, the fevers and pains and the cancer. He remained silent. He didn't cross himself. She stared at the rosary hung on a nail over his bed.

"I sent all my money, some months," he finally said. "Did you get the money for medicine?"

"Yes. I wrote you to say I was buying food and medicine."

He nodded, biting his lips. "Did you get the money for the roof?"

"Yes." She saw a mesh of thorn scratches like black netting on his wrists. "We fixed the roof. I wrote you that I wanted to come back here. But I couldn't leave her."

He gestured at the plastic door. "We were moving all the time. Two years of bad weather."

He didn't look like her brother anymore. He had been the handsomest in the family, his skin light as burnt flour, his brows fine as delicate brush strokes. Now the frown marks between the brows were deep as knife cuts in a gourd, and his mouth was a crescent slash of worry.

She rubbed her jaw. The swelling was down, but she felt two hard knots like dry pinto beans along her jawbone. *They will stay forever,* she thought. Chips of bone?

"What happened?" he said finally.

In the shard of broken mirror on the orange crate nearby, she studied the green tint along her jaw, the blue circle of bruise left on her forehead. Her own lips were cracked dry, her eyes red.

"The coyote," she said. "While we were crossing. He hit me with a gun." She remembered the blood on the coyote's face. *Does Florencio want Rigoberto to know that we killed a man? I won't tell him. Florencio can say it. Then it will be over. Forever. The Tiltepec men are gone to Fresno. We will never see them again.*

Florencio appeared in the doorway, blurry through the plastic. He searched Serafina's face, then held out the money to Rigoberto, who looked stunned. "The coyote disappeared. We had to make it on our own." Florencio turned to Serafina, who nodded. So he didn't want Rigoberto to know. The journey would be theirs alone.

Quickly, he hid his marred hand in his pocket, and she thought, *Rigoberto saved him; wherever they are, in the cabbage or here, they are like a pueblo.* She said, "Florencio was kind. He stayed awake at night to make sure no one harmed me."

But Rigoberto was rolling the money carefully into a cylinder. "Now we are at zero again," Florencio said, clapping him on the shoulder. "Our favorite place."

Rigoberto went to a corner of the shack, crouching and digging in the dirt. He brought up a coffee can, put the money inside, and said, "I will give it back to Don Rana tomorrow." He replaced the dirt, stamped it hard with his boots, and scattered orange peels and pebbles and a soda can over the spot.

"You have to hide everything," he said. "Los malditos come from the river all the time, to steal our things when we work." He glanced back at the corner. "When I first came, I even buried my spoons and razor every day."

"Your rosary?" Serafina glanced at the plywood wall.

He shook his head. "No one wants that." When she curled on the bed, tired, he said, "Not yet. I can't leave you alone either. Not here. We have to leave soon for the groves. We work all night this week. Don Rana says the wind is coming fast to burn the fruit. Dry it out."

Serafina lay back on the blankets. Her body was melting. She felt each finger and leg and wrist throbbing with blood. She whispered, "Don Rana? He lent you the money so I could come?" She thought his name was the Spanish word for *frog*.

"You will see," Rigoberto said.

She blurted out, "Do you remember, when you left me? For the grapes? And la migra got me? I wrote to you. But I couldn't say it in the letter. I left a daughter. Here."

"A daughter? With who?" His face changed. "Those men from Michoacan in the garage . . ."

"No. I never got back to the garage. La migra came. I wrote you!"

"You keep saying that!" he shouted. "I got one letter! I was working! Sleeping in a barn or a place like this. How could I get letters?"

Serafina sighed, even her breath tired. "I met an American. My daughter is half American. La migra caught me, and she was left behind."

"So many years ago? And you came to find her now?" He shook his head. "I thought you wanted to come to California to work, to put your money with mine and buy a house."

Serafina heard a radio, and men talking in the other shacks. Florencio stood up and said, "That's a long time from now. Now we have to go to work."

A truck honked somewhere. "You have to come," Rigoberto said. "It's dangerous here."

Florencio helped her up. "Stay close to me," he whispered. "I won't let you fall."

Headlights slanted into the orange trees from the dirt road, and moonlight fingered through the leaves. The oranges bumped against her neck and wrist when she reached up into the branches. The dust coated her eyelashes, and thorns pricked her forearms until her skin was dotted with spots of dried blood like black sequins.

Though she was here, in Rio Seco, she couldn't even see the city except in glimpses from the groves. Every day they picked, and even after supper the truck came to gather them from camp. They had to finish the harvest before the rain.

But Rigoberto said a man named Alfaro who drove a Volkswagen taxi would come on Sunday. Then she could go to Yukon Street. To the church. Santa Catarina. She daydreamed that a nun would appear in the church doorway and say to the priest, "Here she is. Remember?"

Rigoberto said, "You can't hope to find her now. She has another mother. Let it go."

Serafina said, "I will go Sunday." She pulled the heavy canvas sack from her shoulder and dumped the oranges into the box. The trees were all the same when she turned — explosions of silver-edged green, the oranges looking like frost in the harsh beams.

The boss's name was Jorge Estevez. They called him Don Rana among themselves because he was fat in the belly, like a frog, and his feet splayed out to the side when he walked. But he rarely walked. He raced through the acres of groves on a motorbike with three plump wheels. They never called him anything to his face. Because he had their money, all of it in cash paid out on Sunday, and he had a gun in his holster.

She found Rigoberto and Florencio by their voices. They were moving the ladders. She waited until they were above her, then picked the low-hanging oranges. Yesterday the wind had blown in the morning, gusts too fierce for work, but all night, the air had been quiet. She didn't talk now. She waited for Sunday. The bag pulled her down like a person clinging to her hip and shoulder. Not a child, but a long white ghost, fat with pulp and rough skin.

When the truck hauled them back to camp, Serafina washed at an irrigation spout and went inside the plywood shack. But her hands were restless, trained to move in a different way in the evening. No tortillas to pat in shape, no blouse to resew, no dishes to wash. The plastic sheet over the door blew in the breeze when she stepped outside. Some of the shacks were made of cardboard, some of sticks tied together with plastic sheeting covering the huts. A dirty, broken couch sat outside one of the shacks.

But no one cooked. They ate at Araceli's place, under the cottonwood trees. Serafina sat down next to Rigoberto and pressed her aching hands to a cup of hot atole. Like home. Araceli had a tiny restaurant, a few chairs and crates and a card table under a plywood roof, where she served breakfast and dinner to the workers who had no pots or pans or grills. There were thirty or forty men here for the Valencia harvest. Araceli's broths and sauces were weak and watered down, her rice dry, but she made tortillas and frijoles negros every day.

If she found Elvia, she would teach her to cook. She wouldn't think about where. Someday. Not here, in the ravine. Someday, she would live in a place with a kitchen again, and Elvia would sit beside her with the mano, rubbing chiles and tamarind and cumin on a molcajete.

Serafina winced, looking down at the rice on her plate. She had to buy a mano, too. She looked up at the dark sky above the cottonwoods.

They heard the whiny roar of the motorbike. Rigoberto said, "Work again. Money."

"Kiss the money": she remembered the coyote's voice. *No. On Sunday, you get paid for all your boxes. Then you get a ride to town in Señor Alfaro's orange Volkswagen taxi. You send some money by wire to Uncle Emiliano, for your tequio. You buy a pot, for your tequio to*

Florencio. And then you will ride to Yukon Street and the church of Santa Catarina.

On Saturday, fog shrouded the groves. Serafina's canvas sack felt even heavier on her shoulder while she crouched to pick low-hanging oranges. Rigoberto climbed the ladder, pushing himself so deep into the branches that all she saw were his shoes on the rung above her.

Once Don Rana roared up to the edge of the irrigation furrows, then stopped. He watched them for a while. He said something in Spanish to Rigoberto, laughed, and roared off.

"He says this isn't jungle fog like you indios are used to," Rigoberto said. "He said it's California fog. It's California's way of fooling you, making you think fall is here. But the wind will be back tomorrow. He says if you want your money, you better finish this grove."

Money. That was all Rigoberto ever thought about, too, all he talked about. He didn't even eat. He lived on tortillas and coffee and anger.

"We have a few more weeks of oranges," he said. "Then who knows what the weather will do? Last year I had saved five hundred dollars, and the rain flooded the fields up north so we couldn't work. No strawberries, no artichokes. Nothing. Just that damn leaking barn."

He emptied his bag into a crate and stopped beside Serafina. "Or someone might call la migra. Someone here. Then he might hide, and while we are trying to cross again, he goes through our things. Or he doesn't pay us for the last month."

"But the people here are Mixtec," Serafina said.

"So? Rana is a norteño from Sinaloa. He's the one I don't trust. And he doesn't trust me."

"San Cristobal . . ." Serafina began, and then Rigoberto cut her off.

"San Cristobal is almost empty. Our mother is dead. I don't think about San Cristobal."

"At fiesta, the priest asked everyone to send money for the church roof . . ."

"I don't have a church," he snapped. "I want a house. Here. So I don't have to move around." Then he put his bag back over his shoulder. "You're going where the government buildings are, and tell them you're from Oaxaca, no papers, and please help you find an American citizen, a girl born here? Why would she want to come live with you? With us?"

Serafina pulled three more oranges from the branch. Her brother's voice was raspy as a new mano stone. He said, "Why see someone if you are leaving again?"

Serafina's anger surprised her, and she pulled so hard on the branch he stumbled above her. "Why see someone if she is leaving?" she shouted up at him. "Is that what you thought about your mother? Is that why you never came home? So you wouldn't have to see her?"

He descended quickly, his bag not even half full. His frown was black when he put his face close to hers, and she saw the dirt collected in his forehead, dirt that he couldn't wash away that first day when she'd surprised him bathing in the canal.

"I saw her every day," he said, his voice deadly, "when I picked grapes and lettuce and sent the money home. I saw her buying medicine and coffee and a stove. I saw you eat the money."

She swallowed the taste of fear that rose bitter as ashes and citrus dust flying through the trees. Money, india. Kiss the gun.

Florencio said, "Don't speak so harshly to her." He looked down at them from the next tree.

"Why should we pretend anything will turn out right?" Rigoberto still stared at her. "No one in Rio Seco wants to see you. They don't mind the hands, but they hate the face. Wait till you get a ride to town and see." Then he said, "I don't know how you slept with an American anyway. How could you be so stupid? Why didn't you go back to the garage?"

"Because I didn't know where it was," she screamed, not caring who heard. "You left me there. You went to the grapes. I was always scared."

"Serafina," Florencio said, coming toward her, but she moved to the next tree, drying her face on the sleeve of the sweatshirt Rigoberto had given her.

"I'm not afraid now," she said. "Don't."

She picked and moved, seeing only the oranges. Maybe Larry's constant chant of money, his novena like Rigoberto's, had gotten him what he wanted. Maybe he and Elvia lived in a big house on a hill far away from here. With pumpkins carved into faces, and a woman with red lips, red nails, and hair curled around her forehead, like in the magazines he used to bring.

In the vacant field near this grove, she saw wild tobacco bushes like the ones back home, the leaves her uncle used to chew. Nopales grew here, too. *Vihnchá*, Elvia had whispered, holding up her finger, and Serafina had plucked out the small red spines with her teeth.

She picked the last of the oranges from this tree, and Rigoberto descended again, his bag so full he hung sideways. "It's true," he said, as if she'd never left. "They don't mind your hands, but they don't want to see your face."

She heard the motorbike cruising along the dirt roads through the groves. Don Rana glared at her, then said something to Rigoberto. Serafina pushed her face into the branches and reached for the oranges. Hand-filling globes, like the *chīhlós* from Yukon Street, the pomegranates whose seeds she'd made into ruby-glistened jelly for the old woman next door. She concentrated on remembering the dusty trail along the chainlink fence, where Elvia's feet had left their prints.

This is my memory, she thought. *My search. Rigoberto doesn't even want to know that her eyes are green. He doesn't know her middle name is Estrella. Our mother's name.*

That night her back ached like fiery ropes were being pulled tight across her shoulders. Her hands were covered with scales of green and black, the citrus oil mixed with juice and dirt, and her forearms were a red mesh of scratches.

Serafina stayed upstream from the men. She wouldn't jump into the swift waters of the canal; she was afraid of the slick-looking mossy sides. She lay on her belly, staring at the surface for a while, and when the irrigation water came streaming from the cement tower into the furrows between the trees, she bent there at one of the arcs and washed her hair, her face, her arms.

With wet braids and stinging skin, she went to Araceli's. Tonight, Araceli had found epazote leaves to put flavor like home into the black beans.

She owed Araceli money. She owed Don Rana money for the canvas bag. She owed Florencio her life. She sat in the blustery wind, the smoke wrapping itself around her hair, listening to the radio someone had hung from a pepper tree branch.

"Por que l'amor de mi alma, solito Mexico . . . viva Zacatecas!" the banda sang on the radio. The last time she'd heard that song, she'd been walking in the market in Nochixtlan, buying chocolate and veladoras. It was an eerie feeling, as if the words and nopales and tastes in her mouth erased the border trails and the coyote.

The wind roared again, scattering the words, and she got up. But she didn't want to go back to the shack. She walked along the edge of the camp, hunching over herself, missing her rebozo. No one wore rebozos here. Don't be an Indian. She wrapped her hands around her elbows.

Elvia would be eating hamburgers, maybe potatoes. Ice cream. Then she would do her schoolwork and watch television, sleep in a room with a pink bedspread and a soft pillow.

Near Jesus's brush-covered cuevo, she looked down the sandy road, the canal snaking green under the flying grit. She heard the whine of the motorbike, and Don Rana shouted at her, "You going to leave down that road? So los malditos near el rio can roast you like a puerco Mixteco on their fire?" She turned to go back, and Florencio was waiting by the irrigation tank.

He had made several trips back to the river bottom, cutting cane stalks and tying them together to add a cooking room to the sleeping room. They sat in the doorway, the light falling through the tall cane stalks. "Are you watching me?" she said, finally.

"Yes."

"All the time?"

"Yes."

Serafina saw that he had laid a circle of hearthstones, round white rocks that looked funny, they were so clean. His mouth grinned, lopsided, but she saw his eyes still waiting. Then Rigoberto ducked inside with an armful of dead orange branches.

"We're going to pretend we're at home?" Rigoberto asked, shaking his head. "The harvest will be over in three weeks. Then we'll be gone."

Florencio only shrugged, grinned again. "Listen. When I was small, every spare moment my grandmother made baskets. For the market in Nochixtlan. I made hats. To sit around was to think of what you didn't have. But your hands gave your mind something to do. Here, when we're done, I'm so tired I think I can't do anything else. But I don't like my hands to be still."

"You won't even be here to harvest your corn," Rigoberto said, but he sat down by the hearthstones. Serafina glanced at the damp circles in the earth outside the shack, the sprouts rising like green rooster tails.

Florencio had carried the seeds from San Cristobal in a plastic bag in his pocket. He had planted the corn the day they returned. "This would be the fourth harvest, at home," he said now. She heard her father and uncle naming the plantings: the cloud planting, the rain planting, the wind planting, the autumn planting. She saw the steep fields around her uncle, the steep banks of tires holding up arroyo walls in Tijuana, and how people planted corn inside the black rings.

"You still believe in the old ways, after all this time here?" she said to Florencio. When she saw him studying the clouds, murmuring prayers, she recognized someone like her mother, who had never changed no matter where she lived, who never let Oaxaca fade like stone carvings worn down by water and wind.

But Rigoberto said, "The old ways stopped working, or half of Mexico wouldn't be here. Hear the story of the Oaxacan ants on the trail to Culiacan? Stepped on. And the trail to Tijuana. And the trail to here. Killing some and they just keep coming. Working hard all the time, and making the big people angry."

Florencio said, "It's easier to be angry. Like you. It's easier to be angry and knock everything off the table with your arm. Then you don't have to wash it and keep it and put it away." His voice was soft and fast.

"Then keep your hands busy," Rigoberto said, standing up. "But if you made hats right now and sold them here, they'd be Hecho en Mexico." He picked up a bag of saladitos—salted plums. "Look. Hecho en Mexico. Just like you. No matter what you do."

When he was gone, she said, "Rigoberto is like our father. He was impatient in church, in the fields. In his own head. He always wanted to be somewhere else. Like Rigoberto."

Florencio lit the fire. The smoke flattened and touched the stones. *The bones of the earth, burning, suffering pain for us. Even here?*

She wanted pots. She took out her molcajete, looking at the blue glass she'd laid inside the stone bowl. She missed her mano—buried in the ravine, covered with the coyote's blood, his disbelieving eyes imprinted in the porous stone when she hit him between the eyebrows—but she couldn't have touched it again. Florencio asked, "You understood him?"

Serafina frowned. How had he known what she was thinking? "The coyote?" she said, and Florencio shook his head. "Oh—Don Rana." She nodded. "Understanding the other words is always easier than saying them. Before, I knew some of what"— she hadn't spoken the name in so long—"Larry told me, but I couldn't speak." She rubbed her fingers inside the molcajete. "El coyote was the first one here, in California, to speak Spanish to me this time," she whispered. "But I didn't understand something. *Reata.* He pulled my braid."

Florencio buried his head in his hands, his long brown fingers deep in his hair, a crow's wing lying in the gap where the two fingers were missing. "Leash," he said. "Or lariat."

She wasn't sure what he was thinking, because he was a man who had delivered the final blow. But when she thought of the gun's metal against the bone of her forehead, she considered the coyote not a man but truly an animal who didn't consider her a woman but something small and helpless with long, braided fur. She rarely let the words into her memory, because it was finished. The *ñū'ún yuu nu'un* had helped her, and she tried to repay them every day.

"He won't expect anything. Your brother. He says there is only today."

"He might be right," Serafina said.

"I think about tomorrow, and next month, next year," Florencio said, after a long pause. "If you look for her, and you find her, I would love her. But if you don't find her, you could still have another child. I would love that child, too. I would take care of you both."

Serafina couldn't look at him.

"I wouldn't leave," he said, softly. "If you wouldn't."

She listened to the wind hum across the cane stalks. She was thirty-one years old. When she'd held someone's newborn in San Cristobal, smelled the warmth rising from hair and mouth, felt the nuzzling head on her arm, she'd nearly collapsed from the hurt. Now she was so afraid she couldn't answer, couldn't even nod or blink away the tears that blinded her.

She got up and walked unsteadily into the next gust swirling through the arroyo.

"Do you need help with tonight's washing?"

Araceli looked surprised. Her face was so plump that her lips looked like a radish tucked into a mound of corn dough. She nodded.

Serafina scrubbed the frijole pot, rubbing sand on the crusted edges. Her eyes dried in the rushing air. She considered Florencio's words. *He is a good man*, she thought. *Maybe I can stay with him.* But she wanted to find Elvia first. She said, "I am coming to the mercado on Sunday."

Araceli nodded, scrubbing the black cast-iron pot at the faucet sticking out from the earth. "While Florencio was gone, your brother told me la migra got you long ago. You never came back, but you wanted to."

Serafina lifted her chin. "I lost a girl. Here."

"She died?"

She felt the poker of heat under her breastbone. "No. The police took me to la migra. She was sleeping in the car. I tried to tell them . . ."

"Oh! Who found her?"

"I don't know." Serafina rinsed sand from the black well of the pot. "She was three." She didn't mind telling this woman, impassive and huge, someone from Nochixtlan who married a man from San Cristobal and then lost him when he found a woman in a strawberry camp up north. "She might not even be here. Maybe she lives in . . ." She thought about all the places she heard people mention. "In San Francisco, or Nueva York."

Araceli said, "I lost a child in Nochixtlan. When I go back, I lie on his grave and cry. I tell him I miss him. He was seven. He had fever. I leave him toys from here. I kiss the stone with his name." Araceli looked up from the grill. "You have nothing to touch. That is bad."

Serafina showed her the barrettes, and Araceli nodded gravely, biting her lips. They cleaned the plywood counter, stacked the few folding chairs, and, finally, Araceli blew out the veladora's tiny dot of flame in a pool of wax. When Serafina got back, Florencio and Rigoberto were asleep. She lay the barrettes along her cheek before she curled into herself on the blanket.

Rigoberto was right. When the money was in her hand, she felt like a person again, not a set of hands covered with clinging black tar and two feet swollen as the fat rind of grapefruit.

And in the Volkswagen taxi, crowded with Rigoberto and Araceli, swinging down the dirt road and then into a neighborhood that looked like a Tijuana colonia, she felt hopeful. Someone would be at the church, or the house; someone would remember her daughter.

In the Mercado Aparecida, she bought a cast-iron pot, the metal velvety black under her fingers. She bought a new mano, rough and too light to her palm. Small bags of spices, several pounds of beans, and a veladora. La Virgen de Guadalupe.

She and Rigoberto sent thirteen dollars by wire to Uncle Emiliano. The money disappeared across the counter, turning into a thin receipt in her hand.

But then she stood by the car, ready, and she couldn't see the right hill. The one with the cross of green, the mark of water. The one she had seen from Yukon Avenue.

Rigoberto told Alfaro, "She wants to go to el centro." He pointed to the tall buildings.

Serafina looked at the huge buildings, thousands of windows for watching eyes. She felt a ripple of fear in her stomach. If they were caught, where would she run? But she had come to look for Elvia. She would have to see the government. She said, "El centro."

They went down streets like darkened arroyos through the forest of buildings, past locked doors and glass windows with painted signs of the government. Rigoberto said, "Condado del Rio Seco. Estado de California. Who would you ask if the doors were open? You? No papers? Mojado . . ." His voice was softer. "Look. Inmigración. Right next door."

She said, "Alfaro, do you know Yukon Avenue? L'iglesia del Santa Catarina?"

When they turned onto the narrow street, she couldn't believe the brown faces, the corn ready to harvest, the children playing in the dirt yards, screaming in Spanish. This neighborhood?

Plywood covered the windows at 2510, and Rigoberto asked a woman across the street who had lived there. His Spanish was good now. The woman shrugged and said she didn't know, maybe Guatemaltecos. Gone now.

Serafina stood on the sidewalk, touching the chainlink fence, looking at the dusty cactus in the back. She walked over to the other door, where the old woman with spiderweb hair had lived. All those years ago, the old woman had never answered her door unless she knew who was there. She was afraid of strangers. Serafina knocked. *Will she remember me? Maybe she is dead now.* She heard nothing, but she smelled something sweet coming from under the door. Grain? Cooking rice? She knocked again, but no one came.

When Alfaro drove past the statue of Santa Catarina, when he parked the car and she saw the oleander hedge, the well-watered grass, she nearly fainted. She wanted to bury her face in the leaves to find Elvia's scent. She fingered the sharp spears, and the bells rang loudly. A nun came out from the side door and stared at her as she moved toward the statue. Then people streamed from the double doors, white faces and brown, and Serafina ran back to the car, too afraid to touch the stone hands.

Florencio's hands were callused rough as stone from chopping firewood for Araceli. When he saw Serafina's new pots, he smiled. "You'll make salsa verde? Like home?" he asked.

But she stared at the cane walls. Of course she hadn't seen her daughter. Of course she would never find her. She wasn't brave enough. Or smart enough.

"Serafina," Florencio said. She touched his arm. If he wouldn't leave . . .

Everything had to be different now from the way it was at home. There were no promises. There was no church. Florencio wasn't her husband. But he had taken care of her like a husband. She closed her eyes. His hands spread across her back, pulling her closer, not as rough as Larry's wrists, not as soft as her daughter's baby fingers, and she tried not to remember anything.

Drylands

WHO CAN fuckin survive without wheels?

Larry sat on the curb outside the hospital. Afternoon sun stung white into his eyes.

The first day Ellie was in the desert, she sat on the curb outside his place, and he watched her for like an hour. She didn't move. What a stubborn kid. Wouldn't say shit to him. Wouldn't come inside, even though it was 106. Finally he went and sat beside her. Ants. So many it looked like the street itself was moving. Like they were moving the world, she finally said. First time she really spoke to him.

It was like she hated him. He couldn't figure out why he did it. But she was his—his bad attitude, his feet and hands even. Jeans, boots, no curls. Those braids, though. Lasso. But she was his kid. Not a son, but not a girl in dresses and ribbons and all that shit. A cool girl. A him-version of a girl. Not blubbering, whispering. Just watching.

Where the hell would she go?

No money to pay the hospital bill. They'd be sending him letters forever, demanding dinero. But he had no address. He'd left the Tourmaline house number, figuring if Callie ever went back, she could see what Dually did when people didn't pay for their high.

What if Ellie had gone back there, to that place?

He started walking. He was in Indio. Only hospital around.

How the fuck would he get to Tourmaline or the Sands, or any-where? Shit. He'd had the truck since he was eighteen, since he got here to the desert after bailing on the group home. Bailing on Colorado.

The September wind stirred up sand on the shoulder of the road. Just like the prairie. The drylands. Outside Nunn, where the wind could blow straight from Wyoming all the way down to the prairie. Down the highways marked off straight and square. State road 198. His mother's house. No car after her old Biscayne broke down. No guy to fix it. Larry hadn't known how then. All he knew was his father had bailed. Part Indian. Cherokee or something. His mother's eyes blue like faded jeans.

That Biscayne would be a low rider's dream, out here. Indio.

He couldn't even take the fuckin bus to school when it snowed. Sometimes it took the guy from Nunn three or four days to plow out to 198.

When his mother died frozen, he walked for two days, to Greeley. Hopped a train. Got caught stealing a Dodge Ram.

Too old to steal a fuckin car now. Too old to hitch a ride to the Sands. Tired of sharing a room with fuckin Warren. Feels like I been sharing a room with him since Saint Thomas. I known him all my life, but I ain't gotta like him. Just like family—just like Ellie. She was mine, but she didn't have to like me.

How the hell can I find her? Walking. First I was strapped down and now I'm floating like a fuckin ghost out here. He heard the creak-ing signs over the road, like drunk baby birds. He knew he was head-ing slowly toward Griffin's place.

He'd bought the truck at Griffin's, when he got off the train to here. Wherever was here. Indio. Longest fucking trains anywhere came through here. He'd seen the sign. Junkyard Dog.

Crate of grapes sitting near the office. Smelling like cheap wine. Griffin bought anything. He acted like Larry was around yes-terday even though it'd been about five fucking years.

"Somebody stole them over to Mecca. Help yourself, Foley."

Tastes like mud. Hot. Like wine pills popping in your throat.

"You need to sit down. In the shade. Where the hell's your Ford? You let that Ford go, you're more of an idiot than I thought. Here, sit your sorry ass down. What the hell happened to you? I heard you had a woman. A kid."

Larry saw Griffin's hands on his hips, gnarled fingers like black-veined tree roots growing into his coveralls. The grape was sour in his teeth.

A couple months ago, one of his teeth had fallen out. Too much speed with Callie—speed made your gums loose and green, made your teeth decide they were bailing. A side tooth. Ellie looked at it. Long yellow tooth in his hand. She looked scared, like it was a scorpion. "Who keeps grown-up teeth?" she said, almost to herself, and Larry said, "What? Who keeps any teeth?"

"I have a kid," he told Griffin. "Don't need a woman."

"Well, I ain't got no kids here, but there's two women yonder. I gotta go. Drink some water, Foley, then come see me."

Larry squinted into the field of dusty windshields. Yonder was a Bronco. He threw the last grape toward the chainlink fence, and he heard a woman say, "Where you headed?"

He could see their faces now, dark because of the shade under the Bronco, or the dirt, or their blood. But one had reddish hair. They lay on blankets, a radio beside the front left tire, an oil pan with ice and beer beside them. A box of clothes. Fuck—living under a fucking Bronco.

He turned away, his head aching. They laughed.

He heard a dog growl near them. They had a dog? Why try to love something when it would die or bail? He'd had chickens in Colorado. Coyotes killed them. A dog. Truck killed it on the highway. A mother. Dead drunk. Dead dead drunk.

Where the hell could Ellie be? "Somebody keeps teeth," she'd said, when he threw his tooth in the trash. "Sandy Narlette kept baby teeth."

"Why?" he said. "For a necklace?"

She frowned. "For a box."

He shrugged. "She's still a foster mom. It's still a group home."

But maybe she'd gone there. When he'd first walked into that yard, seen Ellie with the other kids under that mulberry tree, he knew it wasn't a group home. It was a family.

That's what she missed so bad—a crowd of kids, no relation, a woman who thought she was some kind of angel. Taking any child, acting like it didn't matter. How could you love anybody that wasn't your own blood? Flesh and blood. Ashes to ashes. Sins of the fathers. Dust to dust. The Bible verses from the group homes he remembered. The whippings with belts and cords and paddles with verses carved into them. The one piece of chicken. The lonely bone.

He ran away from the group home once. Before he met Warren. He was watching the trains, and an old guy came up behind him. Larry thought, *Fuck, this guy's gonna kill me, or I'm gonna kill him.* Old guy with silver hairs like staples along his jaw. Old guy said, "Look. Watch him."

They saw a young man with a ponytail, long and straight like winter wheat, jump onto the slow-moving train. "See where he's goin?" The old man grinned.

"No."

"I asked him an hour ago. Said he was goin wherever. Nice place, huh?"

Yeah.

Wherever. Good place to go.

Formica

IN THE BEDROOM where purple night air drifted in through the screen and no one else breathed now, Elvia dreamed that her mother ran along a canyon like the Tarahumara people she'd seen on TV. Red bandanna over her hair, rope sandals on her feet, she padded along a trail. Elvia sat high on the path, watching. Ruby said this wasn't the real dream, only the entrance. Elvia lay down on the dusty path and told herself to sleep, curled like a baby.

Then her mother lay in a tub of water, her hair loose on the surface, floating like black roots. Her hands bobbed, too, palms down, and Elvia thought she was dead, her fingers motionless but for the water swaying. Then her mother smiled, looking down at her fingers spreading wide, the backs of her hands rising from the wet.

Elvia slept for nearly two days. When she woke, she heard crows screaming outside, and she remembered the flock in the pecan trees near the river, flying over H8red, dropping black wing feathers to drift through the palm frond roof and land on Michael's hair, disappearing.

The other twin bed was empty, and there was an empty crib against the wall. She touched the walls and imagined their breaths, hers and her foster sisters', condensed under the fresh yellow paint. Yellow. Safe for boys or girls. For any fuck-up kids who might show up.

She had examined her tattoos in the small mirror. They were

dry-scabbed, the coating over them thick and grainy as a layer of de-composed granite. *I didn't put the Vaseline on them like I was sup-posed to,* she thought. *Now they're probably gonna disappear. Fall off with the nasty scab. Then I'll lose the moths, too. My mother's and Mi-chael's.*

Now she looked at Sandy, across the table, then at the nest of spaghetti on her plate. Sandy moved her water glass back and forth. "When you first came, years ago, you didn't talk at all in the begin-ning." She touched Elvia's fingers. "Just like this time."

Elvia shook her head. She didn't know how to explain any of it.

"So start talking. You're not a little kid anymore." Sandy bit her lips, then touched them with the napkin. Cloth napkins with the same blue flowers, a little paler from washing.

Elvia glanced at her knuckles. Sandy's eyes were the light blue of the napkin-flowers. Her hair was still brown, her hands moving restlessly over the wooden table shined with lemon oil. Elvia re-called that, rubbing the oil in circles every Saturday. Chore day. She remembered the two big bedrooms in this house, the kitchen with the old white refrigerator and old white stove. This table, with only one place mat now.

She hadn't seen Sandy's husband, Ray, yet, and Sandy's bed-room was a different color now. Lavender and white, instead of green. The bedspread was covered with daffodils, and Elvia hadn't noticed any man things around. No wrenches or pliers on the coun-ter, no oil cans or car magazines on the steps. She'd looked out the kitchen window at the closed garage. It had always been open, with Ray working on classic cars men brought to him for restoration.

"Where is everyone?" she asked, putting her clean plate in the wooden dish rack, nearly silver from years of dripping water. Leaning against the rounded edge of the counter, the same white Formica with gold flecks, she watched Sandy wash the pot.

"So you ask questions first? Then it's my turn?" Sandy grinned.

"Nuni," she said suddenly. "We had canned corn because all the kids would eat it. Once you were sitting right there on the counter, your favorite place, and you pointed to the label and said *nuni*. But when you tasted it, you frowned like you'd never eaten it before. Rosalie said maybe you ate corn on the cob."

"I don't remember that," Elvia said. Rosalie—in the girls' old bedroom, there were only two of Rosalie's horse figures, some horse books, and her collection of boots lined up in the closet. She said, "You're all alone."

"Yeah." Sandy nodded, and that was it. *She always has an explanation for everything,* Elvia thought, when she followed Sandy outside. *But not now.*

The pink climbing rose sprawled on the trellis. "Dreamweaver," Elvia murmured.

Sandy's smile was broad as always, her lips cushiony-wide and the chapped marks like tiny fingerprints. "You remember that, huh?"

Elvia remembered the roses in heavy bloom along the driveway. Cecile Brunner, the small pink flowers smelling of lemon. Moon Shadow, glowing purple. Peace, with flowers that changed colors in clouds or sun. Sandy cupped a rose and shook out a spider. Elvia said, "Did you name her Rosalie because you always loved the flowers?"

"I didn't have any roses until she was about two," Sandy said, moving the hose so the water dripped onto the woody base. "I was tired just from trying to take care of her. Trying to know what to do. Rosalie's been in college for a year now. She wants to be a veterinarian. You know she likes animals way more than people." Sandy shrugged, but her blue eyes turned dark as the water in the puddle at Elvia's feet.

All those years, Rosalie had adopted birds with broken wings, lizards with chopped-off tails, cats who lived in the arroyo on the cans of food she left there. "She was good at school, good at science and math," Elvia said. "But sometimes she liked the cats better than us."

Sandy smiled now. "You know what? She was mad at me because all her sisters came and went. I think she dealt better with animals."

"She was happy when I left," Elvia said quickly, thinking of the

arroyo, of all the times Rosalie said, "They're my real mother and father. Biological parents, okay?"

"She acted like that, every time, but you didn't hear her crying
in the bathroom," Sandy said, brushing a spiderweb from the yellow
stucco. "That's where she'd cry, when one of you left, because she
thought I couldn't hear her." Sandy breathed hard. "You stayed here
four years."

"When we were like, nine or ten, Rosalie used to get mad cause
we ate so much. All the snacks. She didn't want to share."

"Rosalie wanted more the day she was born. Her first words,
practically. 'Mo juice, Mama. Mo watty.' That was water. 'Mo paty.'
That was paper." Sandy hugged herself, moving the hose with her
toe. "And then with cookies, 'Nuddy one.' God, I haven't thought of
all those words in a long time. Remember Chrissy? She couldn't say
any r sounds. You guys teased her about Barbie, cause she'd ask . . ."

"Gulls, let's play Bobbies." Elvia laughed. "All day."

When they sat on the steps, Sandy's face looked gaunt, the hollows of her cheeks black in the faded light. "All you kids were different. Rosalie wasn't big on touching, even though that made me so
sad. You didn't mind it. I think your mom held you a lot, because you
were used to hands on your hair." Sandy smoothed the end of the
braid, her fingers soft on Elvia's back. "The first time you came, I
used to lie down with you. You were scared, crying out in your sleep.
You missed your mother." She paused. "You were loved, Elvia. You
might not believe it, but I do."

"How do you know?"

Sandy hesitated. "I don't know if you'll understand." She
propped her arms on her knees. "You'd eaten. You weren't sure
about my food. When kids have been neglected, like starved, they
look at any food in a certain way."

Elvia thought of Lee's kids, of Jeffrey. She understood fine.
"Did I eat?"

"Eventually. And when I touched you, especially when I tickled
you, you didn't pull away."

"I didn't expect you to hurt me?" Elvia whispered.

Sandy nodded. "You'd been held and touched plenty. My hands didn't scare you. And you laughed." She nudged a pill bug off the steps. "Then you left after a year. You were gone almost four years."

"Did you get tired of me?"

"No, the social workers thought you wouldn't talk here because I couldn't speak Spanish. But when you came back, the worker said you hadn't spoken Spanish where you went."

"Why'd I come back?" she asked.

"I had asked for you. You kept moving around, and they wanted you in one stable place." She turned Elvia's face with her finger. "You never called me. While you were with your dad. Now you show up here in his truck, pregnant, looking awful. It's your turn to talk."

Elvia stretched out her legs. "I didn't call because we moved all the time." "She's not your blood family," her father had kept saying that first month. And then Elvia had decided that if she heard Sandy's voice, she'd be even lonelier. She remembered feeling very old, for the first time, staring at the Sands Motel pay phone, knowing she'd hurt Sandy's feelings to save her own.

"The truth?" Sandy said firmly.

"I didn't want to miss you." Elvia looked at the arroyo, at the fields pale with dry grass.

Sandy said, "Your dad didn't tell you about your mother? You didn't look for her until now?"

"He said if I wanted to be Mexican like her I better start picking crops or cleaning toilets."

"No—he wasn't that mean."

Elvia felt it in the back of her throat, like the iridescent floating top of root beer. She missed her father. How could she explain the feel of her father's rough hands over hers on the steering wheel? "He's not a good guy. I mean, to everyone else. But he is to me. We used to laugh about everything. Eggplant. Stupid commercials. He took me to the ocean once, and to the mountains." She knew Sandy wouldn't think he was a good father. "He got mad when I asked too many questions about my mother. I guess cause he didn't want me to get hurt." She paused. "But he was always in fights. And his girlfriend was into speed. Smoking it. And he was, too."

Sandy said carefully, "Not you. You didn't smoke anything."

"Not me."

"Because you know what that would do to a baby, right? I didn't even take aspirin when I was pregnant with Rosalie."

Elvia said heatedly, "So you were perfect, you ate everything good, and Rosalie has a huge college brain." Then she paused, adding softly, "I probably messed up. Already."

She told Sandy everything, the whole story from the beginning. The arroyo in Tourmaline, the cigarettes making smoke people to keep her and Michael company. The speed lab, the vapors she'd breathed in, the little girl. Then Mecca, and Tijuana, and Michael's face in the river bottom camp. His sad eyes, the moth dust of his memory.

"So you think you're five months along? Take a pregnancy test. And tell your dad."

Elvia lay her head on her arm, looking away. "I don't want to tell him."

"He's your legal guardian. You have his vehicle. You haven't thought about that?"

"What about my mom? If I find her, she could be my legal guardian." She took a deep breath, watching pepper tree branches wave like dark strands in the breeze. "You know the church where she left me. It's on a paper somewhere, right?" She kept her voice steady. "What did you do when I cried for her at night?"

Sandy sighed. "I put my hand on your side. You were so thin my fingers felt like they fit between your ribs."

"I didn't eat at all?" Elvia thought she smelled lime and cinnamon and corn. She watched the heavy nodding roses, the soil going black with wet.

"You ate. You were just skinny. Jade wasn't. You were all different. Your feet, your hair."

"You had all of us, and you remember all that? How do you know which words I said, the ones from my mom? Moon and sleep? Did you just say that to make me feel good?" Elvia watched Sandy bite her lips.

"I thought you knew me better than that," she said, turning off the water. "You should remember I never lie, not even to make someone feel good. Come here."

Inside her own bedroom, Sandy opened a closet, and Elvia saw stacks of shoeboxes with names on the ends—some she knew, some she didn't. Christine, Tammy, Ozelle, David, Billy, Jade, Danny, Bridget, Patrick. Elvia.

They sat on the bed. Some boxes had only a few pieces of paper, a toy truck, tiny socks, or a drawing. Jade's box had costume jewelry she loved to collect, and snowflakes she cut from white paper. Chrissy's box had Barbie clothes Sandy had made, with careful stitching on the skirts, and papers from the speech therapist, and a tiny envelope of baby teeth.

Elvia held her own box in her lap. Sandy's eyes glowed with tears; she held her lip tight between her teeth. "That's what Ray couldn't understand," Sandy finally said. "How I fell in love with every kid, and how I don't mind crying every time they leave. Even every time I get these out."

"He left?" Elvia asked. Ray. She and the other girls never knew what to call him. If they called her "Mom," were they supposed to call him "Dad"? The girls rarely saw Ray, since he was always at work or in the garage working on the cars. So they didn't call him any-thing—just said, "Here's your dinner," or "Mom says can you fix the toilet again?"

Sandy stood up and went to the window, blew a few leaves from the sill. "Yup. He got tired of doing the hokey-pokey with kids. With me. He's doing the pokey-jokey with someone named Bonnie. Open your box."

Elvia's box was full of watercolor pictures she and Rosalie had painted one summer, and pebbles and rocks. The beginning of her collection—such ordinary pink and white and gray gravel, stuff Ray probably bought for the driveway, and she'd been sure they were valuable. Baby teeth, a tie-dye tee shirt she'd made in school. Sandy pulled papers from beneath the shirt.

"Social worker stuff. And I wrote down some of those words you said, because I wasn't sure what they were at first and then I thought they sounded beautiful. I never heard any words like that since. Not Spanish or French. My mother was French. Your mother . . ."

Elvia looked at the rounded writing. "*Sándoo.* Wash. *Cu-shu.* Sleep. *Yoo-oo.* Moon." Her chest tightened like when she'd inhaled the smoke from Michael's wild tobacco cigarette, and then she felt a couple of hesitant pokes against her left hipbone.

Was it because she was finally sitting down? Or because she was scared again, this time scared that she was ready to give up on her mother? Did the baby come alive only when fear made her blood sound different in her veins, in the sac-thing around its head? Elvia put the lid on her box, pushed it across the comforter.

Sandy sat down on the bed again. "You know what? Every one of these kids was different. What their moms ate, what they did—all that was in them. Look, your baby's already getting fingernails and eyelashes and bones from you. And from the father. Does he want the baby?"

Elvia said, "No. I think he wants me to—" She didn't want to say the word. Abortion. "He's scared about Pampers and Cahuilla stories and songs. And he acts like tweaker tribe now."

Sandy held up her palms in confusion, and Elvia knew she wouldn't know *tweaker, fader, sketcher*—all the words for people using speed. She added, "He's only halfway around. He likes to stay high. I left him your number. His name is Michael. If he calls."

"Okay," Sandy said. She pulled her hair into a tighter ponytail, her wristbones showing like marbles under her skin. "What do you want? Here?"

Elvia stared at the face she'd seen whenever she tried to conjure up her mother. Blue eyes darker than Callie's, eyelids lightly purple, forehead with freckles like sand. She had wanted a quiet room, food, and the washing machine. Sandy's voice. Home. "I don't know," Elvia said.

"So if your mother's not here in Rio Seco, I'm just the backup mom? Food and a bed?"

Sandy had read part of her mind, as always. "No. I—I wanted you to tell me what to do."

"Okay," Sandy said, bringing out a home pregnancy test from the bathroom. "Pee on a stick. One minute. Blue stripe."

"Why?" Elvia swallowed nervously. "I already know it's true."

"Yeah. But I want you to pee on the stick and get started with the official, gross, undignified part of being a mother. You get pee tests and blood tests. You go to the doctor. Everything hurts from now on. It's not mystical or romantic. It's not about drinking tea or dreaming."

Sandy doesn't know anything about dreaming or being Indian, about the desert or my mother or Michael. She has a box with my baby teeth. That's it. Elvia grabbed the test and went into the bathroom. She peed on the plastic wand like the directions said. She felt way past stupid. She carried the stick out to the kitchen. "Here. It has pee on it."

"Pee doesn't scare me. And it better not scare you." Sandy didn't glance at the stick yet. "What scares me is teenagers—" Sandy made her voice high and girlish. "We were just kissing and something happened. I don't know, whatever."

"You're old. How would you know what they say?"

"I'm thirty-eight. I know cause I said it. I got pregnant with Rosalie. Everybody knows what happens. They kiss you and it feels good. End of thinking. But not end of story."

Elvia looked away from Sandy's reddening eyes. "That's why you and Ray got married?"

"Yeah. And he didn't understand the icky stuff, didn't want to do it." Sandy pointed. A blue stripe had appeared on the stick. Under her pee.

Elvia stared at the window screen, filled with evening blue, the black branches waving past. Doctors and tests and hospitals. She bent and cried on the counter, smelling the Formica, the remnants of onion and garlic. "I can't do this. I can't."

"You're already doing it," Sandy said calmly, her hand on Elvia's shoulder. "You didn't get high. You tried your best."

"I could still—" Elvia cast about for words, her breath ragged. "Girls talk about getting it taken care of—"

Sandy whirled and went to the porch. When she came back, her face was pink, the cords standing out in her neck. "You have two choices if you don't want a baby. You think I'm gonna tell you about conception and life, all that. No. It's *your* life I'm worried about. If you think you're five months pregnant, you can't even have an abortion. And if you'd tried to have one, you might never have gotten over it." Sandy rubbed the hair from her forehead. "Damn, Elvia, it's the one thing in life you can't change. Ever. Your other choice is to give the baby away. But you were pregnant once, you had a baby in there, and you'll never change that."

"My mother changed it," Elvia cried. "She left!" She remembered the numbers on the curb, the dusty yard where her footprints had been erased a thousand times.

"So you want to give the baby away?"

"I don't know." Elvia couldn't lift her face from the gold sparkles.

"Elvia, you don't even want to talk about it. How are you going to love it?"

"That's what Michael said," Elvia murmured finally. "How am I gonna know how to be a mother if I don't even have one."

"You do. You have two. She's out there. Your mother has never forgotten you. That's what I'm trying to tell you. Never. Mothers can't forget."

Elvia washed her face in the sink. She stared at the blue-striped stick. No abortion. No erasing the geode, pulling it out like a hollow sparkly shell. A baby. A person. Getting bigger and bigger, moving more and more, with a brain that knew something, even inside. No choice now. She had to have the baby. Whatever happened, she would never forget.

Sandy said, "I'm right here. You feel okay?" She bent down to lift Elvia's face.

Elvia felt only the smallest stirrings now, down by her bladder. *You don't have fingernails yet? Not yet?* She stood up, unable to meet Sandy's eyes, wondering if the vanilla and sugar and flour were still in the cupboard near the stove. With sprinkles for all the birthday cakes.

"We can call a social worker on Monday. My friend Les. See what he says about looking at your file, trying to find your mom." She paused. "I know you were found at St. Catherine's."

Elvia opened the cupboard and touched the spindly birthday candles. "So you want me to find her? You don't want me to stay here?"

"Oh, Elvia, you know I'd be happy if you stayed here." Sandy lifted her chin to the window. "But we can't just pretend . . ."

"Pretend somebody left me in your driveway?" Elvia said bitterly. "Not now. I'm too old."

"Your father still has—"

"I can be sixteen. I'll be an emancipated minor."

"Impressive term. I've heard it. But we don't even know—" Sandy sighed. "I gave you that August birthday. Remember? You don't even have a birth certificate. Even your father doesn't know when you were born." Sandy folded her arms. "But you're his kid. Still."

Elvia was silent. She took out the green bowl where she'd watched lumps dissolve into batter when she'd first sat on this counter and touched the gold sparkles, where she'd heard her mother's words disappear in her head like poured honey, falling in ribbons and melting into itself without a trace.

She slept on Saturday morning, the heavy light in the bedroom wrapped like a blanket around her legs. She woke once with the word *nunī* echoing in her head. She hadn't taken her candle from her backpack. She wished she could pray to a corn goddess. Maybe her mother's tribe had a corn goddess. Maybe her mother was Maya, like Hector joked. He said, "Now there's more Maya in LA than in Mexico." She'd never find someone in LA.

When she went outside, Sandy was sitting on her two steps, staring across the field.

Elvia said, "I never know when I'll fall asleep, or wake up."

"I remember. Once when I was pregnant with Rosalie, I was watching Ray work on a car." She pointed to the driveway. "He was putting on glass packs. They make the exhaust real loud. And he revved up the engine over and over. I sat here dead asleep for about two hours. I woke up and had little dots of oil on my legs."

Elvia said cautiously, "I always wanted to ask you. How come you only had Rosalie?"

Sandy stood up and brushed off her robe. "Because that's how life went." She went inside, and Elvia stared at her father's truck, a pale hulk beside the house.

Suddenly she felt so tired that she leaned against the same wall where Sandy said she'd slept. Sandy always knew what she was doing. She knew how to be a good mother. Elvia felt her way along the wall back to the bed that already smelled like her, and she lay there thinking of Callie and Tina Marie. Where were the babies? They were better off without their mothers.

Late in the night, she heard a powerful engine, and she thought it was her father, there to pick her up. Pressing her face to the screen so hard she smelled the rust and dew, in the same spot where she'd rubbed her forehead years ago, she saw Ray, his wide shoulders and brown hair slicked back, shiny. He stood in the glow of a streetlight shining onto the driveway. "Whose truck?" he called softly, and Elvia heard Sandy's voice from the porch steps.

"Somebody's visiting me."

He nodded. "Yeah? That's a hell of a truck. A '62 Ford. Seems like I've seen it before." He stood with his hands in his pockets, his head still bobbing slightly.

"Maybe," Sandy said finally.

"Just came to pack up some more tools. I'll be out of your way in a minute. You and your guest." He walked down the driveway, and Elvia heard the garage door sliding open. Sandy wanted to make him jealous? He couldn't have been gone that long, if he still had things here. She listened for Sandy's shoes on the gravel, too, but she heard the front door close.

Before dawn on Sunday, she couldn't sleep any longer. St. Catherine's—people would be around on Sunday. She left Sandy a note and backed the truck out, hearing the screen door slam. Sandy was on the porch. Elvia didn't look back. This was it. The last chance.

Rumbling down the street, she passed a yard where a woman stood like a ghost in a white robe, holding a coffee cup, her light brown face contorted with tears. Elvia took in a ragged breath. Was the woman Mexican? She saw a black bun when the woman turned away.

The orange groves were deserted, the long green hallways where she and her sisters used to run, pretending the irrigation furrows were racing lanes. She saw more groves across the city, on the eastern hills, and the river bottom laid out in a dark swath far below her. Fog clung to the eucalyptus and palms, where Michael might still be sleeping in the mist-filled branch room. Or he might be anywhere—just like her father, her mother, everyone else.

When she saw the white tower of the Spanish-style church, in a panic she thought: *Who taught me that finger thing? Here's the church, here's the steeple, open the doors, look at all the people. A foster mother. The big lady with the broom hem.*

She jostled over the speed bumps and parked the truck near a hedge of oleander with dusty leaves. She ran her hands along the bristle-trimmed top of the hedge. Here?

The big front door was open, and the sanctuary was cool. The stained-glass windows were bright as kaleidoscopes on one side, dark and indistinct on the other. Someone was humming.

An older woman was replacing the water in the bouquets near

the altar, her gray hair floating and bobbing like a cloud. Elvia said, "Excuse me. Can I talk to the—priest?"

The woman turned, startled, her lipstick bright red, her brows penciled black. "Oh, honey, he's not here right now. It's too early. I'm just getting everything ready for mass."

"Do you know—is he the same priest that was here like, twelve years ago?"

The woman shook her head. "No, Father Mulcahy left, well, I think nine years ago? He went to Louisiana. Father Parks has been here since. We had an interim priest for a short time and . . ."

Elvia wouldn't cry. She nodded and went back outside. Near the street was a statue, a woman with her hands outstretched and limp, like the begging women back at the border. The same curve of finger. Elvia touched the cool white tip of a thumb.

She stared at the hedge, imagining her tears floating around the baby like pearls. Pearls weren't real rocks. They were collections of calcified oyster spit around an irritation, she told herself calmly. An irritation in the belly.

I'll tell Sandy I give up, she thought, driving up the street. *Now what? Now you really want me to stay?* She hesitated on the porch, hearing voices through the screen even though she saw no social worker car. A woman said, "All week I think about the stuff I'll get done when he's gone, and then I take him to his dad's and I miss him so bad I have to sleep with his pajamas."

"For the smell," Sandy said.

"Yeah. It's one night, and I wander around like a zombie. I can't even breathe right when he's not there. Bugging the hell out of me."

When they'd finished laughing, Elvia opened the door. The ghost-robe woman Elvia had seen down the street sat at the table, sipping from a coffee cup, her hair still in a bun, her face carefully made up now. Sandy said, "This is my friend Enchantee. This is . . . this is Elvia."

Not your daughter. Not your friend. Somebody who just showed up one day. Elvia went into the bedroom, listening to their voices float down the short hall.

"A new shelter?" Enchantee said.

"No. She was one of my kids for years." Elvia heard Sandy sigh. "Broke my heart when she left with her dad. I haven't had anyone stay that long for a while. Because everything's so unsettled with the separation." She paused. "Ray got a condo with Bonnie the blonde. And I guess she doesn't like oil stains, because he rented a warehouse to work on his cars."

"Damn. All those Chevies, the Impalas, all the low riders and classic cars Demetrius and his brothers sold. Always some guy waiting for them to finish. The perfect engines, right?"

Elvia remembered Ray and a guy named Demetrius, a brown-skinned man with a ponytail and broad back, working in the garage on a pale blue car with fins that looked sharp enough to cut. So Enchantee's husband was gone, too.

"Yeah. All their hoods up like those cheap clip-on sunglasses. I used to look at the engines. The hoses were all tangled up like those pictures of your small intestines, and then you had—I don't know, oil filters or bigger things that looked like stomachs and livers."

Enchantee laughed. "You're crazy, Sandy."

"Of course I am. I had oil and grease outside, poop and pee in here. All my kids and their stomachs sticking out, the way you could see tangled-up veins in their foreheads and wrists." It was quiet, and then Sandy called, "Come get some breakfast, Elvia."

Elvia got a glass of orange juice. "Good," Sandy said. "Calcium for the baby. You think all this we're talking about sounds frightening?"

Elvia didn't answer. She stood near the window, eating toast.

Enchantee smiled and shrugged. "Teenagers always think if they pretend something isn't there, it disappears. Like dirty dishes."

Elvia slammed the cupboard door. "I don't need a lecture. I've been taking care of a little boy practically by myself. I saved a little girl's *life*."

Like they're gonna scare me, she thought. *Hell, no.* She stayed in the bedroom all day, staring at the dresser drawers where her things used to be. She slept, hearing crows, dreaming about one circling over her. She woke breathless, her scalp prickled with sweat, more fear than she'd ever had deep inside her breastbone. But no one kicked her, or even shivered.

When she walked into the kitchen that night, she said, "Sorry I was rude to your friend. And you." Sandy nodded. Elvia said, "But I went to the church and the same priest isn't even there now. And you guys were joking about poop."

The smell of lemon oil floated around her. Sandy said, "Okay. Do you want to stay?" Elvia nodded. "Then we have to talk to social services. And you have to do something about that truck in the driveway."

Elvia was so surprised she hiccuped. "Why? Because Ray saw it?"

Now Sandy looked surprised. But all she said was, "Because you're driving a vehicle that could be considered stolen, your dad is a scary guy, and I can't get in trouble with the county."

"Oh, yeah," Elvia said, stung. "More fuck-up kids might show up. He gave me the truck."

Sandy blew a little air out when she laughed. "Right. I guess you forgot. The biggest rule in this house was no lying. Remember why? I don't think you do, because back then I wouldn't have put it to you this way. I'd have just said because it's wrong, because it'll hurt you later, because I said so. Now that you're going to have your own baby, I'll tell you straight up: because it insults me. And I'm a short woman who's never done anything except raise kids, cook, clean, and wash, so people insult me all the time. I don't need it at home."

"No one's here to insult you now," Elvia said. "Maybe Rosalie got tired of hearing about laundry."

"Yeah. There's just me—today anyway. And you. And your baby." Sandy paused. "Tomorrow, we can make a doctor appointment. Then go down to social services. My friend Les can see if your mother's in the system. Maybe she's had other kids, maybe she still lives here." Sandy paused. "Then we can return your father's truck. I know he's not the easiest person in the world to talk to, but we can tell him—"

Suddenly Elvia couldn't stand Sandy's patient tone, her almost-bandage voice, as though she felt sorry for Elvia's pitiful life. "My dad's probably in Florida." She stood up. "I heard Ray talking to you last night. You sounded like you wished he'd come back. And I don't want to mess up your life more than it already is. An illegal fuck-up foster kid." She headed for the bedroom that used to be hers.

"You're not a fuck-up. I said it, okay? Look, you don't even have a driver's license, do you?"

"I forgot. Gotta go by the rules." Elvia wanted to laugh. Her father wasn't big on rules. Neither was Michael. She closed the bedroom door. Laying out the last brown and green glass-gems and her moonstone on the bed, she tried to pray one more time, like in the motel, in the desert. Sandy didn't know what her life was like. She didn't want Sandy to return the truck and see the shabby motel. She didn't want to be feral. Years ago, Ray had called a shelter kid "a feral child. The kind I don't know if you can help." Elvia had asked Rosalie what *feral* meant, and Rosalie said, "Like wild dogs that live in the arroyo or groves. You can't make them live normal again."

I have to do this by myself, Elvia thought. *Figure out what's normal, for me.*

She heard screaming in the middle of the night. Stumbling to the door, she saw a man handing a kicking child to Sandy. The boy yelled and flailed his wrists, and Sandy's hands ran down his wind-milling elbows until she'd trapped them in her arms. The man said, "Baby sister's gone. Dish drainer marks on the back of her head, Sandy. Father gave her a bath. Drunk. This one's two. On the kitchen floor staring at the sink when I got there. You're gonna have a long night." When he turned to put down a bag, he saw Elvia. "Who's that?"

Sandy's voice was high. "Just a friend's kid spending the night,

Les. I have plenty of room." The man looked hard at Elvia, and then he reached for the doorknob.

She thought Sandy would call her to help when the car left, but the boy's wail was regular as a car alarm now, and then Sandy took him into her bedroom and closed the door.

Elvia stayed awake until dawn, hearing the cries muffled and slowed, Sandy's voice soft and indistinct and constant, like clothes in a dryer. Her bandage voice. *She doesn't need me. She does this all the time. For anybody who's messed up. All the same. We're all here for a week, a month. Then somebody's supposed to want us. But I'm not a kid now. I already have my box. We all get a box. Then we have to go.*

She got her clean socks from the laundry room, the white washer and dryer where she used to fold clothes at night, looking at the highwire moon through the wispy curtains.

Quietly pushing open Sandy's door, she heard their heavy, sleeping breaths. He had dark blond hair, a butch cut like dust on his skull, his body curled tight away from Sandy's. She lay on her back, her arm beside him, the pillows stacked around them. So he wouldn't fall, Elvia knew.

She went outside to put her backpack in the truck. Sandy's roses were bright as pinwheels in the streetlight. The white dead-end rail was like a crooked picket fence against the vacant lot. She walked through the dry foxtails to the arroyo, in the space worn down by her sisters' sliding feet. She wondered where they were—Jade, Chrissy, Bridget. The light snaked down the arroyo, illuminating the dry sand. A shopping cart lay on its side like a sleeping animal.

When she passed Enchantee's house in the truck, she saw the blue Honda pull out and blink headlights at her. Enchantee waved and Elvia waved back. But then when she got on the highway heading toward the desert, she saw Enchantee still behind her.

She pulled onto the shoulder and walked back to the Honda. "What are you doing?" she shouted.

"Giving you a ride back to Sandy's. She called me and said you'd be leaving." Enchantee had on sunglasses, a white scarf, and red lipstick. She looked like a movie star.

"Who said I'm going back?"

Enchantee shrugged.

"She's trying to run my life. Rules and doctor and school. Pretend to read my mind."

Then Enchantee grinned. "That's what mothers do. If you want one, I'd go back if I were you."

"That's you." Elvia waited for a convoy of semis to pass, wind thundering against her. Enchantee's scarf waved like a flag.

"Sandy's worried." Enchantee pressed two twenties into her hand. "If you won't let me drive you, do what you gotta do, have a good lunch, take the bus back here."

Elvia looked at the money. "You don't even know me."

"I'm your aunt now, whether you like it or not." Enchantee grinned, her white teeth, maple skin, and red lipstick bright in the morning sun.

"Yeah, you and Sandy really look like sisters." Elvia rolled her eyes.

"Hey," Enchantee said, her voice suddenly harsh. "My mother left me with my aunt when I was born. I had three cousins who weren't anything like sisters I'd want. I'll take Sandy anytime. And I taught myself to be a good mother. I hope you figure it out." She pulled back onto the highway, leaving Elvia standing near brittlebush and discarded tires.

Hector's aunt told me the same thing. She said who takes care of you is the mother.

Driving through the Sandlands, down the curving highway, she knew she'd leave the truck, whether her father was there or not. She wouldn't cry. She was trying not to remember that night when her father had brought her this way and she'd imagined the night-lit trucks were Christmas trees hurtling sideways through the valley.

Santa Ana

WITH EACH STEP over rocks and dry stems, Serafina had imagined herself on a pilgrimage, like women moving on their knees up the cobblestoned streets until their legs ran with blood. Or a donkey, carrying baskets along the mountain trails, plodding, head down.

Now she was lost. The labyrinth of streets, the government buildings, the idea of asking strange Americans about her daughter—she was as lost and afraid as before, when she'd panicked and sat down on Larry's green couch. And Florencio wouldn't even leave camp, for fear his luck was used up. Rigoberto said she was wasting her time. How could she think clearly when she picked oranges every day until the citrus oil covered her arms and her full bag felt like a person on her shoulder? And the wind blew every afternoon, whirling through her head with the wild rustling of palm fronds and eucalyptus, brushes sweeping away her thoughts. The government had a building for children, she was sure. For lost children. Americans lost their children all the time. She could buy false documents from Alfaro—Araceli said an identification card was fifty dollars—and then present herself at a government counter to ask about Elvia.

Rigoberto said, "Waste fifty dollars for that? For someone to tell you, yes, your daughter is living with someone else. In a house. With a bed."

Last Sunday, she had slept through Alfaro's honking taxi call, and Rigoberto hadn't awakened her. She'd opened her eyes in the shack, covered with fine sand from the fierce gusts, not sure where she was. Then she remembered the wind from before, when she and Elvia had watched through the window as palm fronds and newspapers and tumbleweeds cartwheeled past them.

In the hot plywood near her face, thousands of woodchips glowed in the afternoon sun. What did Elvia remember? Serafina remembered her own mother taking her to the river, showing her the round stones she said used to be jagged, before water took away what it wanted and made sand. She remembered her mother's hands over hers on the metate, on the mano.

She had to make money for the documents, and make offerings to those who could help her.

Before dawn, she stood outside at Araceli's place to shape breakfast tortillas. Behind her, the sunflowers and tobacco still reached green and tall, but the October wind bent wild oats and foxtails to the ground and loosed their sharp seeds through the camp. Between gusts, it was quiet in the arroyo, but not like San Cristobal. For long moments, all Serafina would hear was an eerie hawk cry or the clink of Araceli's pot lids. But behind those sounds, a helicopter hovered somewhere, car engines raced down a distant street, trailing sirens.

When she wasn't in the orange trees, she was here—tortillas in the morning, sauces for dinner. Araceli paid her cash each night. She had made mole coloradito for Florencio and Rigoberto after that first Sunday, when she had carefully picked all she needed from the Mercado Aparecida bins. The new mano was rough in her fingers, and the ancho chiles ground into a paste looked so much like darkened blood that she had to close her eyes.

But she ground harder and harder, adding the tomatoes, then the raisins, peanuts, and almonds, the thyme, marjoram and cumin, peppercorns, and last, a bit of chocolate and sugar. When she mixed in the broth, smoother and thicker, the fiery smell rose into her nose and mouth and she breathed it in to erase everything. Everything.

Everyone else could smell it, too. She added the chicken

pieces, and when Florencio and Rigoberto had dipped tortillas into the sauce, several other men stood near her lean-to clutching dollar bills and asking for just a small plate, their eyes hollow with memory.

Because Araceli cooked large amounts of food, but nothing that tasted enough like home, Florencio said, their bellies were full when they headed to the groves, but their hearts still ached. He took Serafina aside and said, "None of us is going home. Maybe for a long time. Maybe forever. We have to do what we can here. Do you have enough mole for them?"

Then Serafina thought, *Araceli will pay me. I know it. I can do this every day.*

For three weeks now, she'd awakened long before dawn, just like at home, and made more than a hundred tortillas, turning them on the hot metal griddle Araceli had placed over the fire. The new plywood shelter was held up by a pole and a pepper tree. To the thick bark, Araceli had affixed a picture of La Virgen de Soledad, the patron saint of Oaxaca, her pale face above the gold-embroidered black robe severe and serene at the same time. Underneath, Araceli put fresh flowers in a soda bottle: wild mustard, sunflowers, and yerba buena she grew in a coffee can.

"I brought the seeds from home," Araceli said to Serafina. "Yerba santa, epazote, and aguacate. The last time I went back, I knew I needed them. But I can't mix them like you do."

Serafina finished the last of the tortillas as the men crowded around the grill, and Jesus said, "Chilaquiles today, no?"

She nodded. She'd made everyone's favorite breakfast with the leftover coloradito. Torn tortillas, the red sauce, and white cheese in layers. Everyone ate so quickly that the only sounds were Don Rana's motorbike and the truck rumbling up the grove road.

When Serafina was in the trees, the wind began and she closed her eyes against the grit rising from the furrows. She did not need to see the oranges anyway; she could feel for them by bumping her fingers until she plucked hard and mechanically dropped the fruit into the sack. Today was Friday. They worked Saturday, too, and then Don Rana would pay them. On Sunday, she would wash all the clothes in the canal, hang them on the ropes Florencio had strung between the trees, and hope the wind didn't take them. Rigoberto said the wind had a name. Santa Ana. She thought of all the places here—Descanso, San Jacinto, Los Angeles, Rio Seco. Everywhere seemed like Mexico, with the same names and plants and faces, if you stayed out of sight. There were camps all over California where you could disappear. Now everyone was talking about Santa Maria and Guadalupe, where Rigoberto said they would have work in the strawberries soon.

But she didn't want to leave. She was making a plan now, slowly. She could find work here, maybe she could cook somewhere. She could buy the falso documents, pay someone to translate at the government buildings. She had even thought about looking in bars this Sunday for Larry. He wasn't a child. He might be easier to find. Larry Foley. She could remember only parts of him: the eyes green as new corn, their corners laced with red when he smoked in the truck with his friend; the hands veined with engine oil; and how he'd laughed and swung Elvia.

She wasn't paying attention when the whirling dust devil came from a barren field left fallow between groves, whipping her hair around her face like a strangling mask for a moment. She held on to a nearby tree, choking on the dust, sure that los aires, the spirits everyone talked about in San Cristobal, were trying to tell her something. All this wind was a bad sign. Back home, the air was calm and quiet and damp. Rigoberto said, "It's just Ana. Does that make you feel better? They named a wind after a santo?"

She heard a high whine, and the dust dervish spun away from her and zig-zagged crazily across the road, picking up speed, and then disappeared into the grove.

Don Rana stopped his motorbike in front of her. "The trees—they kill it," he said slowly, nodding at the dust devil. Then he motioned for her to get on the back of the motorbike.

Serafina didn't move. Her head burned black, and she looked at the gun on his hip. No. This couldn't happen to her again. The arroyos, the hard hands clubbing her on the head . . . There was no sense in running. The motorbike idled along beside her. If he wanted sex, why didn't he go to the Tejana women who came every Saturday to the end of the ravine and lay down on blankets for ten dollars? No. She wouldn't even look at him.

But Don Rana said, "You have to cook, no? Mixtecos work better when they eat." He spoke slowly and she understood. "Plenty more work after dark. Goddamn wind slows us down."

She was still afraid, the whole time they rode through the grove roads, leaving roiled clouds of dirt behind. But when she got off the motorbike near camp, Rana said nothing, just hunched over and whirled away.

When she got to Araceli's, the older woman shook her head. "Nobody has any money yet, and I didn't see Alfaro today. We have to make do with this." Serafina glanced inside one pot at the rice flavored with bits of onion and a sheen of yellow cumin. Araceli pointed her knife at a pile of nopales, and Serafina sheared off the tiny red spines with her own knife.

The ruby-red fruit of the nopales by that back fence, the jelly she'd made for the old woman . . . Could she possibly be there? That first Sunday, Serafina thought she'd smelled the oatmeal scent of years before; back then, the old woman never answered the door. But she crept out at dawn to water. Could she leave a note on the door? An offering of jelly for the old woman? She looked up the hill at the green trailer sitting half hidden near a cottonwood. An offering of nopales to Don Rana? She knew he could speak English. Maybe he could write, as well.

Don Rana sat outside his trailer with two other men, all wearing pointed cowboy boots and western shirts with pearl buttons. They stared at Serafina when she approached. Their eyes were light as toasted bread, their norteño faces suspicious.

"Fucking indios," one of them murmured.

"I brought you some food," she whispered, knowing she couldn't ask him anything now.

"Nopales? Shit, I ate enough cactus in Sinaloa." They all joined his laughter. "I wouldn't touch that fucking green pile now. Crazy Mixtecos. I only eat meat." He put the plate on the ground, and a small dog came out from under the trailer and sniffed the rice.

"Remember the fireworks?" Rigoberto said, when she told him what had happened. "Do you?"

Serafina nodded. When they were small, the government had taken away half of the land around San Cristobal, sold it to someone. The people got on a bus to Oaxaca City and camped out on the church steps in the square. The second day, soldiers came and set off fireworks all around the church, calling it a celebration but accidentally hitting two men with rockets.

"We weren't invisible at home," Rigoberto said. "We were irritants. Tin cans in the road. Shoot at them. Run them over. But here, we are invisible."

Jesus said, "Except when someone stumbles on us by accident." He scraped the bottom of the rice pot. "Then someone kicks the can to the roadside. He cannot send soldiers. Not here."

Rigoberto shrugged. "Why should he? We don't own the land. We only move across it. Back and forth."

Serafina remembered the smell of the fireworks, the deafening sound, the older women screaming, the soldiers laughing. But when they were scattering off the steps, her mother had pulled her inside the church. "Here," she said, shoving Serafina in front of the Virgen. Furtively, her mother rubbed something over Serafina's face, then knelt and prayed silently, her lips moving. When the shouting outside grew louder, she pulled Serafina up, and Serafina smelled the pollen of lilies, saw the yellow stain on her mother's fingers.

Yellow, she thought all night. *My rice wasn't yellow enough, not like the marigolds and gladiolas under the feet of la Virgen de Soledad.* Florencio watched her while she sat on the bed, combing her hair. Rigoberto left, probably for the Tejana women. She had heard him tell Jesus, "I don't want children. I can't afford it. So I have to pay. The Tejanas cost money, but a mother is much more expensive."

Don Rana and his friends had spat the word. *Mixtecos.* The visiting priest who had come to San Cristobal only once a month had hated Mixtecos, too. He would stand in the church, glaring at the villagers. The church walls were an affront to God, he said.

The old priests had ordered the church constructed over the tombs of dead Mixtec rulers, on the very wall of mosaic stones over the burial grounds. Serafina had often stared at the east wall. In the moss-black niches where statues of Spanish santos looked out, her uncle had pointed to garlands of flowers and grapes for fertility carved into the stone. On either side, El Sol y La Luna gazed at each other. The sun, god of man, and the moon, goddess of woman. The priests had been oblivious, her uncle said, to the Mixtecos laboring on the facade.

She felt Florencio's hands on her shoulders, resting cautiously. Larry's lips had frightened her, rough mustache bristles and pressing teeth. But she'd kissed Elvia a hundred times, loving the feel of her lips on her child's skin.

Then she had tried to kiss the hands of Santa Catarina. The night she lost her baby.

The rice had to be gold for an offering. She would do everything right on Sunday. When Florencio turned her toward him, she made the sign of the cross, quickly, her thumb to her forehead and breast, shoulder to shoulder, and then she kissed her own thumb, her lips soft against the thumbnail.

Florencio embraced her now, and she wasn't afraid. She let her lips go soft against his. She felt his mouth warm on the scar at her temple; then he kissed her jaw, lightly, not hurting the pebble of memory inside.

Amarillo. She ground the yellow chiles guajillo with white onion, with cinnamon and cloves and cumin and garlic. When she added the rich gold chicken broth, the mole was bright as beaten gold. She dropped in a pinch of masa. Corn. Her offering. Remember? *Please.* That was all she had been able to say.

Don Rana was alone. She saw his nostrils flare when the plate was set on his wooden picnic table. The mole amarillo filled the plate like a hot sun. "What do you want?" he grumbled.

"Please, write," she said carefully. "In English."

"English? Fucking Mixtecos. You can't even write Spanish. You want English? For who?" He bent his head to the plate and took a spoonful of the sauce, and when he looked up, his lips gleamed. "For who?"

Mrs.—My dauter and me live here 12 year pass. Did you seen her? I am her mother. I will come here. Sunday next.

"Sign it," he said, watching her carefully after he handed her the notebook paper. Serafina looked at the penciled words, the square letters. The old people at home had always signed with their thumbs. Her own mother had been so happy when Serafina wrote her name, the last year of school. She took the pencil and wrote under *Sunday:* SERAFINA ESTRELLA MENDEZ.

When Alfaro's taxi came, Rigoberto shook his head. "I don't have money to waste," he said. Florencio said, "I have to repair these." He held up the canvas bags, and she took a long breath and got in beside Araceli. Their eyebrows shot up. "You can't go around the city alone," Florencio said. "I will—"

She shook her head. "I can do this without you." She closed the taxi door.

After she and Araceli had bought supplies at Mercado Aparecida, Serafina went inside the American market called Vons to buy something they would all think foolish. A magazine. A woman on the cover with smooth yellow hair and pink fingernails. One hand rested on a pumpkin, the other on a boy's shoulder, and all three were grinning.

In the taxi, Araceli watched her silently. Serafina opened the magazine, trying to remember how she'd felt that day so she could say the right prayers now. She looked at the pink cheeks and blue eyes and hands placing bowls of salad on wooden tables. *We are not from another universe,* she thought, staring at the pumpkins with carved faces. *We use pumpkin seeds in moles. We eat the same food. We both have gods. La Virgen, you are here. Even if Elvia is eating food at a table like this,* she prayed, *please let me see her again.*

Walking into the bare yard of 2510, looking at the boarded-up windows, she surreptitiously scattered pale masa around the two cement steps and below the window, hoping the ground would accept. Then she carried the bowl of amarillo she had reheated over the fire only a short time ago, and left it on the old woman's steps. Tucking the note underneath, she laid beside it a sprig of wild yellow mustard.

Mukat

ELVIA REALLY was the past. She couldn't believe it. The Indian man in the office said, "No, the customer from number eleven has been gone for nearly three weeks. I have not seen him." He frowned. No red kiss rested between his brows. Then he closed the door.

She stood underneath the neon, a scroll of dull white worms in the sun. The Sands Motel. The pink night-lit sign had been exciting when her father first brought her here three years ago. He'd gunned the truck on the freeway and sung along with Sammy Hagar—"I can't dri-i-i-ve, fifty-five!" Then he looked over at her and grinned. "But I will for you. So you won't get scared. So you won't ever have to see cops."

He looked for me for months before he found me. Even if he didn't always act like he wanted me. But he never left. She touched the door to number 11. *I'm the one who left.* What did Callie say? "You think this is a bad life? Nobody touches you. You don't have no marks, okay?"

But now I have a brown line under my bellybutton. What would he say if she found him, if he saw her belly now? "Get rid of it?" She'd have to tell him she couldn't. He might say, "Give it to the foster mom—Sandy. She's good with kids."

She was good with me. And school starts next week. Elvia wanted to wake up in sheets, eat Corn Pops, get dressed in clean clothes, and go to class. Be bored in English, look forward to Science. Come home and put her papers on a table. Eat chips.

Kips, kips. Doggie. She didn't want the crazy Callie life, or the crazy Michael life. She stared at the doors, like red sticks of cinnamon gum. Number 12 was open. Boots were outside.

Elvia parked at number 9 and crept near the door. Asshole Warren. She could hear his voice. He was talking to the TV. "Fuck she did, Leeza," he said, and then, "Oh, man," when Elvia knocked on the metal jamb. "You're alive."

"No shit, Sherlock," Elvia said. "Where's my dad?" His face was blank and unshaven, and she thought, *Why isn't he at work?* "He went to Florida, right? Tell him I brought the truck when he comes back. I'm leaving the keys with the lady in the office."

"Florida?" he shouted. "What the hell? I ain't seen your dad. He took off lookin for that guy Dually. He thought Dually stole his truck. And you."

Elvia studied the beer cans on the rug. "Me?"

"Yeah. He said Dually must be lookin for payback. The girlfriend owed him. Took off the day the truck disappeared." Warren peered out the door. "Holy fuckin shit. *You* took the truck."

Elvia looked away from him, the pinkish skull like rose quartz, the few black hairs gathered into a ponytail. "I stole myself. Tell him I'm sorry. About the truck. About everything."

She opened the glove compartment, looking for the purple velvet scrunchie. A magazine fell out, tied into a tube with Christmas ribbon. A note said,

Elvia. I can't be your real mother. Not even your fairy godmother. But backup mother is fine with me. Look at page 109.

Warren said, "I can't fuckin believe it." Elvia tucked the magazine into her backpack and went to the motel office. She didn't see the woman with the red kiss and long skirts and sad eyes. She dropped the keys through the door slot, figured she could walk to the bus station in Tourmaline. Five miles. That couldn't bother the baby. She used to run that far two weeks ago, when everything was different.

.   .   .

On the bus, she watched the smoke trees fly past. *My dad's in the wind—your dad's in the trees. He says baby trees have to live downstream from their mother, but this is for real, not a story. I can't live with my dad, or with Michael. Not at the river. Not at Dos Arroyos. I have to go back to Sandy's.*

Does she want me to give it up to a family? Every time Elvia thought of the trilobite tracing its feet across her, inscribing something inside her, on her bones, she didn't think she could really leave the baby with someone else. When the baby found out, when the child or teenager found out, "Your mom couldn't handle you, couldn't take care of you," she knew just how it would feel. The way she'd felt in the foster homes. Like a hollow, ripply husk, like the waxy pale insides of a pomegranate, the ones she'd seen picked clean by ants and dried by the sun.

Sandy wasn't home. Elvia looked under the green pot for the key. No note inside. Back on the steps, she looked at the wild tobacco bush near the arroyo. The yellow tube-flowers really looked like macaroni. Michael had smoked wild tobacco since he was ten, drunk jimsonweed tea many times. What would dreaming do to your brain? The third level? So far inside yourself you could see people from your past, from your actual memory, inside your cells?

The wind ruffled rose petals onto the driveway. She opened the ribbon-tied magazine.

Melanie Griffith, a boy, and a jack-o-lantern with an intricately carved face. Grinning. She wants me to learn how to cook? How to put on makeup? Elvia turned to page 109. A little red baby the size of a Barbie doll lay on its mother's bare chest, the tiny black-haired head like a stone pendant at her collarbone. Elvia couldn't believe how small the arms and legs were, bent like a frog's. The baby's skin was so thin you could almost see the blood pulsing inside.

"Miracle of survival," the article read. "This baby was born early, at only 23 weeks, and her very life depended on her parents' love. They held her, skin to skin, for seven hours a day to calm her, to help her grow. And their devotion worked."

Elvia touched the photo. The baby could have fit into her father's hand. Her tiny fist reached through a wedding ring.
Fist. Her baby had fists. Feet. Twenty-three weeks. That was
why Sandy gave her this. April—it was halfway through September
now. About twenty-two weeks. Or more. The baby didn't look like a
trilobite floating around inside her, with blind eyes and nubs and
tadpole feet. The baby looked like this. A person. A squirming, pirou-
etting, hand-tracing person.

A white truck parked at the curb, with designs on the doors.
Powder-puff painted trees and lettering: ANTUAN'S LANDSCAPING.
Hector got out, and Elvia laughed with relief. "You drive?" she called
to him.

Then she noticed his haunted red eyes, his scratched face, his
arms black with scabs. "Me and Michael been working trees for this
guy AnTuan. Trying to save money for the baby. But Caveman and
Michael got a motel room and mixed the medicine with speed.
When mano woke up, Caveman was gone with the red bowl. And
the money . . ." Hector wiped his face, and she saw palm bark shreds
on his hair. "Mano drank too much of that stuff. He's in the trees
with his chete, yelling shit nobody can understand. I can't talk to
him."

She hurried to the truck, and Hector drove into the foothills,
steep streets lined with jacaranda trees. "This guy Darnell hired us,
but Michael took off with his truck. We been up in Grayglen all day,
and Darnell showed up. Says he's gonna have to call the cops cause
Michael's 5150."

Pulling into a long driveway, Hector pointed to a large Spanish-
style house. Six palms were trimmed like shorn pineapples, and Michael dangled near the house, slashing at fronds, shoving off the
trunk with silver gaffs flashing as though he were some kind of bird.

A black guy stood in the driveway next to an old truck. "You his
wife?" he said. "He's ballistic. I didn't even know he spoke English.
We hired them off the street, thought they were Mexican."

"Wife?" Elvia said, watching Michael wave the machete. "He
said that?"

"Look, I'm Darnell. I own AnTuan's. I don't know why he stole my truck, but here he is stone trippin, talking about, 'My lady's gone, the truck's gone, my money's gone.'"

Michael's braid flew around his shoulders. He didn't look down, didn't see her. Darnell's arms were scratched, too. He said, "I got three girls. You're havin a baby—I'll cut him some slack about the cops. But he needs to quit. The homeowner's gettin nervous, and I'm liable."

A blond woman, cell phone at her ear, watched them from the front door. *She could be calling the police*, Elvia thought. Michael would go to jail for being high, if nothing else. Elvia stepped around the fronds, woven almost like rough baskets as they'd fallen. "Michael," she called, as close as she could get under the rain of bark. He slashed with the machete, and only three fronds were left on the tree, standing up like electrically charged hairs. "Michael!"

He glanced down, and his mouth opened. *"Mukat!"* he cried, voice thick like a stranger's. He was five or six levels away from her, from earth. *"Mukat!"* he cried again, mouth stretched thin in amazement, both hands going to his head as if he felt pain, and he fell backward, the machete flying over Elvia's head, the rope around his waist catching him, slamming him into the trunk.

Elvia put her arms around the tree. "Get the machete," she shouted to Hector, putting her feet on the wedge-steps of spongy gray bark. She had climbed this kind of palm with Rosalie, in vacant lots. Michael was dangling upside down. The bark rubbed against her belly, and Hector climbed under her.

"Lower him," Darnell called, standing on the grass with two Mexican men and a blanket.

Elvia wrapped one arm around the trunk, shoving her other hand into Michael's armpit, trying to pull him sideways. Once Jade had gotten scared halfway up a palm tree, and Elvia got her down. But she was eleven then, and not pregnant. And Michael might be crazy—he might hit her. But his eyes were closed, blood striping his neck. He was so heavy.

Hector was just below her, bracing his knees around the other side of the trunk. Her foot brushed his shoulder. He cradled Michael's back with his arm just under hers, then cut the rope with the machete. They both sagged under Michael's weight, and the bark dug inside her thighs. "Slow," Hector whispered.

Darnell shouted, "I'm a firefighter. I've done this before." He had climbed under Hector. "Let him down on me." He grabbed Michael's knees, and Elvia let go.

They laid him on the blanket, and Hector reached up to help her down. Her skin hurt, her chest hurt, and she knew there were bark imprints on her belly. She steadied herself against the trunk, knowing if she'd had to choose, to let Michael fall or fall herself and hurt the baby, she would have let go.

The blond woman came running onto the lawn and said to Darnell, "Oh, my God, I called 911. Is he okay? I can't speak Spanish. Tell his wife I'm so sorry."

Elvia crouched beside Michael and he opened his eyes, dark as oil, covered with a film of red. "*Mukat*," he said, struggling against Darnell, who was trying to look at his arm.

"I think it's broken, but it's like he doesn't even feel it," Darnell murmured.

Red lights and sirens twined through the trees. "Who's Mukat?" Elvia whispered to Michael, but his eyes flickered in their sockets and he turned away.

The paramedics pushed everyone aside, and Michael fought the restraints. Darnell helped get him on the gurney, and the doors closed. Darnell said to Elvia, "County General. He's trippin big time. You're his next of kin, right?" He frowned. "What was he callin you?"

Mukat. "I don't know," she said. "Maybe an Indian word." Next of kin? His grandfather. And the baby. His blood family. She looked at Hector, his arms marked with the scratches of palm bark and devotion, his eyes on her.

The blond woman approached Darnell and said nervously, "These are your workers, right? My husband hired you. I just called him at his office, and he said to make sure and give you this—for your trouble." The woman's eyes were hidden by her sunglasses. She pushed an envelope toward Elvia. "Habla ingles?" she said. "So sorry."

Elvia touched the perfectly trimmed hedge, where the shorn leaves held only a few drops of moisture, and then she pushed the envelope into Hector's hands. She nearly ran to Darnell's truck. "Why'd you do that?" Darnell said, starting it up.

"Hector needs the money. He doesn't have a home yet. Like I do."

By the time they got to County General Hospital, the nurse in the emergency room said, "That crazy guy? With the long braid? He got off the bed and walked out the door."

Darnell said, "He had a broken arm."

The nurse shrugged and glanced at Elvia. "Maybe he had a broken brain. You can't make people stay if they're determined to leave."

Elvia told Darnell, "Thanks. I can walk." She faced the setting sun and headed down the long avenue toward the river.

The evening had autumn chill around the edges, and she shivered. *Do you shiver inside, when I'm cold?* she asked the baby, trying not to think about what she might find at H8Red. Her knife was loose in her hand when she went down the tunnel of arundo cane, passing a ghostly figure pushing a shopping cart loaded like a burro.

The camp was dark and deserted. Michael could be anywhere. The branch shelter was missing a wall, and burned sticks were scattered in the fire pit. *Someone else could already be claiming this place,* she thought, afraid, and she turned to go back. When she neared the road again, she heard rustling footsteps coming toward her, and she gripped the knife tighter.

"Elvia?" Sandy called softly. "Elvia?"

Her heart pushed painfully against her chestbone, and she felt a small thump on her hip, but this time she imagined a tiny elbow. Sandy's chapped lips were held tight in her teeth, her hands buried in her jacket, and Enchantee was right behind her, keys held in a spiky fan.

"Are you crazy, coming down here?" Elvia said, teeth jostling against one another.

"Are you?" Sandy shot back.

"It's wild life down here. And you look . . ."

Sandy said, "I look like a mom. A pissed-off mom in Keds and jeans, with pepper spray."

Elvia looked away, at a tiny fire in the distance, under the freeway bridge. Michael was at the next level now. All alone. *Looking for his mother*, she thought. *Not me.*

Sandy waited until they got to the 7-Eleven before she pulled Elvia close to her. "Three Mexican guys came to my house in an old truck. One guy said his name was Hector, and you were in trouble. He said you might be at the 7-Eleven. And the guy in there, Mr. Singh, said he'd seen you making phone calls. A girl with purple hair pointed us down there, where you might be. She looked so rough." Sandy paused. "Did anyone try to hurt you? You looked scared."

Elvia shook her head. She pointed to the small black canister in Sandy's hand. "Who were you gonna spray?"

Enchantee said, "Oh, she's used it before, little girlfriend."

"Two months ago," Sandy said. "On the father trying to push past my door to grab his son. His son with a broken arm and bruises all over. I sprayed the dad in the face, and my aim was fine." She hugged Elvia tight and then started walking again. "Just fine."

Día de los Muertos

SOMEONE HAD started a fire in the river cane. Serafina heard sirens while she stirred rice. She shivered so violently that Araceli said, "A spirit? Next week is Día de los Muertos. I will see my son."

But Serafina had heard the twirling rope of sound around her neck while she lay at the feet of Santa Catarina.

Her prayers had not been answered. She had been to the old woman's house two times, leaving amarillo and then tunas jelly. The nopales were harder to find now, and when Rigoberto had taken her to the end of the arroyo, where it fanned out into the river, he'd pointed to a slope of cactus burned and carved with initials. "I saw the American malditos here. The children with purple and green and yellow hair. They chased off some Guatemaltecos."

Serafina had plucked the few red fruits, boiled them and added sugar, poured them into a jar. She'd prayed to red, since yellow had not worked. She had laboriously copied the note on another piece of paper and carried it with the tunas jelly and a sprig of magenta bougainvillea creeping over a fence on Yukon Street. October. When the pomegranates, the bougainvillea, the tunas all turned red. Elvia had loved the riot of color, pointing to everything and shouting, "A. Apple! Red! The bed is red!"

She had knocked and knocked. Maybe the time wasn't right, but Alfaro came only on Sunday, and he came only at ten o'clock. After a while, she had left the note and offering. She had gone back to the arroyo and cried until she thought her face should be red with blood.

The rain came suddenly, the wind still hurling tumbleweeds through the camp but turning cold and then throwing water, too. The drops splattered onto the plywood roof of Araceli's, where Serafina made tortillas that steamed in her hands. She thought, *The old woman might be dead.* The amarillo plate was gone, but anyone could have taken it from the doorstep. She would find out today, the fifth Sunday she'd been in Rio Seco. She placed another tortilla on the comal and looked at Jesus, huddled nearby. Jesus couldn't stay in his cuevo when it rained, Rigoberto said, because the walls could turn to mud and bury him. That had happened to people.

"It's a male rain," Araceli said.

"What?" Serafina said, not paying attention. She thought she heard the grove truck. But today was Sunday. Araceli said, "When it rains like this, too hard and noisy and pounding on the ground and then running off like nothing. Useless." She laughed. "The female rain is what we need. The soft one that sinks into the earth. You can work better in the female rain."

"We aren't working today," Serafina said.

But Araceli nodded. "Yes, you are. Look."

Don Rana shouted from the truck cab for them to hurry up and get in. The wind had desiccated the rind earlier, and now the water would make mold on the skin. He got out and banged on plywood, kicked in plastic sheets. "We have to finish this week! Get in the truck, goddamnit! What's the Mixteco words for hurry up or I'll shoot your indio asses?"

When Serafina was in the trees, reaching for the slippery fruit, feeling the drops slide off leaves and trail down her neck, her anger at Don Rana and the invisible owner of the grove felt like a band tightening around her forehead. Like the tumpline she used to carry a heavy load of wood on her back in San Cristobal, she thought, pulling at her skull. *My head is the strongest part of me. Not my hands.*

My skull. Like the sugar skulls Araceli bought for her son, to leave for his spirit. My forehead is glittering like sugar.

The oranges were shiny with rain. "At least we don't have to wash them off today," Florencio said, passing behind her. "Maybe we'll be done faster."

"Not fast enough to meet Alfaro in an hour," she said. She stepped on the leaves that had swirled dry under their feet all this time, now curling in the wet. *Tree after tree, like corn plants at home,* she thought, picking and moving. *Coffee and corn at home. Cotton and grapes here.*

"Why are you so angry?" Rigoberto said, climbing past her again. "An extra day of pay."

"Because it's Sunday!" she cried. "My only day to look for Elvia."

Rigoberto stopped, incredulous. "You haven't come to your senses? You'd rather miss a day's pay to chase the past? Forget yesterday. Make money while you can."

"Don Rana didn't even pay us Friday," Florencio said from the next tree.

"He'll owe us now for two extra days," Rigoberto said. "Be glad we're working. This is just a one- or two-day rain. In November, the real rain will come. Maybe El Niño storms like last year." He looked at Serafina. "No rain in Oaxaca," he said. "And too much here. This year has to be better."

"After the harvest is done, do we stay and cut the branches?" Florencio asked.

Rigoberto shook his head. "I heard Don Rana say they have a truck now that trims the top off each tree. Goes right down the aisle." He stared into the shaking branches. "Strawberries. In November they plant strawberries."

Serafina looked at the thick-skinned orange in her hand, the dimples filled with black dust that turned to dark tears under the rain. Strawberries—red like the tomatoes they'd picked in Culiacan, where their hands bled, where her mother had buried two baby girls and grown a silver stripe in her hair and lost part of her mind.

Rigoberto said, "More money. Put it in the wire at the mercado. All that money going to San Cristobal, and no one is there but Tío Emilio and old women." He wiped his face. "We pay for a memory. San Cristobal is everywhere else. Here and Guadalupe and Fresno and Soledad."

Serafina said, "There is still the house." She thought of her mother's bed, the crumbling adobe walls, the roof of the church.

But Rigoberto shook his head and started picking again. "I'm not going back to that house, so I'm not going to fix it," he said. He raised his chin at her. "You're going back? You'll take her back there, when you find her? Your daughter? You think she'll like San Cristobal?" His laughter was mocking.

Serafina didn't answer. Her bag bent her back like an old woman's. Like the woman on Yukon, who might be so old that this lost Sunday could be the day she died. Serafina felt a gray mist like a dusty screen door closing in her mind. When they had a break, Florencio said, "I could walk with you to Yukon Street."

She knew Alfaro's taxi had left the empty camp. She touched Florencio's wet shoulder and said, "It will be too dark then." He smoothed her hair. "You walked with me all the way here." She left her fingers on his shirt until they reached the next row.

The dead leave their homes in *ñú'ū anima* on one special day, to visit those they have left behind. This year, the dead children would return on a Friday, and the adults on Saturday. Serafina began to prepare the altars. Florencio and Jesus had built the wooden shelters, and Araceli had helped her buy the candles and paper flowers and incense, and the new plates.

Serafina had put one new plate aside, to take to the old woman's house this Sunday. She prayed the woman was still alive, but she would make an offering here to her soul. When a person was that old, the spirit sometimes hovered.

She would not make an offering to Elvia's soul. Here in Rio Seco, she felt sure that her daughter's spirit was not floating, that she was alive.

Serafina put a small table in front of the altar she had decorated with red and yellow paper flowers, with candles and green crosses Rigoberto had woven from palm fronds.

Two plates, with tiny tortillas she had held in her palms, and two cups of milky atole drink, the first food her baby sisters would have been given when they left her mother's breast. A doll made by Araceli sat between the plates, and the steam moved over its small face like fog.

In the morning, the atole was cold, its surface shrunk lower, and she thought of the sweet fragrance her baby sisters had drunk. And somehow, the fog had come again in the morning, as if the atole steam had thickened and remained in the pepper branches. A few hours later, the sun came out and drank the fog.

Serafina began to make salsa verde, for the first time since her mother's death, for her mother's visit tonight. She ground the green chiles outside near Araceli's kitchen, moving the mano slowly. She added the small fringed leaves of cilantro and the large flat leaves of yerba santa, telling her mother where the plants had come from, the pots with seeds brought by Araceli from Oaxaca. Florencio had asked only for frijoles for his father, and the black beans simmered with epazote and dried, crushed avocado leaves on the low flames.

Suddenly a gunshot sounded in the river bottom, not far away, and Serafina heard Florencio and Jesus yelling. She ran into the shack to crouch near the bed. But they were laughing when they came into the camp. Hesitating at the doorway, she saw them dragging a pig. "A wild one, so the meat will be lean," Florencio said. He nodded at Rigoberto. "He borrowed Rana's gun."

"Don Rana let you?" Serafina asked, incredulous.

"I gave him five dollars," Rigoberto said, letting a grin break his face. "I promised him salsa verde. So get going."

Eugenio had been a butcher in a carniceria near Nochixtlan, and he cut up the meat and began salting it with Araceli's help. Serafina stirred the bright green salsa verde, waiting for the pork that would swim in the sauce. She began to make fresh tortillas, the comal smoking hot.

The helicopter whined overhead like a giant wasp. "La policia heard the gunshot. They don't care about us as long as they don't see us. If they see us, we make them angry. Put the fire out," Rigoberto said softly, and she poured water on the low flames. The men all huddled under the trees, and Serafina stayed motionless with Araceli under the plywood shelter until the helicopter circled a few more times and then droned away toward the city.

It is like home, she thought, washing the last of the clothes in the canal, sitting back to rest before she draped them on the pepper tree branches. She went inside the shack to clean the grit that collected on every surface. She shook arroyo sand from the blankets, thinking that if she had a broom, she might really believe she was back in San Cristobal, with joking, laughing-loud men around the carcass of the pig. Like fiesta, where meat made the men's voices sing and boast. *You make your home wherever you are.*

There were no graves to decorate that night. She knew her mother's friends were putting flowers and candles on her headstone, and she hoped someone, maybe Alba, was honoring her father and Luis at their places. She paused, remembering with a jolt of pain the long walk to the corn fields with her brothers, her mother's fingers in her hair. Then she finished setting the plates of food out on the altar for them, with the sugar skeletons Luis had always loved as a child. She placed tortillas wrapped in a cloth at the center of the offerings and turned away.

They heard the roar of motorbikes just before dark, and Serafina said, "Don Rana's friends have the tricycles now, too?"

These bikes had two wheels and three rangy teenage riders with long hair trailing from their helmets. They tore through the grove road and stopped abruptly at the edge of the arroyo, one rider pulling off his helmet and staring in surprise at the ground damp with blood. The pig's carcass lay nearby. "Shit," the boy said. Then he looked down at the camp. Serafina saw a small and pointed goatee, like a mouse hanging from his chin. "Damn," he said. "Beaners."

They raced off, laughter trailing, and Serafina turned to Rigoberto.

"Frijoles," he said. "They called us frijoles." He went out to Jesus's cuevo and stood watch for a long time.

In the morning, the fog was thicker, draping itself in the branches and along the gray shedding skin of the eucalyptus, as if the camp were still full of spirits. The mist had risen from the river bottom, as though a water god had breathed all night in the cane. Serafina's heart beat fast. She might find out now. She had made the offerings. Sunday. Serafina took the air into her mouth. Even though it felt dry, more like smoke and not the gentle wet veil of San Cristobal, she believed it was a good sign.

She rode silently in Alfaro's Volkswagen. She had begged him to come at dawn. All week, she had tried to make the balance of the world right. The meals she cooked, each orange she held, each word she said, each prayer. Now the clouds were not descending from the heavens, but sifting from the sand, and she wondered if that was proper. For this place, she thought it was.

Yellow. She had thought the pale creamy yellow of atole would be right, since the child spirits had drunk some. She held a jar of the atole in her lap. At Mercado Aparecida, she bought masa for the week, and cumin, and then she saw a boy reach supplicating hands to a box of Cap'n Crunch, begging his mother. Serafina remembered how much Elvia had loved the sweet yellow corn, how she herself had tasted the gold dust on her teeth.

Alfaro stared as she scattered the cereal around the steps and foundation of 2510, praying that the ground would accept this offering, remembering the tequila she had poured here so long ago. Slowly, she approached the other door, her hands trembling, her heart shaking, too. The woman's silvery hair was pressed like a dandelion ball against the wrought-iron screen.

"Serafina Mendez," the woman said, nodding. "Sunday."

"Sorry," Serafina said. *Sorry for last Sunday, when you might have been waiting. Sorry I was in the oranges.* She could only say it again. "Sorry."

Serafina held her breath as she stepped inside. The woman looked as she had all those years ago, her eyebrows paler red, her cheeks wrinkled as balled-up tissue. But Serafina realized she was as old as the grandmothers in San Cristobal who only grew a little shorter and more stooped each season, but whose eyes were sharp as ever.

The woman smiled and said, "Picante."

The plate was clean, a faint trace of the amarillo like pollen stains on the white plastic. The woman said, "Good, but picante." She walked to her tiny kitchen table, picked up a jar, and showed it to Serafina. Salsa. The thin finger pointed to a thermometer on the jar's label, red nearly to the top, and a word there. "Picante," the woman repeated, as if she liked to say it. Then she turned to reach for something on the shelf, and handed Serafina the Barbie.

Serafina put her hand to her chest. Elvia's doll. The one Larry had brought that day, with the long black hair like hers. She had held it when he drove away. Serafina pressed her nose to the silky braid Elvia had been trying to weave. The woman said something to Serafina, then pointed out the door. *She found it in the yard*, Serafina thought. *That day. After I was gone. After Elvia was sleeping so peacefully in the car, waking up to someone else's face.*

She bit her lips so hard she tasted salt. Then the woman said, "Naked," pretending to shed her blue housecoat, and Serafina realized the doll had no clothes. The plastic skin was cool in her fingers, the legs thin as cinnamon sticks. The woman shrugged, as if to say all children liked their dolls naked, and Serafina smiled.

She picked up the bag at her feet. The atole, wild tobacco flowers of palest yellow, five oranges, and a piece of paper. Rigoberto had shaken his head, but he'd copied the name of the nearest street to the camp, Palm Avenue, and drawn a small map of how to get to the arroyo. He had even drawn a tiny orange tree and a ladder small as a staple. Until she'd watched him bend over the paper, Serafina had forgotten that when they were children, he'd wanted to be an artist. To draw cartoons.

"My dotter," she said to the woman. She made a visor with her hand over her eyes, pretended to look at the street, then pointed to the paper now in the woman's hands. "Ice," she said, knowing it didn't sound right. "Verde," she whispered to herself. Green eyes. She looked about wildly for a moment until she saw the cactus growing on the fence. She pointed to it and to the woman's eyes, which were dark as olives.

The old woman nodded and said, "Daughter." She circled her eyes with her fingers, like binoculars, and said, "Your daughter."

The Heart's Fontanel

"I CAN'T DO THIS," Elvia said angrily in the waiting room.

Sandy looked up from her magazine. "You could do the river?" she said quietly. "That place didn't scare you? This place does?"

Elvia realized the other women had also glanced up. Two were speaking Spanish and had matching huge bellies. A very large blond woman sat with a car seat near her ankles like a pet dog, except a baby's face showed, pink and tiny and clenched shut.

"I mean this," she whispered, snatching up the medical forms on her lap. "I don't know anything." Mother's medical history. Father's. The questions about diabetes and cancer, heart trouble. Elvia didn't see boxes to check for mother's invisibility and father's wildness.

"And here—the baby's father." She touched palm bark scratches on her wrist. She'd told Sandy what had happened to Michael. "I write: Gone. Booked up. Might never see him again."

Her belly was now a harder, rounder mound, actually sticking out when she sat like this. The thumping seemed to stay on the right side. Sandy put her hand on Elvia's knee. "You do the best you can," she said. "With the forms. With everything."

Elvia shivered when she was naked under the papery gown in the examination room. She jumped when the door opened. The doctor's skin was brown as agate, her head covered with a bright purple wrap. "I'm Josefa," she said. "Spanish or English?" Her accent was soft.

"Where are you from?" Elvia asked.

Josefa grinned. "Panama. You?"

Elvia looked away. "Wherever."

Her white coat came closer. "And how many months are we? We're this big and on our first visit?" When Elvia shrugged, Josefa frowned.

Sandy said from the corner, "My friend Enchantee recommended you."

Josefa said, "I delivered her son. You're the grandmother?"

Sandy said, "I might be." Elvia saw a look pass between them. "I told your receptionist, I'll pay cash until I get Elvia in the system. She's my foster daughter."

Josefa nodded slowly. She said to Elvia, "What a lovely name. So you didn't come in all this time because you were busy, Elvia?" She did something with a machine, something crackling, and then she touched the lower part of Elvia's body, moving her hands. Quickly, she put some kind of warm jelly on the skin and then a black suction cup. Elvia tried to move, but Josefa shook her head. Elvia heard static, then a loud beating, fast as knuckles on a door. "See? That's a heart. A person. Someone you can't be too busy for now."

A cricket heart, pulsing near her backbone. A baby curled around the sound. When the doctor lifted the stethoscope, Elvia felt a tremor. She looked at her blank doughy skin—the roof protected her, then this ceiling, then her skin, and the baby's back, covering the heart.

She couldn't swallow, she was so afraid. The magazine picture—the reddish thin skin covering bones and heart like see-through cellophane. *This is my baby. It can hear my heart. It has my blood inside its own heart.*

The doctor said, "We'll do a few more things, but since we don't have an estimate of due date, we need an ultrasound right away, to check the size, and other things. Now let's do the important stuff to check on you, Elvia."

All the important stuff hurt. Blood tests, then Josefa's hand in-

side her. Elvia squinted until she saw red, and Josefa said, "Relax, relax, we'll have to teach you to relax." Elvia felt something like soft
foxtails brushing her forehead, and Sandy said, "It's just me, getting
you to focus on something else besides what's scary. You'll have to do
this for the birth."

She reached up and moved Sandy's fingers from her skin. *I
have to do this by myself,* she thought. Josefa said, "No, no, loosen
up." Elvia saw a candle flame in her head. When she blew out the
fire, the wick still glowed hot, and she was amazed at how much light
surrounded the pinprick of red, how completely dark it was when it
cooled.

"Total would be better." Sandy glanced at the Corn Pops in Elvia's
bowl. "Total has iron."

"I ate raisins. At the river." Elvia took a spoonful of the big puffy
kernels. The newly cold wind rattled the windows. Michael might
be freezing somewhere, Hector, too, but up here—she and Rosalie
and Jade used to stand outside and let this wind shove them like
dolls, wanting the invisible force, knowing they'd hit the fence and
not really blow across the groves.

Sandy sat down with her tea and toast. "Raisins are good."

Elvia finished the last bite of cereal and put her head in her
hands. The table was smooth. "I'm bad. I wanted to drink the medicine. Try to dream about my mother."

Sandy sighed. "But you didn't."

Elvia buried her face in her arms then. "I knew the hot sand was
bad, too. But for a while I wished the baby wasn't there, so I could
stay with Michael and dream like him."

"That's what you feel worst about . . ." Sandy laid her hand on
the table near Elvia's fingers, but she didn't touch her. "That you
wished it would disappear? Oh, babe, you think you're the first pregnant woman to wish for a while that you weren't?"

Elvia wouldn't look at her. "You love kids."

"And when I was pregnant, sometimes I wished I wasn't.

Wished *hard*. Especially when my feet swelled up the size of Wonder Bread loaves." Sandy poured more tea. "Elvia. Are you sure you want to be a mother now? To keep the baby?"

Elvia frowned at the milk in her bowl. "What do you mean?"

"You could still give the baby up for adoption." Sandy stopped. Elvia felt the feet kicking Corn Pops around her hipbones.

Sandy's hands were still on the table, the thin skin covering raised veins like blue-green tributaries. Her own map. Elvia thought of Tina Marie and Callie. "My dad's girlfriend has a son. But she gave her girl away. Everybody gives their kids away—to someone like you."

Sandy kept her voice even. "Did you like her son?"

"Jeff." Elvia thought hard, staring at the wood grain. "He'd be falling asleep next to me, and his hand would open up so slow. Like those flowers in the science movies. And I'd put my ear on his back—I could hear him breathe."

"Like a stethoscope." Sandy nodded.

"Yeah. I'd poke his arms and legs. Like—not wobbly fat, like a grownup's."

"Thanks," Sandy said, making a face.

"No—I mean. You know. And it wasn't muscle either. Baby rubber skin."

"Did you *like* him?" Sandy leaned forward, touching her fingers to the crumbs near her plate.

She had—he was a human science project. She liked to observe him. She said hesitantly, "Jeff would ask for stuff all the time—juice, crackers, Honeycomb. Toys he saw on TV." Elvia remembered the dark living room, the shuddering air conditioner, Callie on the phone or trying to watch TV. "His mom would always say, 'You're gonna have to wait.' The more he asked, the madder she got. Why didn't she get the juice and crackers before her soap started? Or get up during the commercial? Because he was bugging her. He acted cool with me. I wasn't his mom." She looked down at her shirt. "I always thought, if you're gonna be the mom, just do it right."

Sandy got up to put her cup in the sink. "Right. If the mom can. I guess you know how much work it is, then. It's never over, either. Look at how old you are and I still . . ."

"I'm not your daughter," Elvia said, quietly.

"I know."

"Why are you letting me stay?"

Sandy leaned on the counter. "If you *are* going to stay, I have to be your legal guardian. Whether you keep the baby or not."

Elvia looked outside at the palm fronds blowing sideways, like giant toothbrushes planted all around the lemon groves. "What will Rosalie say? You're getting a replacement kid?"

Sandy didn't answer for a long time. She washed out her cup, turned it upside down on the drainer's white ridges. "You think I'm going to say something like, 'You were always my favorite,' or 'I always loved you best.'" She stood near the window. "No. I loved all you kids. Rosalie, you, the one who just left. Not all exactly the same. I just—this is what I do. I wouldn't mind helping you take care of the baby. I like talking to you and holding kids and cooking. I even like the laundry. When I'm in a really weird mood." She laughed.

"I don't like laundry." But she meant Callie's clothes in the tub, not the moonlit laundry room here. "And I don't want to go to pregnant high school. Continuation. They probably don't have any science. They probably figure we learned enough biology on our own."

Sandy folded her arms. "School isn't an option. Whether you keep the baby or not, school's a requirement."

Elvia nodded. She washed the dishes, hearing the windows rattle again. Back then, when they were all lying in the bedroom, Jade would cry at the sound, and Rosalie would say, "It's only the Santa Ana, dummy." Jade would ask, "Is that a monster?" and everyone would laugh.

She said, "When I first left, when my dad came, I was happy I wouldn't have all those rules. Like yours. I could eat doughnuts for breakfast. Not Cheerios and orange juice."

Sandy said, "I know."

Elvia dried her hands. "Some days I missed the rules. And the pillow and the folding. Some days I didn't."

Sandy said it again. "I know."

When she got out of the shower and dried herself, pieces of black bark clung to the towel. Frightened, she looked in the mirror. The three moths were still vivid, their yellow wings outlined in blue, the tiny red dots of antennae like pinpricks of blood.

Back in Mecca, Tiny's home was printed in cloudy blue letters on her belly so her kid could see where he was from before he was born. *Michael isn't even a name on my arm. Just a moth.* She touched the moth wings. *This has to be my place. My mother can stay here, on my shoulder.*

She heard a loud engine in the night, and she woke, startled, thinking it was her father.

In the hallway, she heard Ray's voice, and saw his arms around Sandy, who leaned back against the kitchen counter. She turned away, her face burning. Not at the thought of them doing anything, but at the way Sandy's eyes had been closed, lavender like she hadn't slept for days, and the way her mouth had been open like she couldn't breathe. But she hadn't been pushing him away. She held his back so tight his shirt was dimpled around each fingertip.

Elvia felt achy between her legs, where Josefa had put her fingers, where the baby would come out. That would hurt a lot worse. She lit a candle, but she didn't pray. She just stared at the light, tested how close she could get her palm to it before it burned into a needle of hot.

"Hey, the fathers don't have to come here. They did it, too."

The other new girl, besides her, was Marisol, who tossed her tall bangs and sat down hard, her belly nearly touching the table. Marisol was mad that her boyfriend got to stay at Linda Vista High and she'd had to transfer to Jefferson Continuation.

Elvia looked around the classroom. Fifteen pregnant girls. All colors, all sizes. Marisol said, "The guys here, they all got kicked out of school for fighting or drugs. So they're all like, criminals, and we're just pregnant, *simon?* Big deal."

"Simone?" A girl with blond hair streaked green and blue frowned. "Who's that?"

Marisol rolled her eyes and sighed. Elvia remembered Hector saying it was the cool way to say "yes" in Tijuana, or in Mecca. *Sí. Simon que sí.* Had he found a school? A good geography teacher? She could tell she wasn't going to study rocks in here.

The teacher smiled and said, "We have two new girls. Elvia Foley and Marisol Lopez. I'm Mrs. Hernandez. And Marisol's got a point. You're just as scary to some people as the gangbangers. So let's talk about that."

"Let's not," said the rainbow-haired girl.

Marisol said to her, "You looked scary before you were pregnant, huh?"

Mrs. Hernandez shook her head. She turned to Elvia. "When's your baby due?"

Elvia felt everyone's eyes on her. "Maybe January."

"And is the father still in school?" Mrs. Hernandez asked gently.

Elvia shrugged. The rainbow girl said, "My baby's dad is dead. Crashed his car. Asshole."

A girl with brown skin and gold-beaded braids said, "You shouldn't say that. The baby can hear you." She pointed to her belly. "Her daddy's doing time at St. Jude's, but I still love him."

Some girls had black lipstick and hickeys dark as plums. Three wore restaurant uniforms, and one had chapped lips like Sandy's. Sandy had looked tired this morning, but all she'd said was, "Enchantee's going to drop you at school. I'm trying to figure out . . ." Sandy had gone into the garage, and Elvia watched her rummage around for something until Enchantee honked the horn.

Elvia began to fill out the paper Mrs. Hernandez had given her. "What do you want to do with your life? What kind of job do you dream about? Maybe not for next year, but for the future?"

Elvia wrote,

> I always wanted to be a geologist. I collect rocks, and I have a book to identify them. In the desert, I've seen geologists working construction sites. They take samples of the soil and rock and make maps for the site. That would work for me.

She handed in the paper. The girls talked about clothes and CDs and "my baby's daddy." A few said it over and over. "My baby's daddy does this and he says that . . ."

The guys weren't husbands, or even boyfriends anymore. They were daddies, even if no one knew where they were. They still got to be daddies. It was just biology.

"Where did you leave the truck?" Sandy asked, not raising her eyes from folding laundry.

"At his last known whereabouts, okay?" Elvia looked up from her homework.

"So I got these," Sandy said, finally sitting down. She laid two driver handbooks on the table. "One for you, and one for me." She shook her head. "I know it's breaking the rules big-time, but I thought maybe you could teach me to drive. Out here, where I can't hurt people."

Elvia laughed. "And what are we driving?"

"I asked Ray to get me a car. A Honda or something reliable."

"Why didn't you learn to drive?" Elvia said, serious then. "How could I teach you?"

Sandy sighed. "Ray tried to teach me on a stick shift. He kept yelling every time I stalled the car out. So then I had Rosalie, and Ray drove us to the store or the doctor. Then you other girls came. I'd sit in the driveway, I'd see all your faces in the back seat and I swear I pictured you flying into the glass if I blew it. I just froze up. Ray took us on errands."

Elvia teased, "Learner's permit means I drive with a licensed adult."

"Yeah, well, I've got a license for foster care. Maybe that'll have to do."

That afternoon, Stan the social worker came to talk about a boy named Shykim. From her room, Elvia heard him say, "What are you doing with this girl? You don't have legal guardianship. No parents?"

"She says her father took off."

"And you can't find him? Employer, driver's license, friends. Plenty of ways to find a dad." Elvia heard Sandy say, "I have to let her figure it out. She's fifteen, okay?"

Stan's voice was gentle. "It's not like you, Sandy. Do you still want the shelters?"

"Yes, I do. I do," she said. "Just let me work this out."

Maybe she could find my dad, Elvia thought. Search the bars, look for Dually's truck, go up to him with his venomous blue eyes and say, "Seen Larry? He'll be a grandpa soon."

Did Sandy really want to be a grandmother? Even if the ultrasound showed a baby with no arms or a head like ET's? From all the fumes and hunger? A baby with nubs for feet? Maybe she shouldn't go to the appointment. Whatever was inside her was what she would get.

At dusk, a silver Honda Accord pulled in to the driveway, and a red classic car parked on the street: bright hood, shining doors, a blond woman with black sunglasses at the wheel. Elvia watched from the screen door. Ray got out of the Honda and walked over to Sandy, who was sitting on the porch steps folding maternity clothes from Enchantee.

"Laundry, huh?" he said, resting his foot on the bottom step. Elvia saw his tanned arms, his hair combed back carefully from his forehead. He looked good for an older man.

"Friday night car show, huh?" Sandy said back, her voice light as flying leaves. "Bonnie looks fresh from the salon."

Ray glanced at the clothes. "How's Rosalie? She hasn't called me for a few weeks. I know those dresses aren't for her. Our tomboy vet who only wears jeans."

"Rosalie's fine. She's coming home for Thanksgiving. These are for Elvia."

"Elvia?" Ray said. "I remember her. Her dad had that . . ." Then Elvia saw him nod. "That was his '62 Ford over here. Great truck."

"Yeah. The Honda's for her. Thanks."

"Yeah, it was nice to see you the other night," Ray said softly. "I'm glad you called me."

"But I'm not Bonnie. I'd rather paint quarters than my finger-nails."

"What? I thought maybe you needed the car cause you were getting a job."

Sandy kept folding, but her shoulder blades moved in irritation. "I had a job, all this time. I taught kids to talk, okay?" Sandy glanced at the idling car. "Rosalie, all of them. Right here on the damn steps. Hours of sitting here listening to them babble. Doggie. Moon. Big truck. Daddy. Somebody has to talk back. Kids don't just pop out, open a beer, and read car manuals."

Sandy put the pile into the basket. "While you were in the ga-rage, I taught them to cross the street without getting hit. We looked at dead animals down on Topaz Street. I taught kids not to be road kill." She stood up. "No big deal, not like selling cars or building freeways, huh?"

"Sandy," Ray said. "I know all the stuff you did. I'm just saying Rosalie was grown and gone, and I wanted to do something differ-ent." He tossed the keys into the basket. "Enjoy the Honda, babe."

Elvia watched Ray get into the car. Sandy said loudly, "And I tried to teach them to be honest so they wouldn't steal your damn cars. That takes forever. And nobody notices."

Ray and Bonnie made a U-turn at the dead end and cruised down the street, Ray's hand rising above the roof to salute. Elvia opened the screen door and said, "Was some of that for me, too?"

Sandy clenched her fists on her hips, wetness remaining on her cheeks after she'd wiped her face. "Yeah. Just so you know."

.   .   .

Elvia's candles had burned so long that the glass cylinders were blackened. Veladoras. Tía Dolores had these in Tijuana. Lena had them in Mecca. And the date workers had them in Tourmaline. She touched the prayers printed in Spanish and English: MERCIFUL VIRGIN MARY OF GUADALUPE, SHOW CLEMENCY, LOVE, AND COMPASSION TO THOSE WHO LOVE YOU AND FLY TO YOUR PROTECTION.

Clemency. She looked up the word in Sandy's dictionary, the same one she and her sisters had used in elementary school. "Clemency: mildness in judging; mercy." Judging? Who knew what her mother had been afraid of? Whom she'd loved? Elvia remembered the clicking sound of beans, falling from her mother's fingers into a bowl. She knew she'd heard that.

In the kitchen, she opened the cupboard where Sandy kept dry pinto beans in a Tupperware container. Sandy didn't cook them often; she used them for school projects and teaching kids to count. Elvia poured them through her fingers, listened to them nestle into the pot. *My mother never taught me to make beans. But Hector showed me, at the river. Maybe Tía Dolores taught him.* Elvia added chili powder in the same fingerfuls he had, and garlic, and water.

She cleaned the floor and washed the towels. After two hours, she ladled out a spoonful of the plump, muddy-brown beans. They seemed soft, so she brought her face closer to the spoon and blew to cool them. They seemed to breathe, their inner flesh expanding out of the petal-thin outer hull. She pulled away and they shrank back, the hulls closing again.

She tasted one bean, curled on her palm. *The baby will be Michael's brown and my brown, his hair and my hair, his blood and my blood. Cahuilla and Mexican, Mexican and white. I can't give it to someone else. What if it's a girl, and white kids call her beañorita? I have to be around, tell her who her parents are, her grandparents. "You're a California baby," I'll tell her. Yeah. Mexican and Indian and desert-tanned white. Beañoritas don't pick grapes. People like me and maybe your grandma pick them. Indians don't all wear feathers and skins like in the movies. Indians like your dad live right up there on the mountain. Your grandpa does. Your other grandpa lives in the desert. Maybe you can meet him someday.*

And one grandma lives right here. With us.

I have to be the real mom. The real mom is the one who takes you for shots. Hugs you for your bad dreams. Sueños malos. The first and second levels. I can do this. I can do laundry and doctors and hugging. Sandy taught me how to hug. I hugged Jeffrey, and the little dime-eyed girl. I hugged Michael. I can hug my baby.

She watched Sandy come up the driveway from Enchantee's house, her pale round calves under her skirt, her light brown ponytail sideways in the wind. *She's the one Tía Dolores talked about,* Elvia thought. *She's real enough for me right now.*

The grandpa on the mountain, she thought, nervously driving the Honda past the dump and through the canyon. *And maybe your father. I don't know.*

Smoke came from the adobe chimney, and Michael's grandfather Antonio stood in the doorway as if he'd heard the car. He lifted a finger in greeting. When she got inside, he was sitting at the table with a turtle-shell rattle and a piece of paper. "He knew you would come. He left you a note. Ventana is way out in the desert, near the border."

E—I am in Ventana and other places. Why be around and you don't need me? Nothing for me to give you. Tell my grandpa the turtleshell rattle is for the baby. Cause if I die they burn it. It was mine when I was little. Can you put dust on my moms stone. Sometime. You know. Maybe I'll see you.

Moth dust, she thought. "He called me *Mukat,*" she said. "Is that 'Mother'?"

Antonio sighed. "He wasn't talking to you, then. *Mukat* is part of the creation, part of us. Cahuilla people. He didn't tell you the story?"

"No." Elvia held the rattle, feeling the palm seeds move inside. "He told me other stories."

"*Mukat* holds the sky in place with his hand. His fingerprints are there. You can see them at night. The stars." When she stood up to leave, he said, "You come up here anytime. I'll teach you and the kid about acorns. Teach you how to use the rattle."

She drove to the cemetery, got out and touched the plaque, but the leaves looked undisturbed, as if no one had slept there recently.

"But how come you only had one kid, if you know everything about it?"

The waiting room for the ultrasound appointment was empty, and Elvia was nervous. Sandy said, "I guess you don't think what I did was hard enough, compared to what you just did. Living where you were, with your dad and then at the river."

"The wild life," Elvia said, looking out the window at the bird of paradise bent in the wind.

"Okay." Sandy looked at her watch, then at the ceiling. "When I was pregnant with Rosalie, Ray fooled around. He slept with some woman who gave him gonorrhea. You heard of that?" Elvia nodded. "It scarred me up. I couldn't have any more kids." She pulled at her lips with her teeth again. "Finding that out was the hardest thing I've ever done, and that's all I can tell you."

"Scarred up inside?" She didn't want to picture it, especially imagining the ultrasound going through her stomach, showing what? Her sack? Her bones? The baby's bones? "Did you ever tell Rosalie? Is that why she doesn't want to hang around here? Or get married?"

"Rosalie never asked me anything," Sandy said, sadly. "She finds it in a book. And no, she doesn't want any babies. Not for a long time."

"All Callie ever said is you're only a place. A place to put their thing."

Then Sandy laughed. "I don't believe that. I think there are nice men out there."

Elvia folded her own arms. "I think Stan the social worker has a crush on you."

"I haven't even thought about him." Sandy pursed her lips, and her smile went lopsided.

When it was her turn, the technician put warm jelly on Elvia's skin and then pressed the remote-control thing into the slime. She had told Sandy to stay in the other room.

When her heart beat fast, the belly-thumping began in earnest. *Don't get mad at me,* she thought, *this is for you.* But there was nothing to see on the screen, just a bunch of spiderwebby-looking veils and dark spots, until suddenly the woman pointed and said, "Spine."

An unclasped bracelet of pearls, lying curved and waiting for a wrist. Then the bracelet moved. The baby moved. The technician moved the remote on her belly, pushing hard, and Elvia saw the baby's head, small as a Ping-Pong ball, outlined in ghostly white and full of frightening black.

"Do you want to know the sex?" the technician said. "I need to make a note for the doctor."

"I guess. I just want to know everything's okay," she whispered.

"I can't tell you that. The doctor will talk to you when she gets these. But I'll give you pictures of some of the things we can see today."

"Okay," Elvia said. She thought she saw white-pea toes, but she wasn't sure. She couldn't stop staring. *What if Michael and I really messed up? In the old days, if something was wrong, you didn't have to see terrible things before they were even born.*

In her bedroom, she studied the arrows the woman had drawn to—a knee? A curve of skull?

But what was inside the skull? Had she hurt the brain, or the heart?

She slept, the pictures in her hand. When she woke up, she went out to the kitchen table and silently laid the pictures before Sandy. She stared at the baby. Everything looked fine.

"Even if I go to college someday and you help me take care of it . . ." Elvia laid her head on the table. "Why did she leave me?" Her voice hurt her throat, tearing hard.

"That's the child's point of view," Sandy said, her own voice shaking. "That's how you see it, and it has nothing to do with you. It's inside *them*. The ones who leave. It's what *they* did." She held Elvia tightly, her knobby wrists hard on the side of Elvia's head. "You have to think about yourself now. Not your belly. Your own heart. What you can and can't do."

"I thought about it already. I can do it. But I need help."

Sandy nodded, but she was quiet. And when Sandy went outside and picked up the hose, Elvia felt strangely calm. She looked at the pictures again, the ghost baby.

She made a plate of cheese and crackers and apple slices and sat down to watch TV. *Sabrina the Teenage Witch.* All the kids in high school worried about parties and cheerleading and science class. *I have to go back there,* she thought. *Next year. And the baby will stay with Sandy during the mornings. Then I will come home.*

Shykim came while Elvia was at school. He was one, with eyes light as amber in a brown face, and a thumb purple from sucking. Sandy said his mother had left him in his crib for two days, and a neighbor found him. He freaked out around five o'clock, when Elvia was doing her English, and Sandy said, "Les told me he falls asleep every time they drive. We can't do that yet."

Elvia took him, hoping he didn't kick her in the belly, and held him carefully while she got into the Honda. He banged the steering wheel with his hands, his hard little feet on her thighs, and suddenly his legs would collapse, and she'd hold him up until he caught the grip again.

Sandy sat in the passenger seat, staring at the gas pedal and brake. "Ray always got nervous, and then he'd talk real loud like I was deaf," she said, watching Shykim pound the wheel.

"My dad was patient," Elvia said. "He started showing me how to drive when I was three."

Grit from the wind peppered the windshield, and Shykim stared in wonder at the leaves flying across the glass. Sandy said, "After we go back to Dr. Josefa again, you see her once a month or so. If everything's okay. Then you can take a childbirth class. They give you a free car seat."

"I know. Three girls in my class already have other kids." Shykim bounced on her thighs, and the baby kicked from inside. A strange feeling—like stones landing all over her. "This girl Tiffini, she's giving up her baby so she can go to college. Marisol was on her case. She said only the mother can raise the kid right."

Sandy shook her head. "Pretty obvious that isn't true by what we see at my house."

"But how could you really love a baby that wasn't yours? I mean, love it for life?" Shykim backhanded her with flailing arms, then banged his chin on the wheel and didn't even cry.

"If the baby lived with me, it would be mine. For then. That's how I always looked at it."

"But it wasn't. Yours."

"After I—was sick, from Ray, I told myself I'd take care of any kid like it was. Big or little. Boy or girl." She propped her knees on the dash. "You sound like your dad. We had this conversation when he first found you. He said I couldn't love you like he did."

Elvia felt a hard fist in her throat. She handed Shykim back to Sandy and went inside. She studied her desert stones, then put them on the windowsill. She listened to Shykim fuss in the crib all night, his diaper rustling, his sucking sometimes so hard he whistled.

Pinkeye

No CLUES in the truck. Larry yelled at Warren, "Go inside and watch somebody screw!" He didn't want Warren standing there in the Sands parking lot grinning, so proud he'd been keeping an eye on the truck for a few days.

He'd been walking along the fucking railroad tracks forever. Every piece of broken glass glittering like diamonds and cubic zirconshit. Ellie'd explained the rocks to him all those times, sitting next to him on the couches where they'd lived. Diamonds are the real thing. The earth makes them, with heat. They're just coal. But a guy could buy a cubic zircon and maybe a girl couldn't tell the difference. Totally fake. "How do they make those, Dad?"

Huh? How the hell should he know? Larry tried to think of all the rocks he'd lifted, all the sand he'd shaken out of his boots.

Ellie would sit there with magazine ads, showing him jewelry. "Look—tanzanite, amethyst, alexandrite. Here's tourmaline. Who looked at those rocks and knew you could cut them up and make something sparkly?"

Larry saw the palm frond tails in the truck bed. He opened the dash, but nothing was there except a purple hair thing. All his old stuff. And a pack of Marlboros. Ellie didn't smoke. A receipt for Taco Bell in Rio Seco.

Ellie must be looking for Sara. Maybe she'd still be in Rio Seco. He held the Marlboros. Sandy Narlette, the foster lady? She didn't smoke, either. Someone else did—a guy. A guy needing steel-toe surgery.

But Ellie'd brought the truck back. Warren said she'd told him to say she was sorry. Sorry.

Driving fifty-five, nice and careful, through the valley and the Sandlands toward Rio Seco, he gripped the wheel, the smell of smoke and oil and himself coming off the black ridges under his palms. He'd thought it was wrecked: either Dually had trashed it and lit it on fire, or Ellie had crashed it into a ditch. He hadn't wanted to picture her face bloody from the cracked windshield.

That was the scary shit. The only part he couldn't do. How he hooked up with Callie.

He'd been cool with Ellie at first, two beds in the Sands, heating up chili on the hot plate, pouring milk in the Cap'n Crunch every morning before school. Then she woke up before dawn one day whimpering like a dog, trying to be quiet, he could tell. "I can't see," she finally said, and he told her, "Hell yeah, you can't see cause it's four in the damn morning."

When he turned on the bedside lamp, he saw her eyes swollen and crusted shut with yellow gunk, like she'd been beaten up and then somebody poured glue on her lashes.

He panicked. Never seen anything like that. Was she fuckin blind? All he could think was, *I bet that foster mom would know what to do.*

But he wouldn't say that to Ellie. He put a wet washcloth on her face and told her he'd go get some medicine. But when he left the Sands, door locked tight behind him, he realized the only place he'd seen a doctor was the emergency room all the way in Indio. He stopped at the Cabazon Market down the highway for a pack of Tareytons and a beer to clear his mind, and Callie came up next to him while he held a jar of Vicks, wondering if Ellie just had a cold, if you could put Vicks near eyes. "Hell, no," Callie said, hands on her skinny hips when he asked. "Sounds like pinkeye. No big deal. I'll come help you out."

He bought her a few beers, some tequila the next night, and like every time, you get drunk or smoked or whatever, you do it in their motel room or the truck or wherever, and then they cry. All the ones he'd ever met—Sara, Callie, the redheaded woman under the Bronco. He thought of his mother—getting out of a truck, crying, the snow falling or the wind blowing and she'd come up to the front door with her black eyelashes smearing oil onto her cheeks.

Pinkeye—no big deal. He'd thought Ellie was blind. All that scary stuff about having a kid—pinkeye that disappeared, coughs that got quiet with NyQuil, fevers and homework and going to the laundrymat on Sundays. He could handle that. What got scary was Ellie's face getting beautiful, guys staring at her, her staring at him like a statue when she asked about her mother. He coasted down into Rio Seco, remembering Sara's blue eye makeup that last time he'd seen her. Made her look blind. Or half dead. What if she was dead, after all this time? Wherever she'd gone, it couldn't have been easy for her. He drove toward Yukon Street without thinking, but when he saw the duplex, he didn't stop. She wasn't here. He didn't want to knock, to see a slice of the same dark linoleum and curtains like nubbly thick dust, think of all the doors and floors and rooms he'd lived in.

Wherever. Good place to go. Where would Ellie be? Who did she love? A guy? No. Who?

The woman he'd wanted to call for help sometimes. Sandy Narlette.

He tried to remember where it was. Lemon groves. Topaz Street. Driving nice and slow, nothing for a cop to notice, he cruised up through the blooming trees with white star-flowers along the road. Then he saw the mulberry tree, remembered all the kids playing in the roots, eating Crackerjacks, Ellie's hair in a ponytail. Her face when she saw his truck, when she saw his tattoo.

He stopped at the curb, remembering that first day, Sandy Narlette like a mother mockingbird and he was a crow. Wanted to peck him on the back, chase him out. But he had the information from social services. She let him sit on the steps and talk to Ellie.

Why? Why had he come for her?

He didn't want her crying in some stranger's house, fighting for food, wondering every day why somebody who shared her blood didn't give a shit. But when he got here, to Sandy Narlette's, he knew that wasn't how it was. Ellie had been under the mulberry tree.

No one was there now. Clothes jumped on the washline in the yard. Her black tee shirt, her baggy jeans. Ellie was here.

He saw Sandy Narlette coming out of the screen door, in her jean shorts and tee shirt, hair in a bun, a total mom type. Not a mockingbird, diving onto his back, but a statue, like that saint woman in front of the church he'd passed today, on Palm Avenue. Standing there holding a dishtowel while he walked up the driveway.

"She's fine."

"Yeah? She been here all this time?"

"No. She was with a group of kids."

"Boys?"

"Two. And girls, too."

He could see her holding something back. He didn't even know her, didn't know how to get an answer out of someone like her.

"She was worried about you being mad."

"I'm her goddamned father." He didn't say the rest—*I'm supposed to be mad. I'm supposed to take care of her.*

Sandy's eyebrows raised up like women's did. He heard a kid murmuring in the house, like when Jeff used to wake up. Making bird noises. "She wants to stay here, for a while anyway. She just wanted a stable place for . . ."

"I was doing my best, okay?" He could tell she was holding back. "I would a killed anybody even looked at her wrong. I was trying to keep her safe. Hell, when the truck was gone, I thought she was dead." He felt his eyes go hot red. Fuck if he'd cry. He looked past her face, all soft and melted at the corners of her mouth, like she knew everything, everything about pinkeye and kids and stone-faced teenage girls. The doorbell was the same, that kind that lit up at night like a fiery ember in the plastic plate. The same as when he'd sat here in the evening trying to get to know his kid.

Cabazon

"Your father came here after you left for school," Sandy said. Shykim cruised around the table, grabbing wooden spoons and spatulas, smacking imaginary ants.

Elvia calmly got a stack of cookies, then stayed at the counter, remembering the smoothness of the dragon on his arm when she finally touched it. "He knew I'd be here?"

Sandy bit her lips, leaving tooth marks that slowly disappeared. "He said he thought you might be dead at first. He was crying."

"Crying?" Elvia tried to picture her father with tears instead of an angry squint. "He came from Florida? When I went out there to give him back the truck, he was gone."

"He didn't say where he'd been. I asked him where he was living and he said, 'Same old place.' I asked him if he'd gone away before, and he said, 'I didn't go far enough.' Then he left."

"What does that mean?" Elvia sat down on the couch. "Not far enough from me?"

"I don't think so," Sandy said, helping Shykim up. "He came, right? He said he couldn't believe you ran away, and he wanted to make sure you were okay."

She wasn't running back. She just wanted to see him. Tell him she was sorry.

She left before dawn. On the highway, she felt an exhilaration mixed with fear. *When I see him, he won't believe how I can drive.* Then she thought, *He'll see my stomach. The baby.*

The wind picked up again as she drove through the Sandlands, pushing tumbleweeds and palm fronds across the road. She glanced up at the cleft of green where Michael might be sleeping in his trailer. East toward Tourmaline, the sun was only an eerie tin thread in the desert.

The sign was rocking at the Sands Motel. No blue truck. The quarry was deserted, where the wind flung gravel against the windshield and she could barely turn around in the parking lot. On the highway, the sand made a glistening sound against the car doors, and she remembered all the winter sandstorms she'd watched from different windows. Her father used to say, "That sand can wreck the truck's paint job in an hour. And man, people always crash in sandstorms."

She thought of the grapevines in Mecca, sand shifting the rows where they'd all bent and crouched and talked. "Go outside and you could die," her father would say. "Your mouth and nose would fill up with sand. You'd be buried and nobody'd find you for a year." If no one had ever found the dead woman in the desert with the burnt-bark face, she would be covered in drifting sand. No one back in Mexico would ever know what happened to her.

She would never know what had happened to Callie and Jeff, to the dime-eyed little girl. In the sullen dimness of Tourmaline, she saw a green car and new curtains at the old house.

She drove to Palm Springs, trying to remember the name of the construction company, but she could barely keep the wheels on the road in the blowing sand. She couldn't drive around golf courses looking for new cement pipes. Back on the freeway, with fewer golden sand clouds rolling across the asphalt, she pulled off near the Cabazon market to buy a soda, and on the frontage road she saw the truck, the rust sheen like ancient turquoise.

Elvia drove into the old motor court, "Cabazon Inn," looking at the thick curtains over the cottage window. What if he was sleeping, after a long sketch? She gripped the wheel.

He peered out his door right away, his face suspicious and hard as always. *He must still owe somebody money*, she thought. *Somebody must be mad at him.*

When he saw her, she couldn't smile, couldn't wave, couldn't move. He walked over to the car, his boots untied, the laces grinning wide. "Nice car," he said into the window. A new scar on his nose, a fingernail moon over the bridge. A bare patch on his temple, where the hair had been shaved off and thin glittery stubble covered a red line held together with black string.

"Stitches," he said to her stare. "So you made out okay, huh? You don't need shit from me, so what are you out this way for?" He squinted in the gust that blew between cottages.

"I do need something," Elvia said slowly, her fingers tightening on the wheel.

"This your new dad's car?" Her father looked out at the street. He didn't tell her to come in. He was dressed for work. Flannel shirt, jeans with faded-white knees.

"Sandy's not—she's separated." Elvia swallowed the hotness that had started aching behind her jaw when she saw the scars. "Have you seen Callie?"

"Nope."

"Do you ever think about her? And Jeff?"

"Nope." Her father put his laced fingers behind his head and his chest expanded for a minute. She couldn't believe he'd cried at Sandy's house—not with the way his face looked now. "No, I don't, Ellie. If I tried to think about all the people I've hung around, remember all of them and what they did or didn't do, I'd be 5150 certifiable."

Elvia heard trucks rumble on the freeway behind the tamarisk trees. "Yeah," he said. "That's what I'd have been. If I thought about your mom."

"Or me," she said.

"I think about you. All the time." But he didn't look at her.

"I think about everybody," Elvia said in a rush. "Their faces and

their names. The foster houses. Everybody at Sandy's. I think about
Callie, and Jeff, and Lee, and her girl."

His new scar turned whiter when he frowned. "You don't think
I missed you? All that time, you don't think I got used to seeing your
face, even if you weren't always thrilled to see me? I got used to your
voice bitchin about dinner or whatever. You're my kid, okay?"

"I'm fifteen. I'm gonna get a learner's permit."

"Yeah. You can drive, for sure. I didn't think it was you took my
truck. That's how I got messed up." He touched the shaved side of
his head. "I was so fuckin worried, Ellie. You were gone. I thought
Dually took you, for the money Callie owed him. I went crazy, went
to his house lookin for you and tried to kill him. But it was the other
way around. He almost killed me."

Elvia stared at the scars and put her face in her hands. "I'm
sorry," she whispered. "I brought the truck back. I didn't know."

"Yeah. I was in the hospital for days." He bent down to lace his
boots. "I gotta go to work."

"At the quarry?"

He shook his head. "Nope. Indian Wells. Another golf course."

Elvia said, "Dad. I want to stay in Rio Seco. For right now. I want
Sandy to be my legal guardian. Don't get mad, okay? I want to . . ."

He shrugged, his lips set tight under the mustache, and inter-
rupted her. "I tried my best, Ellie. I guess you told me how you felt.
You were sayin I was a fuck-up dad. You booked up. Just like her." He
took out his wallet, the same soft-worn leather that wore a white
square in his jeans. He pulled out another ID card. "I never gave you
this cause I didn't want you starin at her face, gettin all worked
up over somebody who was gone. I found it in the kitchen, when
you guys disappeared. Burnt-out candles. Like some ceremony. Like
hasta la vista, baby."

A small dark face, with triangle cheekbones and chin, a fright-
ened look, two wings of black hair and a thick braid. SERAFINA
ESTRELLA SOLORIO-MENDEZ. SAN CRISTOBAL YUCUCUI,
OAXACA.

"But you look like me, too," he said, and the dragon's tail curved from his tee shirt sleeve like a faded green grin. "You got a lot of me inside you. Drivin. Talkin shit. Bein alone. I love you, Ellie." The wind blew a veil of sand around the corner. "Have a good life," he said, turning toward his truck.

"You know where Sandy lives," she called. "You can come see me. You found it before!"

The truck shivered to life, and the deep stutter inside the hood sounded the same. For a moment, Elvia wanted to jump into the passenger seat, crouch down under the dashboard shelf, the dark space like her favorite cave smelling of fresh unsmoked cigarettes and cement dust. Then the truck wheeled past her when her father pulled onto the road.

He hadn't seen her stomach. Her baby. *That's better,* she thought, wiping her face. *You'd be just one more person to forget,* she told the baby, which was moving inside her like someone tracing a finger on a window. *Once I see your face,* she thought, *I'll never lose it. Never.*

But he loves me. I'll come back, here or to the golf courses in Indian Wells, when you're born. I'll show him your face. Maybe you'll have green eyes. Maybe not. But you have his blood, too. He can't lose you so easy.

I'll put my whole name in the telephone book, when I get a place. Elvia Estrella Mendez Foley. She felt the ID card sharp against her leg. *Anybody comes looking for me, my dad or Hector or even you someday, when you're in college or something, you can find my name and address right there. That easy. Let your fingers do the walking. Here I am.*

Cloud People

THE PIERCING WHISTLE sounded like a mountain flute from back in Oaxaca. Jesus shouted.

Rigoberto grabbed Serafina's arms, and she heard the Broncos roaring through the groves. Everyone ran down the arroyo to the tall cane where the riverbed began.

Shouts, bullhorns. No one moved. Then, after an hour of hiding in the cane, they heard rumbling in the distance. Not la migra's Broncos. Louder. When Rigoberto ventured back, hiding along the arroyo, he saw the bulldozers.

They returned to piles of wood and plastic lying half buried under mounds of dirt pushed ahead of the blades. Only Araceli's plywood shelter was still standing, because it was protected by the trees. Don Rana was nowhere to be found, his trailer up on the hill empty.

"Don Rana probably called la migra himself!" Rigoberto shouted, kicking the metal door. "He has my money! He worked me like a burro since I borrowed to pay for you!"

Serafina felt the blood whorl around her jaw, her forehead. She was angrier than she'd ever been at her brother. "Paying for me?" she shouted back. "Like a turkey or burro? I'm not an animal. I'm your sister. I got here myself, and I gave you back that money, after—" She stopped, looking at Florencio. The coyote was theirs alone. Forever. "Your money?" she hissed at Rigoberto, who stood open-mouthed. "I cooked every day, after I picked! I put money into the can. I sent money to San Cristobal with you."

Jesus said, "Maybe one of those boys on the bikes called." She remembered their faces when they'd seen the camp, the pig's blood. They were all silent, looking down at the arroyo, seeing how it looked from the trailer. A collection of trash flung around by a flood. "Maybe the owner himself called," Florencio finally said. "Not the one with the baseball cap and white hair. The other one we never saw. That happened to me in the peaches. And once in the grapes. Maybe he didn't want to pay us."

As they wandered around the camp trying to salvage what they could, Florencio listened for the Broncos of the immigration men. They might come back. Serafina dug through the sandy earth for her rosary, but she found only odd things: the blue stone from the desert, a tangled blouse, a box of matches, and one spoon. Rigoberto used a pickax, frantically turning the dirt until he found the coffee can with his and Serafina's money. The bulldozer had pushed the mouth closed, and he pried it open. The dollars were folded and dry.

But Florencio's things were gone. All of them. The corner of the bulldozer had driven them into the side of the arroyo. And Jesus's cave had collapsed under the weight of la migra's Broncos parked at the edge of the camp. Jesus couldn't even lift the splintered trap door.

"We don't have time to dig," Rigoberto said. "They'll be back. We have to go to the strawberries now. Guadalupe."

"You are asking la Virgen . . ." Serafina began, and he cut her off.

"The town of Guadalupe. The strawberries in the north. Let's go."

Florencio nodded. "We have to follow the crop."

Serafina went to Araceli's shelter. Araceli was packing her pots into a box she'd found on the roof. "They left it on purpose," Araceli whispered. "Because they know we'll be back. Or someone else will be back, to pick las naranjas. Next season."

Serafina looked at her own pot, her metate and mano. "Are you coming to las fresas?"

Araceli shook her head. "Fresas are too hard. So much bending. The people are angry and tired. Most of the time they would rather drink than eat." She closed the box. "I'm going to find a room here. Cook in a taqueria. Maybe El Rey." She touched Serafina's arm. "If you come back, leave me a note at the mercado. I will try to help you."

"Serafina!" Rigoberto was calling her.

She had no choice. She couldn't stay here alone, and she didn't want to try to survive without Florencio now. She was used to his arms, his watchful eyes, his presence near her. But she would be back. She stared at the tree trunk, where the image of la Virgen was still praying, where the candle flame had gone out. The barrettes were in her pocket. The helicopter was a drone in the distance.

The teenage girl was beautiful, her black hair collected in ringlets on her head, her white quinceanera dress a swaying bell of satin layers with pearls along the neck and bodice. She held a parasol over her head when she walked down the dirt road between the shacks in Guadalupe. The girl's parents beamed at her tiny waist, her shy smile, at the boys who watched her.

Serafina pressed her fingers hard to the corners of her eyes. It would have been rude to cry when she saw the girl. She sat in her doorway of damp gray wood. Twenty rooms in a row on this side of the dirt road, and twenty on the other side. A woman with five children sat across from Serafina, her long hair in a braid, her baby at her breast. They all watched the girl walking carefully over the ruts in the road, holding up the hem of her dress.

Jesus stood beside Serafina, his lips thin as a splinter, staring at the rhinestone tiara, at the proud father. After weeks of oranges, he had nothing to send home for his daughter's quinceanera.

They had gotten here three days ago, after traveling two nights by bus and foot. The other people in this camp had been here for a month, preparing the fields, tearing out the old strawberry plants. Guadalupe was flatland strawberry fields and row houses, a small downtown with bars and stores. Serafina watched the girl reach the end of the road and turn to wave.

Elvia was fifteen now. She had never had a quinceanera. *She might not even know what it is,* Serafina thought, watching the lace hem disappear. She went back into her room.

Florencio and Rigoberto were talking to the foreman at one of the fields. They had worked Thursday and Friday, punching holes in the plastic-covered rows with a metal tool. She had walked behind Florencio in the mist of this valley near the sea, pushing the cold iron pipe down, taking two steps, pushing it again. Her arms ached. The perfect rows were covered with beads of dew that leapt onto her shoes when she punched. The dark shapes of people moved slowly ahead of her, stiff and straight like soldiers.

But after they finished, it would be time to bend and crouch, to set the young strawberry plants into the holes, then to weed the furrows with hoes, and then to bend again and pick each berry, careful to keep the green fringe like a crown. Florencio said when the crew bosses checked, if your box wasn't perfect, you weren't paid.

The room had a hot plate and sink at one corner, three beds, and a toilet behind a curtain. She picked up her comal and put it over the gas burner. Even her wrists hurt, when she mixed the masa and began to make the tortillas. And she felt the salty thin taste rise in her throat—the unease sent to her mouth by a baby.

She knew that's what it was. She had been weak and dizzy the whole time she worked her rows, and in the predawn darkness, she'd bent over the sink at the smell of coffee drifting out all the windows in the row of rooms. She'd been able to eat only a tortilla or two. She tried to recall when she'd known, with Elvia, but that only made her sad.

A boy called to her in Spanish, from the doorway, and when she turned, he held out a dirty hand in supplication. He must have been watching her make the tortillas. His eyes were cloudy gray, his skin cafe con leche. She put two tortillas in his fingers and he blew, running away so quickly that she could see only his bare heels, like the tiny pale doughballs in her palms.

When Florencio came in, she was holding the barrette.

She looked at the fan of lines beside his eyes, the eyes always steady on her face. No one else ever *saw* her—not her uncle, or Rigoberto, or Don Rana. Not Larry. They saw her hands holding tortillas or oranges. They saw her back bent, her head bowed. She could love Florencio, because he looked at her as closely as her mother had, but without frowning wild fear.

"You lost the other barrette?" he asked.

"No. I left it. For an offering," she whispered as he sat down on the bed beside her. "I always have to choose. My father and Luis died, and I had to decide. Stay with my mother or go with Rigoberto. Then I stayed there, in Rio Seco, with Larry. But I had Elvia." She paused. Her hands' sweat, dirt, salt, and lime hadn't corroded the silver. It was Mexican silver, from Taxco. She knew because the woman who'd sold her the barrettes, in the parking lot at the linen plant, had said, "Taxco. Yo soy de Taxco."

Florencio took the barrette, held it across his blackened hand, and nodded. "You want to go back. To Yuu Sechi."

"When the strawberries are finished," Serafina said. "And you can build me a *ñíhin*, with the cane from the river. That's the best."

Florencio looked at her in astonishment. "A *ñíhin*?" A sweat house where women went after childbirth, to cleanse themselves and restore the balance of hot and cold in their blood?

She nodded. In San Cristobal, she would have waited another month or so, then told her mother and mother-in-law, who would have told everyone else. It wasn't right to announce it like this. But this was California. She and Florencio were living as husband and wife, but without a pueblo. There was only Rigoberto, who was like the always-complaining old woman of this new pueblo. That made her smile.

Florencio smiled, too, rubbing his forehead, leaving a streak of dirt. "A baby! When?"

Serafina tried to think. "August," she finally said. "The same month I had Elvia."

She took back the barrette, rubbing away the brown smudges from his fingers.

"We will go back before then," Florencio said, holding her now. "I promise."

After a while, he left with a handful of tortillas to find Rigoberto. The warm stripes of silver turned cold when she dropped them into her apron pocket. She had bought the apron, a broom, and masa from the mercado. The masa flattened in her hands, and she laid another tortilla on the black circle. She had made thousands of tiny suns, and each one was gone in minutes.

Then she swept the wooden floor, raised the broom to the ceiling, and thought about her prayers to la Virgen, like thousands of straws tied together in a huge broom to collect spiderwebs from the corners of the sky.

The fields were covered with rows of plastic that shone dull silver in the sun, like the tin roofs of San Cristobal. When she walked beside Florencio, moving down each row to plant, she blurred her eyes until she saw home. This was home, with him, for now. Until she could go back to Rio Seco in a few months and try again.

Thunder rang through the valley in the afternoon, and she sat with the men around the flimsy card table covered with food. "Do you remember the stories our father and Uncle Emiliano would tell, when we were small and afraid of the *kanara* thunder?" she said to Rigoberto.

He smiled a little then. "The *ñū'ún savi*, the saints of the rain?"

She nodded. "They bring rain by climbing the mountaintops and smoking the seven cigars, making the clouds thicker and thicker until the rain people get drunk on the tobacco."

"Then they shout. *Kanara.* Like fighting drunks." He looked at Florencio. "Your grandmother told that one, too?"

He nodded. "But she was always worried about offending some santo, always afraid. Especially of the *ñū'ún yuu nu'un.*"

Serafina thought about the hearthstones she'd revered all her life, at home, in each camp. The sooty stone that had saved her life in the ravine. The fierce rocks where she'd cooked her food. "You have to make your sacrifices properly," she said. "That's all."

She had tried her best, in Rio Seco, amid the ruins of the bulldozed camp. She'd had only a few minutes. *Soko*—presenting something to the gods. A sacrifice. Remembering how in San Cristobal people put things in branches, in tree trunks near the corn fields so the santos could better see their offerings, she looked at the tiny wooden shelf nailed to the tree. *Itun, iti, itā,* Serafina thought. Corn, candles, flowers. She found one dried tortilla under the stove where someone had dropped it, and she cracked it into pieces. At the edge of the trees, she grabbed a stem of wild sunflowers, the only thing still blooming. She lit the veladora.

Speaking slowly, respectfully, she said, *"Ka'a maa kao."* Alone. We are speaking alone. To all the gods and saints, all of them in the sky and earth and wind who might be able to see her and see Elvia now, at the same time, she said, "Please. She was my *anima*. My soul." She had no photo to prop against the candle, where they could see it, so she found a scrap of paper and pencil in Araceli's box and wrote carefully. ELVIA ESTRELLA MENDEZ FOLEY. B. 8-20-80. With a piece of red cellophane, she wrapped the tortillas and blue stone and paper, and one barrette. She kissed the bundle and then the image of la Virgen on the candle, and she left the tree without looking back to see how small the flame burned in the dusk.

Starla

"WE CAN ONLY tell you what we don't see. I don't see a penis."

Elvia looked up at Dr. Josefa, who was studying the ultrasound photos. "It's a girl?"

"It says here you wanted to know the sex, right?"

"I really wanted to know if the baby had two arms and two legs. And about the head."

Dr. Josefa said, "She has all those things. And she looks okay. Normal size for six months. You said April. That makes her set to debut in January. Now lie back."

She measured from navel to pubic bone again, saying, "Yup. Growing. Good. Legs up."

Outside, Elvia said to Sandy, "No, I'm not used to it yet. And yeah, I know I have to expect worse. Just let me drive, cause I can't take all the jerking right now."

"What a smart-ass. We have to meet Enchantee at the doughnut shop."

At the plastic table, Elvia listened to the woman behind the counter talking to her son in rapid bursts of throaty language. "She's Cambodian," Sandy said, sitting down with buttermilk bars.

Elvia took out the map of Mexico. She'd found Oaxaca, all the way at the southern end of Mexico, but no San Cristobal Yucucui. The town must be so small it was invisible.

"It's so far," Sandy said, leaning over the map. "How did she ever make it here? She must have been so afraid."

Elvia studied her mother's face on the ID card. She did look afraid, her eyes wide and stunned. Elvia touched the towns, comforting because they didn't move. "I can't even say these names. Nochixtlan. Tlaxiaco." She tried to imagine the houses. Was her mother there, married and happy with kids? Four? Four daughters who looked like her, lived with her, helped her cook?

Or was her mother in Rio Seco, just down the street from where she used to carry Elvia around in the yard and cook cactus, when she lived with Larry Foley and he was wild?

"My dad never called."

Sandy said, "Your father hasn't called *yet*. I think he will. He's just mad because he was so worried." She put down her Styrofoam coffee cup. "I was mad when Rosalie left. I still get mad at her sometimes, when she calls to say she met some nice family with horses up in New York, and maybe she'll spend a white Christmas with them. It's so hard when your kids leave, Elvia. You might as well start getting ready now."

"Me?"

"For when your daughter leaves." Sandy moved the doughnut crumbs around. "The process is already set in motion. She's coming. She has to leave one day."

"Great." Elvia saw sugar clinging to Sandy's fingertips. "Then why do it? If it's so hard?"

Sandy shrugged. "Few days or years of happiness. Pieces of time." She watched the woman behind the counter fill a sugar jar. "I don't know. I'm not sure at all what to do with you. You've been through hell in a week. Do I act like everything's right on schedule, or let you know how scared I was?"

"You were scared?"

"I thought you wouldn't come back from the desert. I thought your dad might go nuts when he saw you and say you had to stay with him."

Elvia said, "He was pissed. At me."

"Well, I was scared you might decide to stay on your own. I thought I'd get one of those phone-booth calls again."

"I'm staying with you." She took a bite of the buttermilk bar. In her backpack was another map—one from Hector, showing the room he'd rented in Agua Dulce with two men from Michoacan.

> I don't have a troca, so I hope you come see me. I will cook for you and the baby. Teach you all the sauces. I could be rent-a-dad if you want one.

She would visit Hector and tell him Michael had been calling someone who held up the sky. She would let Hector hold the baby and draw it a map of the world.

"See?" Sandy said. "I'm scared now. Look, I know just what to do with babies. And little kids. I can read their faces. They love structure. Just like you did, so long ago. Even when you first showed up. But you're a teenager. I haven't had someone your age in a long time."

"You had Rosalie."

"I haven't said the right thing to Rosalie since she turned twelve. All I did was irritate her. She wanted me to leave her alone so she could read."

"I don't want you to leave me alone." Elvia put her hands over her stomach. The baby—she—liked buttermilk bars. "Long as you don't act like I'm stupid when I do something wrong." She looked at Sandy's bitten lips and wide forehead. "If it's really a girl, I want to name her Starla. My mother's middle name is Estrella. I know that's 'star' in Spanish."

Enchantee came in, and her son, Demetrius Jr., looked at Elvia but then quickly ducked his head. *He's only eight, but he's already embarrassed like all the other guys,* Elvia thought.

"D'Jr. needed a pair of jeans, but he stayed as far from me as possible while he picked them," Enchantee said, sitting down. "So I went to the baby department for my thrills. Look. Hooded towels, so the baby's head stays warm. These always make me cry. Booties and onesies and cloth diapers and creepers. I had a good old time."

"Thanks," Elvia said, touching the soft yellow towels. "It's a girl."

"Oh, break my heart," Enchantee said. "But I love the hardhead I got."

D'Jr. brought her a doughnut and rolled his eyes when he said, "I'm outside."

Enchantee shook her head. "Can't be seen with me. And look, Sandy. Brought it from his dad's house. Carrying it around like the Bible." She took a car magazine from her bag. The cover showed a black, lowered truck with yellow flames on the doors, and a blond woman wearing a tiny yellow bikini. "Implants. I gotta tell the boy nobody's chest looks like that." They studied the cover, and Enchantee said, "This chick isn't even aerodynamic. Please." Enchantee patted Elvia's shoulder. "See you two tomorrow."

When they'd left, Sandy said, "Where now?"

Elvia watched the small woman at the cash register, her hair in a bun, her eyes dark and sad when she slid a cup of coffee into a shrine on the counter. A stick of incense released a trail of smoke. Cambodian—but she was tiny, brown skinned, and delicate as the photo. As her mother.

"I want to go back to Yukon Street," Elvia said. "Show somebody the picture. Even if they don't speak English, maybe they'll know where she is." She didn't need to look at her mother again, the startled eyes, the mouth parted in fear.

The duplex yard was full of Mexican kids playing on old scooters and skateboards, and wet laundry hung from the chainlink fence. Elvia stared at the kids, who stared back when she knocked at 2510. When the plump woman with curly hair answered, Elvia said haltingly, "Es mi madre." She held up the ID card. "Aquí?" She swept her hand down the street, into the air.

The woman shook her head and closed the door. Elvia went to the sidewalk, staring at the swordlike irises near the steps of the other door.

Sandy said, "One more try?" and went up the steps with her. "Excuse me, ma'am," Sandy called toward the wrought-iron screen. "Can we ask for your help for a minute?"

A face vague as a cloud finally appeared behind the screen, swaying sideways, and then the old woman said, "Blue eyes. Oh, my Lord, green eyes. The Indian's little girl. You're here. Oh, you're not little anymore." She opened the door. "I was prayin for you, darling. Come in."

This lady? Elvia thought, *she knows?* She felt cold, small fingers pull her inside.

At the small table covered in blue-checked oilcloth, Elvia stared at the old woman's hands. Brown spots, round as baby pancakes, covered her skin. The woman bustled about, putting water in a kettle, setting out fragile cups with red roses and gold rims. She stopped once and said to Elvia, "She's just as wee small as me. Your mum."

Elvia said, "I think so. I'm not sure." She put the ID card on the table.

"Of course she is, dear. She was just here. Your mum."

"She was here?" Elvia felt suddenly panicked, looking around the room crowded with dark furniture. What would she really do, if her mother walked up now?

"Just two weeks ago." She turned to Sandy. "Sit down, dear, sit. I wouldn'tve opened the door if I hadn't heard your voice and seen blue eyes. No one speaks English here. Just brown eyes on the street now. Do you know I haven't spoken a word for five days? Gas man come five days ago." She stared at Elvia. "Never forgot this one's face. Eyes like home."

"Where is home?" Sandy said, taking the cup of tea in the delicate saucer.

"Ireland, dear. But I've been here fifty years. Yank husband brought me here, and I couldn't get back. That's what comes of waitin on a man, darlin. Just like your mum used to wait on your dad. Not that I know him, no, but I'm just sayin that's what I saw." She picked up the ID card. "That's her. Oh, so tiny."

"Where is she?"

The old woman said carefully, "I wondered what become of you, after you were lost."

Elvia stared at the small bright eyes in the papery drapes of skin. "You knew?"

"Oh, it was a heartbreak," the woman said, putting her teacup down. "Just a heartbreak, and I felt it was my fault. My husband, see, he was Air Force, went and got killed in the war. Only other person I knew then was Sister Margaret at Saint Catherine's, and I only seen her on Sundays. There was a few Irish here, but they moved. I rented my place next door, but people was always comin and goin, and they got rough sometimes."

Sandy said, "It must have been scary to be a woman alone."

She nodded. "I never answered the door. I'd walk to six o'clock mass at dawn and nobody saw me. And I'd water early, before the sun come up. An old woman is just a bother or a mark to people, I know that." She touched the ID card. "But your mum, she brought me jelly. Your da, he was never around much. When he was, oh, he got loud with his friends, and I did see plenty of beer cans. They worked on a black car with the loudest motor. And your mum—I'd watch you two from the window. She'd collect cactus, tellin you not to reach for it, let her do it."

Elvia looked out at the cactus lining the fence. "We ate it?"

"Yes. Fruit, like a red apple, but different. Brought it to me in jars. Cause your da had disappeared and there was no money. I knew that. She was speakin some shushy deep-in-the-throat talk. And she never did once raise her hand or her voice to you." The woman smiled, her expression distant. "You was like a starfish stuck on a rock. Holdin her braid. Oh, I wanted a girl like you so bad, to hold on to me like that. And that's why I feel so bad. Responsible."

"Why?" Elvia shivered slightly.

"Oh, she was cryin at times, I'd see lights at night, candles and such, and I heard her must've been prayin. Then the car—she'd get in that black car and go up and down in the driveway. You were laughin so. One evening she was crying, and she put you in the car, and you dropped your dolly. I never saw you again."

"That's when she left me?" Elvia saw it, the hedge and the car. She heard the crickets in the parking lot, saw the moths slant toward the windshield. *She left me. It was too much.*

"Oh, love, you were in the car. Sister Margaret told me what happened. She felt so bad. She was in the rectory, and your mum wrecked the car. Not hard, but I guess Sister heard a crashin noise, and teenagers had been speedin in the church lot before, so she called the police again. She was watchin out her window. I guess the police saw your mum and she run, screamin in her talk. Sister Margaret told me the story later. The police put her in their car."

"I was in the car. I went to sleep."

"She was screamin for you, darlin, she must have been. You were fast asleep, love. Sister called the police back for the car—the church didn't want the expense of towin it—and she went to meet them. They found you sleepin, love."

Sleeping under the moths. *She tried to run back? For me?*

"Two weeks ago," the woman said quietly. "She brought me food again. But she come here lookin for you. I wanted to tell you the whole story before I give you this. So you'd know what happened."

Elvia held her breath, touching the paper with the words slanted backwards, printed in capitals, and the picture of a tree with circles of fruit.

He was wrong. My dad was wrong. It was an accident. She loved me. She loved me. She didn't mean to leave me. She cried for me. She came back, to look for me. Elvia held the steering wheel hard, but the baby was turning and turning, nervous about Elvia's fast heart.

"Here?" she asked Sandy. "Way out here?" Swerving, trying to find the dirt road, she finally smelled the oranges.

The orange groves were laid out in huge dark squares, and she saw the wide green swath of cane and grapevine and cottonwood below the sloping groves. "I was here," she said, looking at the canal along the road, the silver stripe of river water in the distance. "We were here."

"Down there," Sandy said, peering out the window.

The car bounced slowly over the ruts in the grove road, and Elvia said, "I was this close to her? I don't see any houses." Suddenly she remembered Hector saying he'd picked oranges and seen a man living in a cave.

"Elvia . . ." Sandy's voice trailed away.

But Elvia stopped the car where the road trailed into the wide ravine. Mounds of trash and dirt and ragged piles of clothing were scattered across the sandy bottom, and scrapwood was piled in heaps like matchsticks. On the knoll above, she saw a trailer with metal-shuttered windows. But no one was here, in this place drawn on the piece of paper her mother had held.

Elvia crouched in the dirt, steadying herself with her palms. She cried so hard that the baby kicked in real distress now, alarmed by her shaking, her huge breaths, her ragged sobs. Sandy left her alone. *She was here,* Elvia said to herself, over and over. *She was looking for me. She still loves me. She never forgot me.*

When she stood up, rubbing her eyes with the backs of her hands, she smelled the sand on her palms, and saw the mica clinging to her wrists, glittering in the noon sun. She felt dizzy, and she stumbled to the trees for their shade.

Under the branches, she saw a strange wooden shelf, small as a slice of bread, nailed to the trunk of the cottonwood, and a creamy pool of wax, a few dried flowers. When she looked up to see where the wax had come from, she saw a glint of red above her. A packet, wrapped in clear paper, glowed in the shifting light through the leaves, crimson like a heart, and when she braced her foot on an overturned orange crate, holding her belly carefully with one hand, reaching for the bundle, the wind seemed to push it into her fingers.

Glossary

MIXTEC	ENGLISH	SPANISH
Anima	Soul	Alma
Chīhló	Pomegranate	
Cuehē cuū-yō	Death	Muerte
Cusū	Sleep	
Huipil	Hand-woven blouse	
Itā	Flowers	
Iti	Candles	
Itun	Corn offering	
Kanara	Thunder	
Lasú	Braids	Trenzas
Náā	Mother	
Ndaha	Hands	
Ndéchi	Where is . . . ?	
Ndixi	Liquor distilled from sugarcane	
Nducha	Water	Agua
Nducha yúján nunī yīhi	Hot drink of milk, masa, sugar, and cinnamon	Atole
Nicuvui nuhundeyteta	The dead become earth	
Ñíhin	Sweat house	
Ñuhun	Fire	
Nunī	Corn	Maiz
Nuñi saha	Corn boiled with limewater	Nixtamal
Ñú'ū anima	Home of the dead	
Ñū'ún saví	Gods of the rain	
Ñū'ún yuu nu'un	Gods of the hearth	
Ñú'ūu cuhu	Two sisters	
Sándoo	Wash	Limpia
Sēhe síhí	Daughter	
Soko	Sacrifice	
Táā	Father	
Ticuāá	Butterfly	
Tiñū'ú xíní	Stars	Estrellas
Tú cuiti	Nothing	
Vico nuhu	Clouds	
Vihnchá	Prickly pear cactus	Nopales
Yoo	Moon	Luna
Yúján	Corn dough or flour	Masa
Yuu Sechi	Dry River	Rio Seco

306